Generational Gaps

by William Boyack

PublishAmerica
Baltimore

First printing

ISBN: 1-4137-7002-9
PUBLISHED BY PUBLISHAMERICA, LLLP
www.publishamerica.com
Baltimore

Printed in the United States of America

For Bob

Acknowledgments

I would like to thank all those who lent a helping hand in the progression of this book. Craig Malloy and Jim Sams, thank you for your input and involvement. Thank you to my wife, Maren, whose patience is endless.

I
The Accident

A small branch of the Defense Research Medical and Technological Institute, located near Los Alamos in New Mexico, rested in a place called "The Ranch." Michael Heimer, grandson of the notorious scientist who participated in the Manhattan Project in the forties, was the new director for special programs. Dr. Heimer rubbed his temples, as his grandfather might have, to search for the holes in the theories setting before him. Terms such as "space-time continuum" and "relativity" may be blurred and migraine-worthy to most people, but his confusion was the equal relationship between the two theories and the quantum mechanics binding them. These were what truly racked his mind at that moment.

Pouring a cup of coffee, he slipped and spilled the cup all over his lap. The final straw to the mass frustration consumed the scientist, forcing him to throw the cup, which shattered against the counter in the small kitchen in the break room. He sat and watched as the mess poured from the top of the cabinets to the floor below. Taking a deep breath, he stood to clean the mess before him. He kneeled on the floor to clean the coffee and the remnants of the mug from the various surfaces of the kitchen. The boiling coffee was almost melting the cheap paint on the top of the cabinets where the cup hit.

On the floor he spotted a small chunk of fallen and forgotten cheese, which had not even been phased by the fluid. Standing slowly, he moved to the table and thought back to his father telling him a story regarding the idea of the implosion device.

"True genius is found in the awareness of existing ideas. The combination of these things create the recipe of epiphany. God is the only genius. The scientists who are declared brilliant were those who only paid attention to the patterns of their creator."

Thousands of principles flowed through Michael's mind as he ruled out the unrelated ones and kept the potentially associated principles stored in the back of his mind. Finally, he rushed to the cabinets and screamed in excitement

"Doppler!"

Reaching for the phone, he dialed and instructed the receiver to get everyone to the lab immediately. Standing in the kitchen doorway, Michael turned to look at the mess he had made. In the similar way that his grandfather had conceived of the implosion device, he believed that he had cured the void of mass argument amongst colleagues. His notorious grandfather had thought of the implosion device during a frustrated moment when he had squeezed an orange in his hand. After he had realized the sticky mess that was created by his own hand, he also realized that explosives evenly surrounding an atomic core were the key to more powerful and more efficient bombs. With a gentle and respectful smile, Michael turned out the door to greet the scientists he had been leading.

Two hours later, all of the scientists had finally assembled. With Michael Heimer standing in front of a large projector, he began his brief as to what he believed the difference to the experiment would be.

"Gentleman, we have created a device that the Defense Department could use to create a massive void in its target. It can destroy without evidence, as well as clear a path as far as thirty miles from detonation, without risks of radiation poisoning or fallout of any kind. We have devised a way to create a highway for soldiers to move quickly from their drop-off to their objective. No more breaking trail, and no more risks of what they could not see from obstructions in front of them. We have also found in it a weapon that would destroy anything in its targeted path without burns, fallout or shrapnel to cause a risk to those not intended.

There is only one problem, which was questioned by one of the head researchers. "What happens to the matter upon detonation? We know that matter traveling at the speed of light squared turns to energy. We do not know what this energy converts into. During our initial testing in the 'cave,' as we so affectionately call it, we have discovered that the pure building block of our religion, science, had been perverted."

Michael shifted on the podium and stared blankly at the wall behind the men in front of him, as if to explain what he believed his answer to be.

"Energy does not disappear, it simply turns into something else, as we all are well aware. We have discovered that radiation from a dying man could scatter about and move upon death. Franklin discovered that built-up static in the atmosphere discharges its energy toward the ground in the form of lightning. Gentleman, energy moves and transfers; it does not disappear, as we have seen with our own eyes in the cave. Where did this energy go? One theory covers that which is virgin ground in the realm of testing, and that is the space-time continuum. This is what I wish to speak with you all about today.

"One theory brought to me by Dr. Edwards discusses that matter traveling at the speed of light squared does not only turn to energy but passes a realm that we know as the STC, the space-time continuum. Previous scientists theorize the STC to be like that of a figure eight, or infinity. It is unknown where on this figure eight the matter might land, or even if it does land. I have an idea that I would like all of you to battle with and prove, right or wrong, and add to the equation. The Doppler effect is the old principle that explained why sound is weaker at a distance and why the size of an object is perceived larger at close range than it is at a distance. Gentlemen, the beacon that acts as the catalyst for our design slows down before it detonates.

"What if the matter, which simply disappears without trace, is not destroyed at a molecular level and turned to energy? What if this energy simply moves from our place in the STC to another? If so, would the distance from the beacon at detonation to the distance of the matter upon receiving the catalyst place it on separate places on the STC? Would objects five feet away from each other be placed hours or decades away from each other? Doctors, gentleman, please add these questions to our equations and give me your best answer."

Michael was about to end the project that was started by his grandfather, who had issued it to a new big name in science, and Michael would take the project from where his mentor and his grandfather had left off, to carry it the distance he had hoped. Almost fifty years in the making, the experiments were still unknown, even to most of the intelligence community. One person outside of the scientists working on the project knew about it. This man was the director of the Defense Intelligence Agency.

In Washington, D.C., members of Congress met to discuss the various bills laid before their desks. Aspects of these bills covered ranges of difficulties, from after-school activities being in place for the varied school districts at an attempt to lower the crime rate, to bills that were there to reevaluate existing decisions made by the bodies of the representatives as well as the Senate. The folder at the bottom of the tall stack before them addressed the issue that the American fighting force had dealt with since the first day of combat against the British regulars over two hundred years before. This file was an appeal brought in by the feminists from around the country.

Democratic Senator Malloy was sweating from the years of action against the very appeal being decided that moment; standing, Senator Malloy tucked his tie ever so carefully into his jacket. Adjusting his jacket along with his throat, he began to speak before the hundreds of elected persons before him.

"Ladies and gentleman, I stand before you today not as an elected member of this body but as a parent and as a concerned American. We have been hard at work all day today, and I hope that the point I make today will be brief and acute to the fabric of the morals that we have lived by for many wars and many more years. This appeal is an attempt by the feminist movement to allow female soldiers an opportunity to fight in our nation's interest by means of combat positions. As our policies currently allow, women are given the opportunity to serve in all jobs the military has to offer except combat positions requiring great deals of physical strength. Our reasons for excluding the female gender from the combat positions was strictly to maintain the strong and fierce fighting force that we have been proud of for over two hundred years. I believe that with female involvement on the front lines, the men will become distracted by the months of built-up 'frustration.' It is only from my own experience with combat in Vietnam, and my experience as a soldier, that I speak my mind. I offer opinions not from a conservative point of view but from the realistic point of view as a soldier. With the way our system is set up now, implementing women in combat arms would require us to place them on the physical grading scale. A separate grading scale for the women and the men would not be able to be tolerated in a combat environment. It is my firm belief that this nation's armed forces will only gain more and more suffering publicly to its reputation by mixing the female gender in combat arms. Ladies and gentleman, I expect you will make the appropriate decision and find the same, if not similar, conclusions I myself struggled with. I beg you to deny this appeal and keep the long-standing tradition in place. I would be heartbroken to find one of our daughters, wives or mothers in harm's way. Thank you for your patience."

Applause filled the capitol building as Senator Malloy took his seat. The decision did not take long to come back in favor for the traditional ways of war. Women were withheld from combat operations until such time that society could accept the notion of having women perform at the level required for the men without bias or alternate scales.

Senator Malloy left the capitol building with his head high, smelling the breeze of autumn. Reporters filled the stepped to catch the final words from the highly respectable and influential spokesperson and politician. No words were given to the press that had not been addressed prior. The senator stepped in his vehicle and instructed the driver to head to the farthest and most remote place he could think of. With creative recollection, the driver silently obeyed.

A short three hours later, the vehicle slowed to a stop on a back road near a short waterfall surrounded by thick woods. The senator took again a deep breath of the fall air and began his short walk to solitude. In his mind's eye, he thought back to the times when men would sit in woods not to think or be alone but to survive. An image of screaming and short bursts of artillery interrupted his peaceful venture. Standing from this place, Senator Malloy stepped up the short incline to the dirt road and thanked the driver. With instructions to stop by the nearest market and on to home, the vehicle began its final journey to a landmark day.

With newspaper in hand from the local market, Senator Malloy read the headline. "Congress to Vote on After-School Activities for Inner-City Children." No mention of the battle he had fought. With a sigh, the senator pushed the newspaper to the side and watched the trees wisp by.

The copy of *USA Today* sat unread, with titles unexplored, on May 21, 2008.

The Beacon or the Oracle?

A small Lear jet soared through Denali National Park destined for Fairbanks, Alaska. The majestic view soared by the windows of the small plane of five men who formed a committee of investigators. Traveling a long distance from the Pentagon, they were finally on the final leg of their trip. They were flying to visit an unlikely soldier who was the only known survivor under forty of the great war, whose cease-fire was almost thirty years before. Understanding how this man survived the war would unlock all issues with national security, even national history.

Beginning their descent, they packed their briefcases with the notes on Staff Sergeant Sands and the Fan Si Pan investigation.

The fourth floor of Basset Army Community Hospital at Ft. Wainwright, Alaska, was where the recovery rooms were located. In one of these rooms was Trevor Sands; the desolate hum of life support systems beeping and pumping drained out the usual sounds of life and solitude in the background.

On the ground level was a small crowd of investigators and family waiting for the doctor's word to allow visitation. Trevor's wife had called in her mother to help her through the time when Trevor was missing. A small group of men was huddled in a corner of the lobby. All of them had to be in their seventies. These men were carefully watching Trevor's wife and mother-in-law. Before they had segregated themselves, each of them consoled Trevor's wife and gave careful gifts to symbolize the grief and concern that they shared for Trevor.

The investigators included two FBI agents who had heard of a soldier who had disappeared and then later fell from twenty-five feet in midair in front of his own home, located in the outskirts of Fairbanks. There were several witnesses, including video footage of Trevor's fall, since it was his daughter's birthday party that day in the front yard of his home. Police detectives were there at the hospital to close the missing persons case; the Army's CID was brought in to do the same.

Trevor's wife was usually an attractive woman, but she bore no attraction now due to the stress that she had had to bear over the last few months. Now she was a tall and flushed woman with months of insomnia. At a young twenty-three years, others would assume that she had not done much in her life. Jessica Sands married Trevor almost three years before and was almost immediately pregnant with their daughter.

Before getting married, Jessi had her own issues. She had experienced dependency problems with drugs as well as alcohol, which began as a way to express rebellion to her strict family. Upon meeting Trevor, she had found a motivation to leave all of the problems behind her. Leaving the small town of Juno, she arrived in Fairbanks and moved in with her friends. Living there, she found herself a job in which she could respect herself. During her first week at work she met Trevor.

Trevor and Jessi met when Trevor was a young private first class. He had been in trouble with the Army because of a stupid prank played by some of his fellow soldiers. They had gone out fishing and left him in the woods to fend for himself. Six days later, Trevor walked into his company, exhausted and weak, after walking back from the campsite more than eighty miles away. The charge of quarters notified their first sergeant as well as Trevor's platoon sergeant. Both had come in to fill out the appropriate paperwork. They instructed the CQ runner to take Trevor to the hospital for IVs and to have the doctor look him over.

His punishment was for leaving the immediate area without a mileage pass and without notifying the proper channels of his location in case of emergency, as well as being drunk under the age of twenty-one; the charges of AWOL were waived, and he was issued an Article 15, which gave him extra duty for forty-five days. Had he have been charged with AWOL he could have expected a dishonorable discharge, or even to serve time in a military prison. The least they could have done for AWOL was give him the same punishment he was issued, but he would have "lost" time on his records, which would come back to bite him later in his career.

On his first night out after the long days of work and extra duty, he went to an all-night diner, where he met Jessica. They had talked all night and every night since then. They moved in together only after a month of knowing each other, and got married six months after they moved in together. The intensity of the relationship multiplied faster than for the typical couple.

She was very much in love with him, and now he was very much in a coma.

Hours passed as the soldiers and family paced the hallway in the lobby. Investigators took shifts there in the lobby. It was a miracle, so far, that the press had not been notified, considering the amount of witnesses and videotape. Press involvement was only a matter of time.

One week later, Trevor woke up to find three men in his face, coaching him to sit up. Nervously, Trevor fought his body to sit upright and motioned for the men to take the tube out of his throat. As one of them inflated the balloon to allow the tube to come back through the esophagus, Trevor gagged and coughed in reaction to the awful sensation. He would have vomited if he had anything in his stomach to spare. Confused and disoriented, Trevor looked around the room and asked one of the attendants what had happened. With all the intelligence gurus occupying the place, they wanted nothing to do with Trevor. They simply walked away and brought the doctor in. The doctor looked Trevor up and down, jotting notes on his chart. Trevor pleaded for the doctor to explain what had happened.

"I'm only going to tell you what I was told. You were found outside your home after falling off something. You were missing for over four months. Your wife called the paramedics, and you were brought here. If you don't know where you were for the last four months, then there is nothing I can tell you that will help. All I know is you fell from something at least twenty-five feet up and ended up here. That was a week ago. You have been in a coma since then. Now you are awake, and we'll fix you up as best as we can. In my opinion, you're lucky to be talking to me. There was a lot of damage. You even managed to get yourself shot. Don't even ask me how that happened. Now, I need you to follow the light with your eyes; don't move your head."

The doctor shined a bright flashlight in his eyes and moved it from side to side. The doctor conducted a short series of physical tests to ensure that Trevor hadn't sustained brain or nerve damage. Trevor passed all of the tests. While the doctor inspected Trevor's body, Trevor searched for the bullet wound. He found it on his thigh. Due to the amount of medication, he felt little pain.

"You would be surprised how many important people are waiting for you to come to. I will tell them you are awake shortly when I have time to get some food in your stomach and complete a work-up. Lay back and rest. You will see your family soon. I must warn you, there are some pushy people who will only let you see your family after they get everything they can from you to explain what happened. I hope for your sake that you have some answers for them."

Trevor nodded and looked around the room almost as if he needed to pinch himself to verify the reality. This was no dream, but there was no way to be sure anymore. The doctor turned to leave the room as every footstep slammed into Trevor's ears. The doctor eased the door shut, but the alarming click of the door mechanism forced Trevor to a place that drowned Trevor in horror.

His eyes were gazing at the green jungle and suddenly he slammed into a void of red as he fell to the ground. Trevor tried to roll into a better position in which to defend himself. The red haze covering his eyes cleared in places to reveal a long barrel staring at him. Closing his eyes, he had one last chance to save himself. Trevor kicked his legs up at the man behind the barrel. The man was forced back and fired one shot into Trevor's leg. Reaching behind his back, Trevor pulled his knife and lunged at the man. He slowly pushed the blade into the breastplate of the man's chest; the grinding of bone against metal was overwhelming. Gurgling blood and spit flowed from the man's mouth as Trevor issued all remaining energy to reverse the thrust of the blade. Finally, the blade stopped, with the tip resting on the ground beneath the man, who now eased his grip on Trevor's shoulder. Trevor, shaken and scared, twisted the blade with all effort to ensure the man would not get up. The slow grinding caused a thunderous crack to emit from the man's chest. Trevor pulled the knife out and fell back with morbid disgust. The blood cleared from his eyes, and Trevor looked around to gain his bearings. Lying on his back, he looked at the trees above, sensing the sick feeling of defeat. Lying next to him was a poorly uniformed Vietnamese officer with a large hole carved into his chest. Stumbling to the riverbank, Trevor vomited. It suddenly seemed like it was years ago that he was at home with his wife, preparing for the upcoming mission he had been deployed to.

After his first meal in who knows how long, and a couple hours of rest, the doctor informed the people in the lobby that Trevor was awake and alert. The first to enter was the CID investigator, who brought with him a man whose agency was not mentioned.

The questions that were asked were of the sort that would make any man, confused or not, shake his head in disbelief. The questions from the CID agent were straightforward and to the point of a missing person case. The questions from the other man, though, were not. Still in a confused haze, Trevor had no inkling of how to attempt to answer the man. Instead, he asked if he could come back after he spent time with his family. The agent responded with the typical "national security, no unauthorized personnel" jargon. The CID agent asked the man if one of them could sit in the room with Trevor while he spoke to his family to ensure that no information would be passed. With that, the agent reluctantly agreed and called downstairs for Jessi and their daughter.

Jessi arrived from the lobby with their daughter, Mali. Standing in the doorway, Jessi looked into the room where her husband was staying. Staring down the agents who were frustrated and short in temper, Jessi sat in a chair positioned next to Trevor's bed. Mali nuzzled into her mother as if she were afraid of her own father. The tension in the room was thick enough to taste. The agents did not speak a word but instead studied the couple to get a reading on what might be said between them. The CID agent briefed Jessi when she was in the elevator. She was simply told not to ask any questions about where he was or whom he was with. She could only talk about things dealing with family.

Tears filled the eyes of the couple as they stared at each other. The overwhelming feeling of relief and love were evident to anyone watching the couple. The baby was silent, probably in confusion, trying to place the face of the man lying in the bed in front of her. Jessi simply smiled and leaned over to kiss her husband on the forehead. Nothing was spoken; the couple simply wanted to touch each other and study each other's eyes. After an hour of smiles and relief, the agents insisted that they have another try at questioning Trevor.

With the only words spoken between the couple, Jessi kissed her husband again on the forehead and said, "I love you, and we will wait for you to come home."

Alone now with the mysterious agent, Trevor simply asked what the agent knew so he would know how to begin filling in the blanks. The agent finally introduced himself as Special Agent Monroe with the Defense Intelligence Agency. Special Agent Monroe told Trevor what he knew.

They had a special project in Vietnam that involved a ship-mounted device that was similar to a rail gun design. It would launch a beacon at the speed of light that would then open up and force the object in its path to travel at that speed squared. It was designed to destroy anything and everything in its path. What they did not expect was that the items or beings in its path would travel along a time line, which was determined by the velocity breakdown of the beacon. Trevor, who was in Vietnam on a humanitarian mission, stumbled along the path of the beacon during the test fire and was then sent with the six other persons in his fire team back somewhere. The DIA had no idea how far back or where. Because of the rotation of the Earth, they could have landed wherever the planet was revolving at the time of release from the time line.

They had tried to calculate the breakdown of velocity of the beacon before it activated its path of destruction. They could not gauge exactly what happened. Since the DIA and the contractors believed the beacon would only destroy the object in its path, they did not factor the theory of relativity. The theory stated that an object of mass traveling at the speed of light squared turned to energy. This also correlated with the theories of the space-time continuum. All of this was soaring over Trevor's head.

The gist of it was that the agency accidentally sent Trevor and his men back in time somewhere. What Special Agent Monroe needed to know was not how, but when and where.

Thinking back, Trevor forced himself to a place that seemed like a strange dream. Images flowed through his mind, and he tried to sort them out to discover when the beginning was. Then a sickening feeling passed over him as he recalled the horrifying and heroic moments that he had lived in such a short time. Closing his eyes, he told the agent to find something to record with; he doubted he would be able to recall it again.

The Hangover

Trevor kissed his wife goodbye as he loaded his truck with his gear. As she patiently waited for her husband to come back and give her one more kiss goodbye, the voices from the television distracted her shortly when she realized they were now talking about her husband's unit.

"Soldiers are being sent to North Vietnam as a contingency force. Though all diplomatic means are being used to ensure that these soldiers are there only as a contingency force, there is talk on Capitol Hill of the possible use of Special Forces to ensure the resolution of the hostage crisis in Vietnam. Reports of special operations groups being sent or even considered are unconfirmed. We go now to our military analyst, Colonel William Butler. Colonel, what is your opinion? Do you feel that Special Forces will be used in Vietnam, or do you think that this problem can be dealt with diplomatically?"

A skinny man with obvious experience was standing in front of a large television with images of Vietnamese men running in the streets with machine guns. The colonel had begun to respond when Trevor rushed through the door, delivering his final kiss goodbye. With a tear teasing out of Jessi's eye, which Trevor had anticipated, he wiped it off gently. Looking at his wife in a very observant way, Trevor closed his eyes as if to take a picture to remember. Turning toward the door, Jessi rushed him from behind to deliver a tight hug. Holding the hands of his wife, Trevor peeled their bodies apart and walked to his vehicle, looking back at the nervous woman.

In Vietnam there were several factions of NVA and Viet Cong roaming through the jungles. Most of them were harmless now, but every once in a while they got an itch they desperately needed to scratch. In this case it was refusal of demands made to the American embassy there. The remaining factions were nothing more than common terrorists. The groups had begun an assault on the embassy and started up a small conflict once again in Vietnam. Several U.S. officials were executed and many more held hostage. As preparation for peacekeepers and, more than likely, Special Forces, units have been inserted to evacuate the American personnel and key figures that were non-combatant. Supporters had been targeted and supply lines had been attacked.

NEO (Non-Combatant Evacuation Operations) was the operation that Americans conducted to eliminate the risk of needless civilian lives lost. The American people and the politicians did not like watching their own people on the news being shot, bombed or held as prisoners. It was more political than anything else. When Washington received their numbers of American casualties, it helped them sort out civilians and soldiers.

The 1st battalion 17th Infantry Regiment was selected for the Pacific region support. Stationed out of Alaska, it placed them a hop and a skip away from the troubled region.

Trevor boarded the CH-47 Chinook heading to Eielson Air Force Base from Ft. Wainwright, where they would link up with a C-5 Galaxy cargo and passenger plane, one of the largest in the Air Force inventory. From Eielson they would fly to Los Angeles, California, for refuel, then to Guam, where they would transfer to a C-130 passenger plane to Da Nang, Vietnam. The flight was long and boring. All the soldiers were thinking about the battles that were ahead and the friends they might lose along the way.

From Da Nang they moved to the backs of five-ton trucks to take them to the confined area loaned to the U.S. by the Vietnamese government.

That was where they received their operation orders and further instructions as to the specifics of the mission. Major Freeman of the Battalion's S-3 (operations section) was briefing the men in place of the commander, who was working with the local government as to the smoothest way to evacuate the personnel without ruffling any feathers.

Major Freeman was a skinny man who could run like the wind. He never tired and had a great sense of humor in times of crisis. Always at ease and usually straightforward, he pulled C Company's first platoon aside and instructed them to the specific mission in which they were assigned. The platoon's mission was to find one man who moved from hut to hut within a fifty-kilometer radius. This man was an American-born scientist who moved to Vietnam after facing the embarrassment of a failed experiment of cold fusion that proved to be a falsehood. He was a man of genius, but a man who could not handle failure. He was a person of valued importance who would be difficult to acquire.

Trevor linked up with his alpha team, who would be going on the hike through the woods with him to search for Dr. Sung. He looked around at his men. Corporal Boyd was a longtime friend of Trevor's, as well as his alpha team leader. His machine gunner was Baxley, who traveled with his assistant gunner, Private Malloy. His rifleman and radio telephone operator was Private Wilson. The grenadier, who was responsible for signals, concealment and high explosive grenades, was Private Himelrick. Private Trits, who maintained a high level of fire when the medium machine gun was not necessary, operated the light machine gun. These seven men would travel together to track down and extract the notable scientist.

Trevor listened to the order and observed his area of responsibility. After briefing his men, he began his movement to find Dr. Sung. The six soldiers moved toward the last known address of their designated person, who was about thirty-five kilometers away from their present location.

As they broke a trail through the dense trees, they gained a bearing to Dr. Sung's hut and begin a straight movement. After an hour, they reached a large gully they would have to walk around. Losing three hours on the timetable, they crossed the gulley and begin working their way back to the bearing from which they started. Stopping for chow, they sat back and watched the sun force itself through the curtain of trees above them. Suddenly they heard the crack of what sounded like a recoilless rifle in the distance. Snapping their web gear on, they positioned themselves in a small perimeter as Trevor and his RTO (radio telephone operator) begin a small recon to see if they could identify the location of the sound. Moving due south of his men, he headed straight to what the map showed as the Black River.

Spotting nothing, the two men returned to the perimeter after they reported what they knew about the fire. Because it was possible that they were receiving fire, Trevor thought it to be a good idea to zigzag on their way to the perimeter to avoid snipers and trackers. As they moved northeast, they crossed something that would burn forever in the mind of Trevor and Wilson.

A clear-cut path burned into the ground that stretched for miles was in front of them. Informing the TOC of possible PIR, or pertinent information requirement, they began to take a closer look. Wilson went down on the ground to provide security for Trevor as he closed in on the closest tree to the path. The tree was severed vertically in half with no saw marks or burn marks. It was simply dissected down the line as if it were simply pulled apart and sanded down. Perfectly smooth. All trees, rocks and even a tiger were on the side of the path in this manner. Squinting against the sun that faced him, he spotted a hut that was cut in the same way as the tree and tiger. Calling Private Wilson to follow him, they moved to the hut. Wilson looked below his feet as he walked alongside Trevor. He noticed that the trees and tiger were not the only things damaged; the earth looked as if an enormous bulldozer had dug through it. The ground was perfectly level, with no sign of grass. Worms were protruding from the earth, dissected in half. The trail of death led from three hundred meters behind them to two hundred meters to their front. Once they determined the area clear of hostiles, they began looking around. Private Wilson was first to notice and called the attention to his squad leader. Under a chair was a man who was sliced in half at the hip horizontally. Blood was pouring from the man and filled the floor of the small hut. Portions of the man's stomach and lungs were beside him. Wilson, who had a strong stomach, reached under the man. He pulled a bloody ball from underneath the carnage. Holding the dripping wad, Wilson unfolded it to reveal the man's wallet. Pulling out the driver's license from Utah, the picture was suddenly clear. They had found Dr. Sung.

Reporting this information back to the TOC was extremely difficult. Trevor had no idea how to describe Dr. Sung's death, let alone describe the path that led to him. All they knew was that there was something that they were probably not supposed to see surrounding the area in which they occupied. With every creative effort, Trevor pulled the hand mike from Wilson and began to call the tactical operations center.

"Buffalo 33, this is Diablo 11, over."

"This is Buffalo 33, over."

"Hey, Buffalo 33, I got a mess here. I found our package and, well, he's pretty dead. Be advised, there is something here that Buffalo 2 needs to look at. Prepare to copy grid, over."

"Diablo 11, send it, over."

"Grid as follows. November-Zulu-three-three-five-seven-eight-two, over." The over-enunciated numbers were scribbled on a form and given to the intelligence officer

"This is Diablo11. Do you need me to stand by for Buffalo 2? Over."

"Diablo, wait one."

Trevor waited for the response. The horrific view before him was enough to terrify anyone. His stomach was growing weaker by the second, and he only prayed they would tell him to return to base. Breaking the silence, the TOC informed him that it was okay to clear the area and that the intelligence officer would be out there when he finished his meetings to look for himself. With relief, Trevor replied and delivered Wilson his hand mike.

Trevor pulled out his ICOM, which was used for communications between small parties, such as squad leader to team leader. Staff Sergeant (Ssg.) Sands instructed the men in the perimeter to move to the previous rally point that was established. He would meet them there to move back to the TOC.

At the rally point, Trevor handed Wilson the ID, which proved Dr. Sung was the man they were sent to acquire, and began the movement back to the TOC. Covered with blood and dirt, they looked like they had just been through a battle themselves. With the egging on from the other team members, Wilson and Trevor were still in shock enough not to talk about it.

Walking their journey back to the TOC, there was a loud report just like the one from before. No later than a second after they heard a shot fired, they were thrown into unconsciousness, as if someone knocked the life out of them all.

Wilson was the first of the group who looked up to find only Sands lying directly to his side in a large hole, seemingly a crater from artillery. No one else was with them when they were hit. Shaking Trevor, Wilson screamed in panic. Trevor opened his eyes and grabbed Wilson's mouth to keep him quiet.

After Wilson had taken a few breaths to calm down, Trevor let go of the boy's jaw and sat down, holding his rifle. Anxiously, he keyed the hand mike to the aging ASIP radio to contact the TOC, but there was no answer. Wilson tried the alternate frequency, but there was nothing. Frustrated and in pain, the two men sat down to wait for the TOC to contact them. Moving out of the crater, they walked a few meters and patiently stared at the pit in which they had awakened.

Two hours passed as the men attempted to associate themselves with the map by the terrain, with no luck. Lost, hungry and hurting, the two men passed the time with sleep. Hiding themselves and their equipment in the brush, they closed their eyes in slumber.

A cloud formed five feet away from Trevor's head, about six feet off the ground. Becoming more and more dense, lightning stirred inside the small marvel. Buzzing and static surrounded the area as a flash of light woke the men instantly. Lightning stirred all its might and hammered the ground, leaving a fog of dust. The dust settled, and all that was left was a hole similar to the one that Wilson and Trevor had woken up in. Slowly moving to the side of the hole, they saw nothing but dust and smoke. A slight sound of groaning and coughing was heard. Wilson jumped down to find the source. It was their squad automatic weapon (SAW) gunner, Private First Class (Pfc.) Trits. Pulling him out of the hole, Trevor grabbed hold of the top of the web gear and pulled him to fresh air. Trits was disoriented and bruised. Treating him for shock, they pull the young man under a tree and try to compensate body temperature. It took nearly an hour for Trits to wake up fully and speak.

Almost fifteen hours had passed when all the members of the team had arrived in the same strange way. All of them were conscious and alert. None of them were aware of what had actually happened. Putting their heads together, they attempted to determine their location using the GPS and their maps. Nothing matched. Their GPS was not even working. Perhaps it was the electrical interference from the storms, Trevor thought. The men slowed their thinking down and ate their rations. Once they realize that they were lost and alone, they decided they would try something else in the morning.

Sleeping soundly, they woke to the sound of automatic gunfire. Quickly and instinctively, they moved their positions in a perimeter and waited for something they could see. By the rules of engagement, they were told that they could fire only if they were being fired directly upon by the few remaining Viet Cong. Under no circumstances were they to fire against Vietnamese nationals. The nationals were not known to fire weapons; if they were scared they would throw rocks or maybe a Molotov cocktail, but mostly they would just scream and wave their hands around. As of yet they had nothing in their sights. Anxiety rushed through them like a strong wave. The men were confused, in pain and now in a firefight they couldn't see. Each of them were praying in their own different way, hoping to gather the slightest bit of clarity on the situation.

Trevor ordered the men to pick up and move away from where they had fallen. Perhaps the storms drew too much attention to their location. Walking in a standard wedge formation, they moved to the direction they last knew the TOC to be. As if they weren't in a bad enough situation, the men found themselves staring blankly at a river that they had never crossed from this direction. Painfully retracting all that had made sense a day prior, they set up security where they were, hoping that someone without a weapon would find them and explain what the hell was going on.

Aching heads, bleeding ears and noses seemed to be all that was left of the unexplainable landing into the holes in which they awoke. The slightest sounds and light shot through their mind like a rusty nail, forcing its way downward through their skull. Corporal Jonathon Boiyd sat next to Trevor. Corporal Boiyd was one of the team leaders in Trevor's squad. His team was the only one of the two in the squad that was selected to go on the mission. The other team on the squad was in the rear, pulling roving security at the TOC. Corporal Boiyd managed to muster enough courage to ask Trevor for permission to take two men and conduct a recon up the riverbed. Denying Boiyd's pleas, he instead ordered all men to their feet as they headed upstream to find a village.

Fishing villages in Vietnam would always be located at the edge of the river itself. These villages were typically filled with skittish natives who may have never seen Americans before in their life. The Americans that they had heard of had always been the brutal force that fought their fathers and grandfathers. They heard only what the traders or passersby said to them. They had no radio and no television. Poorly educated and strong-willed, they would help anyone in need, even through the pain and anguish their ancestors may have caused.

As they crossed a danger area in which there was an open space leaving them all without cover, they entered the wood line to find themselves at the outskirts of one of these villages. Trevor halted his men and placed them in their security positions. Moving toward the village with his RTO, Wilson, he was greeted with every woman taking their playful children in their homes and the men moving toward them with rakes and sticks in hand. Trevor looked back at Wilson as he slung his heavy weapon behind his back slowly to show a sign of non-hostility; Wilson did the same. What looked like the strongest and the oldest man in the village was the first to greet the Americans. The younger men were yelling under their breath as if to not draw attention, but their tone was loud and clear enough to be heard by everyone within the immediate area. The older and wiser looking man reached for Trevor's hand and escorted the two Americans to a shack, where they offered them water. Trevor smiled curtly to the older man, followed by the most complicated conversation he would ever have.

Motioning with his GPS and compass, he tried to express that he was lost. He pulled out a map and gestured for the man to show them where they were. The older man looked at the map in confusion and handed it to another native. This man was short but built like a lion, with very lean muscle and enough mass to throw his weight around if needed. This man looked the map over and frowned.

Looking back at Trevor, he said in English, "You in the Fan Si Pan Valley," and pointed a finger at their location at a sharp bend in the black river. Trevor's brow squinted with confusion.

The man stood to leave the shack, turned back to Trevor and motioned for him to follow. The man pointed upriver and said something unclear. Trevor squinted, leaning the right side of his head toward the man to hear better over the white water of the river.

"I say, you must help us! Vietnam Congsan from Hanoi treat us like pigs, they raid our village, they rape my wife and shoot my animals. My son beaten because he say bad things to VC soldier."

Trevor took a deep breath and turned away from the river and away from the man's tears. With the intensity of the events and things that Trevor had seen, he began to feel nauseous. Closing his eyes and bending his knees, he vomited on the river-beaten rocks. Wilson stared blankly upriver at the smoke coming from the trees. Very faintly, they heard small arms fire. Looking around, Wilson was half-tempted to kneel down and join Trevor.

Begging for clarification, Trevor asked the man, "Sir, you mean the terrorists? I thought the actual soldiers were non-existent."

The look in the stocky man was one of shock and humor, as if he was trying to keep from laughing. It was unbelievable that these Americans were telling him that there were no soldiers. It was more than he could take. Spitting toward the river, the man turned to the village and stomped off.

Walking back to the wood line, Trevor searched his mind, trying to find the words to explain to his men what made no sense. Frustrated and confused, like much of the past thirty-six hours, Trevor decided to sit the men down and explain what was told to him.

How was he going to explain that they were now on the other side of the river with no recollection of moving, had woken up in what had to have been a grave, and that there was clear evidence that the VC were still terrorizing these people after all these years. The elder had asked Trevor to stay nearby to help defend them. Trevor tried to explain that he must not get involved. The elder pulled several pictures of Americans at a dinner table with him that were apparently taken three weeks before. The men signed the back and dated it June 12, 1969.

The men sat back and took a deep breath of the humid jungle mist. Looking down, they all sat silent for several minutes before the first of them spoke. Corporal Boiyd stood and put a cigarette out with his boot.

Looking to his right, he said, "You can't seriously be considering what the senile old man was saying, are you? There is no fucking way that these people have any clue what time it is, let alone what date. As far as waking up where I did, fuck if I know. Probably some mortar fire and artillery knocked us out from the concussion. Blasts could have thrown us in the craters left from other rounds."

Trevor had heard enough. Holding his hand toward Boiyd, he interrupted.

"Hey, Corporal, you were the last to land, so you have no fucking idea what happened. Wilson and I were first here, and I know for a fact the artillery or mortars had nothing to do with what happened to us. If it were arties, don't you think we'd be dead? I know you didn't see, Boiyd, but the rest of us did. Arty did not create a friggin' cloud out of thin air and burn a hole in the ground where we all woke up. Boiyd, something happened to us all that I have never heard of. You boys know me. You know I'm an all or nothing guy. If it is going to be fucked up, it needs to be severely fucked up. I am not going to create problems, but I assure you that something over our heads happened, and we all have no clue what."

Boiyd considered these words and began, "Okay, Sergeant, we have no idea what happened to us or know why the hell we are on the wrong side of the river. What I do know was that we can't help any of these people. We do what we are supposed to, gather information and give it to higher-ups. I'm sure that UCMJ would screw us if they found out we were killing people to help a village that I'm sure they don't care about. Let's find out where the fuck we are and then figure out what we do while we're here. There's no way we could be where they say we are. Dudes don't just walk around on one side of a river and end up on the other more than a click upstream. I want proof. For all we know it could be some fucked-up village with people just screwin' with our heads. They could have gassed us, brought us here and then decided to mess with us! I'm just sayin' we should find someone that we know is credible before we start believing this shit that I'm sure we are imagining."

All the soldiers nodded in agreement; Trevor was in full agreement as well, so he made his decision.

"I agree with Corporal Boiyd. We will wait until we find someone who is credible and without leaving ourselves open for criticism, whether they are fucking with us or not. We have one ration per man left, and they have offered their food. We should at least eat with them and test the waters there a bit more. We also have to consider the pictures that they showed Wilson and me. They were of U.S. soldiers who looked to be dressed in old uniforms with the

A-1's. The damn thing was dated 1969. Now that is just another thing that they have to screw with us, but I almost feel more comfortable with going what we went through if it were thirty years ago. Let's ground our gear here. Wilson, you stay as weapon guard, and Trits, you bring him back chow. Let's move."

Dreams Abroad

Smoke rose from the watchtower designed to observe the trainees for air assault. The instructors were studying one of four students who would walk away from the course with the highest honors. All types of soldiers could go to this school. Infantry, medics, field artillery, supply clerks and three truck drivers filled the class. The students were enduring a gruesome twelve-mile road march, the final phase prior to graduation. A thick haze of fog permeated the long gravel road where the twenty-five candidates marched. At the pace they must keep, some find it better to jog every other mile to make the time required; others insist that they could maintain the pace by walking. Twelve miles in three hours is not a difficult task except for the burdensome weight of the rucksack and combat gear.

One of the students ran the entirety of the 12 miles to ensure her first place across the finish line. Never in her life had she failed to meet a goal that she made for herself. Growing up in Papillion, Nebraska, A.J. Segal didn't have much knowledge of places outside her community. When she was fourteen she had watched a young woman on television, cut, beaten and exhausted, get carried out of captivity in Iraq by several Special Forces men and a "Chinook" CH-47 helicopter. A.J. watched intensely as reporters speculated as to what happened to her. Regardless of what the reporters thought, in A.J.'s eyes a hero of inspiration was born.

For five long years she trained to join the Army to prove herself to her ignorant father. As a child, her father would sit her down in the living room and teach her the "facts of life." She would sit for hours at a time and listen as her father instructed her in Racism 101. She would learn the abridged history of the United States and learn that the black men and women in the States were the cause for the fall of the white dominant society. These ideals had never latched on to A.J.'s personal ideals.

In high school, Segal found the only true friend she had ever known. Her friend's father was an Air Force major assigned to Offutt Air Force Base in Omaha, Nebraska. Segal would spend many nights at her new friend's home, her life finally one of friendship and peace, until her friend came to the Segal house unannounced. A.J.'s father answered the door and let the young girl into the living room. Segal had come down the stairs to see who was visiting when she walked in on her father teaching her friend how the black people were at fault for every disease and political downfall in the nation. Segal's friend left the room in tears and ran home, never to speak to Segal again. A.J.'s father then continued to scold her for allowing "that animal" into the home. Segal lost her only friend, and she lost her because she was black.

Segal was running the final stretch of the twelve miles to finish her goal in achieving her air assault badge. As a truck driver, Segal was not permitted to attend combat-specific schools. As a woman, she would be at the bottom of the list for all other schools. This was the unwritten rule in what she called the "law of the buddy boys." She had spent five years driving trucks while her head was filled with dreams of carrying her battle buddy out of danger. She had dreams of jumping from a large cargo aircraft with a hundred other soldiers to the combat zone below. Her heart was always Army, but her dreams belonged to the infantry.

As the end of the road march, the first person across the line was given points that would factor in who left the school with honors. Through the thick haze, the instructors at the finish line could hear the grunts of two soldiers as they approach the end. The exhausted form of a soldier penetrates the thick haze as the swift soldier crosses the line at a low time of two hours and one minute. Second place was running as fast as possible and finished only forty-seven seconds behind the first. Both soldiers sit at the field across from the finish line and remove their helmets. The first place winner reveals his face from the balaclava that protected him from the bitter cold of Alaska's early October morning. The face belonged to Specialist Tad Harrison, an infantryman from one of the local battalions. The second place winner was A.J. Segal, a soldier with remarkable strength for a truck driver.

That day she felt like a failure for letting a man beat her at a simple road march. However simple it was for her, the next person to cross the finish line arrived almost forty minutes after she had crossed. Looking over to Tad Harrison, she felt a huge kick to her ego as she set next to the one who defeated her. She realized that she would be runner-up at graduation. Even through the regret that weighed heavily upon her, she sat back and closed her eyes as she waited for the others to finish.

The Reunion

Sitting at a large table only a foot off the ground, the men looked around very carefully at the men who had told them stories of aggressors that hadn't been around since the seventies. At least half of the men had horrid scars that were visible; it was safe to say that they all had scars that were not as obtrusive. Did these scars come from Viet Cong torturing them for information, or did they simply come from the hard life of living in a fishing village? The area of the village and the damage to morale was consistent with everything that Ssg. Sands had always imagined. He had never been in combat before, and this was more than his senses could take. He could taste the death.

Trevor had seen a documentary of Vietnam in 2005. From what he had seen, the area had turned back to its origin. He saw rice paddies filled with woman and children harvesting and maintaining. The men were not walking around with rifles and grenades; they were building huts and running plows. This was definitely a different world.

Trits packed up a plate of rice and some food he couldn't describe if he wanted to, and he definitely did not want to. Thanking the hosts, they begin moving back to the wood line to get the sleep they desperately needed. Wilson was first to get sleep, since he had pulled the last guard shift. Wilson was a small young man with no experience. He was very intelligent and very book smart; his common sense, however, was lacking. Laying his head down, he seemed to fall asleep before his eyes finished closing.

Trevor ensured all of the guys were taken care of and security was in place. He had the machine gunner and an assistant gunner on guard. Whomever they woke up would take the place of either gunner or AG. Trevor instructed the gunner to only fire as a last resort. A medium machine gun was a typical weapon carried by platoon-sized elements. Anyone who studied American tactics would know that if they were to come across medium machine guns, they should assume that they were up against a platoon instead of a fire team or squad.

Trevor walked back to the village with rifle in hand to speak to the natives again. Walking down the path, he turned to face the hut of the eldest, who was speaking with the only villager who spoke English. Looking at the translator, Trevor asked him to translate something for him. With a nod, the man stood to explain what Trevor had said to the elder.

Trevor began, "Please tell him that we are in great debt to him for his hospitality. We must speak, and I wish that neither of you repeat to anyone what I am about to tell you."

The translator passed the message. A moment later, the elder and the translator agreed. Trevor lowered his head, racking his mind to find the words to explain what he knew had happened.

"Sir, I know what I am about to tell you will seem crazy."

Trevor looked back at the translator; the large man wasn't missing a beat in translation. Hesitantly, Trevor continued to tell the tale of where he was and where he and his men woke up.

After an hour of these men thinking of the conversation that had just taken place, they let it sink in with awe that could not be described. Finally, after what could only be described as a painfully short list of possible courses of action, the village elder explained to Trevor that the American Special Forces came by once a month to gather intelligence from the village of VC and NVA activity. Trevor asked permission for his men to hide in the woods outside of their village until the Americans came by again. Once the elder briefed Trevor as to what side of the village was a highspeed avenue of approach for the VC and which side the Americans usually came by, Trevor decided to place his men to the southeast of the village, near the Black River. Trevor did not want the SF to think they were VC and open fire on his men, likewise with his men to the SF.

It seemed that the green berets were his best chance to get out. It was perfect in his mind. Special Forces could possibly manage to get his men out without raising unnecessary eyebrows. Trevor gently bowed toward the elder, as he believed the custom to be. The elder bowed back, as well as the translator. Turning to leave, Trevor noticed a sling sticking out of a small closet by the door. Trevor recognized the sling type and asked the elder, without facing him, where he got his rifle, hoping the answer was from the SF. The elder confirmed what Trevor hoped. The M16A1 assault rifle rested where Trevor found it. Trevor smiled at the antique weapon and left the room.

Walking back toward the perimeter, Trevor gazed at the skies above him. The romantic inside of him was hoping that his wife was holding their daughter and not worrying a bit about him. Trevor had an issue with a premature declaration of his death when he was in Bosnia. He was on a peacekeeping mission when a rocket-propelled grenade (RPG) missed him by inches. Through the dust and rubble, his friends thought they had witnessed his demise. When the Army had a chance to sift through the rubble, they didn't find him. He was found walking back to base camp after they had sent a death notification to his wife thirty-six hours prior. They rushed him to a telephone and he managed to contact his wife while she was on the porch steps with the post chaplain. She was hysterical when she answered the phone. The chaplain had just attempted to console her when Trevor eased her mind over the phone with one sentence. He simply spoke, and his voice soothed her heart. In her emotional confusion, she managed to lose control as she walked back to the chaplain and landed a solid punch to his face. The poor man spun to the porch, having no idea who was on the phone or what the current situation was.

Closing in on the perimeter, Trevor eased to where the gunner and AG rested, pulling security opposite of the village. Since the gunner did not know that their squad leader had left, Trevor low-crawled close enough to the position to holler out his presence. The gunner responded with the challenge as Trevor replied the password. Now clear for Trevor to enter the perimeter, Trevor found out if anything had happened. From what the AG had said, absolutely nothing had happened.

Sleeping soundly for the remainder of the night, Trevor allowed his men to continue sleeping through the better of the day. Fifty percent of the men would rest while the other half would pull security. For evening chow, the women from the village brought the men some nicely flavored rice with pork strips. The soldiers consumed each morsel of food as if this were their last. The women brought the men some wine and some rice pudding, an extremely rare treat considering their poverty.

Some of the women helped the men mend their blistered feet. These were the younger men who hadn't had a chance for their feet to harden from the hundreds of miles of marching or running that the men use for training. Trevor and Boiyd, even Baxley, the M240Z machine gunner, had feet hard enough to walk on nails. These poor kids were still getting to the point where they could just get their boots on and walk.

Weeks passed, and Trevor felt the dire need to train these men much better in the ways of recon and reaction techniques. Trevor taught them the best ways to conduct a close-area recon as well as preparing ambush sites. The next few weeks were spent improving and honing their techniques. The tactics used by U.S. soldiers have always been redefined after the failures of past wars and conflicts. Most of the changes made in the tactics come from the lessons learned from the Vietnam and Iraqi conflicts. The Joint Chiefs of Staff organized a massive undertaking by having all tactics rewritten to allow for the faults found in the tactics to guerilla warfare as well as aircraft. The greatest changes made were pertaining to the way men would initiate contact. Instead of being an aggressively offensive force, the U.S. instilled the need to teach and concentrate on defensive doctrine. Countless attacks to United States soldiers were from falling into the traps that the VC had lured them into. A popular trap was to use a man who would act as a lure. Once an eager lieutenant or sergeant would see this man, it was common for them to give chase. The lure would run directly into an ambush that would be in place for the platoon or squad. The lure would then trade places with someone on the ambush line and go out to find another unit to kill. Other crude tactics used by the Viet Cong would include small children and women. They would commonly threaten to kill their entire family if they did not do what they were told. Some of these things varied, from delivering grenades in hand baskets to American soldiers while they were passing through a village, to infecting women with a severe sexually transmitted disease and then having them sell themselves to soldiers. Instead of killing the horny soldiers, they were taken out of action while being treated for their STD. This method of using prostitutes proved to be the easiest and cheapest delivery of biological weapons, not to mention a way to financially contribute to the war.

Concentrating now on fine-tuning the young soldiers' weaponry techniques, Trevor managed to get an AK-47 from the village and practice its use in case the soldiers needed a backup weapon. Practicing with blocks of wood, the men would learn ways to use C-4 and claymore mines. The men practiced their hand-to-hand combat skills as well as bayonet techniques. Road marching early in the morning and running in the evening, the men were all equipped with the thick skin and endurance necessary to survive the jungle and a war. The confidence in the men grew with every difficult task set before them. Along with the confidence, arrogance began to shine through.

The training they would conduct now would involve the weapon systems, which were still new to the Army's arsenal. The rifles each man carried were extremely heavy but had more firepower than any of the old systems in the past. The M252-A was a 5.56mm rifle with a 20mm grenade launcher above the rifle barrel. The grenade launcher had a six-grenade magazine and fed like the prior model automatic rifles. The magazine for the grenade launcher rested behind the pistol grip with the 30-round rifle magazine in front of the grip. The safety selector switch was located within thumb's reach of the firing hand, while the barrel selector switch was located to the side of the trigger housing in front of the safety. A rechargeable battery was encased in the butt of the weapon, which charged when the weapon was moving. Simply swinging the rifle, or any typical movement from marching, would charge the optics that consisted of a laser range finder, video, day optics and tracker. The video feed led directly to an eyepiece, which was mounted to the helmet on the opposite side of the night vision. This feed would allow the soldier to fire the weapon while only exposing his rifle. He could easily stand at a corner of a building, exposing the weapon, and see exactly what he was aiming at through the eyepiece.

A small computer display was mounted to the key leader's wrists that displayed the latest intelligence update from the TOC and would allow messages back and forth using everyday relay chat services, which were sent through an encrypted signal. Trevor had such a device on his wrist, and so did Boiyd. The new technology that they were issued only two years prior still had some bugs that needed worked out. Since they had no contact with the TOC, let alone use of their GPS, the time came for them to find their own techniques that would keep them alive and safe during their excursion. They had decided to prepare the villagers in advance in case they were ever attacked by instructing them to get down on the floor and do nothing at the first sign of attack. Trevor assured them that all would be okay and that their men would take care of them.

Baxley, the medium-machine gunner, had the old M-240B with some modifications made to it. The machine gun would have the same optics and feed that the rest of the men had except that Baxley had one more feature on his optics. He had the ability to detect thermal images. Seeing through no more than one foot on concrete, the figure of a man would provide him with the ability to protect men from a distance through buildings. The rounds he fired were penetrating explosive rounds that comprised of a regular full metal jacketed round covered with an impact explosive that would blow a hole in a concrete wall and allow the bullet to fly through, still following the same trajectory.

With these weapons they would be more than competent in any conflict from the Third World country they now sat in.

They were now encircled in their perimeter, which was still located to the south end of the village near the river. They were sharpening their bayonets and, once again, counting their ammo.

Patiently waiting for the Special Forces team to make their monthly checks on the village, Trevor began to prepare a wish list for rations and ammo; the men finalize it with replacement gear such as ponchos and socks. Hopefully, the SF would be helpful in supplying them with items needed to survive in case the SF could not help them with extraction.

Eating the meals which they had grown to love from the village, they prepared their new schedule for sleep and security. The village elder, whose name they still could not pronounce, told them that the SF should be there tomorrow or the next day, usually arriving at night. Hopefully, they would soon meet.

About four hours after nightfall, Trevor was sitting under the hut where the elder lived, hoping that the SF team leader would come over and get their information about VC activity in the area. Another hour passed, making it 12:30 a.m., and still no sign of the green berets. With the elder now sound asleep, Trevor crawled out from under the hut to check on his men.

Slipping into the night and silently through the jungle, Trevor maneuvered his way past the booby traps that he had set on the eastern edge of the perimeter. Stopping to check the area, he heard a slight snap of a twig no more than ten feet to his front.

Deciding to stay low and not move, Trevor considered it may be one of his men urinating. Ruling that out because he had designated the slit trench to the south side of the perimeter, he listened ever so closely for another sound. He could hear a slight hiss on the other side of the tree he was hiding behind, but he could not place it. He heard it again. Just then Trevor knew exactly what that sound was. It was someone's breath.

Filled Generational Gaps

Jumping up in a fluid motion, he raised his heavy weapon to the ready position only to meet a barrel touching the flash suppressor of his own. Both men behind the weapons took a deep breath in shock. Looking even closer at the man in front of him, he lowered his rifle to have the barrel pointing to the ground. Trevor looked at the man in front of him and spoke.

"You Spec Ops?"

The man lowered his rifle and replied, confirming Trevor's hopes; they both looked at each other in a rush from almost killing their own. Trevor, who didn't smoke, offered the man a cigarette he was given from the villagers. The man took it, nodding in gratitude. Trevor asked the man to follow him into the perimeter along with his team. Staying put, Trevor waited for the man to gather his team, and they linked up with Trevor to enter the perimeter.

As they approach, Specialist Baxley was heard from the perimeter in a whisper.

"Ninth hole!"

Trevor replied, "Always rough!"

The green berets look at each other with recognition of standard operating procedures of challenge and passwords for entry. Entering the perimeter, Baxley looked up at the men who were looking down to him, trying to place the night optics that they have not even been issued.

Now sitting around in a circle on the inside of their perimeter, the men simply stare at each other. The green berets had no idea who these men were, but they knew that the equipment they had was far more advanced than their own. This was what made the Special Forces hold tight and speak not a word.

Trevor's men were silent because they were sitting with the most elite soldier, by reputation, that they had ever seen. Trevor looked around to find the highest ranking man he could see. The only problem was that these men were wearing no rank.

Looking closely, they all looked like the complete expert in their job. Ruling out the leader took some time. Trevor was tired of staring and decided to cheat.

"Which one of you is in command?"

One man raised his hand. He looked like the others. Worn out and battered, he still managed to have a surprisingly cold gaze in his eyes. No matter what he had been through, he looked like he had chewed it up and spit it out, eager for more. The rough man inspected Trevor and his men, trying to size each of them up. He still could not figure out Trevor. The leader of the elite soldiers stood to introduce them.

"My name is Paul, and these are my men. This is Lars, our medic. That is Cooper, and the skinny one there is Ward. They are the weapons sergeants. Rowdy over there is our operations guru. He follows us around and keeps us in line in case deviations need to be made from our mission. Now you know who we are. Would you guys mind explaining who the fuck *you* are?"

As Corporal Boiyd spit some tobacco juice onto the ground, Trevor stood to speak to Paul. Pulling Paul aside, Trevor asked him if he knew of a place where the security was not as necessary. Paul looked at him to see if he was kidding. With the stern look in Trevor's eyes, Paul opted to indulge in his curiosity.

"How long you boys been in this site?" Paul asked

"A little over a month now. We arrived with little ammo and one-day rations. We were hoping you could help us out and have a cache delivered."

Trevor's men leaned in to listen for the answer. Paul's face frowned as he decided to have one of his men pull security. He placed Lars at the twelve o'clock position and escorted the rest of the men into the village.

Inside the stocky translator's house was a small hatch that led underground into a cellar. This was used to hide the children when the VC would raid the village. Here the men could talk at a regular volume. Here they could get to know the answers that each had for the other.

"Who are you guys?" Paul asked. "What agency are you with? By the rank I can tell you are supposed to be Army, but I do not recognize the uniform or the unit patch you wear. Why are you here in this area? Most of the fighting is south of here. No one is insane enough to be this far north."

Trevor answered, "We are light infantry from Ft. Wainwright, Alaska. Sorry, I must have heard wrong. Did you say fighting?"

Paul looked at Trevor as if he had two heads. Paul was not about to answer that question until he was sure of the line of questioning. Trevor continued.

"Paul, excuse me, what's your rank?"

"First Sergeant."

"Okay, First Sergeant—"

"Just Paul."

"Sorry, Paul, our understanding was that there were only a few separatists and no fighting except for the embassy. How far south, and who is involved? How long has the fighting been going on?"

Paul squinted his eyes and dropped his view to Trevor's wrist computer. It was as if Trevor had spoken to him in Arabic.

"Embassy? What fuckin' embassy? What the hell are you talking about? Who are you and why are you here?"

Trevor composed himself and began to explain his understanding of the whole mess they were sent for.

"Excuse me, Paul. I am about as confused as you seem to be right now. If you don't mind, let me sit here and explain what I was told. My understanding is that there is an American embassy held by VC and NVA separatists who had killed several officials after they had refused certain demands. They were holding several dozen American hostages and threatened to kill them all if we did not deliver. Our unit was sent here from Alaska to ensure that this area's special interest non-combatants were evacuated. My latest intel sent me off to find one man, who we found dead. We then were heading back to our TOC when we were somehow knocked unconscious and left in a hole. That was about a month ago. First Sergeant, I have no idea what had happened since then. We would practice recon techniques and go on forced marches to keep in shape, usually traveling through where our TOC used to be. Nothing is there, but there are villages we haven't been through before. We were hoping you could shed some light as to what the fuck is going on."

Paul looked over to his men to get a reading of their reactions; they were about the same as his, confused and cryptic. Paul began to study the men in better light. Those weapons, what the hell are those? He looked at the blended black and green uniforms, of different material than his uniform. There was something on Trevor's wrist that seems to come straight out of a science-fiction movie.

Trevor noticed the glares and the incessant research that Paul was doing to his men. What was he looking at?

Paul leaned over to Rowdy, the intelligence escort, and whispered in his ear. Trevor could not hear, but he knew by the eyes in both men that it could not be good. Trevor leaned forward to inquire.

"Paul, excuse my interruption, but is there something you find difficult to understand about our situation? I can't help but feel like we are something that you have never seen before. Would you mind enlightening us about what your thoughts are?"

Paul moved his head back from Rowdy's ear and looked around for support. With a slight nod from Rowdy, Paul explained.

"Son, you are carrying weapons that seem to be way out of our league. Your uniforms are something out of a movie, and your helmets look like something an alien would wear. You ask me to shed light on the situation? Son, I beg you to give me every single detail about where you are from and what you are doing here!"

Trevor was now the man looking to his squad for support. Boiyd gave Trevor a glance that insisted on every detail being revealed. Trevor bowed his head and held it just below the muzzle of his large weapon. Thinking of a way to make this easier, he considered a way to break the ice without insulting the men in front of him. Looking up, he brought his weapon to his lap and cleared it from all rounds. Looking at Paul, he gently tossed the weapon to him. With a reactive catch, Paul was thrown by the surprising weight. Studying the grenade barrel and the rear magazine for the 20mm high explosive rounds, he suddenly looked like a child in a candy store instead of the rugged warrior.

Paul asked questions relating to what the barrels were for and the caliber of each. Trevor described the weapon straight from the technical manual. Describing the weapon as a gas operated, air-cooled weapon with selectable barrels firing a 5.56mm round switchable to a 20mm grenade launcher. Operation of the separate weapon systems were switchable by barrel selector lever. Both 5.56mm and 20mm weapons fired semi-automatic by way of safety lever. The optical scope was powered with a kinetically charged battery located in the butt of the weapon. The words flowed smoothly over his tongue since it was something that was drilled into all of their heads. Each of the men raised their eyebrows as Paul held the weapon up high.

Trevor motioned for each of his men to give up their weapon to the man in their front. With each of the Green Berets looking at the weapon in front of them with great diligence, Ward, one of the weapons sergeants, held Baxley's weapon up. The medium machine gun was like nothing he had ever seen before. Baxley leaned over and activated the thermal scope. Ward jumped back in excitement as he raised it up. Spotting the translator and his wife, he moved the weapon toward other huts. He could spot all men and women in the village. Slowly, he lowered the weapon down and handed it over to Paul.

Paul leered through the scope and looked around as Ward had done. Lowering the weapon quickly, he turned to Baxley.

"Hey now, when was this made?"

Baxley replied quickly that the weapon with the optics came in to service in the spring of 2005.

The five green berets looked at each other in disbelief and tried again to evaluate the men in front of them. Not knowing what to say or do, they simply lit a cigarette and passed it around.

It's funny how the most common of things can bring a group of men who were stubborn in their ideas and in their training together. These men, still looking at the interesting weapons in front of them, took it as if it were just a drop in a very large bucket of strange phenomena that inhabited the jungle. Paul leaned over to Cooper and told him to go get Lars. This was something he wanted the whole team for.

Paul looked over at Rowdy to see how he was taking the story that their fellow Americans had just told them. Rowdy was concentrating at the floor of the small cellar, trying to find the words to explain his plan for the change in mission. He wasn't sure exactly how to go about this. These men had seen too much to disregard what they had seen.

Rowdy was thinking, If these men were telling the truth, when did they come from? How would his higher-ups handle the situation? Would they simply ship them back to a lab and have their shrinks test them and call it good? On the other hand, would they laugh at him and never support a thing he needed for the rest of his career? Rowdy decided to keep the entire thing quiet and just ask supply for the ammo and rations that the soldiers were so desperately going to need to survive the jungle and the VC. Trevor's men could not have picked a better place in Vietnam to arrive; Viet Cong typically were fighting south of that spot. At the moment, Trevor was so far behind enemy lines that this would be the last place anyone would come to look for Americans. They should be safe from the conflict, but alternatively, how were they supposed to get home?

Rowdy joined the conversation.

"First of all, gentleman, I need to know exactly where you came from. A little more than just Alaska. I know you understand what it is that I am asking. If you were to send a letter home to your family the day before you got here, what would you date it?"

The Green Berets looked at each other, and everyone watched Trevor and waited for his answer. Hesitantly, Trevor answered, "Sir, I expect that I would have dated it May 21, 2008."

Rowdy shifted his head into a solemn nod and replied.

"Well, son, you are definitely a long way from home. It doesn't make sense, no how. It sure does explain your toys and your uniforms. Welcome to the Vietnam War. You have just landed smack in the middle of 1969."

Trevor and his men were in shock at what they heard. Out of the mouth of the skeptic, Boiyd muttered something that didn't register in Trevor's mind until a moment later.

He had heard, "That would explain a whole shitload now, wouldn't it?"

Our Fellow Americans

With the painful truth out, Rowdy didn't speak a word for a long while. The men in the cellar all had an icy presence about them. Trevor's men were worried about what Paul's men were going to do. Paul's men were concerned about being this close to people from the future. However, their weapons and their equipment were nothing they had seen before.

Cooper was continuing the previous conversation to Himelrick, the grenadier. The weapon he carried was similar to the rest except that it had a 40mm barrel for larger grenades. This barrel was below the rifle barrel and had no magazine for the launcher. Himelrick explained the types of grenades that he had on his person. He had the high explosive, used against light armored vehicles. Explaining the flechette and flares, Cooper was in weapon heaven.

A flechette had small chunks of metal that fly at an object while spinning at great speeds. Though very bad for the barrel, it was great in a tight pinch. Flares were designed for signaling. Himelrick reached in his assault pack and placed ten smoke grenades in his vest. These were colorless smoke for screening and concealment. He also had red, yellow and green smoke for different signals to either his team or approaching aircraft.

After "show and tell," the men were much more relaxed since they were all proven experts in their own field. The Green Berets were far more experienced than Trevor's men were, but they did not grow up in the Army learning from all the mistakes made in the war in which they all sat.

Now that all the men were relatively comfortable with each other, they had to decide what to do. Rowdy, who simply sat back and watched the men bond through their equipment and their stories, was comfortable in the fact that however the men got here, he had to find a way to help them. Knowing only one person who could help them, he promised himself not to let these men slip away like so many soldiers before.

Walking back to the perimeter sight, they discussed absolutely nothing. The jungle seemed to have its own language. They had stayed in it long enough to become fluent in the hisses and the chirps. The occasional silence was when they needed to be the most alert. The greatest survivalists could tell you that the woods know everything, you just need to know how to listen to its advice.

Only a fool would believe that good things happen when the sun comes up. Every morning while sunrise was taking place, soldiers were at a hundred percent security. All men were in fighting positions, ready for combat. In the past, soldiers were typically attacked when the sun came up because that was when a good percentage of men were groggy and their eyes had not adjusted yet. As a result, American soldiers wake up a couple hours before dawn to be awake and alert when it is time for stand-to. Stand-down occurs an hour or so after they were at full alert. Then they go back to normal duties.

On this particular morning, Paul and his men were at stand-to with Trevor's men. Since they were in an area where there were high risks of enemy, they were paranoid. That morning they had a good reason to be.

A shrill scream sounded from the translator's hut, and his wife ran out from behind the hut with blood on her face, pouring down her front. She collapsed to the ground to reveal a man standing behind her, his rifle smoking. Immediately all the soldiers raised their weapons to take aim but did not fire a shot. Reluctant to give away their position, the men were drawn between helping the kind people who fed them and saving their own lives. Three minutes passed and at least a dozen men filed into the center path between the ragged huts, splitting off and entering each hut to complete the raid of the simple village people. The concern for their village friends overwhelmed Trevor. He decided to execute the plan that he had laid out for his men and the villagers.

Trevor stood up to get his men ready to move when Paul grabbed him by the leg to stop him. Trevor delivered a cold look through Paul, taking no advice from the elite soldier. Whispering into the ICOM, he called Himelrick and Baxley into position. They had explained to the villagers that if anything ever happened like this, to lie on the floor no matter what happened. Paul was not aware of this plan.

Baxley moved into his support by fire position, which was established about a week ago. Trevor ordered Himelrick to launch five smoke grenades into the four corners of the village and one down the center. Once they were all smoking with a brilliant white haze, Baxley laid down a grazing fire, killing everything standing at three feet and higher. With the villagers, hopefully, lying on the floor, they should be relatively safe. With strafing streams of 7.62mm explosive-tipped rounds flying through the huts, you could hear the shrill cries of death from the invading pillagers. Baxley had spotted targets through his scope in the form of red blurs shaped like men. Anyone standing belonged to him. All persons that he saw duck or lay down after firing became his target. After Baxley had fired for just less than one minute, Trevor called a cease-fire. At this point they would move through and clear the buildings themselves. With the enemy being at a minimum, the risk should not be as evident.

Working in two teams, with Baxley still mounted at the support-by-fire position, Trevor began moving his men through the village.

Not missing a beat, Paul moved his men to the edge of the nearest hut to prepare to help. To Paul it seemed as if this were something that these men did everyday. It was amazing how these men would simply clear a room and move on to the next with no effort at all. These men were definitely trained well.

Corporal Boiyd, Wilson and Malloy moved to the elder's hut to search for him after the buildings were clear of hostiles. Trevor, Himelrick and Trits moved to the other side to search for the survivors.

Trits sat outside the door of a hut to maintain rear security; a man slowly walked up behind him with a rifle bearing down at his head. As the man centered a careful aim on Trits, he placed his finger on the trigger. Trits turned to find the man bearing down on him as a loud burst shot out and covered Trits in a morbid blanket of blood that flowed from his head, down his neck and trickled to his waist. Trits stood to find Baxley's machine gun smoking after firing a short burst into the man lying on the ground behind Trits. A faint smile was given to Baxley as Trits collected his composure to assume rear security once again for that hut.

Five minutes had passed, and the smoke still hazed within the village. Without the wind, the haze hung over in its humid and choking fog. Through the smoke, Trevor and his men escorted the women and the few children out of the haze and into the perimeter, which most villagers didn't even know was there.

Setting down a small child who was cut from the flying debris of the hut, which was pounded by the explosive bullets, Trevor leered at Paul. Slowly standing from his crouch, Trevor eased over to Paul to begin his explanation.

"These people are the ones who made sense out of a senseless situation. We prepared ahead of time what we would do if something were to happen to them. First Sergeant, don't ever hold my men back from their orders again. I swear to you I will never hold your men back. My men are alive because of these people. We are here for no other reason than to pay them back. We have no orders. We have no mission anymore. We are here to survive and to pay our debt. I mean you no disrespect, but if we could get along in this regard we will be much more beneficial to each other. Remember, First Sergeant, that my men are trained in a completely different manner than yours. My men are trained by tactics that solve most of the mistakes that soldiers made here in Vietnam. Do we have an understanding?"

Paul looked blankly at Trevor while trying to digest the words that had just flowed out of his mouth. Thinking back at the things his men had accomplished, he tried to recall the sort of mistakes that Trevor referred to. He could think of a few things that he would have done, in retrospect, which would have kept some of his men alive. What if all the generals and commanders sat together at the end of this war and rewrote the tactics and training for the soldiers to come? Were the soldiers he saw before him the result of that training? With this on his mind, Paul shortly agreed with Trevor. The two leaders would not interfere with each other's operations again.

The villagers cried and shivered after the fleeting scare in the center of the perimeter that had been widened to allow more people in. There were two deaths, including the woman who the men had seen first, and her husband. Only two deaths among the villagers before Trevor's team annihilated the invading force.

After sitting down once again with the security higher than before, Trevor ordered his men to give him an ACE report. An ACE report was a quick evaluation of the soldier's ammunition, casualties (if any) and equipment. This was a fast way for the leader to assess damage and reconsolidate as needed. The report came back and Baxley was hurting for ammo. The rest still had six magazines per person.

Day turned to night when Trevor relaxed the security. Paul pulled Rowdy aside to talk about what they could do for Trevor. They walked to the river and gathered water as they discussed.

After an uncomfortable moment of silence between the two men at the edge of the river, Paul finally broke the ice with the inevitable question hanging over them both.

"Do you believe them?" Paul asked.

"Ya know, I wouldn't have if it weren't for their equipment. I would be going through hell right now if I had just woken up somewhere I didn't belong. The man isn't more than twenty-six years old. He isn't even born yet according to his story. I just don't know how to help them. Do you honestly believe that *higher* would approve an evac for these guys? I know they would just laugh their ass off at me if I even asked for an evac this far north. Hell, you can't get an evac for soldiers in a unit that doesn't exist, let alone is born yet. As far as the cache, I already made the call. One C-130 should be dropping it off tomorrow morning. This is the grid where the drop zone is."

Rowdy handed Paul the paper and began asking him what he thought of the situation.

"To be deadly honest, I don't know. They aren't from our Army. They must be from something else. They are obviously American, but that doesn't mean they aren't CIA. They might have the night vision that would kick the shit out of our starlight scopes, but why would they be here waiting for us without asking or giving information? If Trevor's men are from where they say then it would be the only thing that actually makes sense in its own fucked-up way."

Rowdy replied, "Well, I suppose we should get back and give Trevor the good news about his supplies. I'm sure he'll want to know."

With that, the two men left the riverbank and moved toward Trevor's men to deliver the good news.

Trevor had a slight smile of disbelief about him. Rowdy hadn't talked much since the night before and, all of a sudden, a cache that would save all their lives was only one night away. On the other hand, it would make more sense for these men to use the cache as a payoff to be able to leave them here. They would all surely know tomorrow afternoon.

Trits was sitting on the side of their dugout position, repairing a malfunction with his weapon. Because Trits had the light machine gun, his rate of fire was not set at only semi-automatic fire. He had no grenade launcher to his weapon and carried much larger magazines to handle sixty rounds of ammunition. The problem was in the magazine well. A spur of metal protruded from the well, preventing any magazine from entering and loading. Cooper, one of the weapons sergeants, sat next to Trits to help him solve the problem. As a weapons sergeant, Cooper carried an elaborate tool pouch to modify and fix weapons. Part of this was a small file, which he used to wear away the spur from the well. After testing the action and loading, Trits thanked the man. The two men sat on the side of the perimeter and stared into the dark jungle in front of them. With the woods lying wide-awake, as were the animals of the night, they listened ever so carefully to the wild.

Guerillas in the Mist

Staff Sergeant Lars Madison, the skillful medic of the Green Beret team, had found his "battle buddy" in Trevor's men. Cpl. Boiyd, who was preparing his equipment for the night, happened to be from San Antonio, Texas, the same town as Lars. It seems that the homes of the two men were only a street away from each other. Even though forty years separated the men, they seemed to be closer than they had felt to home in a long while.

Boiyd, who lived on Pendragon Street all his life, played basketball at the same high school where Lars attended, and ate food at the same old restaurant. Memories of the home Boiyd felt that he would never know again flowed through his mind.

Both men recollected their time in San Antonio and compared the differences between them to the current times, which were dramatically different. With a smirk on both faces, their eyes wandered into the distance.

Boiyd's eyes automatically focused on a figure that looked like a bush, but seemed to sway with a wind that wasn't there. Waiting and whispering to Lars, they hoped to confirm their suspicions.

Paranoia rushed through the men; Boiyd called Trevor on the ICOM at a small whisper. Trevor eased to his knees and gently poked Paul on the leg. With instinctual response, Paul rolled slightly to Trevor and brought his weapon to a ready position. Trevor high crawled to Boiyd's position. Once Boiyd briefed Trevor to what he thought he saw, Trevor sat back to study the wood line in front of him.

"Do nothing, and keep the villagers calm!" Trevor quietly ordered.

"They're just scouts. We can't give up our position. If they come through here, silent kills only. Only fire back when one of them fires from inside the perimeter. Understood?"

Paul looked at Trevor in confusion.

"What if they fire first from there? Why wait until they fire from inside?" Trits asked.

Trevor whispered, "Sometimes these guys will walk around, and if they have no idea where you are they will fire a shot at nothing. Soldiers think that they are firing at them and that they are compromised, and they end up giving away their position by returning fire. By waiting until they are within us, we limit the chance of them doing a recon by fire. Silent kills will limit their buddies hearing something and rushing to us."

Paul practiced the close kills quite a bit, but he never would have thought to wait for them to know where they were. He had assumed in the past that they saw them and opened fire. Now Paul thought back to some of his own mistakes in this regard.

Watching the bushes that they suspected as helmet dressings, they prepared their weapons silently. After only five minutes, one bush stood up to walk forward toward them. Behind him were three more figures. Trevor made a hand signal, which meant that they would do nothing under any circumstance until he snapped his fingers. The first man pressed his foot only inches away from Boiyd's face. Stopping, the man looked around at head level. The man turned to wave the men behind him through. Moving forward, the first man was now at the rear of the perimeter. The three, who were in a small file formation, entered the perimeter. Trevor looked Boiyd in the eye. He issued a hand signal, which Boiyd didn't understand. Issuing the signal a second time, he got a confirmation. The confirmation did not come from Boiyd; it came from Lars, who was still beside Boiyd. Lars drew his knife from his sheath. Waiting for the eyes of Trits and Cooper, he then carefully stood placing the blade to the rear of the man's neck, lifting up. Trits, hesitantly, took his bayonet and simply stabbed the man from behind and through the front of the man's trachea, twisting the blade. The groan caused the point man to turn, only to meet Paul's machete swing across the man's neck. Blood sprayed across Trevor's face. Trevor snapped his head up in time to watch the man's head simply roll off the shoulders, hitting the jungle floor with a dull thud.

Trevor signaled the men to maintain near security to the front to ensure no one else was coming. After an hour, he placed the men on watch, three on and one off. They would rotate through to ensure all men managed some rest. They couldn't risk moving the bodies until morning.

Trits was still frozen, staring at the man he had taken down only an hour before. He shook from the adrenaline that rushed through his veins like nothing he had ever felt before. Cooper slid himself next to him and noticed that a tear was passing over the camouflage face paint. He thought about what to say, assuming that this was Trits first kill by hand.

"Your first kill?"

Trits nodded slightly.

"I know how you feel. It's hard, but I'm sorry to say it actually gets easier after a while. You killed a man today. It doesn't make you more of a man; it only makes you a friend."

Trits looked over at Cooper without understanding.

"You see, your buddy Himelrick was in front of him. If you hadn't done what you did, Himelrick would have been stepped on. The man would have seen him and killed him. You stopped that and saved your friend. You were a man before. You are a friend now."

Trits looked at Himelrick, who was sleeping where he was an hour ago. With a smile, Trits repositioned his rifle with a newfound confidence. Trevor looked at Cooper and delivered an approving smile.

The men had bonded through their trials. Bonded even past time. Because of the horror of combat, the man who defended another's life every day proved he was the truest of brothers.

Over the horizon, the sun began to penetrate through the dense jungle canopies onto the faces of the bodies, which still lay on the ground. It seemed that with just a little sunlight, an odor of death rose with the humidity. With all men awake and all men alert, they lay down in their positions to prepare for the ritualistic stand-to.

The Yellow Brick Road

Paul made a suggestion to Trevor that they relocate, since there was an obvious attraction to the area that they were in. Rowdy wished to see the "holes" that the men had landed in and hoped that they could stop by there on the way to the new location.

It seemed that the only casualties from the village were the translator and the wife. Even the elder made it through the attack. There were several wounds from Baxley's fire through the village. Broken wood, acting as shrapnel, pierced through skin like warm butter. They had all done what Trevor had told them to do. Once the smoke hit they all hit the ground and waited for the dust to settle. They were told not to get up until the Americans escorted them out. They had all done well.

Today the soldiers instructed the villagers in one last thing to do. If anyone were to come in asking about them, they were to begin crying as if the soldiers had just terrorized them. They were to complain about their raped women, beaten husbands and slaughtered livestock. The destroyed village from machine gun fire was to be blamed on them completely. Hopefully, the VC would not harm them if they thought the villagers were already victims.

The men began to hide their presence in a position they had been staying in for over a month now. Laying the sod that they had peeled back when making their positions would cover the worn earth that a month of laying on would cause. Baxley picked up all the expended casings to the rounds he had fired, along with the links. They had used a tree branch to sweep away the footprints along the paths as they left; there was little trace that Americans had occupied the area.

The villagers waved them off with the haunting sense of both fear and regret. Trevor looked back, smiled and watched as some of the men in the village took the four bodies left by the night recon somewhere for hiding. Trevor shook his head as he turned to take his men to safety.

All of the current intelligence showed that the cache point was in another area that was supposed to be secured. What Rowdy was not sure of was where exactly this location was. This was an area that this specific team had yet to explore. Walking through jungle was like walking with kids holding on to your ankles. It's slow and exhausting, as the soldiers constantly hacked through vines and stepped over entanglements on the ground. The men, however, seem to weave relatively easily through the trees and obstructions in their way as if they had belonged to the jungle.

Over fifteen hundred meters was being cleared through while they continued to push toward the place where Trevor's men had "landed." An hour and a half later, they arrived at the spot in which they woke over a month before. Paul had his men place security around the area in case the arrival of Trevor and his team drew the attention of the enemy to the area. Rowdy and Paul gazed into the deep hole where Trevor said he woke up in. Paul had seen many craters caused by artillery and bombs, but this one didn't have the blast pattern you would usually see with such explosions. It was a clean-cut hole with no sign of the missing soil.

Rowdy was convinced. He packed up his camera after taking several shots of the phenomena and cued Paul to move out. They began heading south to the cache point. Trevor and his men seemed to walk backward as they took their last look at the womb of their new life.

With the images of the holes drilled into all of their minds, the walk to the cache seemed much shorter than the fifteen miles that it was in actuality. Well camouflaged and on its side, the cache was much more than Trevor could have hoped for. They had enough there to set a base camp where it sat. Three or four shovels, a couple thousand rounds for everyone, new weapons, grenades, LAWs (light anti-tank weapons), C-4 explosives and claymore mines were in the stash. Early warning devices such as flares with trip wires and materials to make their own were in high supply. With all the excitement from Trevor's men, they didn't notice Rowdy's frown as he looked around the area. Rowdy began cursing under his breath when Boiyd looked back in wonder. Boiyd finally understood what was missing from the package: food. Boiyd grabbed Trevor by the arm and they all began searching the underlying area for the second drop that should have been in place. Without the villagers feeding them, the men would have to survive on the abundant boar that inhabited the area. That meant fire that would give away a scent and smoke. That was tactically unacceptable.

After a half-hour of cursing and searching, the men found nothing; they were only interrupted by an aircraft flying overhead. The men fell to the ground without movement so not to draw attention to the air. It was unlikely anything could have seen them through the jungle canopy, but they wanted to play it safe just the same.

The plane passed and circled over the area. With a loud crashing and cracking sound the men rolled out of the way just in time to avoid a large palette and box slamming into them. With no markings, only the camouflage that the first package had, the men smiled with a hungry passion as they realized the gift that was just given to them. The food was here, and they were saved.

Rowdy placed his hand on Trevor's shoulder in a way only a concerned father would. Trevor looked back at Rowdy with a curious wonder.

"How the hell did you manage to have this much sent? There is no way that you told them about us, and I doubt that you guys get this as a typical drop-off. How did you do this?"

Rowdy answered, "I told base that we found a village of people who had been feeding us information since the beginning. We told them that they wanted to join the local rebellion and needed some training supplies and combat equipment for thirty men. They didn't ask any questions except for 'are they serious and are they a risk to us.' Once I convinced them, they OK'd the shipment. This should last you guys long enough for me to do some homework and find someone who can help you. We will be leaving tomorrow night to make the movement back to base. I will send a team out once a week to you to check on your status. I will also make sure that they know to refer to you guys as 'indigenous personnel.' Don't worry. These guys know when we are taking care of our own. They won't ask questions and they won't bother you. They may come in for foot powder and c-rats, but that should be it. Just make sure you are dressed in the uniforms provided and carrying the weapons in the crates. This will prevent them asking too many questions. I am just not sure how to describe you guys. I may have to warn the team coming out, but I assure you that your team will be safe. If you need more ammo or food, let the men know when they come by and they will tell me. I'll take care of it."

With a grin, Trevor shook the man's hand and thanked him. With that, they sat around the cache and discussed the best place to be avoided. With a devilish smile, Paul looked up. Trevor shook his head and laughed.

Placing their entire cache in the trees and building what they needed to hide there would be extremely difficult and tedious. On the other hand, it was perfect. In this area there were multiple canopies of low-lying layers. The trees were growing together, it seemed, to where all of the large leaves developed into blankets. If they were to build above one of these layers, they could have perfect camouflage from underneath. Men could walk by and not see a thing. Just so long as they kept watch and knew when not to talk, they should be safe.

Paul's men provided some help and the security for Trevor to begin their movement. They would use the palettes for platforms of their "tree house" and build a small bunker out of the ammo cans filled with dirt. Ammo would be placed evenly throughout the span of their aerial strong point.

Drawing the layout in the dirt, Trevor made it clear to begin cutting the wood needed from the higher points of the trees. They would have rope ladders and connect the trees together with small boardwalks. The platforms would wrap around the trees to provide their fighting positions. Some of the low branches were tied to the positions to allow a man to pull the branch out of the way, allowing the soldier to have line of sight with his target. The plan wasn't perfect, but it was the best they had.

By the next afternoon the cache was transferred to the trees, and the men began making their own living areas, since they would most definitely be there a while. On the ground, the men ate their final meal together. They didn't say much, but they were grateful that they had the pleasure of meeting and knowing each other. Paul and Trevor exchanged looks of dutiful respect and admiration. Paul leaned to Trevor.

"You know that if I ever need someone in a jam, I'm going to ask you. What better person than one who was trained by our mistakes!"

There was a hint of condescension in Paul's remarks, but the words were understood. Trevor replied, "Don't worry. If I ever need someone to catch bullets for us, you'll be the first on my list. You don't want to waste perfectly good soldiers like us on the regulars, do you?"

Both men laughed as Trevor continued.

"Seriously, though, I have learned a lot from you and your guys. You'd better come by again if nothing more than to party. You bring the fireworks and I'll keep a beer chilled for ya."

Trevor laughed.

Both men would probably sell their rifles and a testicle for an ice-cold beer. Two hours later, words of good luck were exchanged, and they shook hands. Trevor and Paul turned away from each other as their men followed them accordingly. This was going to be the first night Trevor's men would be alone without the villagers or the berets. Trevor had been waiting for this moment. The moment where he would finally see how well he trained his men. Discipline was going to be the only difference between life and death for his men.

Death from Above

One week passed by very slowly after the green berets left Trevor's men with the cache. It had only been three days, and the encampment was almost completed. The men working all day had developed systems of pulleys that allowed them to bring the wood to the high levels of their new home. Once they connected the seven trees together and encircled them with boardwalks and platforms, they found their own fighting positions and living quarters high above the ground instead of in the foxholes they were trained to fight from.

Trevor had decided to ask the men, who would arrive on Monday, to contact Rowdy and ask him for steel plates to provide armor from receiving fire, which would occur from below. These plates would be mounted to the bottom of each platform that the men would fight from and sleep on.

The men had developed the skeleton of the web of positions by finding the largest tree and encircled the other positions around it. The center held the majority of the supplies as well as their squad leader. The position north held Cpl. Boiyd with Spc. Baxley to the south. Baxley's assistant gunner occupied the east position of the medium machine gun, and Pv2 Wilson in the northeast position. Himelrick and Trits covered the west side. With this set, they had experienced people evenly surrounding the area close to the newer soldiers. The automatic weapons were evenly distributed according to the likely avenues of enemy approach.

The men had finished with the rough work of the positions and began working on camouflaging the undersides of the platforms. This was the difficult part; the men must camouflage the positions while still allowing the brush to move to allow clear shots from above. This was done with the twine and rope that was provided in the cache.

The area itself had been very quiet, and the men were beginning to get relaxed with the noise discipline. Trevor had planned to speak to the men and attempt to scare them straight. Without the fear, his men would surely die.

With the positions finally camouflaged after the fourth day of being there, Trevor was well pleased with the work the men had done. They had set up their ponchos to provide rain protection above their sleeping area and placed sleeping mats in front of their weapon system. The machine gun, mounted to the tripod, was angled in such a way to allow the weapon to fire straight below them. Trevor prepared interlocking fields of fire as he rounded each fighting position. He had set their limits of fire by direction and by marking trees ahead of them so they could all visually see the right and left limits of their positions. By simply stripping the bark on the trees, Trevor made it clear to each man that they were not to fire farther than that point unless the man beside him were killed.

By interlocking these firing positions forty meters in front of the positions, it reduced the chance of enemy grenades to be thrown onto their position. It also provided double the fire superiority in favor of the Americans.

Trevor briefed them on the work for the upcoming day while seated in the center platform with his men. Trevor began.

"First off, I am proud of each of you. You worked your asses off, and that will prove worthwhile in the upcoming days. I expect all of you to remember that we are not on some FTX behind Eielson Air Force Base. We are in a combat zone. You must maintain noise and light discipline the entire time you are here. No more jokes. No more laughing. The next person that violates this will be punished painfully. The next bastard that decides to shout out for someone to come to you, I will personally shoot you myself. I will not risk everyone's life for one man's lack of discipline. Everyone clear?"

Nods from all men were followed by the notorious Army "Hooah."

Trevor continued.

"We have a few days before we get our first of many visits. I expect all of you to maintain the impression made to First Sergeant Ricardo. These men are the elite soldiers. They are bending over backward to help us because they think that we are elite as well. I love that they think that! Now, I know you men are tired, and I know you are angry, so am I, but you must maintain discipline or you will get yourself killed. This hellhole is unforgiving. Remember your training and remember your buddies. Each of you volunteered, even for this; don't forget that. Most of the soldiers here today that we share this nightmare with have no choice. They were drafted. I expect that you lead the way and remember that you are all representatives for *our* country. Now, first guard shift will keep watch until 0200 hours. Second shift will pick up then. Wake up is 0545 hours. I want you triple S'd before stand-to. That's shit, showered and shaved. Obviously, we have no showers, but I need you to do your best. You don't want the kind of shit crawling around your nuts that the jungle has for you dirty bastards. Get clean so we don't lose you to disease instead of a bullet. Is everyone clear as to what I expect?"

The men delivered a hasty nod.

"Okay. Second shift, hit the racks and get some sleep; you have an early morning. Dismissed."

The men scattered about silently as they thought about the bacterium that had built up on their body since they had last washed. Hopefully, Trevor thought, they are scared straight.

The night was silent as they shuffled to their positions. They all knew that at the first sound of weapons fire to wake up and respond accordingly. In the jungle, no one really sleeps; they were just in a place in their mind where the horror of combat was not as evident. Resting their bodies for the day ahead, the men slowed their minds to allow the peace they did not have with their eyes open.

The posted man next to each man would wake the second shift. The shifts worked out so every other man slept while the other was awake. Only averaging four hours of sleep a night, the men still found the energy to fight and to work.

During stand-to there was silence, even from the birds who usually chirped at the sight of the rising sun. Normally this was a key point to be paranoid. Today it appeared to be nothing. Perhaps the animals slept later today than the days before.

Again, ready to work with security in place, the men felt as if they were abandoned from the world in a place that the world forgot. Trevor instructed the men to walk their fields of fire and finalize the range cards, which they prepared. The range card was a laminated form that each man carried in his helmet or in front of his weapon system. On this card they drew their areas of responsibility in regard to their weapons, exactly as they see it from their position. Dead space, which was an area hidden from sight in their position, was annotated. Their right and left limit was marked and symbolized with the making or terrain feature on the ground and direction. Each were assigned primary and secondary targets. The purpose of this card was grim. It was designed to allow a man who would replace a soldier in case of death the ability to know everything that the fallen soldier was responsible for, and terrain that may obstruct the ability to fire.

During the process of range card preparation, the men were instructed to garden. This was where the men would walk out as far as they could while still able to see their own position and clear the area to limit the dead space. That way they could easily fire at a further distance to prevent the enemy reaching hand grenade range or a range that would allow for an easier target for an enemy rifle.

The soldiers took turns working on their fields of fire; the men completed the clearing before their scheduled lunch break. Trevor walked each lane to ensure the clarity of the field and the job done by not making it obvious. Trevor instructed the men not to cut trees halfway up but instead attempt to uproot the smaller ones and thin out the branches. They were to rub mud on the places they cut to make it look as if it were cut long before. This would prevent the enemy from being suspicious of current inhabitants. Hiding all of the cut branches and uprooted small trees a hundred yards to the west of their position, Trevor planned to create one last thing.

Trevor pulled Cpl. Boiyd with him as he showed him what he wanted done. The final project for the day was to find a way to hide enemy bodies away from their position so as not to alert new enemy to their occupation. Cpl. Boiyd pulled two men to help. Boiyd decided to use the cut limbs and trees as camouflage for a small pit they were going to dig. The rough lumber was set aside the digging area, and the men got to work.

Sweat poured from the men as they hacked through the vine-infested ground. After three hours of hard digging, the men dug a hole large enough to fit as many as a dozen men. The brush would cover the loose dirt that would be thrown on top at the end of the burial.

Moving the hundred meters back to the shelters, Boiyd remembered the one thing that they had not done yet. He remembered because of an old habit his squad leader drilled into him, walking to avoid trip wires.

No claymores or early detection devices were in place yet. Boiyd rushed to Trevor to remind him.

As Boiyd explained what he felt was missing, Trevor agreed to employ the APERS (Anti-personnel) mines but did not authorize the use of early warning devices. Trevor explained that his goal was to avoid conflict, not to advertise their presence with the use of flares or chemical lights. If the enemy walked past them it would be preferred.

The claymores were placed on surrounding trees, tied at a forty-five degree angle toward the ground. They were wired one per position, in case of enemy overrunning their position. The surrounding trees were about fifteen meters in front of each position. The detonator, a hand trigger or "clacker," that sends a small electrical surge through the line into a blasting cap screws into the mine. Upon detonation, it would detonate a pound and a half of C-4 explosives, sending approximately seven hundred steel ball bearings at high velocity into anyone who was within fifty meters at a sixty-degree fan.

Now that they had clear fields of fire, camouflaged positions and claymores wired, they were ready not to touch ground for quite some time. Each position was set up with a small latrine, consisting of a hole in the platform with a small plastic bag. The men could urinate from the platform onto the ground, but feces had to be in the bag to avoid odor. These bags would be collected daily and taken to the enemy burial pit.

Resting, the men take turns eating their rations. Worn down by work and exhausted by stress, the men had no problems with their upcoming sleep that night. It was only 2045 hours, and the first shift for night security was steadily on guard.

Night vision had a tendency to give a person a headache, for two reasons. Some mounts were a plastic hoop that straps to the head of the person. These were affectionately called "skull crushers." The other factor for the headaches was the green light of the monocular night optical devices. It covers one eye while the other was open. This was designed to allow depth perception, which was lacking in the PVS7B models. Because of the variant lightness in separate eyes and the different magnifications seen in each eye, long viewing would create one hell of a headache.

Pfc. Trits rubbed his temples, hoping to massage the pain away at midnight. Through the darkness he heard a slight whisper. Readjusting his nods, Trits scanned the area for enemy. With nothing showing, he slowly and quietly pulled the twine to allow the brush below him to shift, revealing more of the area; nothing showed. Looking to his rear, he tried to flag down Baxley. Baxley looked back to find Trits signaling him that he heard something. Easing the safety to "fire" on his machine gun, he leaned forward, forcing the gun to point down. Nothing showed. Baxley had been taught that the machine gunner never fired until he had no choice. Machine guns of that magnitude were typical of a platoon position that would carry two. By giving his equipment away early, the scouts or point men would run back to the main body, informing them of the estimated size of the element in which they had made contact with. It would be ill-advised to be a fire team making contact with an enemy who had prepared to encounter thirty heavily armed soldiers. With that in mind, Baxley placed the weapon back to "safe" and reached for the M-16A1 he had taken from the cache. He scanned the area; he still could not find a thing. He turned back to Trits, who was about to lose control. He signaled to wake the man next to him. Baxley passed the signal around to Wilson, who also woke Trevor. Low crawling to Baxley, Trevor stopped to peek below the boardwalk. There was nothing.

Easing next to Baxley, Trevor asked for a SITREP. Baxley only reported that Trits heard something. The paranoia seemed unjustified, but they all knew what efforts they must go to not to be heard when they walk. The slightest sound could be the only one they would hear from the enemy until a shot was fired.

Trits turned toward Trevor and Baxley, signaling what he saw in his sector. Trevor rushed silently to his position and found a single man frozen still in the middle of the path, seemingly scanning the area. Trevor instructed Trits not to do anything until the lone soldier fired. Ignore him if he shoots only a couple times. Study him.

The man below took a single step, only to follow by three shots at ground level. The man waited for a moment and continued through the area. Trits' nerves were at its limit. Trevor placed a hand above him as he jumped. The jump caused a tree to shake, alerting the man below.

The man slowly walked directly below the moving branch. He inspected the limb and the tree it was connected to. With unwavering patience, the man stood and stared. Trevor was desperate to shake this man off; he signaled to Malloy to be ready to make a silent descent behind the nuisance.

Trevor's fear was that the man was a lead for a larger element. Malloy was prepared; he held on to a rope to ease himself to the ground and held eye contact with Trevor. Trevor silently instructed Baxley to keep an eye on the man while Trits kept his SAW on the path he had come from. All other men scanned their sectors, prepared for the worst.

The soldier leaned to either side to get a better angle to what he might have heard. Himelrick began to load a full magazine into his weapon by pressing the magazine release button on the right side of his M-4. The magazine slid out of the magazine well as he placed it on the platform. Himelrick replaced the empty well with a thirty-round magazine, but he kept the release button depressed to avoid the clicking sound of the button when the notch touched on the magazine. He locked the magazine into place and faced forward again to pick up security. He shifted his body into his rifle as his foot pushed the half-empty magazine closer to the edge of the platform. With more effort to lean into his rifle, his other foot pressed the side of the magazine and shifted it ninety degrees, placing the item halfway over the edge.

As most things do in the woods, shifting and swaying with the wind was natural. This next breeze would doom someone that night. Malloy looked back in time to see the mag as it slid off the edge of the platform and spun toward the ground to the side of the awaiting man.

In a fluid motion, Malloy leaned back off the edge of his own platform and swung from the rope toward the man, letting go only within inches of the man himself. Malloy pulled the bayonet from his teeth and pressed his blade slowly in a downward motion, into the soldier's neck, severing his spine. Now that the man was silent and in a brief moment of paralysis, Malloy finished him off by slashing at his throat.

Malloy stood up after a moment to study his act. The lowly private first class looked up at his squad leader with the great pride in taking care of his team. That young man had moved like an elite soldier you only see in movies, and risked everything because he was told to. Without any hesitation, he did what was needed to defend his team.

Trevor looked down at the young man and signaled for him to return to his post. With it still dark, not knowing if the dead enemy soldier was a point man of a larger element, he ordered all men to maintain security. The death of that man might make things very difficult or it might have been their saving grace.

Their position was about thirty-five kilometers east of Vientiane on the border of Thailand and Laos. The Mekong River ran along that border. The river itself was only about five kilometers away from their new location. The main problem in this area isn't the VC but the mercenaries that traveled in that province. Some factions of Special Forces groups would do the bidding of various agencies.

Trevor had not a clue as to what agency had their best interests in mind, not to mention who even knew of their presence. The maintenance of the security in this area was an absolute priority for the variables who marched all day to find something of value to kill.

With dawn approaching, Trevor made the call to rush that body out to the pit. Boiyd took Trits and Malloy to drop the body off. The two young men swung down from their positions, picked the man up and placed him in his proper place. The dead weight of this man was a struggle; they managed to carry him the distance as well as have their weapons at the ready.

Boiyd began to chuckle at the thoughts in his mind.

"Hey, Sarge, you remember that tattoo I got before we got out here? I thought it would make me a hard ass. Take a look again."

Boiyd pulled his sleeve up and showed off the tattoo on his arm. The tattoo showed a skull with a black beret, the head attire worn by all soldiers. The beret originated with the US Rangers. The Special Forces had their green berets, the Rangers had their black. Underneath the picture on Boiyd's arm it had something in quotes.

"Death from above, Sergeant. Just like what Malloy did."

"That's exactly what we should call this place. DFA. It's about as appropriate as you can get."

The two men smiled with the irony of a common quote that they had never seen more true. The soldiers in 2008 didn't see as much of the horror of war or the morbid nature of combat. Their missions were primarily peacekeeping or NEO. Only a few years prior did combat come back into the picture, when the soldiers from all over were sent to Iraq to help liberate them from Saddam Hussein and the rest of the Middle East from terrorist factions. Now that they were in 1969, they had to go back to the worry regarding communism.

The men rested in the noon sun only hours after the wandering enemy had strolled into their camp. The men had nothing left to prepare. Today was the first day at the DFA where they would rest and pull security. Their discipline in regard to noise and light during the nighttime hours were still maintained. These men had earned their rest.

They had only a few days before the team would come and check on them. Hopefully it would be Paul's men, but he knew that there was little chance for that. Trevor, too, went to sleep. He dreamed of his wife and his daughter; he forgot his place and pondered on what they might be doing now.

Meanwhile, Back at the Ranch

Richard Meyers was the typical stereotype of a scientist that people would make fun of. In public, the majority of society would lift an eyebrow at the sight of him; they would laugh at the lab coat and pocket protector that he adored. At work, his diligence was revered by the quiet agency in which he worked for. He would always be the man who would come through with the missing pieces to the theories that the staff would come up with. Richard was now the man who would be the only hope for Trevor's men, who were stuck in a world thirty-nine years behind.

After Richard had come up with the idea and delivered it to Michael Heimer about the probabilities of their device in relation to the four-dimensional STC, Richard had never left Michael's side. Michael had decided to run through all the data on the testing that they had done on the hills of Vietnam, which was ensured by the State Department of its clearance, and found that the hills were indeed not cleared.

After discovering the lost team and the dead American scientist in those hills, Michael didn't leave his work for a minute to find a way for these men to come home. The best plan he had was potentially disastrous to the fabric of the STC. Knowing nothing of the practical mechanics of this theorem, Michael was completely hesitant to the tampering of a device that utilizes and travels along these paths amongst a theory, which before now could never be proven or analyzed.

Richard entered the large laboratory inside of the compound known as The Ranch. He walked along the metal walkways to the main chamber, where Michael waited. Richard drowned himself with a large and saturated cup of coffee. Wiping the sweat off his forehead, Richard Meyers sat beside Michael to attempt to finalize the data from the tests.

Each man at the desk knew that there was a modern-day group of soldiers who were sent back in time somewhere. What they were not sure of was when and exactly where. Michael stood from the chair to go to the break room, where he had received his epiphany, and try to recreate the mindset that offered him clarity before. Richard followed him but stopped at the doorway to watch as his project leader attempted to set the mood that he was in before. After several minutes it was not Michael but Richard who thought of what was missing in the recovery of these men. Richard thought about the psychological reasoning that these men might consider when they realize that they aren't where they belong. Most men would try to find the place that was steady in their life. The place that they would consider home and fight their way to it no matter what date it was. Whatever they do, they must do it at these men's homes.

Richard pulled out his notebook and began writing his thoughts. After he completed writing the various ideas that flew through his mind, he dated it 05 July 2008, over a month and a half since the men's departure. The beautiful thing about the recovery of these men was that if they could figure out how to control the time and date when they opened the rift, it would not matter how long it took to recover them. They could in turn recover them to the day after their departure. Even if it took the scientists at The Ranch fifty years to figure this out, the men would only know the time they were gone before the rift opened for them. They would then come home whenever the rift released them. If they do this right, the men would come home and their families would not be fifty years older while the men were only months older than when they left. Richard smiled at the thought of the men's hopes in his notebook and shared his thoughts with Michael. With excitement and a glimmer of hope, Michael began to think and realized one thing that shot the hopes down for him.

Looking over at Richard, he said, "Richard, if we had figured this out, we would already have seen these men on the news or in the reports that they are now at home eating dinner with their families. I'm sorry, but we will not figure this out. Here is the bitch of it, though, if we read in the reports that these men came back, would we still work to find a way for them to come home a day after they left? If not, they would never get home. If we had sent them back when we read they returned would we have two sets of each missing man when we follow through? Should we leave the mission alone when we read that we were successful? Perhaps history or even these reports will change the second we figure out how to get this job done."

Richard squinted at the new thoughts on the subject and took a sip of water. The flow of the cold fluid poured down the man's throat and gave him comfort to know that every step they made toward the discovery of the creation of a rift could change the history in their hand every day that goes by.

The Stronghold

Today was the day that the men had been waiting for since Paul and his entourage had left the men with the supplies needed to survive. Today would be a highly anticipated day for these men to talk to men of their own nature. With a feeling almost like Christmas morning, the men woke up early and waited for hours until stand-to. Once the sun had risen completely, the men tried to imagine the look on the soldier's face when they asked where they were from. Deciding instead to keep the low profile of the no-name soldiers in contemporary uniforms, all men took turns changing their uniforms to the new and clean 1969 jungle fatigues with load carrying equipment (LCE) and ammo pouches. With the men positioned, they await their predeceasing comrades. Each man looked about for any sign of activity. Trits, the first to hear the brush rattling from the northwest, alerted Trevor to the activity ahead of him, Trits turned back to notice that the bushes ceased their movement. With an anticipated plea of excitement, Trits alerted the bushes that they were there with an exaggerated attempt to whistle like a bird. Trevor threw a small piece of wood over to Trits to get his attention. The irritated squad leader shook his head vigorously; Trevor ordered Trits to stay down and make not one single move.

Boiyd moved from his position to investigate what it was that Trits had seen. Looking very closely through the dew-covered trees, Boiyd noticed a patch of dead bamboo leaves. In training they were all taught to camouflage there position with brush or leaves. Booby traps were done in the same way.

The key thing was to keep trading out the leaves so that they would continue to be green. A patch of brown leaves in a green field was not camouflage. Boiyd looked at Trevor and signaled that he was going down.

Using a rope similar to Malloy, Boiyd slowly slid down to the ground. His weapon brought back to a ready position, the young corporal stepped on the side of his boots while rolling them to the ball slowly. He had found this to be a safe way to walk quietly. Now in front of the brown patch, he turned to look Trits in the eye and signaled for him to look out for security.

Lifting enough leaves to show a small hole into what was below; Boiyd caught a glimpse of a claymore mine. The mine was not one of the anti-personnel mines that they had placed. The mines that they had placed were located in the trees for an aerial burst to maximize the effect. Sweat poured from his forehead; Boiyd thought swiftly and looked closer at the mine. No trip wire was attached, only an electrical wire that was attached to the blasting cap, which was screwed into the top of the mine. The problem in this case was that there had to be someone with the detonator in order to use the weapon. Was there someone watching Boiyd? Was there a group of people who knew that they were there? Alternatively, had this mine been in place since before they got there? Boiyd had to gamble that no one was watching right now, since he was not dead. By simply pulling the leaves out of the way of the mine, the quick-thinking corporal lifted the mine out of the ground and simply turned it around. After aiming the mine directly behind where it was initially aimed, Boiyd covered it with fresh leaves and moved quickly back to his position.

Trevor gave Boiyd one hell of a questioning look, but Boiyd simply explained that the mine was rigged for a clacker and not tripwire. If they ever used it they would instead blow themselves up instead of the Americans.

Soldiers have always joked about doing that to someone and claiming it to be the most brilliant of the black ops that they would play in the field. During expert infantry badge testing, the grader had turned the mine around on Trevor and claimed that he didn't pull security walking his way back. Since Trevor noticed it before he had simulated the detonation, they let him pass.

With a smile and a pat on the back, Trevor sent Boiyd back to his position, as they would contemplate who it was that may have been watching them. Since the claymore didn't have any markings on it, Boiyd had assumed it was a claymore from the VC. When the men they were expecting finally arrived, they would inspect the perimeter for more mines.

At noon the men didn't hesitate to break open the c-rations for lunch. The men sat back while alternating security, and relearned the old weapons that they had in their hands. Baxley was given a 1911 Colt to replace his Beretta 9mm. The M60 was also issued to him to replace the M240Z machine gun. Himelrick was given the M79 Grenade launcher with an entire case of grenades. Also given pineapple grenades and a variety of smoke grenades, he slung his new M16 on his back and carried the M79 as his primary. The RTO, Pv2 Wilson, would continue to carry his ASIP and ICOM, but he would carry it inside his ruck and not show it when the visitors arrive. All M252-A's were replaced with the appropriate M16A1's. Trits was given a set of bipod legs and extra magazines to connect to his M16. He would keep the weapon on full automatic fire to maintain the role of automatic gunner.

The only thing the men did not compromise with was the new helmet. The steel helmets and the inserts were extremely uncomfortable compared to the light Kevlar helmets they were used to. The men elected not to wear the helmets and decided, instead, to wear the boony caps. These were very comfortable and were exactly what the Special Forces wore instead of green berets or helmets. If a stranger were to look at these men, they would assume that they were all Special Forces. No rank insignias were worn and no unit patch was in place to designate them. They had removed their dog tags since they didn't belong there in the first place.

Once they had finished their food and prepared their new equipment, the men were ready for their visitors. The small unit they were expecting had shown up at about 1600 hours. They were not of the same unit that Paul was from; they were a detachment of the 2nd Ranger Battalion. The Rangers had moved from the east into their perimeter and stopped center mass by the tree, which Trevor was located above. The Rangers were instructed to deliver the challenge at a specific grid coordinate. Their lieutenant pulled his RTO aside and confirmed the grid in which they were standing. The lieutenant looked around and delivered the challenge.

"Two aces!" the lieutenant said in a whisper.

Trevor looked down from his position and inspected the scrolls on their shoulders. With a whisper, Trevor replied the password.

"Three queens take the pot."

The lieutenant looked around and could not place where the voice had come from. All men looked around the wood line and could not spot anyone. Trevor announced himself and began to swing down from his position.

"Coming down!"

With a solid and deliberate landing on the ground he hadn't touched in a while, Trevor looked at the lieutenant and began to size him up. The leader of the small unit took a knee and ordered the rest of the men to form a perimeter around him. With the men in place, Trevor looked to him and spoke.

"Glad to see you boys here. I was beginning to think that First Sergeant Ricardo had blown us off. Before we brief you I need your men to be aware that we pulled a babysitter in the brush over there."

Trevor hoped that the people in this day called wired claymores "babysitters." Since the lieutenant didn't look to be thinking too hard, Trevor assumed that he knew what he meant. The lieutenant instructed his NCO to pass the word around that the area may be mined. The sergeant first class had passed the word around and returned next to his lieutenant. The lieutenant had kept quiet from that time forward, allowing the experienced NCO to do the talking.

SFC Quinn was a badly scarred man who looked like the typical war vet and career NCO. One could easily see him being a sergeant major making the new lieutenants do push-ups for making ignorant decisions. It was extremely evident that he hated officers. Especially cherry lieutenants who disregard experience and rely purely on bookwork and education as the key qualification for leadership. The men around the platoon sergeant had obviously been around him long enough to prove themselves to him. He wasn't rough on any of them, and he cared for them a great deal as if they were his own children. SFC Quinn was the kind of man that kept the United States standing during war.

Quinn leaned past the lieutenant and spoke directly to Trevor.

"How are you and your men on supplies? Paul had told me that your men would be dressed in a surprising way. You seem to be dressed normally to me. Sergeant, I ask ya, are you used to what you are wearing and the equipment that you have in your hands? If you ain't, I'll have my men maintain security so you can get back to what you're used to. We were ordered not to ask questions, so don't worry about my men. Rowdy declared you people top secret, as well as your equipment. I'll cover you for a good fifteen mikes so you can get your shit together. From now on you don't have to put on a dog and pony show together for anyone who comes looking for ya. Stick to what you know and keep your head out of shit that doesn't fit to your training. I suggest you get a move on, Sergeant. I want to debrief you and get your fucking wish list jotted down so we can get this over with."

Trevor thanked the rough man and instructed his men to get on with the changing. With as much fun as the men were having with the antique equipment, they were eager to get their own gear on. Not more than seven minutes had passed and all of the men had come down from their position, almost in unison, with their strange uniforms, equipment and, most especially, their weapons.

Nothing would prepare the experienced E-7 for the look of these men. It was only then that he yearned to ask the questions he was ordered not to. With the sophisticated look of these men and the futuristic way their equipment was mounted to their weapons, it was as if he was watching a sci-fi television show. These were not actors playing the role of the future. These were men trying to play the role of the past.

The first impressions of these men were extremely high. They had sense, tactical experience and, most of all, discipline.

The soldiers looked at each other in a moment of awkwardness and shook the spooky feeling off by turning their attention to either security or the debriefing. Trevor asked the Rangers to move their security into the tree positions so that they didn't draw too much attention to the area. SFC Quinn agreed and allowed Trevor's soldiers to grab one man each and escort them to their positions.

Once security was in place, the Lieutenant and Quinn sat beside the rest of the supplies in Trevor's self-declared command post. Starting the conversation with a supply request, Quinn began to write down what Trevor's needs were. Since they had an ample supply of ammunition and spare weapons, the request was for medical supplies and food. The major item that they needed was iodine for the water. Trevor had drawn out a plan for the current batteries to be used in the ASIP. By having this converter with the encampment, it would provide the group with the ability to call for indirect fire in case of enemy attacks. Supply requests would be able to be delivered by radio instead of taking two weeks from request to delivery. Rope and ghillie suits were added to the list to enhance their position and their camouflage. Additional claymores were something they could use a lot more of in order to enhance their security. They had also requested palettes and steel plating to enhance their position, as well as raw materials to make their own custom mines and explosive booby traps. The likelihood of Trevor using these types of traps were slim, but he always strove to be prepared in case the need arose.

Because they were stranded and had no support except for the few hours a week, they needed even more firepower to protect themselves. Trevor prepared the best they could for a decent meal for Quinn's men, and he made an effort not to talk more than necessary. Quinn could not help but look at the equipment lying around the area. Trevor noticed the man's obvious curiosity and handed over his rifle. Quinn looked up at Trevor as if he had just broken a major rule. Trevor delivered a slight smile and began to explain what each item mounted to the rifle was.

"Don't worry about it. Just don't ask where it came from. This is a PAQ-4 infrared targeting system. It's nothing more than a laser you can't see with the naked eye."

SFC Quinn asked confusingly, "Okay, what's a laser?"

Trevor laughed to himself and answered.

"Shit, I'm sorry, it's a light that travels in a straight line. It doesn't spread. Put these on."

Trevor handed Quinn a set of night vision goggles.

"I'm going to aim at the C-ration next to Malloy over there, you ready?"

Quinn gave a nod as he looked at the C-ration can.

"Okay, you see that dot on the can? Now follow it to the left. Wherever the dot is, the round will fly. Give or take trajectory, of course. It's an easy way to quickly fire at night. This way, when the enemy is firing at anything and everything, I will have the ability to know exactly what I am firing at and they have no idea. With thirty rounds I can take down thirty people without them seeing anything more than the flash from my barrel."

Quinn looked up with a look of awe on his face and asked to see for himself; Trevor handed the rifle over to Quinn and showed him how to activate the beam. Quinn targeted a tree and removed the goggles to see for himself that the beam was, in fact, invisible to the eye. Quinn would be entertained for quite some time once he got to inspect each feature on the rifle.

After their meal and no discussion as to where these men were from, the lieutenant asked if they could rest with Trevor's men for the night so they could leave at first light. Trevor agreed and offered them a night without pulling security. Quinn denied that offer as quickly as Trevor mentioned it. It was typical of NCOs in Vietnam not to allow someone they do not know very well to watch over the lives of their men. If only one man were to fall asleep on shift, it could be devastating to the unit. A single man could sneak through their position and throw a single grenade, killing a large portion of the group. For this, Quinn insisted that his men cover half of the security rotation.

The night was quiet and peaceful. All of the men were rested well, since there were more men for security. Since they all had relatively short shifts, that night was of the best sleep they all have had in a long while.

The following morning, Quinn packed his men and moved out after stand-to. The list of supplies was delivered to Rowdy three days after Quinn left Trevor. The supplies would be dropped within two days after Rowdy received the list. They had decided to drop the cache point a couple hundred meters west of Trevor's location so the drop would not actually fall on Trevor's position.

The drop was made on Friday, and Trevor's men had followed the parachute they had seen fall from the cargo plane. It took another two days to bring all of the supplies back to their position. The first priorities were the explosives and steel plating. They took everything that would either kill them or save them first. Then they concentrated on the food and medical supplies. Sunday night the men had finished installing the steel plates to the underside of their positions and painted it with vegetation inlayed into the plated for added camouflage. They had created another few platforms higher in the trees to store the medical supplies. The area where the supplies were now stored at was renovated to keep the friendly casualties known as a casualty collection point (CCP).

There was only one box in the first supply drop that was not opened. Trevor had not opened it since it was labeled the same as the weapons that Trevor had already issued to his men. With curiosity brewing within him, he cracked open the crate to find four cases of ammo with four separate sniper rifles. With a wide grin of hope, Trevor planned for two snipers to be placed at the CCP since they had a higher position. He selected the two best shooters, Boiyd and Malloy, to be moved to the tower. The rifles were similar to the M24 sniper rifle, which the scouts used in Trevor's battalion. They fired a 7.62mm round and were very reliable. Mounted to the rifles were high-power scopes, which could see very clearly at a mile away. Since the men couldn't see more than a hundred meters in front of them clearly, the snipers shouldn't have a problem with hitting the target when one came into view. They had more than enough ammo to last through two major firefights.

The time had come to prepare the explosives. The formal training for explosives for the infantry was limited. An experienced soldier would know how to arm C-4 or Bangalore torpedoes. The average soldier would only know prefabricated devices such as claymores or anti-tank (AT) mines. Trevor had the fortunate gift of having a father who worked as explosives ordinance disposal (EOD) technician for fifteen years. His father taught him every way imaginable to rig explosives to give the desired effect. Trevor had the skills to design shape charges and concussion blasts. He also had the ability to design trip wires to act as detonation for a variety of explosives. The main project now was to create a "Bouncing Betty" that was more powerful than the ones mass-produced for the Army.

A very small charge of C-4 was in place to blast the device upward. Trevor used cloth and gunpowder to make a fuse. Tying the fuse in with the C-4 underneath the main charge, Trevor had the other end of the fuse rigged to a blasting cap, which was embedded into a can with pellets from shotgun shells as well as ten-penny nails. The initial blast forced the can into the air upward, allowing a delayed detonation of the large charge to allow shrapnel from an aerial burst. This would cause much more damage than a ground burst.

With the claymores fired from trees and these mines, which would place when the threat grew higher, the security and efficiency of the small perimeter would be greatly enhanced. The men were now properly prepared for whatever might come their way.

The Big Bang

Since Quinn had left the DFA, Trevor had run several tests on the explosives that he feared might draw attention. Nothing had come out of it, but since a team would be coming out today to check up on them, he strengthened the security around the DFA. It was closing on noon, and the morning sun begun its relentless pouring down of heat. With the incredible humidity, rain was a common hassle with the men. The men had constantly fought against rust and corrosion with their weapons. They were on their last leg of patience. Growing tired of the heat and the consistent feeling of abandonment, the men drove on knowing that their lives would not end but just continue elsewhere. Worst-case scenario was that they would wait the war out until the cease-fire, hike their way through Thailand and find a way home by way of Hong Kong. Best case, Rowdy came through and found a way to send them home secretively. In either case, none of the men would see their families again.

Boiyd discovered the first movement through the wood line. Passing the words down from the tower to Trevor, Trevor instructed the men to hold their positions until the identity of the men was known. Though the movement was only known by the shifting of the trees and brush, it was Monday and they were expecting their check-up team.

A man stepped out of the trees and stopped to look around. Trevor stood to find himself exposed through the large leaves of the DFA. As the man on the ground looked up to identify the movement, Trevor hadn't a second to prepare himself to see the man's head explode with a large red burst. Falling back to the platform to attempt to grasp what it was that had just occurred; he looked up in time to find Malloy reloading his rifle. Just as Trevor was about to holler up at him, a loud scream from the wood line overwhelmed their senses. After the sound of the scream, a dozen men charged through the brush to the south east of the DFA. Firing upward at the trees, the attackers were relentless in their charge.

Without order or hesitation, Baxley replaced the M60 machine gun with his M240Z and began to spill the lead at an unbelievable rate of fire down on the men. With the first burst, five fell to the ground with bullet wounds entering from top to bottom of their bodies. Boiyd and Malloy opened fire to hit the men at a distance when Trits noticed a man on a radio at his end of the DFA. Taking a close aim, he fired a burst with his M16 and missed the man as he leapt into the woods. Himelrick was the first to notice as he launched a grenade into the woods and watched as white smoke filled with a red haze of blood from the impact of a grenade.

As the dust settled from the sudden strike of these men, it was safe to assume that they had heard the testing of the explosives from earlier. Trevor ordered the men to reload and wait for a counterattack. After a couple hours of unsettling adrenaline, the men were then instructed to get to the ground and clean up the site.

Trevor supervised the search of what was left of the VC; he piled the findings next to the center tree. Moving the bodies to the pit was a gruesome and exhausting task. When the bodies were placed, the men tried to sweep the bloody earth as best they could to hide the gruesome retaliation. It was then when the men almost killed their only way home.

With a loud rustle in the woods as before, Baxley fired a short burst into the brush to put it at ease. With Trevor, Trits and Wilson on the ground, Trevor instructed the two young men to hold in a cover position as he advanced to inspect the woods. Waving Baxley off, Trevor found Paul sitting there, laughing at him hysterically.

All of the contemporary soldiers in the party came out of the wood line expecting frightened and wounded men. When Paul had seen that no one was injured and Trevor's men had killed twelve with relative ease, he placed his hand on Trevor's shoulder, giving him an admiring smile.

Paul had told his men to help with the cleanup as Rowdy and Paul moved into the DFA. Rowdy was quite impressed that the supplies he had sent to these strange Americans was put to good use. The steel plating had been hit at least a hundred times under the DFA fortification, but nothing had penetrated. Only one injury was found from flying wood; Malloy was hit on the cheek, causing a small cut.

Placing security elements heavily across the DFA, the men were then free to discuss what else they would need. Since Trevor could think of nothing, they had agreed to wait until dusk to prepare their food for the night. Paul pulled Trevor aside.

"We just left our joint operations center. It isn't good. I need to know what you and your men will need for the next month or so."

Trevor asked, "Are we expecting company?"

Paul answered, "Our CO ordered us to avoid coming here because of the latest enemy activity in the area. There are going to be more and more attacks in the area. It seems that good old Charlie ran into the village and saw your handiwork there. I can't express to you enough how sensitive the area is going to be. VC are patrolling and probing the area, looking for anyone who isn't covered in shit by the sight of them. Since last week four villages were raided, and reports show that they were looking for a small Special Forces insurgent in the area. All four villages were destroyed. You must know that there are only three teams, including us, which are assigned to this area. This place is too sensitive to have anyone else brought in."

Trevor lowered his head. "So you're saying that your CO denied you guys to continue to send men our way for support because you need to keep a low profile."

Paul nodded. "You men have stirred the fuck out of the hornets' nest. We're here to make sure that you know not to do shit without a direct mortal threat to you and your men. If we lose you, no one will come to help or even collect your bodies. I am going to do one last thing for you. I will give you our medic to ensure that you can stay in the fight as long as possible. Aside from that, we can't send any more caches or provide you with indirect fire. I'm sorry, bud."

Trevor looked around at his men. All of them were wiping down their primary weapons and keeping their secondary close by in case of attack. Boiyd reassured Trits of their chances of evacuation while Baxley made sure that his assistant had the rounds counted and prepared for another firefight.

Looking back over to Paul, Trevor replied, "I never expected you guys to carry us through this. We're more than in your debt for the help you've given us. I ask only one thing, and I know how bad it could go if you approach the wrong people. I need you to convince Rowdy to contact some of the highest levels of the intelligence community and see if there is anyone who is working on the type of project that I described to you. If they pass the report of us to the people who assume the project in our time, perhaps they might find a way to get us back. I need the people in my time to know about us and know what happened. For all I know we are nothing but MIA, and without good reason. Please convince him to try, even though it could hurt his reputation."

Paul raised his head toward the tops of the trees. Light beamed off his face as he replied, "I can't guarantee that he'll do it. I can guarantee that I won't leave him alone until he does something. Just stay here and stay safe. When things blow over we'll do everything in our power to get you out of this hellhole. If we can't, I'll send word and provide you with a route so you can make it out yourselves. Just stay alive until we can get to you. Now, before we head out tomorrow morning, I need to know how much ammo you spent on this last fight. We'll provide you with what you lost. It's not much, but it is that best we can do for now."

Trevor turned behind and asked Boiyd for an ACE report. Boiyd began asking around. The count came back at seventy-four 7.62mm and only twenty-eight 5.56mm rounds, and one 40mm grenade.

Paul's eyebrows rose as they did at the realization of who these men were. The controlled rates of fire and weapon use were incredible. The average soldier around that time would expend as much as five to ten times as much to kill the same amount of men. With the battle lasting less than a minute, Trevor's men completely decimated the entire patrolling squad.

With the realized capabilities that his men had shown, Trevor couldn't help but smile in pride.

Paul collected all of the spare magazines from his men and gave them over to Trevor. Paul stared into the young man's eyes in front of him; he realized that these men were probably the only ones this far north that could go the distance.

Trevor's men had found enough pertinent information requirements (PIR) from the fallen VC to send back to the JOC to help with strategizing the placements of the VC and the NVA in the north.

Rowdy joined in on the stockpile of information, no matter how trivial; he pulled a series of maps from the obliterated RTO's gear and laid them out. His eyes were drawn immediately to a route marked leading straight to the JOC located in the outskirts of Dien Bien Phu. The aging soldier spit out the wad of tobacco from his mouth and leaned over to get Paul's attention.

"Paul, if these slanty-eyed fucks get their hands on the command center for this area, they'll know where we are and kill us all, even here at the DFA. According to this map there are several units moving from Hanoi to patrol from every direction around Dien Bien Phu. This group here had gone from Hanoi northwest to Fan Si Pan Mountain and moved southwest from there to get to the JOC. We are only two and a half days walk from there. Who knows how many units have made it closer. I'm sorry, Paul, but this says that there are five more patrols following behind this crew. We have to leave now! I have no fucking clue how many are going around through Laos to make it to the JOC. I only count seven routes marked here. No one is stupid enough to plot every route on a map that could be compromised, even these fuckers. Get your men together; we leave now!"

Paul shied a glance over to Trevor, who had listened in on the terrifying conversation. Trevor's face was completely flushed with fear and anticipation. Paul didn't say a word; instead, he walked over to Lars and directed him to the tower above the DFA. Without hesitation, Lars picked up his medical gear and climbed the rope ladder up the DFA. Trevor packed the PIR up in a rucksack and handed it to Cooper.

With a slight shove against the rucksack, Trevor looked to Paul and said. "Just leave. I can't have our only out getting shot up. From what I know, the VC will sacrifice security for time. Stay away from the rivers and trails, haul ass and get us home."

Paul rallied his men to his position and filled them in on the need to rush their movement. Trevor glanced a thankful nod over to Rowdy, hoping that his look would be burned into his conscience. He would decide how far to take their welfare.

Rowdy didn't even say good luck; he simply tapped Cooper and Ward on the shoulder and left the DFA moving due east to get to command. Paul slowly stood to follow them as he looked back at Trevor's men as if they were already dead. Paul turned back to his small team and rushed forward to take point.

Trevor looked uneasily over to Paul. Small firefights were manageable for his men, but he couldn't do what he had seen in the movies. Trevor had seen the kinds of battles on film that lasted for days and did not end. In the same regard, Trevor figured that movies had experts help with the technical details. If he were to adopt some of the ideas from the movies, he could have an edge on the enemy by being unpredictable. In the same regard, Trevor was already unpredictable to the enemy and to the friendly forces by having the training and technology that they lacked. Perhaps he had the edge anyhow. Would his men be able to handle this on top of the stress they were already under? They had done well so far, and they believed that they would go home…eventually. Perhaps the motivation would be greater with the added stress to the men.

Trevor now studied the faces of his oblivious men who knew nothing of the terror they were likely to go through. Common phrases came to mind as he decided the best way to prepare his men for the upcoming days. Trevor decided to begin his preparations and rallied his men to the center tree.

The History Report

Richard Meyers ran through the hallway with a paper trail billowing behind him. He ran to find Michael with new information and data, which could bring great ease in bringing the men back. What he had discovered was a way to determine exactly when these boys were sent to. By knowing the exact location of the men, and the location of the ship that fired a test of the beacon, he figured them to have landed in the summer of 1969. He only needed Michael's help to determine the exact location and date of where and when these men were.

Richard invaded Michael's office with a stack of papers. He had just left the lab after finalizing the formulas with the other overworked scientists. With a smile on his face, Michael began to feel an actual hope for the men who were stranded in another time. The time had come for the massive project of determining the precise location that these men would have been released from the quantum foam. By calculating the exact distance between the men and the beacon upon activation, they relied only on their unproven formulas to make their determinations.

According to the data, after two hours of scribbling on scratch paper, the two men had established that these men were released southwest of the Fan Si Pan Mountain in the farthest north of Vietnam.

Richard didn't hesitate and moved straight to Michael's historical records. In these detailed books, Richard read through pages upon pages that referred to any actions from May to September of 1969 in North Vietnam.

Michael sat back in his chair and watched Richard as he tore his books apart. Without speaking a word to each other, Michael waited until Richard had completed the destruction of his office before asking what exactly he was looking for.

When Richard had enough historical data and time line information to help with his case, he began to explain himself to Michael. Michael had begun twisting the ends of his mustache habitually as he pondered what Richard was saying. Standing to an empty wall, Richard stapled some of the clippings onto it for tracking purposes. Michael studied Richard intensely as the clippings began to cover the entirety of the once empty wall. Michael waited until Richard was at a breaking point before instructing Richard to get with DIA to request the pertinent top-secret information from June 1, 1969 to October 31, 1969. If they had told anyone responsible for anything of their situation, and that person believed them, they would be declared classified and filed accordingly.

His eyes wandered along the wall where he had placed the clippings of his records; he noticed something that stirred his stomach. Comparing the entry on his wall to the location data on his desk, he felt a great pain for these men. Dated August 31, 1969, he read about a massacre of top U.S. officials from an unexpected raid of a major command center in Dien Bien Phu, Vietnam. Leading generals as well as several battalion commanders were slaughtered. All classified information for operations within Vietnam was compromised, leading to the precise ambushes and strikes killing over two thousand soldiers from all over the small country, North and South. The men were located within the attack pattern leading to the command center.

With the realization that these men might be dead already, Michael needed some proof. This would have to wait until the classified files were opened for him. Spending the day reading over the unclassified attacks over that summer, Michael tried to find an abnormality about the men he had begun to feel responsible for. Seeing nothing as of yet, Michael felt a great pain as he looked into the files of the men who were sent. Staff Sergeant Trevor Sands, married with a daughter. Wife named Jessi, daughter named Mali. He lowered his head, picked up the phone and dialed a number, feeling foolish.

Jessica Sands stared blankly out of the window from her overstuffed loveseat, the cooling coffee held tight in her hands. Her peace was in the comfort that her husband was merely lost and not dead. She searched her heart for the strength not to cry; her thoughts were abruptly disturbed by the ring of the telephone. She stood and walked slowly to the phone to answer.

"Hello," she answered somberly.

On the other line was Michael, who dialed without planning what to say.

"Yes, ma'am, is this Jessica Sands?" Michael blurted.

"Yes, this is she."

"Ma'am, my name is Michael Heimer. I…I know where your husband is."

The line was quiet for a long moment before Jessi responded.

"Is he okay? Where is he? When is he coming home?"

Now frantic and crying, Jessi began to beg the man to tell her more.

"Ma'am, I really can't tell you anything more. I just want you to know he is alive and I am trying to get him home soon. Please know that we were doing everything in our power to make it very soon. I am truly sorry, Jessi, but I can't say any more."

"But…"

"I have to go. Please just tell Mali that everything will be okay."

With those words, Michael hung up the phone and expected to be crucified for the breach of security. Michael poured a small glass of bourbon, sat back and drank his mind to numbing ease.

Jessi placed the phone on its base and sat back down on the couch. Now confused and hopeful, she wrote down the name Michael Heimer on a napkin and placed it in the drawer in the side table. She looked over to Mali, who was playing with her teddy bears, and allowed the tears to flow once again. Jessi didn't have the heart to hold her and promise that everything was going to be okay. Deciding instead to go outside and smoke a cigarette, which she had quit two years before, she tried desperately to relax. Jessi decided to take her mind off things by going inside and finishing the plans for her daughter's birthday scheduled for the following day, with or without her husband

Three hours passed from when Michael had called Ssg Sand's wife. He was prepared to have to call her later for the bad news that they have failed. He sat back in his office chair and tried to search his mind to find the answer he was looking for. Instead, he gave up and laid his head on his desk, falling fast asleep.

Richard stood over the sign-in desk in the office of the DIA representative and filled out the release forms for the documents he needed so desperately. Richard was utterly exhausted from explaining what their status was to fifty different people. Now that they were in his hands, he waited until the morning to deliver them to Michael. Hopefully they would be able to find a pattern of mobility in these men to help determine where they would be to create a return rift. Currently, Richard didn't even know for sure that they were mentioned or even referred to in the files that would be the destiny of the stranded soldiers.

Making History

Trevor sat down beside his men, leaving security aside, and briefed the young men about the new intelligence received from the bodies. With several attacks in the future inevitable, he emphasized the importance of the level of preparation they needed to ensure everything was in place. With the thirty mines that he had made from scratch and the claymores, their ammunition should be conserved quite well. The only thing they have left was to clear the battlefield to allow the men to fire at the enemy from a greater distance. To do this they would need to clear a mind-numbing amount of trees. The fallen trees would also act as obstacles to slow the movement of the assaulting forces.

The use of a detonation cord to take the trees down was the only logical and easily concealed way to handle this massive project. Trevor began handing the spools out to the men to circle the perimeter surrounding each tree at a forty-five degree angle at the base of the tree. Ensuring that the det-cord was camouflaged after the trees were wrapped, they planned to blow the wood line at the first sign of a large hostile force. With any luck, the blast should take out several men with large falling trees coming down on top of them. The following force would not be able to maneuver easily past the logs and branches. The machine gun would then be allowed to plow through the enemy with minimal obstructions. That was the best way for Trevor to channel the enemy where he wanted them without the use of constatina wire.

The young Americans spread around the perimeter, moving as fast as they could to get the area prepared. Three men wrapped the trees while another three buried the mines in between the estimated falls of the trees. Trevor circled around the area to ensure that the det-cord was camouflaged as well as the mines. With any luck the attack would be sooner than later. It would be in the men's best interest to be fully rested when the patrols rolled through. The final touches were completed to Trevor's satisfaction. Trevor moved the men back into the DFA and linked up with Lars, who had been pulling security around the area while the men were working.

Baxley prepared his position by placing several open crates of belted ammo next to him. He placed a generous streak of oil along the guide rails of the machine gun and ran the charging handle repeatedly to spread the oil for performance. Malloy finished the positioning of the tripod to allow Baxley greater ease in elevating the gun up and down. The traversing bar was well oiled to reduce the resistance in moving the gun from left to right. Once Malloy completed his task by arranging the ammo that Baxley had set out so that he could reload the weapon quickly, he began preparing his own weapon. He set aside several magazines of ammo next to his position, scanned his sector and positioned the contents of his pockets in a way that allowed him to be in a comfortable position, providing him with less distraction during his firing.

Trits was debating whether to remain faithful to his SAW or provide automatic fire with an M16. Opting instead to keep an M16 locked and loaded next to him, he positioned his SAW on the platform while nailing small blocks in the front and to the rear of his bipod legs to reduce them from slipping when he leaned into his weapon.

Trevor arranged all of the firing devices in a way that he could easily determine which firing set went to the appropriate claymore mine. By arranging it in a small map on the platform in front of him, he should be able to detonate them quickly. The greatest unease was that he didn't know what size element may cross their path. He was prepared for a small company, he felt, but he did not want the mines to be tripped by a surrounding squad and wasting them all.

Trevor racked his mind, trying to think of the things he should have taught his men; gratefully enough, he could actually think of nothing that wasn't covered at least once. They were now prepared for whatever might come their way for the next week. The sky began to darken as the sun passed through the dense layers of trees below the horizon. It was now that Trevor was grateful for the edge that they possessed. The edge was not their training or their lessons from clever movies or military lectures; it was their own great desire to live. A cornered beast had always become the most innovative and fiercest fighter. The time had come for the men to rely on their night vision, which did give them an edge over the wandering men walking blind into their web of death from above.

Trevor walked around the perimeter in the DFA and issued the men the extra batteries that he had brought with him. He carried enough to have every man observant at night for the next month. It was now that his habitual preparedness paid off. He checked above the DFA on the snipers and the medic; he ensured that they had the line of sight needed to be the most effective. Their line of sight would be completely cleared when the trees fell as they sat in their boxed-in positions, which provided them cover as they fired from the firing point on each end of the box. Trevor had decided to box them in so that the casualties, if any, should be protected from stray rounds. No grenade could be thrown this high, and not many VC had the capabilities of grenade launchers. Even if they had, lobbing a grenade into this box at the maximum ordinate of the grenade's trajectory would be a difficult task for even the most experienced grenadier.

Lying in their positions, waiting for the smell of death to wreak the DFA once again, the men became anxious for the fight. Each man released their tension in their own way. From rocking their leg back and forth to constantly repositioning their entire bodies, every man kept great care to not make any noise as they moved their various ways. Trevor had found himself switching the safety of the detonator in his hand back and forth from safe to fire. As he caught himself, he placed the clacker on the platform in its appropriate position. Now sitting quietly, listening to the sounds of the jungle, Trevor prayed in his heart for the men who followed him through the reaches of imagination. Each man was now thinking about the long-humored phrase "There are no atheists in foxholes."

The noise of the jungle had put the men at ease, as it usually did. It reminded Trevor of a noise box that he had kept in his daughter's room at night, filling the room with the sound of a brook and the chirping of birds. The soothing sound of safety had made each man stop their nervous movements and eased their hearts. The men were at peace with where they were and what was about to happen, until the soothing sound of the jungle ceased.

With the silence creeping into the nerves of all men, they all begin scanning their sectors with their night vision religiously. Trevor had explained beforehand not to fire any rounds until either mines were tripped or the detonation of the trees had taken place. It was believed that no one could see the men before the men fired their weapons. The enemy would have no idea that men in trees were watching the minefield. Most men fired reflexively at body height. Their minds revert to what their frame of reference was and retaliate in the same manner in which they believed their attack was coming from. Not many men think objectively and wait until they knew where their attack originated from before they react.

At the edge of their positions with anticipation, the men waited until their ability to fire came. Almost simultaneously, Trits and Baxley signaled to Trevor with an infrared flash that they had spotted a patrol. With Baxley and Trits on almost opposite ends of the DFA, it was clear that they were about to be surrounded as Trevor had thought. It seemed that the RTO that Himelrick had killed during the first patrol had actually managed to call in a position to his higher command.

Trevor held the men steady with his hand in the air. When Trevor's hand fell, it meant that he was about to blow the det cord for the trees. Before he did so, he needed to wait until enough men were spotted, so not to waste a perfectly designed plan he could only use once. He would sooner blow the claymores than the trees. Trevor scanned the men who had the best eyes on, and they signaled that they spotted seven men. At that moment every man around the perimeter spotted men. The count rose quickly to twelve men. With more and more men coming out of the wood line, carefully scanning the area as if questioning the intelligence they had received, they declared the area clear for more men to come out. When the count was nineteen men, Trevor opted to blow the trees.

With a slight twist of a ring and a push, trees shook with ferocious power as the percussion of the blast threw the men to the ground before the trees could. Collapsing all around their perimeter, screams and thunderous crashing drowned out the orders from the commander. The men who were in too close for the trees to affect them were completely shaken with terror. Frozen in their steps, Trevor reached for two claymore devices. Placing the devices from safe to fire, Trevor squeezed the grips three times as the mines detonated from the edge of their trees, raining ball bearings into the remaining six men who were spared from the falling wood.

With leaves still settling their way to the ground, it was up to the snipers to determine if there were any threats remaining from the ground. By the lack of firing, Trevor had hoped for the best. It was less than a few seconds before everyone was startled by Baxley's machine gun strafing past the fallen trees into the darkness. The bodies slammed into the ground with ear-piercing screams. The count grew larger and larger, and Trevor became almost panic-ridden when he heard two of his mines shatter the peace at the end of the machine gun bursts. No sounds from any man followed the explosions, which told the men that it was an effective kill.

It had come, the humid smell of flesh burned by blasts and blood boiled by the heat of the jungle. They had waited for what seemed like weeks; Trevor kept his men in control before asking for situation reports. Only fifteen minutes had passed but the time had seemed to pass slowly enough to place the men back in time once again. With the silent and dulling scenes in front of them, Trevor requested their ACE reports. All men were well prepared with ammo, no injuries, and all equipment was intact. Sighing with relief, Trevor instructed the men to prepare for a counter attack. As the men checked their weapons, they began scanning their sectors once again. That was the painful part of combat. That was when you knew that there were people after you but you didn't know if you killed them all. The need for closure grew by the second.

Himelrick signaled to Trevor for permission to launch a grenade into the woods to probe for more. Trevor thought this over and decided that the men had plenty of opportunity to detect the flash from their muzzles. Trevor nodded gently toward Himelrick as the dull *pow-thump* of the launching grenade flew down into the far reaches of the fallen trees, impacting into a sharp and radiant blast. Nothing. It was then that Trevor felt even more uneasy. He decided to hold the men tight until morning. At first light the counterattack would begin, almost guaranteed to be at stand-to. Right now, if there were remaining forces, they would be scanning the area from the safest distance they could think of with a stolen starlight scope. Because of the lack of a clear picture with that device, Trevor felt comfortable that the men on the ground were much more nervous than he would ever be tonight.

With the adrenalin wearing the nerves of the men down to marrow, Boiyd called from the tower under his breath that he spotted seven men surrounding one single man. They looked as if they had just begun the planning for the counter attack. Trevor smiled and decided to place his men in the single basket up above. The snipers would take one man each while Malloy would give his M4 to Baxley to take the third. Himelrick, Trevor and Lars would take three more, leaving one unassigned.

Trevor said with a smirk, "First one to get the last man gets a full night's sleep."

With a gentle laugh from the soldiers, they took their aim and, at Trevor's count, they marked the target with the IR beam. On the second count they would take their assigned man out and draw on the seventh. Trevor began his count.

"Okay, men. Three, two, one." The men marked their target.

Trevor eased his voice for the second countdown.

"This is it. Three, two, one. Fire!"

With what sounded like a single shot, six men fell to the ground with shots to the head and chest. Another single shot rang out in unison from the six weapons as the remaining man was thrown back over the bodies of the men around him and fell to the ground over six feet from where his head was once positioned. Malloy grinned at Trevor, asking who he thought was first.

Trevor smiled back and said, "I was. We will all get sleep tonight in turn. Malloy, you go first, then Boiyd. Lars, you third, then we'll rotate whoever was up here clockwise, starting with Baxley. Sound fair?" The men nodded with pride swelling within them. As Trevor climbed down from the tower, he told Trits and Wilson to get two hours of sleep. Without hesitation, the two boys' eyes rolled back into their skull as they fell into slumber.

Trevor leaned back into his position and began to scan the area further. Once again, in his heart, he prayed, thanking God for the successful and well-planned battle that they had just won. If it weren't for these specific men, they could have easily failed and not made it as far as they had. They had managed to make it through two firefights and two instances where close kills were necessary. Each time they came out with no injury beyond a minor scratch. It wasn't the training, he decided, it was the men.

Reeducation

Richard was fast asleep on an easy chair in Michael's office. Michael obsessively watched the papers on the wall. He rose from his desk to stretch his legs, walked to his coffee pot and poured himself a generous cup. Even when drinking his coffee, he stared at the wall. It was when he had looked down at his watch that he missed the one thing he was looking for. An article had disappeared. There were no longer typed words on one sheet. Dropping his cup to the floor, he turned to slap Richard's leg. Richard jolted from his sleep and found a bright-eyed physicist staring at him with only one thing to say.

"Go now! This information is gone; there must be a new file in the archive. I need this file now! Go, goddamn it!"

Richard slipped his shoes on and rushed to the door. As he ran down the hallway to the underground garage, he realized that he hadn't a clue what Michael was talking about. What missing file? Richard knew he had taken them all from the periods covered. What was it that Michael wanted?

With desperate avoidance of the eager scientists left back in the office, Richard started his car and peeled out of his parking spot, heading straight out of the compound.

At the DIA archive, Richard was greeted with mixed looks. Since he had been there the day before to collect a large variety of highly classified files, the assistants and the various deputy directors were not too eager to help him. He expressed that he was missing one file that he did not collect the day before. If he could get the last remaining file from the periods he was searching for, it would not only save his job but very well could save his life, considering his superior's excitement back in the office. The clerk headed back to recover a single file folder, returning with a single file in his hands. When Richard saw this, he couldn't believe his eyes. This file was not there yesterday. Upon signing the voucher for the file, he asked the clerk for the last time it was checked out. The clerk scanned his records and showed that it had been checked out twice prior.

With the file on the passenger seat of his car, Richard drove like a mad man back to the compound to deliver the file to Michael. Sharing in the excitement that Michael had exhibited back in the office, it was all Richard could do to avoid opening it. Pulling into the garage, Michael parked and ran as fast as he could up the stairs to Michael's office.

Michael stood, waiting, as Richard entered the room.

"Is this it? It was there?" Michael asked excitedly.

Richard placed the file on the desk and Michael picked it up and held it reverently in his hands.

Richard replied, "I know I took all of the files they had yesterday."

"Well, when I saw the information utterly vanish from the files on the wall, I assumed that there had been something else written to cover the events of that day. Nothing I had covered it. Someone wrote this file that hadn't done so before the men did something different to the original chain of events. If someone wrote the file, than someone must have done research on this file since then."

Michael opened the file to find several pictures and began reading aloud as Richard closed the door to the office.

"Dated for events of August 29, 1969," Michael read.

> By the order of Major General Hayes, I, Cwo. William Glitson, have been issued the task of compiling the data to the best of my knowledge of the events occurring on this date. My presence was not at the site during the events of this day, but instead during the aftermath. Ho Chi Minh loyalists issued the main attack after receiving word from a patrolling radio operator of an American stronghold. During a previous attack of the stronghold, which I had witnessed, information was gathered that showed their intentions to attack and destroy the covert joint operations center outside of Dien Bien Phu. It was this same information that was gathered the

> day prior that made me inform the JOC by runner to avoid compromised COMSEC and intelligence. Once I had made contact with the JOC we received word that a massive firefight and evidence of explosions were coming from the same vicinity of where we had just been. We were instructed to wait twelve hours and return to the site to investigate. These are my findings.

Michael took a deep breath and took a sip from his coffee, now cold. Looking at Richard, he noticed that his partner's eyes were fixed to the back of the folder that Michael was holding. Turning back to the file, he continued to read.

> Forty-seven NVA and VC were found dead outside of an American stronghold. Injuries present were consistent with machine gun fire as well as mines. Fifteen men were later found buried under fallen trees that were blasted at the base when it proved strategic to the defending force. Seven men were found who were killed after the main attack while planning a counterattack. These men were killed by combined sniper fire.
>
> On the arrival of myself and the spec ops men that I was with, we received fire from an estimated platoon of enemy personnel. Enemy machine gun fire as well as grenades pinned us down. It was the unnamed American forces, who were fortified well enough to provide support, who managed to kill all but five men. These five were held prisoner and have been turned over to military intelligence. Total enemy killed is confirmed at ninety-two. American losses total at zero. One injury was received from the weapons sergeant that was with my escort. His wound was to the left thigh from shrapnel of a grenade.
>
> In conclusion to these findings, the Americans, who will be named in a later document, have killed ninety-two enemy personnel who were en route to destroy a highly covert JOC, which had been proven to be the backbone of the special operations missions throughout Southeast Asia. As far as these Americans, once approval is granted by the query I intend to recommend their leader for the Medal of Honor; his men will be recommended for a Silver Star and a Distinguished Service Cross. My findings show no foul play from the American forces. Closing date is November 1, 1969.

Michael sat down in his chair as he and Richard seemed to sigh at once. Michael looked over to Richard, whose eyes were still fixed to where the file once was.

"These boys are in a world of hurt. I have never seen battle reports with these results. This Ssg Sands must be one smart son of a bitch. It sounds like the man who wrote the report, William Glitson, had been working with them. By the sound of it, he's protecting them. Get me the career file on him. Let's see if anything had changed in his file. There must be more changes in our files. We just have to look for it. If he kept these men as classified as he implied, we should be able to find evidence of them as well as complete information in an inquiry that he said was going to take place. I need you to look for the minutes from the inquiry." Michael continued to search his mind to think of anything else that would show something.

The scientists in his team had been working double shifts since the accident occurred. The greatest advance that they had made was devising a method to develop the system at a smaller scale. Instead of having the weapon mounted to a battleship, the device would be able to be fired from a Stryker. This gave Michael great hopes in getting these men back. It was then that his idea hit him like a sledgehammer.

The Aftermath

Hours after the battle, Rowdy arrived to the DFA. They were pinned between the fallen trees when they were attacked by another platoon-sized element. Trevor had ordered Baxley to pick up his gun and move it to the east side of the DFA to lay fire down toward the distracted platoon. It had taken longer than usual to get effective fire from the position, but eventually fire superiority was gained and they defeated the platoon. Five men stood with their weapons in the air, surrendering themselves to the defensive Americans.

Trevor ordered the men to take their positions and prepare for another counterattack. Lars climbed down from the position and asked Trevor's help to get his men out of the fallen trees. Trevor climbed down the rope to follow Lars to his men. Hurdling over these large trees, the two men made it to Paul's position. Trevor was not prepared to see the amount of bodies in the trees around his position closely. The blood-painted earth was an appropriate frame for the bullet-torn bodies of the intermingled VC and NVA. Trevor approached Paul's men and helped lift Cooper, who was hit with grenade shrapnel in the thigh. Trevor walked the men back to the DFA; he could not escape the horror of the men on the ground. Stepping over bodies, Trevor hooked Cooper into one of the ropes to pull him up.

Instead of the typical congratulations or pats on the back, the men sat silent. In Paul's mind, he recollected the vivid realities of previous firefights and battles in his past. Trevor couldn't help but realize the desensitization that television and movies had on the public. Looking at the bloodbath below, he now faced enough spilled blood to last two lifetimes. He would never look at war the same. His mind and his own life were forever perverted by a simple mistake of being at the wrong place at the wrong time. Movies of war now passed his mind as he laughed at the great understatement of the smell of war and the feeling of horror. His heart went out to the men who he knew were going to be greeted with spit and animal blood at the airport on their arrival home. People would curse at them and call them names for doing what their own country had told them to do. None of these men had a choice of what to do; none of them were there to stop the communist spread of Southeast Asia. The men were here because of orders and threats. They stayed alive because of each other. Their new brothers in combat had saved themselves with laughter and with hope. These men fought for those things, not for policies.

The silence was broken when Rowdy asked for details about the evening's events. When Trevor told him, step-by-step, of the order of events, Rowdy looked to Paul in amazement of the men. After a long night and morning, mostly waiting for fights, Paul offered to have Trevor's men get sleep as his men pulled security. Without argument, Trevor agreed and had his men take their rest behind their positions. Paul sat next to Trevor as Trevor placed his head in his own hands.

"I'm not sure what the fuck I'm doing here. I never have been in combat before, man. My men are doing what I tell them, and I have no fucking clue of what I'm doing. I know what the books say for me to do, I know what I've done in training, but I've never done it with the bodies and the smell. Paul, I need to get these guys out now. There is no way we can hold out till the end. That's six years too fucking long."

Paul darted a glance at Trevor.

"Six years? What the fuck do you mean six years? You are telling me that our fucking country is wasting ten fucking years on this hellhole?"

Paul was furious. Maintaining discipline, he kept his shouts at a low volume. Kicking the tree to his back, he leaned against it, looking down. A slight tear rolled down his rough face and fell to the platform at his feet.

"How many of us die? How many friendlies die in this place?"

Trevor thought hard. He was always bad in history and did not study well. He did recall one of the notes put at the end of a movie he just saw before he left.

"I'm sorry, I don't remember how many, but they built a huge wall in Washington, D.C., and all the names of the dead from Vietnam are on it."

Paul didn't move. The strength that he had to continue the fight had fallen from his heart. His drive to lead his men was gone. Now he knew how it would end; many more men would die, and all they had was a wall. The hopes of all soldiers going home soon had slipped through the cracks of the platform below him.

Nobody should know their own destiny or their fate, the thought of failing in an episode in which you risk your life habitually. The men's hope of home and of victory had been the driving force of all men in the distant jungle to continue every day. In truth, when the metal meets the meat, the men fought for each other, fought for the man, black or white, next to them. In the end, the men fought for the one color that joined them together; they fought for the color green that they killed for.

Paul stood tall to hide his utter disappointment in the policies leading the timetable. Thinking hard about how to change the result, he turned to Trevor.

"So, since you know how this ends, do you think you could help change it? Do you think that you have changed it already? Shit, man, you have already prevented our JOC from being destroyed. You saved the intel and the men that the intel protects. Fuck it, you could tell us what went wrong and we can change it!"

Trevor looked into Paul's courageous eyes and found the agony replaced with hope. Paul had found his hope in knowing that Trevor held the key to the success in the land they fought in; the land in which they died in. Trevor could change the course of the battles. With his tactics and his knowledge, he could change the past.

Trevor looked from Paul over to Paul's men, who had no idea what was ahead of them. Cooper was tending to his leg while laughing at a joke that Malloy had shared with him. Lars was showing Baxley the best ways to handle sunken chest wounds. Ward was teaching Trits the best way to clean a weapon in the field. Rowdy sat with Himelrick, staring at the bloody earth below. Boiyd, Trevor's closest friend, was watching Trevor from his position, learning what his friend thought as a leader and not a drinking buddy. These men had no idea what was to come. The younger men in Trevor's group had a good idea as to the failures of Vietnam only because it was drilled into them since basic training. Even Trevor only understood what it was he had read about and studied from the History Channel. What else could he have done? The Tet offensive happened about a year before he had arrived. The infamous victory of hill 937 was only a month prior, better known as Hamburger Hill. The majority, if not all, of the American casualties and losses came from small firefights from all over the country. There were not many major campaigns or battles. The fury of guerilla warfare came from having a few men die here and a few men die there. There were no battles where men would simply charge each other to determine the ultimate victory as done in past wars.

Not much could be done to change the result of the war. Even if he had done something, what would that change in the future? Trevor had seen enough sci-fi movies to know that you just can't change the past without suffering consequences in the future. By saving the JOC, what had he changed? In reality, the JOC was not his motivation; his motivation was keeping his men alive. Now relaxing for the first time since the massive firefight, Trevor asked Paul to take charge. With Paul in charge, Trevor sat back against his assault pack and fell asleep.

Each man was expecting to be wakened up at any moment to fight once again. That moment did not come. The men slept for more than six hours apiece. The greatest gift that Paul and his men could have given the strangers was rest. It was not an attempt to be nice, from Paul's point of view. Allowing these men to sleep was simply a way of thanking them for their efforts in saving their lives that day. Paul studied Trevor as a man would study his own son. The bond between the men was surely a bond that could never be broken, despite the different worlds they came from.

Only Saints Wear White

Michael now understood the time line that these men follow in their time in the jungle. By recovering files from various briefings and committees, he had locations and an order of events for Trevor and his men. Michael knew the names already from the missing persons reports, but he did not know if they were together. Now knowing that the men were together and located at a single place for most of their stay, the key report that he had found had a statement that gave Richard and Michael complete confidence.

The report stated, "Upon discovery of the counterattack of the seven American personnel who were the key to saving the covert JOC outside of Dien Bien Phu, it was noted that no bodies were found. One large artillery crater was found, with no burn indications or shrapnel. Since only five VC bodies confirmed at site with no American bodies, the case was left opened for further investigation."

Michael peered at this section of the report for hours. They had mounted the portable version of their "weapon" onto a military vehicle and were going to test the theories of the distance factor by attempting to send an object five minutes into the past. By doing so, the object should appear only a matter of inches away from the position it left. The exciting part of this test was that the barrel should appear inside of or into the existing barrel five minutes before sending the existing barrel into the rift. The most reassuring aspect of this experiment was that they should know five minutes before the test that their test was successful.

As Michael left his office to witness the testing of the device, which they decided to call "MO" for maximum ordinate, he stopped by the recording booth to ensure that all cameras were functional. The maximum ordinate's definition to these men was "the highest point of the four-dimensional space achieved, therefore creating the sending rift. The receiving rift would be at the lowest point of the four-dimensional space. The centerline of the fourth dimension was the time line they follow currently. Every man follows the centerline until it is manipulated. By sending a man to the past, for example, it would keep the man at the maximum ordinate until he was returned to his center time line. By staying at the maximum ordinate, these men could not age, in theory, until they catch up to their time line. Michael took a great deal of comfort in knowing that these men would remain ageless, in theory, until they reach the time and date they initially left.

The key problem of having these men stay in the past was that the future could easily change by their actions. All of the little things could make a big difference. On the flip side, would the events on September 11 have happened if someone knew what flight and what time and date the attacks occurred? Would they discover the ease in killing the key terrorists before they reach a great level of power? If they did so, would someone stronger and even more daring take the dead terrorists' place? If that were the case, the past could not be changed for fear of the changes of the future. Michael decided that he needed to get the men out now.

Sharing these thoughts with Richard as they stood on the test grounds, he pondered on what course of action would be appropriate. With six minutes left until the test began, Michael kept a careful eye on the barrel. Exactly one minute later a small cloud formed over the barrel and began to emit lightning. The earth shook slightly as they watched the ground below the barrel begin to cave on itself. Forming a hole with no loose dirt, the barrel fell in and was lost in a haze of smoke and vapor. It was now time to fire "MO," and there was no barrel to fire at. It took twenty minutes until the hole had cleared enough to see what was inside. About ten feet into the ground were two barrels, one on top of another. It was then that Richard had his idea.

"Sir, I have a problem."

Michael listened.

"Sir, how is the barrel in the hole when we did not fire the test? We never sent it, so how did it get there? Because the barrel arrived, it changed our plans of firing. So, in the future, we did fire it, which caused the test barrel to land, forcing the pre-test barrel on top of it. By this it made us not fire the test. By testing on the barrel we changed the way we were going to do things dramatically, five minutes prior to doing so. If we had someone with the barrel who would move it on landing, away from the pre-test barrel, we could do the test as planned. The test would change, but the test would still take place.

Michael rubbed his temples as he thought about what was suggested. After a moment of thought, Michael offered, “I’ll tell you what. Let me try something and I’ll let you go, if you are willing.” Richard delivered a smirk. Michael sat down with a pen and paper and began to write specific instructions to MO’s operators and to Richard.

He wrote, “In twenty minutes’ time, move the barrel to the opposite side of the vehicle and fire on it. In five minutes’ time, all personnel except for one operator, Richard, and me will clear the scene. All recording devices will be removed and viewing booths will be sealed. Adjust the distance to provide for twenty-minute travel.”

Giving it to the leading operator, Michael instructed Richard to sit on the barrel when it was moved. Michael stood and watched the events take place. The scientists cleared the scene with the cameras. Windows were closed and sealed while Michael waited for the barrel to be moved. One minute before the moving of the barrel, another cloud formed on the site that the barrel was supposed to be fired at. After the cloud had parted from the crater, Richard crawled out of the hole to find a hand leaning over to help him out. The man offering the hand was Richard. In theory, Richard had to be sent as planned or there would continue to be two of them. The Richard from the hole instructed the operator to begin firing sequence as planned at a different location. Richard sat on the barrel twenty feet to the side of the hole and waited for MO.

After four hours of being stuck in a continuous loop of going back twenty minutes, Richard finally begged Michael to give up. Still having two Richards twenty minutes apart in age, Michael had seen the conundrum that he had created. Now an ethical problem existed. Do you kill one of them off, keeping the other alive, placing events back to normal? On the other hand, do you separate the two forever, keeping one of them in isolation with other duplicates that may come after more experimentation?

Ceasing the experiment, Michael decided to kill one off and maintain the other. Reaching for the sidearm of the operator, Michael placed Richard in one of the craters, which now overpopulated the field, and aimed down on his friend. The man in the pit looked up at his trusted leader and realized that he was going to die. Thinking about the things he loved and the work that remained unfinished, Richard realized that he was not going to die but instead just be "shut off." Smiling at Michael with approval, Michael fired a single shot at Richard's head. The man in the hole spun ninety degrees and fell to the floor of the hole. Turning slowly to Richard, who was watching behind him, Michael smiled gently to the friend he had just seen killed by his own hand. Slowly walking past the vehicle, he instructed the operator to fill the hole, burying the body. Richard watched the execution and gave no argument to Michael. Michael turned to Richard and apologized for having to kill him, sort of.

The argument of whether sending someone back to recover or escort Trevor's team continued through the night between the two scientists. If the men at The Ranch could not find a way to recover the men successfully to modern time, then someone needed to go to ensure that Trevor's men did not alter the events any more than they had already, even if it meant killing them all.

Michael decided to go himself, since he had done all of the research of their actions. The only thing left was figuring out how to get the men back. The current theory was to fire two identical weapons at each other that could create a rift that would send a man forward. The rift's strength would be determined by distance. If the two weapons were far apart, it should send the men forward along a trough of the four-dimensional space only slightly. If the two weapons were fired very close together at each other, than it would send whomever very far forward into the future. Michael had issued the order to begin the manufacturing of an identical weapon to be mounted onto a vehicle.

Once this weapon was created they could test it to ensure its accuracy and develop a proven formula for its path. This way they would be able to recover these men successfully the first time.

Michael felt as Dr. Oppenheimer must have felt while he was project leader for the Manhattan Project. Oppenheimer was looked down upon when the world first saw the results of "Fat Man" and "Little Boy" as they rained down upon Nagasaki and Hiroshima, Japan. It wasn't as if they had much of a choice. Japan's mentality during that time was such that would make an invasion too costly for American lives.

The American government even debated whether to invite the Japanese emperor to the testing of a third nuclear device, "Trinity," at Site X in New

Mexico. The cause for debate was the circumstances. What if the Trinity test failed? If it had failed, than the Japanese would think we were incompetent and possibly strike even harder, knowing our nation's ineptitude. The U.S. wanted them to witness the test as an alternate to striking them. If we were to show them what we were capable of, perhaps they would back down and surrender. Perhaps they wouldn't.

Once the bombs were dropped and the world learned of the Manhattan Project, the public found targets of infamy and issued its blame of inhumanity against them. For this, Michael was determined to do something humane in his project, which had initially begun as a weapon. So far his project had sent some people into the past, away from their families, and they had prevented a key attack of the NVA and VC against the U.S. This, so far, was not enough. Michael was determined to get these men to their families in one piece. All of this would happen if his ideas for the return trip worked.

Field Trip

Malloy overlooked the smoldering trees as he continued maintenance on Baxley's tripod. For an assistant gunner, his primary job was to keep Baxley supplied with ammunition and be his eyes while he fired. Because there were so few of them there, Malloy's job had been changed to sniper. With no training or experience as a sniper, only his superb marksmanship, Malloy had been picking up his own techniques on the way as well as what he learned from Cpl. Boiyd. Boiyd had showed him some tips about scanning sectors in five-degree increments so as not to miss the slightest detail in the terrain and possible camouflaged enemy. Boiyd was in the battalion scouts for six months before he was sent back to his company. They sent him back because he couldn't keep up with the physical workouts. His only problem was that he couldn't run two miles in under thirteen minutes. With the field exercises that he had been on as a scout, he picked up several techniques that had changed the way he fired weapons and conducted recons ever since.

In basic training, the soldiers were instructed to fire from a very specific position as they controlled their breathing and their sight picture. The soldiers concentrated so much on the alignment and positioning of their bodies and weapons that they took too long to fire. For Boiyd, he had spent so many hours a day on a firing range that he no longer thought when firing. He saw everything in the field through the rear and front sight apertures that exist in his mind. He could judge where a round would fly by the feel of the weapon at his side. It is when a man becomes this comfortable with his weapon that he becomes a weapon himself.

Boiyd showed Malloy small tricks in staying awake while waiting for enemies to appear in his sight picture. Most of these tricks were those Boiyd picked up from his platoon sergeant when he was a scout. The major one was to sit in an extremely difficult position, a position so uncomfortable that it shoots pain throughout his body while he waited. For example, he would sit with his leg hyperextended, or he would sit on his leg while it was twisted. These positions hurt like hell but keep a man awake long enough to get the shot that could change the outcome of any battle.

Malloy was a coolheaded young man from Los Angeles. His upbringing was violent but he had grown from it. His father, an ex-Ranger in Vietnam, would beat him at every opportunity until he was seventeen and found the nerve to fight back. One day he called his own father outside to settle the stirring resentment once and for all. Malloy, as short and scrawny as he appeared, managed to place his father in a hospital with over a dozen broken bones. Sadly enough, he was arrested, and a judge, who was a veteran himself, offered the young man an opportunity to rehabilitate through the army. When Malloy had agreed, he was delivered to a MEPS center right away to fill out the appropriate paperwork for enlistment. Four months later he was assigned to Ft. Wainwright, Arkansas. The emotions that had consumed him since his arrival in Vietnam was knowing that his own father was in this Godforsaken hellhole with him somewhere. The only peace that he had found was from knowing that ninety-nine percent of the fighting was far south from where they were now. The chances of seeing his father were extremely slim, regardless of whether he was a Ranger or not.

Malloy double-checked the final touches to the tripod and place it in its position as Baxley inspects his assistant's work. With approval, Baxley sent the young man up the ladder to the tower. Baxley had been impressed with the young man since his arrival in the unit. Malloy was a hard worker and eager to learn. Baxley had no idea what his reason for joining was. If he had known it was for disciplinary reasons, it wouldn't have fazed him in the least.

Trevor was recounting the ammunition in the cache and felt that they need about half as much more since the attack that had taken place. All of the attention in the area would be focused on their location. Two men were below, where the first body pit was being dug to allow all of the fallen men a mass grave. In Trevor's mind, a mass grave was something that was always associated with acts of genocide. The Nazis had mass graves for the poor Jews and gypsies. There were similar graves in later conflicts such as Iraq and the African tribal wars. Even in Somalia, graves were found filled with dozens of people who had starved to death. The guilt for creating a similar grave for the VC who were before him was consuming the young leader. He had no choice; it would be a great tactical downfall if he were to leave them where they were or attempt to bury them all.

Trevor finished his count of the ammunition and began to instruct Wilson to fill the slit trench when he heard an unmistakable series of beeping and static. Trevor and Wilson listened in on what traffic was being sent over the radio.

"Red Leg, this is Comanche 20. Fire mission…enemy closing in on my position, break…I need you to light up grid 578844. How copy, over."

"Comanche 20, this is Red Leg. Unable to fire, break…suggest you find alternate support and get the hell out of dodge. Out."

"Negative, Red Leg, I need your support now! Fire for effect at grid 578844. We cannot lose any more men! Fire goddammit! Fire now!"

Trevor's expression hung. He had to do something. Listening in the distance, he could hear the men firing. Trevor called for his men to rally around him. As he continued to listen to Paul's men, Trevor began to plan how he would help. The best way he could help was to get Paul's men to run below them. Hopefully they would not expect an American ambush this far north. Trevor reached for the handset for the radio.

"Comanche 20, this is—"

Trevor tried to remember the call sign that Rowdy had given them.

"Comanche 20, this is Hard Rock 12. Which direction are they from your position? Over."

Trevor waited for a response. Trevor was assuming that Paul would know who they were even though he had used his call sign from back home.

"Last calling station, Charlie is running circles around me. Their main concentration is to the southeast. Why? You have a plan? Over."

"Comanche, I suggest you move to your last rally point. Much more security from where you came, over."

Trevor was referring to the DFA. Paul's men had left the day prior.

"This is Comanche, I copy. Is the site prepared?"

"Roger, file through and you should find some cover, over."

"Roger out."

Trevor prepped his men with the ammunition they needed. The field, where tall trees once stood, was filled with obstacles; the trek through the fallen lumber to catch Paul and his men would be their undoing. Each man was now equipped with their assigned weapon as well as a dozen hand grenades each. The claymores were still available for use, and the steel plating under each man was in good enough shape. They would be fine, Trevor hoped.

It should take Paul and his men two hours running to make it here; this gave them time to arrange the sniper and machine gun coverage that would be needed since they could now see a great distance ahead. Baxley moved his position to the tower with Malloy and Boiyd. Lars, who had stayed with them after Paul left the day before, was equipped with his M-16, which he could fire as well as any sniper up to 350 meters away. Between the four they should be able to provide all of the cover fire that Paul would need when he cleared the wood line.

With the men equipped, Trevor ensured they were all alert and ready for their newfound friends' arrival. Sweat poured from the men as their hearts pounded with more adrenaline. The men prepared for an even bloodier battle for their own survival.

From the Bandstands

Robert was constantly viewing the variety of files, which appeared to change by the minute. Twice a day Robert sent Michael to the DIA branch office to check for new files. Nothing new had appeared, but plenty had changed.

With the body count rising, Robert strived more than ever to get these men out. Drawn between the news of the present and the news of the past, Robert begun to find a mass change in events. The news of the present had yet to change, but if they failed he felt that much would become a mystery. Just like the assassination of President Kennedy and the Roswell "cover up," the public would simply blame the intelligence community for the mysteries and changing events. If Michael failed, these men had the ability to prevent the horrid events on September 11. If that were to happen, the empty space where the World Trade Center once stood would suddenly be filled with the towers, which stood tall several years prior. This was something that the public would not be able to explain or place blame on. Saddam Hussein would have been found and killed long before his prominent rise to power.

Several scientists working with Michael believed that nothing would ever change because the events had taken place. If the men were going to change the events, assuming their recovery failed, none of them would even know of the horrible events. Michael believed that the events would have taken place because the recovery effort had not occurred yet. Theorizing that the changes would be made for all to see was a horrifying thought, but it was a theory that

Michael believed. Richard theorized the opposite. If the events of the past had changed, then all of the events from that point on would simply adapt to the change, and the people's minds with it. The only confusion was why they could see the change of actions and still remember the change.

With efforts of the machines redoubled, Michael strived to solve the theoretical problem and decided to follow the brilliant minds that worked for him and abandon his own thoughts until such time came that it was feasible.

The mounting of the newly developed weapon onto a separate vehicle was complete. The problem remaining was that they would need a third to send the two back. This was turning into a separate problem. The materials for the weapon were extremely rare and expensive. With what had been learned by these prototypes, Michael decided to go another route to develop an array that was directional and reversible. If he could develop this, then the vehicle that this array was mounted to would be able to do the job of three. The vehicle could send itself back and reverse the flow of energy to send them forward. The development was still far ahead and difficult in planning. If his theory were correct, the vehicle would be able to move to the appropriate time and return to a designated time with no one but the operators aware of the elapsed time from development.

Michael sat at his desk and poured a small glass of scotch to drown out the pain of hard thought. As Murphy's Law would have it, the moment he felt relaxed and peaceful, Richard opened the door slowly with a large envelope in his hand.

With a great smile on his face, Richard slid the envelope to Michael. Michael reached inside to pull out a supplementary report from the DIA. With a heavy sigh, Michael began reading yet another report dealing with Trevor and his men.

> From: S.A. Monroe
>
> To: SAIC Intelligence Analysis Section
>
> Subject: Disappearance of Staff Sergeant Trevor Sands and Fire Team Alpha.
>
> Documented from interview with Trevor Sands, disappeared May 21, 2008. Subject was seen falling from approximately fifteen feet from thin air. Subject was in a coma for one week before he was fit to speak about the events that had taken place. A full report of those events is being verified at this time and will be documented in a full report later.

To summarize the events, Trevor Sands and one fire team from C-Company 1-17 Infantry Regiment was sent back to 1969 and abandoned. Through extensive efforts from our scientists at The Ranch, Trevor and his men were brought back four months after their departure. The timing of their return was by the choice of the men.

Trevor's health was unchanged from physicals and lab reports conducted prior to his disappearance. The subject was sworn to secrecy about the events of 1969 and the project that caused the transfer of his men to a previous time line. His men are being contacted now. They were all sent to their homes on an individual basis. Signed sworn statements will be collected and reviewed.

Threats of a leakage of the occurrences are a minimal risk considering the likelihood of belief of such reports by listeners. I recommend a complete release of these men and an awards ceremony for their efforts and struggles at a disclosed location.

End report September 29, 2008."

Michael laid the paper down as gently as possible. With a deep sigh, he stood to face the window and said with a deep exhale, "We will succeed."

Deciding Destiny

It was as if Trevor's prayers had been answered. As soon as it had become too dark to see anything, the long-awaited companions had arrived for support. All night vision and infrared targeting devices were activated. To Trevor and his men it became daylight. To the enemy it was an endless void of nothing. Paul had brought his men into the clearing with his hands above his head. When Trevor whistled, Paul and his men began running and hurdling past the fallen trees to get to the DFA. Once Paul and his team made it to the DFA, the followers had made it to the clearing. Trevor had drastically underestimated the following force. The size of this group had to be at least a battalion. Divided into separate companies and support elements, they came out of the wood line from every edge of the clearing. These men were NVA regulars led by VC operatives. The intelligence of this place was well known to these men. They had made every effort to have the DFA surrounded.

Trevor's mind was racing at a hundred miles an hour. With too many unanswered questions, he had Paul take charge as Trevor climbed the tower to get a better perspective. With the deepened horror of the approaching enemy, Trevor closed his eyes and opted to find the worst threat and hit them at a distance. Searching the edge of the bloodstained clearing, Trevor found what he was looking for…mortars. Raising his arm across Malloy's eyes, they simultaneously acquired targets where the mortars were staging and began firing. Two men fell at the slammed impact of the bullets as the rest of the enemy force laid down to find where the shots came from. Trevor knew there was no turning back now. Trevor fired a second shot and hit what looked like an officer. Malloy kept firing on the mortars. Lars, without night vision, sat back until he could see what he was firing at.

Trevor yelled down to instruct the men to find officers and kill them all. With that, all men scanned sectors searching for the recognizable uniforms of the officer or the man next to an RTO. Within three minutes no officers could be spotted. Malloy had concentrated his fire on mortars and machine gunners. The entire enemy was still too far away for claymores to do any good. Trevor had no choice but to have his men begin killing all they could see.

"One shot only, men. There are too many men out there to waste ammunition. Baxley, I need you to do something for me."

Trevor climbed down form the tower and leaned into his gunner's ear.

"I need you to go down and get behind the closest fallen tree. From there I need you to set grazing fire using your thermal scope." Baxley shot a look at Trevor.

Baxley knew that from an elevated position his weapon would not be nearly as effective. With a lowered head and a quick prayer, Baxley lowered himself down to ground level. Sitting behind a fallen tree, Baxley activated the thermal scope and saw hundreds of figures running along the wood line. Placing the cross-hairs on one end of the figures, Baxley began firing a painfully effective stream of explosive lead. While the snipers were attacking greater threats, Paul's men were assisting with rounds. Paul lowered himself to ground level and gave Baxley more ammunition as well as the spare barrel.

After thirty minutes of fire, Trevor ordered a cease-fire to evaluate the damage. Trevor could find no movement. Paul leaned over Trits and borrowed the night vision. Standing next to Trevor, they both felt an eerie sense that this had just begun.

No sound was heard except for the occasional groan in the distance. Trevor knew that the counterattack was going to take place at any moment and in any direction. Ward had made his rounds to deliver canteens and pats on the back when he heard a sharp snap behind him. Himelrick reacted and killed the man who was creeping in the distance. With the shot from Himelrick's weapon, a second shot, which was thought to be an echo, returned the favor as Himelrick's face shot a spray of thick, matted blood across Ward's chest. Ward reached down to find the fallen boy when he heard another shot. Ward instinctively reached for Himelrick's night vision and his rifle as he screamed to Paul

"Sniper attack, eight o'clock!" Ward raised the rifle and waited for the report of another shot.

Lying in the messy remains of Himelrick's body, Ward searched the field for the sniper who had killed the boy. His only guess was the sniper had fired at the exact location of the muzzle flash. If so, the man down there had considerable talent. Deciding instead of waiting, Ward chose to risk it and fire a shot. Leaning the rifle to his side, away from his body, he squeezed the trigger. Before the sound of his own shot had made its way through the field, a return from the sniper had slammed into the branch where his hand was resting to his side. Ward found the sniper and had only to guess where the head would be in relation to the rifle. With a deep breath, Ward squeezed the activation button of the PAQ-4 and placed the illuminated dot on what he thought was a head. With a shallow breath, Ward squeezed the trigger. It was as if it were in slow motion.

Ward could hear the grinding of the round against the revolutions in the barrel rifling, the short hiss of the round exiting the barrel and the whistle of the round in flight. With his eyes down range, he could almost feel the man, the round flying so diligently through the center of the distant man's neck. Taking no chances, he raised the rifle thirty-five degrees up and loaded a 40mm grenade into the launch tube, aligned the barrel with where the sniper had been, and squeezed the forward trigger. With a loud report in the silence, the grenade lobbed three hundred meters in front of him and exploded in a flash of light and smoke. For a brief instant Ward could see the man lift off the ground with the sudden explosion.

The rest of the men, now safe to fire without risk of that sniper, began catching up with the distraction they had suffered. At least a hundred men had used the opportunity to sneak closer to the DFA. Trevor set his rifle down and reached for the firing device belonging to a claymore mine. Waiting for a dozen more men to reach a set point, Trevor soon found all men within range and fired three claymores, killing all but five men. From above Malloy was firing at several targets in different directions. Below, Baxley was repositioning to cover the south end of the DFA after clearing the north and the east. Wilson was shaking with the steady surges of adrenaline and composing himself with as much discipline as he had in him. Trits was steadily firing into the wood line that Baxley was concentrating on. With Himelrick dead and Ward taking over the position, Paul continued to run ammunition to Baxley. Boiyd managed to take a lower position between the tower and the main platform of the DFA to maintain a flow of rounds toward the soldiers.

After what seemed like six hours in a hellish fight for their lives, the last round flew into the last man in the vast distance. Paul stepped next to Trevor and laid a hand on his shoulder. With the sun pushing through the jungle, finally shedding the light on the field, the men now saw the horrible battle that was fought. Baxley, still lying in his position below the DFA, wiped the carbon from his weapon and the tears from his eyes. With the final touch of a light coat of oil, Baxley put his weapon back together and prepared for another fight. Looking up to Trevor, his eyes showed no pride or pleasure for the end of the night-long battle. His eyes only showed the exhausted relief of staying alive and the pain and fury of knowing his friend was dead.

Trevor dropped onto an ammunition crate and began the steps for the next decision to be made. There was no possible way to clean this mess up. The men lying in the field would not be able to receive burial from the Americans. They would have to wait for their own people who would be looking for the missing battalion of soldiers.

Looking across the field, Trevor let the horror of the blood and the unfairness of the fight sink into his mind's eye. Paul and his men are out counting the dead for the report that Rowdy would have to deliver. Watching the men cross the field among the dead, Trevor realized the one order of business he was missing: Himelrick.

Still next to his position, Ward was holding the boy in his arms, speaking words of courage and peace to him. Trevor fell to his knees as his past months of terror and confusion swelled within his eyes. Trevor wept for the first time since his men fell out of the world they knew and into the hell of the world they occupied now.

With a whistle from Paul, Trevor wiped his eyes and looked below to find a squad of Rangers emerge from the wood line. Weapons were lowered, and the men were brought to Paul. Sfc. Quinn's squad circled Paul as they spoke about the events of the evening. The Rangers were stricken with a dark sense of death as they began to make their way to the DFA. Trevor ordered his men to search the area for survivors and finish them. There were no facilities to handle POWs, and no way that they could afford to let these men live to kill Trevor and his men another day. Breaking the rules of war, Trevor sent his men out.

Sfc. Quinn slowly made his way to Trevor to offer any help he could muster to allow these men time to rest. Trevor agreed to the help as soon as his men finish their duties on the field. Quinn and Lt. Phelps sat beside the young Himelrick and offered help in burial. Trevor ignored their offer, concentrating only on his men circling the field below. So far no survivors were discovered. Quinn caught Trevor's attention when he began to introduce the men that they had not met before.

"Ssg. Nile was killed on our return from our last visit with you. Sgt. Malloy is his replacement. He is trustworthy and a good soldier. I promise you, Trevor, you will get all the help that you need. There are a lot of higher-ups that owe their lives to you, as well as my men. The last fight you had here saved our ops center and kept the information in the center secure. All of our positions would have been compromised and more than likely we would all be dead from ambush or—"

Quinn stopped when he follows Trevor's eyes to the field.

"You did the right thing, Trevor. You fought a hell of a fight and walked away. Those soldiers were trying to kill Paul's team and then you. You saved your men and saved your friends. Why do you look so regretful? You did nothing wrong here! Look around! This is a war. You had to kill, and you *did*! There is nothing to be ashamed of. Now snap out of it and take my advice—never let your men see you like this! They need to believe that you have every answer to any problem. You are their leader. You are now their savior. Now get down there and give your men a pat on the back for the most impressive battle our nation has ever known!"

Trevor raised his head and replied.

"You know, Quinn, I have no idea how many bodies are out there. There are so many that I don't know if it is a hundred or a thousand. It could be a million men out there and there is nothing that we can do for them. We killed them all. My men were stupid kids from back on the block when we got here. Now they are men who will have nightmares that will haunt them until the day they die. I don't pretend to believe that my men are the only ones who will suffer from this. I know that every man that stepped foot on this cursed soil will have these fears for the rest of their lives. It just doesn't seem fair that we don't belong here and the people, who do belong here, in this time, will never receive the respect they deserve. Man, I don't know if I should be talking like this. I don't even know what you know about my men and me. I just needed to dump on someone, man. I'm sorry to do this."

Trevor stood and stretched his body with a deep yawn.

"Well, where do you suggest I begin?" Quinn looked up at him and replied.

"I suggest you get down there and tell your men that they did what they had to. Praise them for their fight and tell them that my men will be covering security to allow you all to sleep." Trevor nodded and smiled.

Turning toward his men, he whistled and signaled a rally to the DFA. With the desperately needed sleep overwhelming the need for reassurance, the men eagerly took the offer and began their first of restless sleep that would follow them through their lives.

Destructive Relationship

With the gift of sleep and the ease from time, the soldiers were prepared to make the decisions necessary for what would come next. Because of the extreme attention that had been drawn to the DFA, it was no longer a safe place to wait things out. There would also be extreme heath hazards by waiting out the war on a thousand rotting corpses, so relocation was obvious and inevitable. The decisions remaining were what location and what efforts needed to be made for extraction. With the heightened sensitivity in the area, would cache drops be available? The discussion of support from Quinn and Paul was unquestionable. There would always be support from these men. However, men are not what is needed to survive in a war. Ammunition and reinforced positions are what is necessary to survive. Food could be gathered from the jungle. Boar and snake, melons and water could all be gathered to survive.

Paul made his suggestion. "Trevor, what you need is to meet with our general. I'm positive that if he looks at you and your men he will know for certain that you speak the truth. I know for a fact that he is one to be trusted, and I am sure that he will give you everything that you need, even evacuation, if you decide. I'm sure Sfc. Quinn, here, will agree with me when I say that I hope you stay with us. You have already made a hell of a difference. If you and your men could change the end of this, think of all the men that you could let go home alive. You could shave years off this war by telling the people who make decisions what it is that happened. Just please consider what this means to us. We need you and your men."

With sudden realization that he was begging, Paul stopped talking. Trevor finished the thought.

"You need us because you feel that we will save all the lives of all the Special Forces teams and Rangers in this area. What you fail to realize is the big picture." Trevor lowered his head and sighed.

Paul looked at Quinn, and they both turned to Trevor.

"Paul, what you fail to understand is that what I have already done here could seriously change the effects in the future. Let me teach you a little history. After the Vietnam War, the Armed Forces suffered its first real defeat. Because of this defeat, they changed our entire tactics and strategy for fighting in guerilla operations. After this war our nation fought in Somalia, Iraq, Afghanistan, Africa, Panama and several others. We won them all. If we felt like a victory was achieved from Vietnam, what lessons would have been learned and what effort would be made to change the doctrine that provided us victory in other conflicts? The lives lost in this one war may never compare to the lives that could be lost by defeats in the others. I feel like changing what happens here would do much more damage than good. Please understand that I will always regret leaving things the way they are when I know the result. I also know that changing things like this can never do any good.

"Now this is the first time, to my knowledge, that anyone had ever had this decision to make. I hate being the first, but please understand that saving lives is what I am attempting to do by not helping. By these battles here I could have already changed the balance of this war's outcome. I cannot do more. I am sorry."

Paul nodded his head and grunted in understanding. Quinn looked as if the thought of all other future conflicts' destiny in their hands was giving him a massive headache. Finally, the men decided to leave the DFA and make the movement to the command center.

Baxley and Boiyd were ensuring that there were no survivors remaining. After two hours of searching, they found no one who survived. Quinn's men were searching the pattern with Trevor's team. In a sudden shock of recognition, Malloy stopped in his tracks and stared at the young man standing in front of him. Boiyd stepped to his side.

"What's wrong with you, Malloy?"

Malloy looked away and replied.

"That man, who is he?"

Boiyd answers. "He came with Quinn. His name is Sgt. Mal…"

The sudden understanding hit Boiyd as he stopped his answer. Leaning closer to Malloy, he asked.

"You think he's your dad?"

Malloy answered, "I know he is. I've seen pictures of him in Vietnam. He looks completely different from the man I know, but it is *him*. I would know those eyes anywhere. Ask him where he's from, will you?"

The sound of broken twigs and brush being shifted shocked the men as a man lunged forward. Sgt. Malloy slammed his rifle hard on the survivor's head and turned toward Pfc. Malloy and Boiyd. Sgt. Malloy smiled a half-grimace and dropped to a knee. Pfc. Malloy ran to him and held him up. Pfc. Malloy pulled his hand away from his father's torso to find it covered with blood. All of the repressed love for his father came back as he cried. His father lay limp in his arms. The last shallow breath pushed past the man's lips as the son held the man's head to his chest. Boiyd lowered his head to Malloy and watched as his teammate vanished. His father's head dropped to the ground as his body settled in its final place.

Baxley screamed to Quinn and to Trevor to come to him. Climbing down a tree, they were stopped by one of Trevor's soldiers. The soldier dropped a man down in front of them and informed Trevor that this was the only survivor found. Thanking the soldier, Trevor looked down to the survivor to offer final peace before having to kill him. The soldier who had discovered the survivor took off the helmet and bandana, releasing short red hair that fell just above the shoulders. She turned to face Trevor.

"Well done, Segal. Now get back to Baxley and see what adjustments need to be made to the tripod."

She nodded. "Roger, Sergeant. Do you want me to handle this one?"

"No. It was my decision to have this done. I'll do it myself. Get back up to the DFA and get some chow. Pull security until Wilson relieves you."

With a swift movement she climbed up to the platform in the DFA and opened up a ration as she had done every day since their appearance in the past.

The Replacement

Memories are nothing more than a complex program that allows a recall of events and facts. It was no more difficult to reprogram the minds of man than the data on a hard drive. Only the natural phenomena of time and manipulation of it could do the complex programming.

The images of Malloy and Baxley training on the machine gun range were replaced. All memories of Malloy as a child, as a man, as a soldier, were replaced in all affected person's minds. The whole of his existence was deleted and reprogrammed by the natural law regarding time. With his father dead, there was no future or past of the man who was his offspring. The boy who was his father, now dead in a foreign field, would never know a family and would never know the change made by Pfc. Malloy's own existence in a place he was not welcome.

A.J. Segal received her wish and became a fighting soldier. Assigned to the 1st Battalion 17th Infantry Regiment, she performed her duties as an assistant gunner. Lying next to the machine gunner that would be her leader, she practiced and tested herself on the functions of the machine gun. She drilled herself on range estimation. She carried the weight through many field exercises and one specific real deployment. Her duty to the team always became the priority in her life. The pride she felt carrying the weapon assigned to defend the squad she was assigned to became her passion and her dream put to the final test.

Here in Vietnam, to find a single man to evacuate, she may have her chance to put herself to the final test of courage and duty. Waking up in a large hole to find her team waking in the same way changed her view on what was possible and what was not. She was a soldier and she was lost. Her squad leader for two years was her only chance of getting home alive. It was up to Ssg. Trevor Sands to bring them all home.

Spc. Segal was combing the field after a long battle, searching for the survivors who might be in hiding from them, from her. Then one of the visiting Rangers was killed, and efforts were doubled to eliminate all possible threats hiding in the field.

The JOC

All team leaders met the following day to discuss the final movement to meet General Hayes. They decided that with the manpower available they could take a relatively direct route. They would leave in four hours' time. They prepared the destruction of remaining ammunition that could not be carried with them. Mines and spare weapons would be carried, as well as explosives that would not be destroyed. Each soldier would carry three days' worth of food and a change of socks. At an average speed of three miles an hour, the men should make the JOC in about twenty hours, not including rest breaks.

Trevor called all of the men to the DFA and briefed them all on the plan of action.

"Our plan is to meet General Hayes and discuss with him in private about the situation. Sfc. Quinn and Sfc. Paul feel strongly that this man could be trusted and will believe us after seeing us in person. We will leave with all the ammo we can carry and enough food for three days. Rations will be eaten twice a day, so bring six. Bring socks and foot powder—this is going to be about fifty miles. Friendly KIAs will have to be left here; there is no possible way we can carry the two bodies without proper support. Does anyone have any questions? Segal, do you have what you need?"

A.J. looked at Trevor and nodded. The contemporary soldiers still felt out of place with a woman on the battlefield, but she had proven herself more than capable. She sat all night on the tower, picking off as many people as she could spot. She had singlehandedly taken out the mortar sections and most officers. All men in this circle respected her as a soldier. Trevor continued.

"Good. I expect that you will help Segal if the weight becomes too much. She has a heavy load with the AG gear, ammo and whatever we need distributed. So help her out occasionally to lessen the load. That load would be painful to all of us."

All of Trevor's men know that this was not a slight of this woman's strength. This was simply what he would say about every assistant gunner. They carry the most weight in a squad.

The men packed the ammo and piled what they could not bring in the center of the DFA. The plan was to destroy the DFA with the ammo so that no enemy force could find themselves a stronghold to defend from.

Trevor placed the charges around the DFA and ensured all men were out of range of the blast. He tied a time-delay fuse to det cord and ended with a blasting cap. Trevor armed the C-4 and pulled the detonation ring, beginning the slow burn of the time-delay fuse.

Ten minutes later Trevor was with his men when they watched the whole of their home explode in a cloud of white smoke. Debris flew around them; they found themselves forced to travel since they had nowhere else to go. Turning their backs on the one thing that had offered them security, the soldiers moved their way into the jungle, fighting their footing with the thick underbrush and vines, which provide a slick obstacle that would follow them the whole of the fifty miles to security…to home.

The teams moved their way through fifteen miles when they decided to find their first break spot. The men stopped in a perimeter as Paul and Quinn discussed the village they were next to. This village had been providing information for some time, and it would be a safe place to find a hot meal and a soft place to sit. Trevor listened to Quinn and Paul and decided to pamper his team with real food.

Paul moved into the village to reacquaint himself with the village elder. When permission was granted from the elder, Trevor filed his people through to the elder's hut for a hot meal. The men suddenly forgot the hell that they had just been through when they watched the children play in the village and the rough civilization that these people lived in. Here they fought for their homes and ate what they grew. These honorable people had only one goal: survive and raise their children.

The rest breaks every ten to fifteen miles provided the teams with the necessary strength to endure the long journey to the one man who could actually help them. The plan was to have Trevor's team stay in the wood line near the security elements of the operations center while Paul and Rowdy briefed the general on the visitors. The briefing would not include what time they are from, only that they were lost and needed assistance. Rowdy decided the best course was to begin the conversation with a covert team sent without the general's knowledge. This should eliminate the risk of the general waving them off without counsel.

In mid-afternoon the following day, the teams made it to the JOC without conflict. As planned, Trevor and his team stayed with the security element outside of the JOC. Paul, Rowdy, Quinn and Lt. Phelps waited for the general to finish a briefing he was giving to other team leaders. Paul leaned in to hear the general better.

"...when it began. All I know is that there are reports of a missing battalion of enemy forces in the area. Radio intercept reveals that the NVA authorities have no idea where this battalion is, only that they are not on the course they were assigned. Apparently, there was communications problem due to the type of terrain. The last word from the battalion commander was that they had made contact with American forces and they were trying to track them down. The American forces retreated to an unknown direction, and the NVA battalion lost communications.

"Gentleman, the only team I sent was lead by First Sergeant Paul Ricardo, escorted by Glitson. I want you to find these men and bring their bodies here. We can't have any remains left around to prove American activity this far north. So, Mike, if you would scan this sector here—"

One of the team leaders coughed in an obvious way. The general looked at the team leader as he followed his eyes to Rowdy and Paul. Frozen in his brief, the general blinked his eyes as if to refresh whom it was he was looking at.

"Well, gentleman, it seems we can call off the search. Please excuse us; I need to debrief these men."

The room cleared, leaving Hayes and the four men who interrupted his brief.

The general looked at Rowdy, gauging the level of concern coming from him.

"Well, Chief, you had best have a damn good explanation for cutting contact with me and blowing off our orders. The last we heard you made contact and requested artillery. Unfortunately, we had to refuse. Where did you go? And who in the hell is Hard Rock 12? We heard them advise you to return to your last checkpoint for assistance. I want the bullshit you have been feeding me to cease, understand? You had best start talking, boy. I am on my last nerve of my generosity. You've only told me that there is a village that wanted training and weapons to help in the resistance against the NVA and VC forces. I have a damn good feeling that's bullshit as well. You best start explaining yourself right now!"

Rowdy took a deep breath and began what he had been rehearsing since they started the journey to the JOC.

"Sir, we lied to you when we requested supplies and weapons for a village. In truth there are seven American men we came across who are on an extremely covert mission. They had little ammunition and food. They were stranded here and left for dead. We helped them with supplies and weekly checkups. They are here with us, and I strongly wish for you to meet with the team leader in private, sir. This is extremely sensitive, and I request that you take my advice." Rowdy paused.

"As for the missing battalion and our movements. This man's team annihilated the battalion along with several mortar sections. The total count of enemy killed is 1,277 men. Sir, these figures alone should be enough for you to meet with them."

The general laughed in disbelief and shook his head.

"Son, you expect me to believe that seven soldiers destroyed half of the remaining NVA forces left in the north? You need to check your bullshit level and try again."

With this, Paul, Quinn and Lt. Phelps answered the general. Paul caught his ear.

"With all do respect, sir, you need to meet these men. When you meet them you will understand and believe everything they tell you. They did, in fact, fight that battalion. They did, in fact, kill every weapon-holding man on that field. All officers were shot and no one survived. These men saved our lives twice directly. These men are responsible for preventing the attacking force from getting here and killing everyone at the JOC. Yes, that's right, they even saved your life, sir. I highly suggest you hear this man out and open your mind to what he needs from you."

Paul was shaking with fury at this man's distrust. General Hayes looked at Quinn and Phelps. Both men were nodding. Hayes agreed with a conceding nod, and Paul left to get Trevor and his team to introduce them to their skeptical savior.

The Prototype

Michael had finished briefing the chiefs of staff about the recovery project, which was underway to acquire the men they had sent to the Vietnam War. It had taken quite a bit of explaining to the generals to convince them that price had to be no object in this mission. Explaining the possible consequences of leaving men in the past who have the power to change the future, for better or worse, was something that could not be left to chance. The chiefs of staff had agreed to allow the budget not to limit the recovery of these men.

The more painful question had troubled Michael's mind for some time. Why have the men in the compound been able to see the changes made from the past? Was it possible that all people would be able to see the changes made? According to Richard, the people in the warehouse seemed to notice nothing by providing a file that was not there the day prior. Only Richard was aware as to the nature of the file's appearance there. This was the first order of business for the day.

Arriving in his office after the conference with the generals, Michael managed to call a staff meeting to prioritize the research. Primarily, they must know why the changes of the past were not affecting the people in this compound. Looking at the men surrounding the large table in the briefing room, Michael began his order of events for the day.

"Good morning, I just left a meeting with the chiefs of staff, and our budget has been approved to endless means to ensure our success. Therefore, we have no reason to worry about lack of money or materials to accomplish the recovery. I believe we have a rough plan for the prototype that will allow one vehicle to do what we had believed to require three. Just a simple loop concentrating the tapped dark energy that had allowed us to build the first device should be allowed to reverse in polarity to bring a positive feed, sending the object forward. I need the R and D group to begin running the data for this plan. If any doubt or thoughts exist, please bring them to Richard or myself.

"Now, our first priority is a challenging one. I have noticed an isolation in this compound that prevents the consciousness of the people within it to change with the events in the past being altered. We are aware of changes, and I must know why. This will require any theory that any of you can think of. So please, speak freely. This is new ground of science that none of us has mastered. In order to ensure success in our mission, we must master the variables of our devices. Now, clear your minds of doubts and fill them with effective thought. I want the project leaders to brief me on all of your thoughts by six this evening. Good day, doctors."

The scientists stood and left the room in a cluttered doubt. Michael and his loyal friend Richard remained. Silent for long moments, they both rose to leave the room to their own offices.

Michael surrounds himself with the documentation of the time line that Trevor and his team had been occupying. Staring at the papers in front of him, he realized a change had occurred when he was not there.

The file had a changed heading referencing another battle. This time about 1,200 were killed. Two Americans were KIA. One of them was assigned to a Ranger team who was temporarily reassigned for northern insurgencies. Due to a death from his predecessor, Sgt. Malloy was transferred to fill in the slot for reconnaissance in the northern territories of Vietnam.

Michael's eyebrows shot up in a sudden recognition of the name. Michael flips through the list of men who were sent back; no Malloy listed. Michael realized what happened. A soldier he had never heard of replaced Malloy, A.J. Segal. With the realization of the drastic change that had just taken place at the moment of Sgt. Malloy' death, Michael picked up his phone and called for Richard to join him in his office.

After five minutes, Richard knocked on Michael's door. Without an answer, Richard let himself in to face Michael's back. Michael offered Richard a glass of scotch; accepting, they both sat down for conversation. Michael began.

"We have a problem. There was a drastic change made during a battle. Get this: these people killed 1,200 NVA regulars with intermittent VC. Two Americans were killed. One was Himelrick, their grenadier, the other was Sgt. Malloy, later to become Senator Malloy. That means his son is no longer in existence. It means that the refusal of women in combat arms was null. The person who was in Malloy's place was an A.J. Segal. A *female* who had been in the service for a little over two years. She was assigned as an assistant gunner for Spc. Baxley. Do you understand what this means? Now that there are women in the Infantry and a whole line of offspring gone, the entire future has changed. The bitch of it is, we are the only ones who know of any change at all."

With a deep sigh, Richard poured the smooth liquor in his mouth and exhaled in a solid comprehension of the effects made by one man's death. The men sat sullen, trying to find a definite answer to the time delay of the recovery process.

Running was heard from down the hall, and suddenly the door burst open. Doctor Hansen, one of the project leaders, was breathing heavily when he announced that he knew why they had been isolated from the changes in the time line. Doctor Hansen placed a stack of rough data that proved the material used in opening the rift in quantum foam had an isotope that radiates within the shielding of the compound. By inhibiting a shift in quantum foam by the concentration of the dark energy cycle, the entirety of the compound was immune to conscious change from the past. It seemed that the changes to the consciousness results from the shifting of the invisible foam that surrounds all dimensional space. In an area where the changes were controlled or manipulated, the change in foam was non-existent. Doctor Hansen continued by stating a further theory.

"Sir, we all agree in this theory. If a man were killed in the past who was originally alive, the offspring he had would disappear. If one of those people who is alive because of his existence were in a confined area where the foam could not be manipulated without a controlled pulse, that person would not be gone. As long as they are in this area, they will continue to live. We agree as well that if that person were to leave the compound, that person would simply vanish and all persons witnessing would see and remember the disappearance since the change in the foam had already taken place."

Michael nodded in understanding as he finally realized the cause for their comprehension of the effects made on the past. Richard simply poured another drink without any response to the doctor's findings.

Now that the question as to their immunity was clear, the larger and more important problem remained. How do they design the new model to implement the positive and negative flow of dark energy? How to concentrate and shape the field necessary to bring the men back? With this on Michael's mind, he had no patience for the importance of the pointless, in his opinion.

Hours had passed and the reports were delivered to Michael. They had prepared rough data for the new model as well as the device, which would have to be designed to flow in opposite directions. The designs look promising and, if lucky, the first test should be able to begin by the end of the week. It was amazing what a blank check could accomplish in a small amount of time.

The next day, approval was given to begin the assembly of the device. It would be mounted to a Stryker assault vehicle and sent to the JOC, where the men were going to be. The final assembly of the device would be finished within twenty-four hours. The construction would consist of a retractable rod with a sacrificial dark energy disk at the tip. The focus of the field would encircle the vehicle and send it to a preprogrammed time. The velocity of the loop would act as the substitute for the distance factor. Because the dark energy loop would be on top of the field, once the vehicle was sent to its destination, the loop would fall to the ground and be left behind. A small stock of loops would have to be stored where the rod would retract to be fitted on for another journey.

On Thursday the vehicle pulled out of the hangar and drove out to the nearest control bunker, where a primate would be placed in the vehicle. The vehicle would be sent forward ten minutes, take 360-degree photographs and send itself back one minute after departure. The staff would sit the moment the vehicle left until it returned. The vehicle must move locations when it arrives in the future to avoid an overlap.

The monkey was belted into the passenger seat. After the test the monkey would undergo several exams to identify physical complications. With only four minutes remaining, Michael took his place in the command bunker. A large digital clock was placed a few meters away from the vehicle to ensure accurate data by photograph.

The time had come for departure. The vehicle began its preparations. The rod began extending with the dark energy loop at the top. With the loud hum of the charging rods, the vehicle began to tremble from the vibrating energy of the surrounding field. A cloud emerged from thin air as visible energy covered the trace of the vehicle. In a flash of what looked like lightning, the vehicle was gone. All staff members took a seat on the hot desert sand, leaving a path for the vehicle to drive through.

One minute later the vehicle arrived fifteen meters away from its departure point with an ecstatic monkey screaming from the passenger seat. The monkey was removed to a lab where tests would be conducted to evaluate physical damages done by travel. The rest of the staff waited the nine minutes for the vehicle to arrive and disappear into what was once the present, becoming the past. As the large digital clock indicated nine minutes had passed, the cloud formed where the vehicle originally left. Once the cloud was cleared, in mere seconds, the vehicle began its photographs of the perimeter. Driving on preprogrammed instructions, the vehicle moved fifteen meters away and disappeared in the same manor. One vehicle remained and two dark energy loops were on the ground.

The following day the results of the lab work from the monkey were delivered to Michael. A large stamp on the cover said all it needed to: NO ALTERATIONS.

To Hell and Back

In the security of a camouflaged tent, lying in the underbrush of dense jungle, Trevor and his half squad was escorted into a briefing area where they would finally meet with General Hayes. According to Paul, the general only thought that Trevor was a lost operative who needed support. Trevor could not help but feel anxious for the man when he heard what it was that he had to say.

Under the light of a red haze, Trevor scanned a small open area to find several men on radios listening in to Vietnamese bandwidths. One man was trying desperately to keep up with the intelligence officer by plotting known areas of interest on the map. In the corner, in front of several wooden boxes, was General Hayes. Trevor found himself standing in front of the troubled-looking man. The man offered a hand, and Trevor took it with a hesitant greeting.

"Good morning, sir, I appreciate your seeing us in this manner."

Trevor let the man scan him and his men from head to toe. Hayes put his hand on his forehead, trying to gain a perspective and clarity that would shed some light to the equipment and units that these men were from. Trevor, who had seen this look many times lately, simply tried to put the man's mind at ease by answering his questions before he asked them. Trevor called his men over to the general and began introducing them.

"Sir, I know how we must look, but before I explain let me introduce my team. This is my alpha team leader, Corporal Boiyd. My machine gunner,

Specialist Baxley. His assistant, Private First Class Segal. My rifleman, Private Second Class Wilson. And finally, my automatic gunner, Private First Class Trits."

The team took their turns shaking the man's hand. The general, showing impressive patience, greeted them all in a courteous manner.

"Sir, we must have a moment of your time and more of your patience. Let me get to the question that must be on your mind. You want to know who the fuck we are and how we got weapons like these, don't you?"

Hayes nodded, confirming that this was indeed his main question.

"Sir, we are infantry soldiers from Alaska. We were assigned to a NEO in North Vietnam when a conflict broke out that would endanger some American lives. I know this makes no sense, considering the situation we are in. If you would indulge me for another moment I will explain further."

Trevor handed Hayes his cleared weapon and began explaining while the general inspected the equipment.

"Sir, when we left our homes and ended up here it was the summer of—"

Trevor found himself hesitating as he took in a deep breath. Rowdy came in to finish the statement when the general did so for him.

"Sergeant, you come from 2008, is that correct?"

Trevor looked at Rowdy. Rowdy denied mentioning it. Trevor turned back to the general, who smiled and nodded in understanding. Handing the weapon back to Trevor, he explained.

"You have someone here who is expecting you. If you will come with me."

Hayes delivered a wry smile and motioned for Trevor's team to follow as they headed outside to a separated underground bay used to hide the general's jeep. Inside was something that shot like a hot arrow into Trevor's eyes. Lying in the bay was a Stryker. Inside was a man wearing a poor attempt at tactical gear. The man standing to the side of the vehicle came forward to introduce himself. General Hayes stood back with Trevor's team and Paul's men.

"Staff Sergeant Sands?" the man inquired.

Trevor nodded as the man smiled a wide grin and stepped forward. Trevor stood his distance with an obvious confusion radiating from him.

The man stepped forward and asked again, "Trevor, right?"

Trevor nodded.

"We have been working diligently to track you down and bring you home.

Fortunately, you have made a big enough noise here that provided us with enough data to know when you will be here. I arrived a bit early to clear some confusion that General Hayes here might have. My name is Michael Heimer. I am a scientist working for the military to design new weapons. When we tested our latest weapon, we accidentally found a side effect we had not counted on. We sent you back to this time line with no knowledge as to how we did so. I am deeply sorry for your unfortunate experience. I can't even imagine the level of horror that you and your men experienced. To avoid anything being compromised in the future, we needed to make your return priority. I'm sorry it took so long. I would have arrived sooner for your return, but I needed a safe place to recover you that would leave no eyewitnesses—" Trevor cut him off.

"Excuse me…Michael, you mean to tell me that you could have pulled us out at any time? Instead, you waited until one of my men was killed and after we were forced to kill over a thousand men! All due respect, but fuck you!"

Michael lowered his head and wiped his glasses off. After a brief moment that seemed much longer, he continued.

"Son, I know how you must feel…"

Boiyd scoffed loudly.

"…but you have to understand that this is the most sensitive project we have ever known. We could not afford to let anyone outside of the intelligence community witness its use. We had no choice. Your existence here has changed everything."

Trevor nodded with little patience.

"You must have a small understanding as to what your presence might change. You happened to kill a little over 1,500 men who were not supposed to die by your hand. Fortunately, the men in this country don't typically have an effect at a global level, but for all we know, their offspring may. We had to get you out in a tactical manner to prevent further change. I am sorry, but this really was the only way."

Michael had expected a different tone when he explained what he was here to do. He did not expect the animosity that he had generated. Trying desperately to empathize with Trevor, he could now understand what this hellish experience must have been like to know they could have been pulled out at any time. They now knew that they could have avoided every painful experience that they had been through if it had not been for policy.

Trevor looked back to his men and then to Paul. Rowdy whispered into the general's ear as they decided something Trevor could not guess. Finally, the general stood back and sent a runner to get something. A moment of uncomfortable silence later, the runner returned with six small boxes. Stepping forward, he moved to Segal. He pinned a medal on her chest and shook her hand with the most gracious words. Doing the same with the remainder of Trevor's men, he came face to face with Trevor.

"Son, I don't care what changed in the future by your being here. I do know that I would not see my wife again, as well as hundreds of my men, if you hadn't fought your ass off here. You are the most impressive soldiers I have ever laid my eyes on. Coming from the Special Operations commander, you must be proud. With that, I present you with the Silver Star. Your men are being awarded the same. If there was a way to honor you more, I would do so. Because of the time difference, it would never come to pass. Please accept this with our most sincere thanks and deepest regrets for your loss. I wish you all a safe journey and a forgetful mind."

The general shook his hand and smiled a deep smile, revealing the deep wrinkles brought by stress and anguish.

Michael chimed in factually, "Actually, General, you would have lived but you lost a leg in the first time line…just so you know."

As he turned away, a loud explosion thundered from outside.

Trevor barked an order as his men took each side of the ramp leading to ground level. Nothing was heading their way, but he knew they were soon to discover another area to raid.

Michael shouted something that Trevor could not understand. After a moment to let things settle in his mind, Trevor realized what was said.

"They can't find the vehicle!"

Trevor moved Baxley to the mouth of the entrance with Segal to his side. After Baxley had been set, Trevor moved to his right to inspect the area. Trevor called Wilson, who now carried Himelrick's weapon. Wilson handed Trevor the grenade launcher and a handful of illuminating grenades. Trevor held off while Baxley searched through the thermal scope. He saw nothing except light yellow shapes on the ground, and he assumed these were the men on the security force for the perimeter.

Several shapes came into focus. Baxley placed his finger lightly on the trigger when he recognized the formation they were in, a Ranger file. Baxley released the trigger and informed Trevor of possible friendlies. Trevor kneeled behind the gun and scanned through the scope. He found what Baxley was talking about. Settling behind the gun, Trevor took a close look and noticed something. Trevor squeezed the trigger, sending a cone of fire towards the red figures. Explosive rounds shattered through the targets as he traversed the gun through the shapes. In a short moment, the shapes were on the ground.

Baxley leaned close to Trevor. "Sergeant, what the fuck are you doing? They were in a Ranger file!" Baxley screams.

Trevor explained, "Bax, those guys were not Americans. They were crossing a danger area the same way, but they were all carrying different rifles. It's okay, I promise you."

Trevor called for his men to come near him as he moved out of the bunker and into the open. As he stepped out of sight of his men, he was struck in the back of the head. Spinning to the ground, he stared down the barrel of an AK-47. Trevor kicked the man in front of him. As the man jerked backward, he fired a round into Trevor's leg. Screaming in pain, Trevor pulled his knife out of its sheath and lunged himself onto the man, thrusting the blade deep into the sternum of the man's chest. With a desperate twist of the blade, the chest cavity cracked with a blood-spraying snap. Trevor fell back and laid his head down. Pushing his head back, he saw several of his men rushing through the jungle wearing night vision. Trevor reached for his own as he spotted several beams cross the jungle. Within ten minutes the small raid was finished with his men victorious…again.

Biting his lip, Trevor cut a strip of cloth away from his sleeve. As he wrapped a field dressing around his wound, he secured it with the cloth. The blood-soaked dressing throbbed with the beat of his own pulse. Picking up his weapon, he found his men and limped his way back to the bunker. In five minutes' time his team was back to the bunker and loaded into the vehicle.

Michael started the engine and listened for the sudden silence surrounding the compound. It was at that moment he finally realized what it was that these men went through on a daily basis while they were stranded. Michael ordered the soldiers out of the vehicle. Hesitating, the team stepped out of the vehicle as Michael prepared his equipment. Directing Trevor to stand in a certain area, Michael raised the rod and directed the loop to concentrate on a directional area. Facing it toward Trevor, he began the sequence. Trevor looked around at the general and his men as the cloud formed around him. In a painful flash of light, he slammed into something, sending a painful shock throughout his body. Trevor opened his eyes to see nothing but a white haze. The smell of home surrounded him as he heard children playing and laughing. A sudden scream and a woman thanking God passed through his ears as he submitted to a deeper sleep.

Debriefing

Lying in the hospital, trying to force the bowl of Jell-O into his mouth, the DIA agent stopped the recorder and leaned forward to wipe the sweat off Trevor's brow. A cell phone jingled as the man stepped back to answer it.

"Monroe," the agent said and then paused. "I understand, sir. When? Uh huh. I'm sure he'd like to know. Yes, sir. I understand, no action. Yes, sir. Uh huh. Good day, sir."

Monroe turned off the cell phone and turned to Trevor.

"It seems that all of your men found themselves in your same predicament. All of them were found falling from thin air in front of their homes. My supervisor just instructed me to take no action toward you and your men. We feel that the likelihood of a leak regarding this issue is minimal since no one would believe it. That doesn't mean you can get on the *Today Show* and start your speech about what happened. I trust you just want to put this behind you, right?"

Trevor smiled as if his deepest fears were at ease. With a nod, Trevor sat up to stretch his neck and a knock on the door sounded. The agent stood from his chair and walked to the door. After a short series of murmurs outside of Trevor's earshot, the agent returned to Trevor's side.

"There is a man at the door who wishes to speak with you. He says you owe him a drink. Do you know what he's talking about?"

Trevor frowned as he shook his head. The agent returned to the door to send the visitor on his way when Trevor shouted, "Let him in!"

Standing aside, the agent let the old man into the room. With a smile, the agent left the room with sudden understanding of who the visitor was.

Taking Monroe's seat, the old man pulled out a flask and offered it to Trevor. Trevor laughed for the first time in a long while as he stared at his new friend. Without a word, the two men sat looking at each other as if it were only an hour since they had last seen one another. For Trevor it had been a week since they were last together. For the older man it had been much longer. Paul reached into the bag and pulled out two cups as he filled them from the flask. With a silent toast, the two men poured the warm whiskey down their throats. Paul laughed loudly and pulled out his family pictures from his wallet.

II
Reorganization

The mind of Dr. Benjamin Phelps had never been sound. Since the rape of his wife four years before, he had withdrawn into his lab, where he was designing what his employers knew to be called "Alphabet." He was a quiet employee, a hard worker and a brilliant man.

On the thirty-second floor of the MedCorp tower in St. Paul, Minnesota, Dr. Phelps was designing a weapon to finally place his troubled mind to ease. Working with a one-track mind, Ben would think of the pain that had hit his life since he was a child. Key images and phrases would echo in his mind. Ben concentrated more on recalling painful events than he did on the extremely hazardous material in front of him. Through the thick level-A suit, Ben studied the red haze of compiled strains of viruses through the high-powered microscope in front of him. The echoes ring through his mind as he stared at the molecular weapon he created.

"Let's play a game, Ben. Do you wanna?"

Little Ben Phelps allows a tear to slip past his eye as his uncle stood over him. Ben's uncle had been playing these games for over two years now. Ben was afraid that he might upset his uncle, forcing the man to become violent. Ben looked as close to the man's eyes as he dared to and answers.

"Yes, sir."

With a smile, Ben's uncle bends down from the waist and explains the rules of the "game."

"Here's how we play. I heard that you have had some problems in school. I am going to say a letter, and you say the one that comes after it. Sound easy enough?"

Little Ben slowly nodded his head.

"Now, when you get one right, I'll give you a kiss. When you get one wrong, you have to take something off. You understand?"

Ben nodded.

"Okay! Let's play the alphabet game."

Studying the biological material in front of him, Ben spoke softly to the oozing agent, "Let's play the alphabet game."

While Ben's uncle was playing his games with the child, Ben's parents were at their weekly social places. His mother would go to play poker with her friends across town while his father would spend his time with some construction co-workers at the bar.

One evening Ben's uncle was playing the alphabet game with Ben when his father came home early. As his father walked into the room to find his brother kissing Ben in a completely uncalled-for location, the father held his place in front of the two and said simply, "That's what you get, boy, for being stupid. If you had a set of balls on ya this wouldn't happen."

Ben's father, drunk at the time, never did anything to prevent his brother from watching Ben. The boy's mother never found out about the abuse, which took place once a week for four years. When Ben had turned twelve years old, he found his father's gun and played a game of his own.

Pointing the weapon at his uncle, as he had seen in the movies, he said in a frightening soft voice, "Sir, you wanna play a game? I know, let's play the alphabet game."

The look of Ben's uncle burned deep into Ben's mind. It was a look of disbelief and complete terror. As the man stammered, Ben pulled back the hammer on the old revolver and raised the barrel toward the man's chest. With the same seductive smile that Ben was given for many painful years, he asked, "I'm thinking of a letter. Tell me the one that follows."

Ben hid the pain of abuse through his schoolwork. Receiving high marks all the way through college, Ben continued his education into medical school and concentrated on pathology. During his second year in med school, he met his wife, Alice. They were married for nine years until she was brutally raped and beaten to death. They caught the rapist in the act of raping another woman.

Blaming his father, his uncle and the rapist for the grief in his life, he discovered that they all shared a common thread. They were all AB negative in blood type. In his own twisted mind, he concluded that all of the AB negative blood comprised the total evil of the world. His gift to the world would be their elimination.

His project now was for a government contract through his company. The project was for prospective biological agents that could concentrate on certain people. With the research in hand, Ben took his work one step further. His project "Alphabet" was named for finishing the AB negatives as well as his revenge for the perverted childhood game. With the plan in his mind, he began injecting the samples into an ice cube located in his coffee thermos filled with Freon. From home he would finalize his efforts to rid the people who would be the greatest threat to him and to society.

13 MARCH 2009
1500 HOURS

Michael Heimer, grandson of the famous scientist who was project leader for the Manhattan Project, listened in on a national security brief. As the politicians and higher-ups in the government's various agencies discussed the events that had taken place the year before, Michael sweat and worried that if any blame was placed, it would fall on him.

Last year, in 2008, a small group of soldiers was accidentally sent to 1969 in the middle of North Vietnam. The experiment was a weapon designed to incinerate anything in its path. With the discovery of harnessing dark energy, they found that they could create a field that would make objects vanish. In actuality, the objects were sent along a time line determined by the distance from the weapon to the object sent. The group of soldiers sent was lead by Staff Sergeant Sands, who was on a mission to track down an American scientist for evacuation.

He found the scientist at the edge of the cleared area the weapon left behind. The man was severed in half, along with the hut he was living in. On the way back to their operations center, a second test took place that had taken them for a horrifying ride to the past. In the fight for their life, they lived long enough for a safe extraction.

The extraction was an even more difficult task than the accidental flight to the past. Dr. Heimer was the project leader working for the Defense

Intelligence Agency to develop this weapon. When the truth of the weapon was discovered, all resources were used to recover the men and master the use of the machine. Finally, the men were returned to their homes one at a time, in a surprising effect that they had not counted on. The first was Trevor Sands, who fell from thin air twenty-five feet up.

The inquiry here was to evaluate the actions taken by the weapon's developers after the accident. Now that the men around the large table had begun their business, they focused on the chairman.

"Gentleman of the committee, I trust you have read the brief regarding the interesting developments that occurred last year. Dr. Heimer, I feel I can put you at ease when I say that you would not be punished in any way for your actions. I commend you for your diligence and the hard work and innovation showed by your team. It seems that something was discovered that requires much discussion.

"It seems that we now have the capability to change events in the future, or present, by manipulating the past. For national security purposes, I know this would be an essential tool to maintain the way of life of the American people.

"Therefore, what I suggest is this. A new covert agency designed to reverse tragedies that would take place in the future. Tragedies that are national or global. Tragedies like the infamous September 11. The director is a man we all know is renowned for his initiative. His actions and decisions during last year's crisis prevented a great deal of potential disaster. I recommend that if future disasters or terrorist acts threaten the lives of this nation we activate this agency to prevent the action from taking place. One step that should be followed is a series of protocols to be developed to allow the senior agent the ability to govern and advise our Congress or chiefs of staff to ensure the prevention of the future disaster he is sent to prevent. Once the event is avoided, he would be sent back to his time to wait for future callings. I would like the panel to vote to enact this proposal of this agency's creation. All in favor?"

The panel all confirmed the proposal of this agency. Certain aspects of the agency were still left in question, but all were agreed that it would be an ideal plan for avoidance of future devastations.

The chairman continued, "Now we must discuss who potential agents should be. Dr. Heimer, who would you recommend?"

Michael took a deep breath and first thought of Staff Sergeant Sands' actions in Vietnam.

"Gentleman, I recommend that Staff Sergeant Trevor Sands and his original team from last year's unfortunate accident be placed on the agency's list of agents. Their discipline and understanding of potential risks to the time line was exceptional. I recommend that Sands be placed as senior agent, with a team to handle tactical responses to prevent future events. He was the only man who had any experience. He also had a superb mind for tactics. He proved that through impossible battles. Responsible for over 1,400 kills in Vietnam while losing only one of his team, he proved himself perfect for the role both as a tactician and as a leader.

"As far as what would be needed, we have already designed a vehicle that would be more than efficient for any situation. We would require a compound in an isolated area as well as a staff of personnel to handle supplies and delivery. I would require a liaison to handle any red tape from the State Department. With my existing team, we should be more than capable for what would be needed. With the help of NSA, CIA or DIA we should have whatever intelligence we would require for a strategic point of prevention. Right now I can think of no one else we would need."

The chairman smiled as if proved right that Michael would be fit for the position. The committee finalized the proposal by assigning a budget to get the agency started. NSA and the CIA would handle background checks on all personnel who would be assigned to the agency. With the signing of the act by the committee, the president would receive the final draft to review and put in effect under the office of Homeland Security, where the new agency would branch. The new agency would appropriately be called "New Option."

21 APRIL 2009
0902 HOURS

On the floor in a narrow basement was a wooden crate the size of a refrigerator. Ben Phelps was finishing the final touches of the device, which could bring down a large passenger plane in a ball of flames. Ben fit the device with a barometer that would detonate as the aircraft descended from cruising altitude. The secondary trigger was a timer that ensured that it was at the proper height and location that Ben was planning for according to the flight plan. The target location was over Omaha, Nebraska. Using the same mentality that the Air Force had during the implementation of STRATCOM during the Cold War, Ben found the ideal central location of the United States. Instead of placing a strategic communication center for defensive purposes, he placed the starting point for millions of deaths and even more sick.

His plan, so far, seemed perfect. He would use the aircraft to deliver the agent to a proper geographical location. An explosion would send the agent into the atmosphere, infecting all who breathed it in. Because it was an airborne disease, the disease would spread faster than the California wildfires of '03. By Ben's calculations, the agent would be proactive for three months until CDC inoculated those unaffected and cured the ones who were infected. In three months' time, all AB negative types should have convulsed their last spasm and drowned in their own blood.

A slight smile for a final revenge passed through Ben as he soldered the final component into his lethal goodwill device. His next step was to prepare the agents for transport. Because the agent would be destroyed instantly by fire, Ben soaked the bio-agent in asbestos and maintained the material in Freon until the explosion. The heat of the blast would break the casing of the container and release the fibers into the atmosphere. The fibers, already broken down to minuscule size, would be inhaled by hundreds, and if he was lucky, thousands, of people. Those people would be contaminated with the agent, and when the dormant phase was complete, the agent would spread to all who were exposed to the initially infected.

The final nail was placed to enclose the crate. Disguised as a soda machine, the explosives and agents were enclosed inside the machine in old soda cans. The wiring was interconnected where the cans touched so that the inspector only saw the cans and machine with no wiring or suspicious leads. Ben had to choose this size because there were limits to what the X-ray scanners could pass through. Something this size could not pass.

Now labeling the crate to a food distribution center in Arizona, Ben was ready to have a parcel service take the package for shipment.

Ben sat at his workbench and lifted a sandwich to his mouth for a celebratory meal. His time had come, and no one was prepared for the revenge of the evil blood that infected the nation and the world. Finally, the evil tendencies of the proud would vanish with the tainted blood that flowed through them. Alphabet would resolve war and hatred. Gangs and random acts of violence would disappear with the removal of the AB negatives. This was his gift to the world, a world without animosity. Ben pulled out a picture of his wife from below wiring schematics and looked deep into her eyes.

"Thank you, darling, for giving me the courage to avenge your death and have my revenge for my life."

22 APRIL 2009
1224 HOURS

Trevor Sands was in his bed in his spacious house in Colorado Springs, Colorado, while his wife and daughter played downstairs. After his return to active duty, he was promoted to Sergeant First Class and awarded the Soldier's Medal as well as the Purple Heart. The Silver Star that Major General Hayes had awarded him in 1969 rested behind a flag case on the mantle in the living room.

Ten months after his return to his unit, he was transferred to the State Department for unannounced duties. He hadn't had any training on the new assignment, nor did he know what the assignment entailed. His only briefing was to keep a pager that was issued with fresh batteries and on his person at all times. His days were at home with his wife and child, while he received his pay as a sergeant first class.

Using this time to its fullest, he spends his time working out, resting and spending the most time possible with his family. He had just taken a trip to Utah to visit his father. Incidentally, this was the first time that his father had met Jessica and Mali. In the country house just next to the mountains, they spent their time camping and hiking. Because of the experience in Vietnam, Trevor had no problem being outdoors, knowing that there was no need to be silent or keep smells down for fear of being attacked. The woods had become relaxing once again.

After his trip to see his father, which lasted a month, he went home and stayed, where he absorbed as much of his family as he could until the State Department called for him.

Trevor sat up and slid off the bed. With a stretch, Trevor stood on his feet and headed downstairs to his family. The sound of laughter emanated from the living room as Trevor crossed the second landing from the stairs. Trevor stood back and watched as his wife was playfully blowing raspberries on Mali's belly. Kicking and laughing uncontrollably, Mali accidentally kicked her mother in the mouth.

"I sowy, Mamma. I sowy. Kiss better, okay!"

The two-year-old kissed her mother on the chin, missing the hurt spot completely, and gave her the biggest hug a small child could give. Jessica laughed at the sweet gesture and assured her child that it was okay.

"You aren't teaching our daughter how to fight, are you?" Trevor said in a sarcastic tone.

Jessica answered, "Oh, please! You have been trying to get her to punch you in the stomach on purpose since she was born! Don't talk to me about egging on violence!"

Jessica fell back to overdramatize the slight push the child had just given her. Jessica grabbed Mali on the way back and brought her down to the ground with her. Trevor walked to the kitchen, where he searched the cabinets for coffee.

"Hey, Jes, we got coffee anywhere around?"

Jessica replied, "No, hon, I think we finished it yesterday. I'll be heading into town here in about an hour to get some more potatoes for dinner. I'll pick some up then. In the meantime, could you fix Mali up a sandwich? I need to get ready to go."

Trevor smirks.

"Ready to go? Who do you have to impress in town?"

Jessica delivered a choice finger out of view from Mali as she skipped upstairs to get dressed.

Here in the valley of Colorado Springs, Trevor had found the perfect place to raise his family. Here they could get the things they needed from society while getting the things they needed from nature as well. It was the perfect place to try to grow some well-balanced kids. So far Mali was the only one; the plan was for two more.

Jessica came down wearing a pair of jeans and a light sweater. She kissed Trevor on the cheek as she reached for the keys. In a whirlwind of kisses, she left the house and pulled out of the drive. Trevor turned to his daughter and lifted her up to his shoulders. Walking into the kitchen to make his daughter a sandwich like his wife said, he felt a dull rub on his hip that he was not accustomed to. Setting his child down, he reached for the pager that was now vibrating diligently at his side.

Incidentally, the number showed the office of the State Department. With the vouchers he was issued he could walk onto any plane going to Virginia and get priority passage.

An hour later Trevor's wife came home. Mali was watching her favorite cartoon, and Trevor was in the bedroom. Jessica entered the bedroom to find a suitcase on the bed and Trevor filling it with items from his drawer.

"Finally moving to your girlfriend's?" Jessica teased.

Trevor replied less humorously, "I got paged."

Jessica's faced flushed with worry. Before she could say anything, she found herself unpacking the sock drawer and placing items in the suitcase. She knew that if he did know anything of what it was about, he wouldn't be able to tell her. Because of the events in the past year, she was sure something terrible and secret was involved, but he never told her what happened. She only knew he was in Vietnam, but she did not know that he was in Vietnam in 1969.

Trevor and Jessica walk hand in hand to his truck, where he threw the suitcase in the passenger seat. Trevor closed the door and held both of his wife's hands. Trevor pulled her in to hold her as he found her head buried in his chest. He whispered in her ear a promise of safety that he couldn't back up with fact. She allowed a tear to slip past her eye as she looked up at him with a smile of courageous restraint. Trevor turned to get in the truck, and Jessica then watched him start the truck and pull away.

22 APRIL 2009
1757 HOURS

Trevor stepped off the plane in Virginia, where a man who seemed to be a veteran in some agency greeted him. The man simply asked if he was Mr. Sands. When Trevor affirmed, the man walked him to baggage claim and waited for the checked suitcase to rotate with the rest. Trevor was unsure of protocol due to lack of education in the procedures of the State Department. He simply asked if the man had any idea what was going on.

The man replied, "Sir, if you don't know, then I know I'm not the one to inform you. Your briefing will take place the moment we get to Mr. Porter's office. Aside from that, I can tell you about everything we see from here to the office."

Trevor had to laugh at the obviousness of it all. When his bag came, the man snatched it from the turntable and headed for the door.

The drive was uneventful, since there were no sights to describe. The man was correct in what he said. When they had arrived, Trevor noticed that the office was nothing more than an average cottage. Inside the cottage, the rooms were fully furnished. An older man and what appeared to be his wife greeted Trevor and his escort. Trevor's escort had opened a closet door and flipped a light switch hidden behind some jackets.

Trevor looked around him and noticed that the light in the closet had a string on it. Without the sense of movement or the hint of sound, the closet door opened into a large room filled with tracking equipment and a conference room enclosed by frosted glass. To the right lay a series of dry erase boards on wheels facing several college-style desks with a digital projector facing a large white screen. In the back right corner lay a video teleconferencing interface. The back left corner had a separate door leading to God only knew where, while the left side of the room was filled with the self-contained conference room.

In the center of the room was the only man out of the organization that Trevor knew. Martin Porter was the man who had explained all that Trevor needed to know in fifteen minutes of his orientation briefing. Since that was the only time he had seen the man, he was rather impressed with himself that he had remembered his face.

Martin stepped forward to greet Trevor. The escort had taken the bag and left it near the closest desk. Trevor never took his eyes off Martin. Martin gestured for Trevor to meet him in the conference room. As they walked into the glass room, Martin began to speak the moment the door sealed.

"Trevor, thank you for coming. I can only imagine how confused you are right now, considering you know nothing of why you were transferred. Let me just say that this break that you had was our nation's way of saying thank you for your service."

Martin had a quality about him that Trevor noticed immediately. Car salesmen have the same quality when they speak to a hopeful client. Trevor sighed and interrupted.

"Mr. Porter, I appreciate what you are trying to do. I really do. Just do me a favor and spit it out. If whatever this is was important when you paged me, and it was important when I got on the plane, surely hours later it would be even more urgent. So please spare me the 'your nation loves you' speech and spit out what it is you need me to do."

Martin laughed with relief.

"Thank God we can just skip the bullshit. I don't really like that speech. See, here's the problem. An American passenger plane exploded over Omaha, Nebraska, a few hours ago. Usually we would assume that it was a malfunction since there were no demands or anything regarding terrorists. Well, some chemical specialists happen to have been out testing their bio-detection equipment when they caught a whole heap of readings coming from the smoke and fallout from the plane. See, the problem is, we don't know what the problem is. There is nothing on the black box to indicate any problem. The plane was fine and then, *boom*, fireball. We believe there is a possibility that a biological agent was on board and set to explode to deliver the agent in aerosol form. I need you to stand by and conduct some serious training until the time comes that we need you. Do you understand what I'm saying?"

Trevor frowned and nodded. Martin continued.

"I think our director should explain further. I was just supposed to break the ice. Let me get him. He should be finished with the intelligence briefing. Stand fast in here."

Martin jumped off the table where he was seated and left the room. Trevor had millions of sudden thoughts rush through his mind. Was he supposed to track the man responsible down and punish him? Was he supposed to collect samples and document its effect? Or was it the one thing he was praying against?

Suddenly, the closet door opened, and Martin and another man came to the room. Through the frosted windows Trevor could not identify the second man. As the door opened, he suddenly remembered who this man was. Michael Heimer, project manager for the weapon that made his life one long nightmare. Michael set a large stack of classified folders down on the table. Michael picked up a USB data stick and handed it to Porter.

"Good evening, Trevor, I trust you remember me. I know you have a lot of questions. Before I get to answering those, I need to know one thing."

Trevor leaned back in his seat, preparing for another sales speech. Michael continued.

"I need to know if you are willing to do something similar to the experience you had last time. The difference is, you will only be sent back to fix things, and this time it would be deliberate. Some are very easy missions, and others, well, others may not be so easy. It would be safe to say that nothing would compare to your last experience."

Trevor leaned forward and realized that this was no speech. Michael was a scientist, not a politician. No, of course, he would skip the speech. Trevor listened to Michael with a newfound respect, forgetting the resentment, for a moment that he had held when he first met the man.

"Nothing would ever be as difficult as what you had to go through before, I give you my word. Do you think that this is something you would be interested in?"

Michael fixed his eyes on Trevor's own. No indication either way was exchanged. Trevor, now uneasy, stood from his chair and paced back and forth in thought. Finally, he turned to Michael.

"You're telling me that you want me to ride your toy back and forth through time to fix things that some agency feels is in its best interest?"

Michael shook his head and replied, "No. What I'm saying is that when something terrible happens, such as a massive strike, we would send you back to ensure that the attack does not take place."

Trevor paces a bit more.

"Will I have enough support?"

Michael nodded with a deepened grin. With that, Trevor stopped pacing.

"I'll do it. I assume this is the whole point in transferring me. Besides, if the future is screwed up by changing the past, I'd rather do it myself than allow someone else to do so."

With a great smile, Michael pulled the white screen down and began the briefing.

"This is the mission."

Michael projected a slide onto the view screen. The slide was a picture of a man in a light jacket. The picture was taken with a telescopic lens; it must have been by one of the agencies.

"This man developed the strongest weapon I have ever seen. He called it 'Alphabet.' Apparently, we discovered through a background check that his uncle sexually abused him as a child. His father, whom he blames, shared the uncle's blood type. After murdering the uncle, he was sent to a home where he recessed his anger and seemingly placed his fury into his schoolwork. He became a well-educated pathologist and had developed some of the most brilliant antibodies and vaccines for some deadly viruses. He was employed by MedCorp and later was contracted, through his company, to develop bio-weapons for the government.

"After college he married a woman named Alexandra, who was brutally raped and murdered. That man, later convicted of murder, had the same blood type as his father and uncle, AB negative. He designed this agent to kill persons with that specific blood type. A psychological analysis discovered that he blames the blood for the evil in the world. This man is a nutcase.

"He delivered the agent in an explosive package on a plane. This flight exploded above Omaha, Nebraska. We believe it was deliberately detonated there as a central location. The agent has already caused about 1,224 deaths in the past few hours. The bio-weapon is still spreading.

CDC is feeding details to the office of Homeland Security, which we work for. So far all who were downwind of the blast have been infected, and the infected persons continue to spread the disease to all they come in contact with. Do you understand so far?"

Trevor looked at the images alternating on the screen of the plane exploding in midair and the bloodied faces of the dead. Trevor cringes at the faces and concentrates on the mission statement in front of him. As he reads it, he finally realizes the truth of the so-called mission.

"You want me to go into the past to make this not happen, right?"

Michael nodded.

Trevor asked, "You don't think I can do this on my own, do you? I'll need people with me to help search. What if I need support from the FBI or something? Why would they listen to me?"

Michael smiled and interrupted Trevor.

"You see, Trevor, about a month ago this agency was created to reverse acts like this. This microchip, which will be implanted into your hand, has an atomic clock in it. This clock would show whomever you come into contact with, who knows to look, the precise time that you follow. It is tamper proof because of a level of encryption that verifies your identity and protects the time and date.

"This chip has a menu option that will provide you with all of the information you require. Just apply pressure to the chip and it will move to the next feature. One hard press will shut the chip down to avoid being compromised. Let me show you. Hold out your hand."

Trevor hesitated for a moment before his curiosity got a hold of him. Trevor held out his hand as Michael brought a small machine out that looked like a gun. With solid pressure and a painful pinch, the chip was implanted. Trevor looked at his hand and rubbed the spot where the chip was placed between the thumb and forefinger on his palm.

"Now press the chip hard for three seconds. Good. Now press it once more. There, you see, that is the correct Zulu time and date right now. That will be consistent regardless of when you travel."

Trevor looked at his hand as a digital display of the time and date appeared, as if written in red ink, on the palm of his hand.

Michael continued.

"Now press it again to reveal the trusted list. This list is all of the people aware of the project who have the authority to do what you require them to do. The chiefs of staff and even the president are aware of the project and of who you are. This list is to guarantee you the ability to bypass all security inside the pentagon as well as the White House. The number for each person on that list is assigned to a pager. Now, this is very important, the pager as well as the number is encrypted. It is virtually impossible for anyone to acquire these numbers. When you dial the number, you must 'key' the pager by entering the five-digit access code, which will not be loaded into the chip. You must memorize this access code. In essence, it is your skeleton key designed to bypass all securities established within the most secret of areas; once verified, they will do as you say to prepare for the event you will be sent to avoid."

Trevor looked at the list of names as it scrolled across the palm of his hand. Sure enough, the president and his cabinet were on it, along with the Joint Chiefs of Staff, including the directors of all of the various agencies. Next to each name was the reserved pager number that all of the men carried in case of Trevor's arrival.

The authority that Trevor would have was overwhelming, but in Trevor's eyes it was a little nauseating.

Michael continued.

"If you'll go ahead and press one more time. Good, now you have a list of twelve addresses for safe houses. In these houses you will find weapons for you and your men, cash and untraceable cellular and satellite phones.

"Here is the one thing I need to show you. Listen carefully, because this is very important. Underneath the garage will be a vehicle similar to the one used to recover you and your men. There are a total of twelve of them all around the country. The only difference between those and the one before is that they aren't military vehicles. They are modified Chevy Tahoes. Each of them can take ten trips forward or back. Now, it is essential only to use these vehicles when you have no other choice and you are at your last resort. Do you understand?"

Trevor nodded and asked, "Sir, you said my 'team.' When will I be able to brief and train the new team?"

Michael smiled and opened the door to leave the conference room. In the back left corner where the door was, Trevor could hear the faint sound of laughter. As Michael opened the door, Trevor found himself inside a well-sized living area. Surrounding a card table were faces he definitely knew. All of the soldiers were playing cards, laughing and smoking. All of them stopped to look at Trevor, and one of them called to him.

"It's about fuckin' time you got here! The pencil neck over there is refusing to tell us shit till you got here. Hey, Doc! You mind fillin' us in now?"

This was the colorful voice of Trevor's close friend Jonathon Boiyd. Trevor turned to Michael and asked him about their briefing. Michael simply said, "They're your team. You brief them."

The door closed, leaving Trevor and the entire team who had followed him into the hell of 1969 in Vietnam. Staff Sergeant Boiyd, Staff Sergeant Baxley, Sergeant Segal, Corporal Wilson and Sergeant Trits all stood to welcome their leader. Moving to the couches, the team and their leader sat down for the briefing.

After an hour of discussion about the mission and the resources, the team all agreed to the assignment. All of the soldiers were around when the World Trade Center was attacked. All of them had seen the terrible and great events that followed. With this New Option they would be the last defense against terrorists and psychotics.

Michael returned to implant the team with a chip loaded with the time and date as well as frequencies to contact each other on. Tomorrow they would begin their training. Tomorrow they would become the elite that no one could question.

23 APRIL 2009
0500 HOURS

Trevor and his team arrive in a secluded training area used by the CIA not far from the cottage. On all four corners of the property housing the cottage and the training area were large beacons that looked like trees. The beacons acted as camouflage against satellites. When a passing satellite crossed over the beacons, a jamming signal made satellites show the area in a grey haze to prevent unauthorized agencies or countries the ability to observe training or spy.

This was the place where the NOs, as they now call themselves, would be trained for all thinkable circumstances. They would be trained in urban warfare, bomb disposal, underwater recovery, reconnaissance and airborne warfare. The training would take months to complete as they observed the events of the world around them.

So far, over 120,000 people were dead around the country. Cases of the disease were reported in China, India and Western Europe. Trevor forced himself to think of the situation as a plot from a movie. With the ability to go back and change everything, there was no point in worrying about the deaths or the sick. It was when Trevor thought of this that he realized he had finally become the detached, cold-hearted man like so many other soldiers before him.

Debating with himself, he decided to use his daily phone call to check on his wife and child. Picking up the phone, he dialed the access number and then dialed his home number. After seven rings, he hung up and decided to try again in a few hours.

So far, his team had begun training in urban warfare as well as hostile aircraft recovery. Their current class was in bomb disposal. The team studied the various types of fuses and triggers, binary devices as well as feints, nuclear, chemical and, naturally, biological. Sniper training would be next week, with intermittent simulations requiring close kills. Trevor leaned to the instructor, a Navy SEAL named Commander Reese, and informed him that they were more than proficient in close kills and sniper activities. Having read the file on Trevor and his team, he agreed with Trevor. The instructor then concentrated his efforts on new equipment, with Dr. Roberts conducting the brief. Commander Reese, the instructor, introduced Trevor and his team to Dr. Roberts.

Dr. Roberts, a skinny young man no older than twenty-eight, brought his equipment in on what looked like a Gurney in the center of the operations room. The team gathered closely around the doctor and looked closely at the equipment that he was to demonstrate. The new weapon that they would be using was a rifle with a retractable barrel. The idea was that close quarters combat required a compact weapon. Long-range sniper purposes require a longer barrel for improved ballistics. The barrel length at center setting was ideal for medium ranges between fifty to eight hundred meters. This rifle required a 7.62-caliber round and had a 20mm grenade launcher, which could be separated from the primary weapon and used independently for any reason. The optics were an improved scope that was equipped with alternate visual settings and thermal night vision, as well as standard scope displays. It was compact and could be linked up to an eyepiece for firing from corners or from the hip. A small camera attached to the scope transmitted visuals to the eyepiece so the user could see what the rifle saw. This mode was effective for urban combat. An infrared beam as well as a visible laser was zeroed to the barrel of the rifle so that it displayed a precise location of where the round would impact. The new and improved feature of this beam was that it took into consideration the trajectory in relation to distance of the round.

Dr. Roberts pulled out a small porcelain object. The object looked like a small cigar box. Dr. Roberts describes this item as a "messenger."

"This item is preprogrammed to transmit directly to its home base, here, delivering a message from one of you. If you require supplies or anything at all, you write it down, place it in here, and push these three buttons on the side here at the same time. Watch this."

Dr. Roberts pushed the three tiny buttons on the side as he stood back. The box formed a small cloud and vanished. As he walked to the corner of the room, there was a platform with the same box resting on it in a thick haze. Dr. Roberts opened the box to reveal a Polaroid photo taken earlier. Dr. Roberts continued.

"The receiver from the operations room locks onto the box's transceiver and ensures that it is released at the same location every time, regardless of time. Since I do not have an implant, I cannot show you another feature. Agent Sands, if you would."

Trevor took the box from the man and held it, waiting for instruction.

"Good. Now for us to send the box back to you, you press the single button on the bottom. The IR port underneath the box will scan your implant for the time and date of transmission. Our receiver will automatically adjust the send time for five seconds after you transmitted. If you will go ahead and try that."

Trevor pressed the button underneath the box and watched as it scanned his hand. Now, pressing the three buttons on the side, the box vanished from his hand and appeared at the receiver. Roberts walked over, removed the Polaroid from before, and placed a folded sheet of paper in the box. He then pressed a lighted button and said, "Transmit." Trevor looked around, waiting for the same spectacle, when he noticed he was already holding the box.

"Why is it here? I didn't see the cloud."

"Well, that's the tricky part of doing this in the present. It took more than five seconds for me to receive and retransmit the box. So, you already had the box five seconds after you sent it. Do you remember receiving it?"

Trevor looked down at the box and smiled in confusion. He did not remember the box appearing five seconds after he sent it.

"I don't understand. I don't remember this thing comin' back."

Quincy squinted as he tried to explain why Trevor could not remember the change that had just taken place. Michael walked into the room after overhearing last conversation. Michael began to clarify.

"Trevor, the implant that we have placed in your hand had some radiation that is designed to emit into your body. When you and your team were mistakenly sent to '69, we discovered that the personnel in the compound were immune to the changes that had taken place. When we discovered that the immunity came from the dark energy fields that radiated through the compound, we decided to include the same form of energy into your implants. This will allow you to watch any changes that you may make to the time line from an omniscient point of view. You must also understand there will be some things that you alone will know at the completion of the mission.

Those of us who are within the cottage here will know the changes, as well as your team, but no one else, including the trusted, will have a clue."

Trevor was now more confused than ever. Thinking back, he asked, "Is there anything that changed with me or my team when we were gone before that we don't know about?"

Michael studied Trevor very carefully and decided that he would tell him in private. Later in the afternoon, the cards would fall, and Trevor would likely have a migraine from confusion.

After show and tell, the men headed to their bunks as Trevor tried to call his wife for the second time that day. There were several rings and, again, no answer. As he hung up, he heard the other end answer. He could not stop the receiver from closing in time. Trevor called back immediately.

"Hello?" a woman said.

"Yeah, hi. This isn't Jessica. Where is she? Who are you? Are you with my daughter?" Trevor asked, desperately confused by another woman answering his phone.

"I'm sorry, who is this?"

"Lady, where is my wife and my daughter?"

There was a pause on the other end.

"This is Becka from across the street. I—I'm sorry, the child was taken to the hospital, and Jessica…sir, Jessica died this morning. She got the bug. I am so sorry; we called everyone in your book. I didn't know where to find you. I am so sorry, Trevor. I'm sorry—"

The voice drifted as the other line disconnected. Trevor shouted, "No wait! Where is my daughter? What hospital? Hello? Hello!"

Trevor slowly placed the phone down and took a step back. Walking back and forth next to the phone booth, a sudden burst of terror shot through his heart. He screamed and slammed his fists into the phone that had delivered the news. Collapsing into the booth, he curled into a ball and cried.

Segal was the first one to reach him. She asked him nothing. Kneeling beside her friend, she held him as the others crowded in silence. They knew what had happened. No one needed to speak.

23 APRIL 2009
1000 HOURS

Deep within the Pentagon, the newly developed sublevels were buzzing with the incoming arrivals of the new National Security Council. The changes that have been made to this council allow all major agencies to provide input as to the regulations and decisions made by the council. Since the creation of the New Option Agency, reforms have been made to concentrate on all possible contingencies of the newly developed resources.

Michael sat on the thirtieth sublevel beneath the Pentagon. In this room, Michael began to explain to the NSC what protocols had been developed to allow maximum security against New Option agents. Michael introduces the prototype of the verification kit that was keyed to Trevor's eyes and implant. Michael places a briefcase on the table next to the Air Force chief of staff. As he prepares for the introduction to the new policies, he studied the face of each man in the room.

Around the table, behind their assigned nameplate, were the members of the new NSC. The appointed head of NSC was the chairman of the Joint Chiefs of Staff, General Maxwell. The chiefs of staff from all four branches of the Armed Forces sit closest to him on either end of the table. The directors of the NSA, CIA, FBI, DIA and Secret Service are alternated on either side of the table. Filling the rest of the seats were the representatives from the president's cabinet, the secretary of state, secretary of defense as well as the national security advisor. As Michael studied each man, he was convinced that these men would comply with the New Option protocols.

Standing from his seat at the foot of the table marked New Option, Michael began his brief.

"Gentleman of the council I am honored to begin the first meeting of the newly developed NSC. I believe our first order of business was to establish security protocols to prevent tampering or imposters. As you all know, the New Option Agency was established to prevent major events against the United States as well as any other nation that was within the interests of national security. In front of you are packets of our newly appointed agents. The special agent in charge of operations is a name you all know well from events that took place last year. I have appointed Trevor Sands as SAIC. He is more than competent and capable of making the decisions that I would expect all of us to lack desire for. He will be trained by new methods to accurately predict any future complications that certain changes may cause by his decisions. His mission is always going to be the big picture.

"The security protocols I recommend involve a designated military person to carry a briefcase containing one of two verification kits. These kits would tie into a large digital clock that we have just installed at the rear of the room. This clock would display the remaining time that Trevor had to adjust the events that he is on mission to prevent. The time the event is scheduled to take place, after his deployment, would be called zero hour.

What Agent Sands would do is perform the necessary verification process to prove his identity as SAIC. Once verified, he would have complete control over all of you. I understand that this is an extreme amount of power for one man, but I must assure you that he will be the only person in the time line of his deployment who has accurate information. I require that all of us follow his instructions to the letter to prevent the mishap he would be deployed to alleviate.

"I trust every man in this room and in this council will trust his decisions. I recommend also that we conduct simulations and training to further learn the capabilities of Agent Sands as well as his team. Right now I would like to go into more detail as to the verification process."

Michael opens the briefcase and turned it around so all members could see. Michael erects a chin rest and lifts the back end of the case to allow the counsel to see the contents within it.

"The first protocol is to verify the ID card that he had been issued, along with a pin number. The scanner will ensure that the smart chip and pin number are accurate. The second protocol is a retinal scan. This kit is already programmed for his optical resonance, so it should work just fine. The third and last protocol is the implant scan. The scan will check the encryption and the intelligence data on the implant. The time, which will remain constant with Trevor, will adjust the zero-hour clock on the back wall. Gentleman, if for any reason any of these protocols fail, the imposter must be eliminated immediately. The level of authority that Agent Sands will hold on deployment is such that we must protect it at all costs."

The staff around the table nod in agreement at Michael's recommendations.

"Today is the first day of the agency's training. Tomorrow we will begin concentrating on the field training. I will send these men two days back three days from now to have them complete a routine sniper mission on our training grounds. I must admit that I am new to the military side of this. Our training officer is a well-known special operative, Commander Reese. Reese is training these men in all aspects of warfare, to include airborne training, aircraft takeover, sniper operations and bomb disposal, as well as foreign weapons training to name a few.

I would like, with the counsel's permission, to send Trevor back two days from now, to tomorrow."

The looks of the council were mixed. Some were straining to comprehend the new line of thinking, while others are thinking ahead, trying to theorize possible complications.

"When Agent Sands arrives, I recommend that he meets with you in the predetermined fashion, as if this were an actual deployment. I think he should be verified with the real threat of failure. Because we have not fully tested the equipment, I think it would be better off that the weapon not be loaded when it is pointed at Trevor's head."

The men around the table laugh at the remark. The chairman of the NSC looked around the table at the faces of the men in their seats. After a thorough evaluation of the men around him, he stood and looked at Michael.

"I think I speak for everyone here when I say that you have done a hell of a job getting this new agency underway. Your selection of staff and agents does you justice. As for the protocols, for a man who hasn't been around as long as we have, I am impressed of the many aspects of security that you have kept in mind. I agree that training and simulations need to be done to ensure that Agent Sands, as well as his team, are accustomed to the deployment process. I also believe that it would do every man in this room a great deal of service if we train with him. Power and responsibility is a dangerous thing to appoint to one man. Through his psychological testing that we had him go through when he returned last year, we learned that he is the type of man who will not allow much to go to his head. He proved himself as a soldier, an operative, and as a diplomat. He would be my first choice for this assignment as well.

Let us schedule his simulation and testing tomorrow in the afternoon. I would prefer if we treated this as we would a real mission. The rest of the chiefs of staff and I will be inside this building. For the rest of you, I recommend you go about your daily business until we page you for the New Option mission. We will prepare a mission for Agent Sands to brief us on. I'm thinking this is going to be interesting; Trevor is going to find out about this mission two days from now and deploy to us tomorrow. Kind of makes your head hurt.

"Michael, again, thank you for your work and for your brief. You have done well, and we all expect great things from your agents. Are there any other items of business that any of you would like to discuss?"

The secretary of state, Honorable Durst, stood from the table and looked at each man in turn. As General Maxwell took his seat, Durst began discussing his concern.

"Men, the president had a great deal of concern about the latest attack. He had expressed his desire to send Agent Sands and his team to prevent the attack. He does understand that there is training that remains. He would like to know exactly when these agents would be ready for deployment. There are many lives that have been lost, and many more that will be if we wait any longer. Michael, when do you feel Agent Sands will be prepared to deploy?"

Michael looked at the secretary and shook his head.

"Secretary Durst, you must understand that whenever we decide to deploy our team, the end result will be the lack of any of you knowing that it had happened at all. My major concern is all of the aspects of certain changes that may cause damage to the future. When I feel Trevor has been fully trained to think and act according to the long-term consequences, I will deploy him. I feel that if he were to simply kill the man and destroy any remaining bio-agents, the long-term aspects would be ignored. Each mission needs to have plenty of study as well as training to ensure its complete success. I would sure hate to ignore the ally to Ben Phelps that we did not think of and have the man strike harder after Ben's assassination. Granted, regardless of what strikes occur after the initial, we will be able to prevent by following deployments.

I recommend you tell the president, no matter when we deploy, that when the mission is successful he will never know it ever happened. All of the lives lost will return to life with no knowledge of disease. Time is something we own, regardless of how many lives are lost by the day. Everything we know will change when Trevor succeeds."

The council members looked at Michael. Michael could see the lack of ability to stop their minds from changing and becoming completely naive to the changes that would be made, even though they would do some of the work to prevent the event themselves. One member, Admiral Jackson, chief of staff for the Navy, had a confusing smile and looked back at the chairman. Admiral Jackson stood from his seat and looked the men in the eye.

"Well, it seems to me that regardless of what we do, we will still have no clue as to the changes. There is something I would like to recommend, primarily to see if it would work. With your permission, General."

General Maxwell courteously nodded his head.

"I would like to change the scheduled meeting with Trevor to occur in fifteen minutes. In my line of thinking, we would provide the work for his arrival once we finished the meeting. Trevor should arrive as ordered. The flip side to this, and I hope I don't confuse anyone, is what if we don't arrange the meeting once he arrives. Would we simply forget he arrived at all? We would have to go through with the planning for his arrival regardless of whether he shows or not. Can we try this and see what happens?"

The counsel looked around, murmuring indistinctly.

One man looked at Michael and asked, "Michael, you and I have never really spoken; my name is John Webb, head of NSA. I think you are the only person who knows the answer to the question that Admiral Jackson has asked. Would you mind shedding some light on this?"

Michael smiled, remembering his own theories and plans from the year before.

"Well, what I do know is what I learned through last year's recovery project. We had the same question that the admiral has. What we planned to do was continue as planned when we received word that Trevor had returned. He had returned months before we had actually set up the vehicle to recover him. Had we never designed the vehicle, he would never have made it home. By seeing that he had arrived, it showed us only that we would succeed eventually. That is the only account I know of, and it seemed to work for us. I don't feel as if I have to remind any of you that this is a new field of study. There are no answers to everything. All we can do is learn from experience and do our best to project all aspects."

General Maxwell nodded in agreement.

"I agree with Michael here. I believe that we should all gain some experience in this. Let us schedule Trevor's arrival with a brief of a simulated mission to deliver to us, let's say, ten minutes from now. I assume that we will be able to come up with a plan and be able to execute it. Let us see what happens."

The council sat at the table in silence as they waited for the ten minutes to elapse. The men were anxious and nervous with high levels of curiosity that were overwhelming. Michael frowned as he theorized possible complications. He can think of none.

Michael handed the verification kit to General Maxwell. The general handed it to a colonel, who was standing by in the corner. Maxwell whispered into the man's ear. The man walked back to the corner, pulled a set of handcuffs out of his belt, and unloaded the rounds in his sidearm. The colonel secured the briefcase to his wrist with the handcuffs and stood by until he would be needed.

After several long moments, the Air Force chief of staff stood and smiled while looking at his watch.

"Gentleman, we should expect a page in 5, 4, 3, 2..."

General Maxwell stood from his chair and pulled a pager from behind his back. With a wide grin and a deep sigh, he looked at the men at the table. All of them were laughing under their breath. As General Maxwell finally realized that Trevor needed to get past the security, he looked at a three-star general and sent him to pick the agent up at the gate.

23 APRIL 2009
1100 HOURS

Sitting at the main gate of the Pentagon, inside of the delivery vehicle, Trevor dialed the number for the Army chief of staff's pager from his cell phone. Trevor climbed out of the Tahoe and walked to the guard with his weapon slung behind him. The guard approaches Trevor with his weapon raised, ordering Trevor to place his weapon on the ground. Trevor placed the weapon on the ground and stepped back several paces. The guard moved to pick up the sophisticated rifle while Trevor followed him to the guard shack.

Within five minutes an armored Chevy Niagara, a new military vehicle contracted from the manufacturer, pulled up to the gate with three men inside. One spoke to the guard and closed the window. The guard turned to Trevor and handed his weapon back to him. With the gate now opened, Trevor returned to his Tahoe and followed the Jeep to the reserved parking area.

The vehicle parked in a reserved space marked "NOA SAIC." The men got out of the vehicle and walked to the main entrance, where they waved Trevor through security. Trevor, with weapon in hand, was amazed that no guard was stopping him. They only looked confused. Trevor walked to the elevator as one of the generals placed a key into the elevator call panel and pushed the down button. A moment later Trevor and the three generals headed down to the thirtieth sublevel, where the security operations room was located.

As the elevator door opened, Trevor found himself in a large room with a rectangular table in the center. Surrounding the walls of the large room were several computer consoles that were staffed with about thirty people. Trevor walked to the conference table as the counsel members stood from their seats to introduce themselves. As Trevor met each man around the table, he looked at Michael, who was among them. Trevor took the only seat unoccupied.

The Army chief of staff smiled with a wide grin at Trevor. Every man at the table knows of Trevor's experience and accomplishments from 1969. They are well aware of his capabilities, even if Trevor wasn't.

General Maxwell stood to begin the simulation.

"Agent Sands, if you would be so kind as to be verified, we will see if that works."

The men around the table laughed, as if all equipment from the government labs were useless. General Maxwell waved a man over to Trevor. The man, a colonel, was standing in a corner with a briefcase handcuffed to his wrist. As the colonel placed the briefcase in front of Trevor, he removed the cuff from his wrist and placed the muzzle of a pistol against Trevor's head. Trevor realized, with a shock, what would happen if the identity test failed.

Shaking the morbid and frightened feeling from his hands, Trevor cracked his knuckles, ready to test the equipment. With the case open, Trevor could see it was the same verification kit that he had practiced with. Trevor placed his ID card in the slot and keyed in his pin number. He then rested his head on the brace, looking at the bright red dot of the laser scanner; a computer generated female voice from the intercom above the table stated, "Thank you for your patience. Please place your hand in the implant verification glove."

Trevor obeyed the omnipotent voice and placed his hand in the glove. After a warm sensation on his hand, the voice stated, "Thank you for your patience. Please stand by for download."

Trevor kept his hand in the glove and waited. Finally, the voice said, "Identity confirmed, Agent Sands. Report downloaded and ready for viewing."

General Maxwell nodded at the colonel, who holstered the weapon and closed the case, cuffing it back to his wrist. Once the colonel was back in his corner, General Maxwell said with a hint of condescension, "You know, we wouldn't have shot you this time. That is what we dictated as the best route to eliminate any chance of imposters. We are excited to see how this comes out. Let us begin, shall we? Give us your report."

Trevor looked at a large digital clock above the back wall. It was counting backward from the time of verification to zero hour of the simulated emergency. Total time remaining was twenty-seven hours and six minutes.

Trevor placed his recorder on the table and pressed record, then he began the simulation first by briefing the staff of the agency's mission.

"Gentleman, the agency I work for is called New Option. It was designed to send a few people to a time line prior to a catastrophic event to prevent the act from taking place. We are in the training phase of the agency's development. Any current problems that exist will be taken care of once training is complete, assuming such action is ordered by presidential authority. This phase of training is purely for simulation purposes.

"To begin the simulation I will conduct a briefing of an emergency that took place in a little over twenty-seven hours, as indicated by the zero-hour clock behind you. When that clock reaches zero, the event will have happened without our intervention.

"By the National Security Act regarding New Option, I am authorized to command this staff as well as the presidency until Zero hour. Due to my lack of experience politically, I will rely on you and your men as well as the cabinet and various agency directors to handle political consequences until my experience is up to par. My responsibility is purely to prevent the action of terrorists or others parties with vengeful, political, religious or any other motive to make an attack that endangers the people of this country.

"With that said, let us begin with the assigned simulation. By my time, I was deployed a little over one hour ago to prevent an action taken by this man."

The face of a middle-eastern man was projected on the screen from the presentation specialist. The staff looked at the man as if trying to place the name.

"This man is responsible for delivering a nuclear warhead over South Dakota. On detonation, twenty-seven hours from now, four thousand people will be killed. The fallout will kill another fifteen thousand within two months. The striking point was the tactical command bunker located behind Mt. Rushmore. With its own nuclear reactor for self-sustaining energy, the fallout was more than the initial radiation released from the device. A training simulation was in progress upon detonation. Four chiefs of staff as well as the national security advisor was killed instantly. Gentleman, we have twenty-six hours and fifty-eight minutes to prevent this act from happening.

"The intelligence we have gathered so far shows that this man is Mustafa

Kamal Suleman. He is a Kurdish refuge who has been living in the mountains of eastern Turkey. He had ties to Kurdish resistance movements, as well as the remainder of Al Qaeda terrorists who have been in hiding. We believe that it was this man, through his connections, who received the device. Through an insider in the U.S. he managed to get the device through customs. We are unsure as to the delivery means as well as insider contact. We do know that his second cousin is residing in Round Rock, Texas. This is all the intelligence we have so far. Gentleman, where do you wish to begin?"

The chairman turned from the picture and asked, "The question is, Agent Sands, where do you wish to begin?"

Trevor looked at the man on the screen and back to the general.

"Sir, I believe that the detonation at Mt. Rushmore was deliberate. We should have helicopters equipped with radiation sensors hovering over the effected area starting now."

As Trevor makes suggestions, staff generals were making the necessary calls to make his recommendations happen.

"Second, I suggest we have the cousin followed by CIA and FBI task forces and tracked to Suleman. Once we find the cousins together, we draw them into a secluded place and hit them both. If the cousin is the only tie to the U.S., we shouldn't have anyone left to follow through after them. Once they are down we should be able to find the device. Either it is on the man or in the house or motel where Suleman is staying. It is not something he will leave sitting around for anyone to pick up. No one can know of the two deaths. The bodies should be covered up and kept away from public eye to avoid anyone avenging them or carrying on with the original plan of attack."

The staff looked around the table, nodding their heads in agreement.

The chairman asked, "Who do you want to handle the hit?"

Trevor answered, "Sir, I need my men or myself to do the hit. I cannot afford any conspiracy theories running around. Besides, we need to be the ones to handle any actual changes so that we are accountable for time line disruptions. Since my men and I are equipped with the implant that radiates some of the same energy required in deployment into our bodies, we are immune to changes and effects. We are aware of all changes when you and your men are not. I will be able to see a newspaper change titles and witness rosters or reports change as a result to the alterations that we make. This is why any direct action must be taken by ourselves, so we can ensure that the event has truly been altered. Let me give you an example of how this may be done."

From his pack, Trevor pulled out the porcelain box. Opening the box, he placed a note inside requesting the front page of today's newspaper. Programming the box for his time and date, Trevor explained his actions to the staff.

"I am writing a note for my men to send me the front page of today's paper. When he receives this note, regardless of how long it takes him, the box will be sent back to me exactly five seconds from transmission."

Trevor activated transmission and exactly five seconds later the box returned on the table in front of him. The staff looked at the box in excitement and wonder. Trevor opened the box to reveal the contents. The front page of the newspaper was folded and placed inside. Trevor unfolded the paper and passed it to the closest general.

"As you can see, I will be able to send requests and receive intelligence and changes. I will be able to monitor these changes and find the most effective way to make sure our actions remain covert."

General Maxwell looked at the paper that was being handed to him with the headline, "Will the Government Do Anything?"

The headline referred to the countless dead from the most recent attack. Looking up from the paper, he asked, "Do you think your team will be able to stop this?"

Trevor replied after a short moment, "I truly hope so, sir. Once we can be sure of our actions we will request to make the change."

"I think you'll do just fine, son. I look forward to seeing you in here again."

"Well, if there is no more input for the simulation, I'll return to the cottage for analysis of our work here. I, too, look forward to working with you men in the future."

Trevor turned to the Air Force's chief of staff and shook his hand. The chief of staff winked at Trevor as if he knew something he didn't. The other generals laughed under their breath and walked to Trevor to shake his hand. Trevor was escorted back out of the building by the same three-star general to the waiting Tahoe for his return home.

23 APRIL 2009
1900 HOURS

Michael had arrived at the cottage and walked into the briefing room inside the basement. The team was at the conference table with Trevor, discussing something that could not be heard through the frosted walls of the conference room. Michael stood outside the conference room and watched the team discuss. Thinking of the paradoxes that he was now in, he laughed at the knowledge that Trevor had no idea that he had briefed the National Security Counsel that morning. He would find out about the brief tomorrow and would be deployed in the afternoon.

The counsel had decided to practice with a real problem to train the rest of the team. The mission would be a bank robbery that had taken place in Fairfax, Virginia. The deployment was scheduled to take place in three days.

Michael folded his coat over his arm and proceeded to the conference room to inform Trevor that he would deploy tomorrow for a meeting. As he entered the room, the agents stopped speaking and looked blankly at Michael. Michael smiled gently and looked at Trevor in an inquisitive way. Trevor blushed at the surprise visit from Michael.

"My team was discussing what you had mentioned before. We would like to know what changes were made that we are unaware of. Would you mind filling us in?"

Michael studied the faces of the team and faced Trevor.

"This is something I would rather run by you in person. I'll let you decide if your team should know."

Trevor looked back at the team and gestured for them to leave. As the team stood from their seats, they walk out the door, looking at Michael contemptuously. Michael took a seat across from Trevor and pulled out a legal pad to help explain the change. Trevor leaned forward, fully attentive.

"Trevor, you are now immune to the psychological effects of changes made in the time line. You didn't used to be. When you were in Vietnam there was a massive change that may be difficult for you to understand. This change will completely go against every memory you have of your team. Are you sure you want to know?"

Trevor sighed, as he expected terrible news. After a moment of thought, he nodded.

"Okay, here we go. Let me begin by explaining the way things were. There was a continuous fight in Congress about women in the combat arms positions. One man maintained the view that women should not be allowed. His name was Senator Malloy. Senator Malloy is a Vietnam veteran who served as a Ranger. When your team arrived in 1969, you had a slightly different team than you remember. Your team members were, Boiyd, Baxley, Wilson, Himelrick, Trits and *Malloy*."

Trevor shook his head with confusion.

"Pfc. Malloy was the son of Senator Malloy. During your last battle, when you were clearing the area for survivors, a hiding survivor stabbed a man named Sergeant Malloy to death. When that happened, Pfc. Malloy vanished. Segal took his place in the team. Segal was allowed in the combat arms position because Senator Malloy was never around after 1969 to prevent females the ability to join those positions. Do you understand? Segal had only been with your team for the last week of your visit to '69. You will remember the day she came to your squad, all the training, everything. She was never there in the initial time line. Is this something that your team should hear?"

Trevor had his head rested on the table as if it would ease the headache he had. His memories included Segal involved with the team since her arrival almost four years ago. He remembered training her and assigning her as assistant gunner for Baxley. Now it seems that she was never there. How would his team handle that? Would they treat her like an outsider when they understood that she was never really there? But in their minds she was; she was always there. How would his team handle this? Should they know the truth about the team?

Trevor stood from the table and walked across the room. Looking through the clear layer of the walls, he could see the team watching his reactions to the news that Michael had just given him. Trevor realized that he could not have the team know the truth in any way. They are in all aspects a team, a family. No, the team could not know the truth. Trevor turned from the window and faced Michael.

"Well, I'm sorry; this is a lot to take. Knowing that one of died and we never knew it. Uh, no, the team can't know. It could ruin what they have."

Trevor took his seat and continued.

"I appreciate you pulling me aside. There is no way they can know. Not yet, anyway. Man, wow. Well, shit, I should probably tell them what I decided. They look edgy in there. Thank you, Michael."

Michael looked at Trevor and smiled. Trevor was truly a man who could put his emotions aside and determine the ethical decision. It may take longer than it should, but the result was always the ethical one. Michael suddenly felt a great comfort in knowing this.

Trevor walked to the door and opened it. As the team entered the room and took their seats around the table, Trevor stood to provide an authoritative standpoint.

"Well, since you all watched my reaction, you know the change wasn't a good one. It does involve a team member here. Because I don't want to see anything change again with the bond you have with each other, I think it would be best for you not to know. Not yet. I know that the curiosity will drive you nuts, but this is something I have to stick with until such time that you develop a bond from new experiences instead of the old ones."

Baxley shook his head and looked at his team. Boiyd, Wilson, Trits and Segal looked at each other and silently decided that they would agree with their leader.

Michael stood and put his hand on Trevor's shoulder, both for support and for a signal to let him speak. Trevor took his seat and listened to what Michael had to say.

"Agents, I commend your maturity on this. Just know that you will know the truth in time. Right now is not the time to risk anything that could damage the morale of this group or this agency. Let us take our minds off this and talk about tomorrow's training.

Tomorrow, Trevor, you will be deployed for a simulated briefing with the NSC. When you get there you will have to go through a verification process. I will let you practice with the kit to get familiar with the protocols. The rest of you will practice with urban warfare. I know you all are efficient with this, but with the test deployment you will have live rounds flying at you.

In two days I will deploy you to prevent a bank robbery that actually happened today. Apparently, four masked men got lucky and got away with over two hundred and fifty thousand dollars in cash. This is not the type of mission that your deployments will entail, but we feel that tactical units, if notified sooner, would handle the matter the same way. Therefore, your mission is to eliminate the threat. If you feel at the time that you can do so with non-lethal means, go ahead and do so. Lethal force is authorized. Trevor, it will be your decision. Here are the times and locations, videotapes and recordings. This should help you plan your attack. I'll get out of here to let you begin your planning."

As Michael stood to leave the room, Trevor followed and stopped him from leaving.

"You know, I think it would be best if you stayed and sat in on some of our planning sessions. We got thrown into your world, so why don't you try ours on for a change? You might like it."

Michael laughed loudly and turned to face the team. As he looked back to Trevor, he smiled and accepted the invitation.

Trevor handed Wilson the stack of photos as well as the video of the surveillance cameras. Trevor stood beside the large view screen where the video and scanner would feed. Trevor had Wilson load the pictures of each of the robbers into the scanner, and instantly the covered faces of the felons were on the wall.

With a laser-pointing device in his hand, Trevor began his initial plan. In the military, this would be called "war games." War games are designed to let the leaders attempt to guess all aspects of the mission that may develop during the execution. This was where guesswork and experience combine to provide a relatively accurate picture of how the mission would result.

Trevor had the men memorize the faces and clothing of each robber. After a few moments of careful study of the targets, Trevor had the video fed to watch patterns of movement and order of events. The video was divided into four angles. Trevor concentrated on one angle at a time.

The four men walked into the bank, faces covered with the stereotypical ski mask, and separated to each end of the lobby. By the way the men moved and covered angles, it appeared that they had combat training. The first man to enter moved straight to the cashier's window and waited until his men called the clear. The second man moved to the right wall and immediately shot the guard. The third man moved to the left wall and secured his zone. The last man to enter stayed at the door to ensure no one left. In seconds, the guard was killed, occupants were on the ground, and the cashier received demands. Their timing was perfect and effective. Within three minutes the robbers had the money and cleared the bank. The police were not notified by the usual alarm activated by the cashier. These men had jammed the signal from the silent alarm to provide them with more time. They didn't wait until they had more money, they simply waited until they had enough to make it worth the job and left.

Trevor looked at the other angles and watched them all over again a second time. Once he was satisfied he began his planning.

"Let's start off with this. We could arrive twenty minutes beforehand and set up positions on the opposite building. When they leave the vehicle to enter, we can disable the vehicle by either explosive means or by taking out the tires or the engine block. When they come out we can use tranquilizers to disable the men until police arrive. The problem with this was that the guard will still be killed. So what we need to decide is to eliminate either the escape or the robbery. We have to maintain a low profile, so that means we cannot be inside the building. So the question is, how do we stop this from happening before they get to the door?"

The team looked at each other when Boiyd stood to look closer at the screen. He looked back at Trevor and asked.

"What if we were to place stun grenades and sleep agents next to the door? We could wire the grenades with remote triggers that could knock them out prior to entering. All we have to do is take out two. It looks like they planned too friggin' carefully to continue while half their cover fire is knocked out. They couldn't do the job with only two people with no notice.

"Once two men or more are knocked out, they should get scared and leave. All we have to do is make the grenades look like they carried it with them. If people believe that they brought it with them and it accidentally detonated, we would maintain a low profile and still have the mission successful. We could easily throw in another grenade into the vehicle when the men are out of it. If they leave one man behind for getaway, he would be too preoccupied to notice a small package attached to the roof. We could be disguised as bums and do the job that way. No one looks at bums as a threat, so we would be fine."

Trevor smiled as the rest of the team nodded in agreement. Baxley gave his thoughts.

"Hey, Trev, why don't we just have each angle of approach covered? Once the men are spotted, we could simply snipe them with either tranq's or live rounds. Real quick, how thick are the walls to the bank? Eight inches? Twelve?"

Trevor studied the doorway and guessed.

"I'd say maybe ten inches. Why do you ask?"

Baxley continued, "Well, we could load our weapons with explosive-tipped rounds to penetrate the wall and simply kill the men from outside. We just have to dress like a tactical unit. We could arrange that with Director Allen. We could fake voice recordings stating plans to assault the bank. We could then prepare ahead of time, preventing anyone from thinking anything of it. From outside we could arrange to have the cross buildings' occupants clear the way for sniper positions from their first-floor window. We just kill the second man first and then take care of the rest. What do ya think?"

Trevor looked around the table. The coordination would be perfect, since it would allow Trevor to work with a director to coordinate an assault. This would be a good way to train. The main question remained whether they should handle the assault by lethal means. If so, then they could easily do Baxley's plan. If not, there was no easy way.

Trevor decided to go with Baxley's plan and begin the preparations.

Michael sat back and watched as the team came together to develop a plan. This was the perfect group of people for an agency like this. They are diverse in thought and mix well in tactics.

The team began their planning by finding building layouts for all surrounding buildings that would have a line of site with the bank. They found the building as Baxley had said, directly across the street from the bank. From there they would have line of site to eliminate all men before they got through the door. The few seconds when the four men were bottlenecked in the doorway should provide the team with the most efficient opportunity.

The team finalizes the plan in only an hour; Michael decided to treat the men with a home-cooked meal. Michael went upstairs to arrange the late meal with the couple in the cottage.

Marla and Walt were more than happy to treat the men to dinner. They then began to prepare the epitome of home cooking: chicken and dumplings with corn on the cob and string beans.

Trevor and the NOs changed into casual clothing and headed up the elevator. Each of the team members brought a gift with them to show their gratitude. As they met the couple in the living room, Walt took Trevor aside to get advice as to what kind of scope to buy for his hunting rifle. Marla talked to the younger team members and showed motherly concern for their mysterious jobs.

Sitting around the table, the team seemed more and more like a family. Michael sat at the foot of the table and watched the team as they jested with each other and kindly thanked the couple for the delicious meal. Michael sat back and began to wonder what his life would be like if he had settled down and had kids. As Michael smiled at the thought, he looked to Trevor. In no other agency was there the camaraderie between all agents as there was here.

Michael pulled out his phone and made three calls. He decided to have the rest of the agency join in for the morale boost, hoping Richard, who hadn't come to work in the cottage yet, Commander Reese and Quincy Roberts would agree to join them for dinner. Michael hung up the phone, sat back and noticed Trevor watching him. Michael spoke over the noise.

"I hope you won't mind, but I invited Richard, Reese and Quincy to join us. It would be nice to have a casual get-together with all of our team here. You don't mind, do you?"

Trevor smiled and shook his head. The two men looked around the table and reached the common mindset that Michael was on. The team would survive any mission; they would fight to the end for each other. These soldiers were the prime example of what soldiers should be for the American military.

Twenty minutes later, Quincy and Richard knocked on the door to the cottage. Michael brought the men into the dining room and introduced Richard to the team and to the couple.

"Everybody, I would like to introduce someone who was essential to your recovery from '69. This is Richard Myers. He is my deputy director as was my assistant at The Ranch. Quincy, why don't you sit next to Marla there in that empty seat. Richard, there is a seat next to Trevor. There is plenty of food, so help yourselves."

Richard and Quincy shook hands with the hosts of the dinner and took their seats. Richard smiled at Trevor, knowing the name and a photograph. He had never met the man he had worked so hard to recover. Richard looked around the table and placed the name with each face. With a shocking look at Segal, she had caught him staring.

"Mr. Myers, did you want to ask something?"

Richard realized he was staring, and blushed as he shook his head and looked away to the plate being passed to him. Richard had forgotten that

Malloy was not to be expected with the group. Remembering the replacement of the boy with Segal, he had not prepared himself to meet the paradox in person.

Reese was not able to make the dinner, which was just as well, since he was the one man that the team already knew quiet well through the training sessions.

After dinner the group moved to the living room to discuss each person's childhood, which was the best way to get to know each other. They shared stories of how their fathers or mothers would be overprotective, and made fun of the irony of how such precautions taken by their parents led them to choose a job of much danger.

After an hour of casual discussion, Marla hinted at the late hour and that she felt tired. Trevor looked at his watch and realized that it was almost eleven. The team thanked the couple for the meal and for the chance to relax. As everyone shook Walt and Marla's hand, they filed to the elevator to head downstairs.

The NOs prepare their equipment for the next day and headed off to their bedrooms attached to the living area. Each room was spacious and provided with cable television and a recorded phone line. The rooms each had an oak desk with a dresser and a well-chosen bed for each person. Trevor changed his clothes and moved out of the living area to the conference room to view the robbery files again.

Michael and Richard were talking in the room when Trevor walked in.

"I'm sorry, guys; I didn't know you were in here. Would you like me to come back later?"

Michael smiled and said, "Not at all. We were actually talking about you. Feel free to join us. I was telling Richard about your mission day after tomorrow. He was a little confused as to what your plan right now entails. I'm sure you can explain it better than I."

"Sure thing. Richard, I didn't get a chance to properly introduce myself and thank you for your work in getting us home. We really appreciated your efforts. I look forward to working with you now. Let me begin by showing you the video feed of the robbery."

Trevor placed the video into the player and turned on the large view screen. The screen split into the four feeds from the original recordings. Trevor activated one view and made it enlarge to fill the screen. Richard frowned as he watched the four men enter the room, shoot the guard and leave the bank with the money.

"Our plan is this. Across the street from the bank, a building has windows facing the front of the bank. We will be able to enter that building early and take the men out as they try to enter the bank. My concern is, again, long term. I was having a thought over dinner that I would like to talk to you about. What if we were to make a plan now to put in action on a daily basis from now on? The plan I'm talking about is a database of all recorded felons and their offspring. If we were to track the progress of the offspring and could send the updated database back to yesterday's date, in theory, an updated database would be on file even now. With this database we could determine if any of our targets would have children or descendants, which could provide a good service worth keeping in the future. That should provide us with better decision-making abilities as to whether to kill the man or use non-lethal means. Am I making any sense?"

Michael looked over to Richard and replied.

"I think so. What you want is a massive intelligence database that will be updated and sent back to be loaded on the console on a daily basis. Is that right?"

"Yes, sir, that's what I mean."

"Well, you realize that we can't update the files to one specific day and expect it to work, unless we specify an exact time to the millisecond. That might be able to be done, but I don't know if it would work. There could be thousands of updates coming into a previous time line at once. That could be dangerous. Unless we were to design a plan that would allow only one update to go back on different days. For example, we make a firm plan to design a computer that can handle the storage. Ten years from now we plan to send the first complete database to this Friday's date. Every Friday from then on they can send an update exactly ten years to the day back. This would provide us with a ten-year outlook, unless you would like more."

Richard thought for a moment and delivered his opinion.

"Let me see if I can explain my thoughts simply. Let's call what we consider the present, the 'present.' Let's call ten years from now the 'outlook.' If the outlook receives updates ten years ahead and update their database, when they send the update to our present we could easily have access a hundred years in the future. If our outlook keeps receiving updates from their outlook, we would have more than just a ten-year database. What I recommend is that every month we receive a genealogical database from our outlook on a drive that can be installed when we have the need. Theoretically, we will continue to receive separate drives with updates forever. Anyway, I like the idea of being able to project the consequence of someone's death, but I think it would require more resources than we have available."

Michael scratched his head as if it would help make a confusing theory make sense.

"I would like to discuss this more tomorrow, but my thoughts right now lead me to believe that there is no such thing as a shortage of resources if we develop a room that can receive packages from the future. If our project is proven a priority agency, then future budgets and equipment can be sent here to allow for a head start on development. I'm sorry, Trevor, but you have a tendency to give me headaches. I want to discuss this in the morning. If you will excuse me, I'm going to bed."

Michael left the room. Richard and Trevor agreed that the idea required more thought and planning than they were capable of. Both men decided to retire for the day and attempt to solve the problem tomorrow.

Trevor went into his room, where he sat on the bed and rested his head in his hands. With a deep sigh he pulled out a picture of his wife holding his daughter on their trip to Utah. Trevor held the picture to his chest and cried himself to sleep.

24 APRIL 2009
0900 HOURS

All of the agents were sitting at the table for breakfast. It was Wilson's turn to cook, and he decided on cold cereal and coffee. He received no complaints, since they were still satisfied with the meal from the night before. The agents simply ate and sipped the stiff coffee.

Michael came out of his room, dressed in the typical suit he preferred to wear. Standing in front of the table, he began the daily brief.

"Today we begin the drills for the plan you generated yesterday. Trevor, you will have to give the NSC a simulated brief of the events covered in this file."

Michael handed Trevor a file filled with photos and statistics of a simulated nuclear detonation at Mt. Rushmore. Trevor began reading the file as Michael continued.

"Implant loading will be at 1300 to give you the intelligence for the brief. I need you to practice with the verification kit as well; we are going to run that drill during the simulation with them. Here is the exact time you need to page the chairman."

Michael handed Trevor the time line information on a sheet of paper. With the completion of his short brief, Michael sat down for breakfast.

Prior to Michael's interruption, the team was discussing how impressed they were with Michael. The team agreed that he wasn't the lying bureaucrat they were expecting. He was just one of the guys, who ate, slept and talked with the team. Michael had earned much respect since the agency's creation.

After breakfast the team headed to their lockers, where they changed into the combat gear they would train with. As they met outside the cottage, Commander Reese pulled into the driveway to take them to the training area.

Trevor stayed behind to practice with the verification kit as well as prepare his brief. The NOs arrived at the training area and dismounted from the vehicle. Commander Reese began his layout for the day's training.

"Before we begin, Baxley, would you mind giving us the breakdown as to the plan for tomorrow's deployment?"

Baxley stepped in front of the team and explained what was discussed in the conference room the day before. Reese listened attentively as Baxley sketched the plan. Once Reese had a firm idea as to the plan, he began to design the day's training around the mission.

The team sat around the training area as Reese began to describe the training exercises.

"What I have in mind today is for all of you to practice your sniper skills. After we do so, we will begin the layout for the mission tomorrow. We will use the live fire shoot houses to prepare. The sniper training will consist of a stable target that will pop-up once for four seconds within a one hour time span. You must hit this target to proceed to the next stage. The second stage for sniper training today will consist of three moving targets that will cross each other. You must hit two targets with one round. For preparation for tomorrow's deployment, the shoot house will be prepared for target's movements into the building. Here we will be able to determine the best avenue of attack. Any questions?"

The team prepared their weapons and began to adjust the barrels for long-distance accuracy. Boiyd raised his hand and asked, "What range will the target be at?"

Reese answered, "The targets will be between four hundred to six hundred meters. I will not give you a precise distance, because I want to see how you adjust for unknowns. Anything else?"

The team stayed silent, waiting for orders to proceed to the range line.

"Okay, if you don't mind, I would like to ask you guys something. Agent Sands, what's he like?"

Reese had never spoken to Trevor outside of introduction, and had not had the opportunity to knew anything more about the man outside of his file.

"Trevor is the only one I would trust to tell me what to do under fire. He planned our defense and protected all of us in Vietnam."

Baxley stopped. The team did not for certain how much about their history that Reese knew. With an uncomfortable look shadowing Baxley's face, Reese detected what the apprehension was about.

"Baxley, don't worry about it, buddy. I am fully aware of your history and of all events that took place. It is because of your files that I volunteered to come here and train you. Don't worry about anything you say to me."

The team relaxed as Baxley smiled.

"What I was going to say was that Trevor planned the defense in Vietnam and guided our survival through one hell of a battle. He is going through a shitty time right now, so he probably won't be himself until the outbreak is reversed. Don't let him know that you know, but his wife just died from the bug. He doesn't even know where his daughter is. He is concentrating only on the work to prevent it all. Otherwise, he is a bad-ass leader. He motivates us all and ain't afraid to do anything himself. He's a good man; don't let his attitude right now throw you off."

The team watched Baxley as he spoke and nodded their heads in agreement. Reese solemnly nodded his head in empathy for Trevor's loss. Turning the mood toward training, Reese guided the team into their firing lanes for the sniper practice.

From the range control shack behind the firing positions, Reese gave the instructions to the agents.

"Here we are, team. Anytime between now and one hour from now, a target will pop up for four seconds. Remember that the round time will vary by distance and wind. Four seconds is not much time. Take this time to adjust for wind as well as for distance. Automatic adjustments are not authorized for this exercise. Manual adjustments must be made. The windsock behind your position will give you the estimated wind speed and direction. The distance for the target will be at least four hundred meters. Make your adjustments now."

The agents make the appropriate adjustments for wind and distance on their scopes. With a ten-mile-an-hour headwind, the round would take more time to hit the target than normal. Reese observes all of the agents as they make their scope corrections through his spotter's scope. Once all of the agents were complete, he began the simulation.

"Lady and gentlemen, be advised that we are going to score by point system. You must hit either heart or head in order to gain enough points to pass this phase. You have four seconds to hit the target in any one of two designated kill zones. The simulation will commence now. Watch your lanes."

Reese watched each of the agents waiting for any one of them to take their eyes off the scope. For twenty minutes no one did. They remained perfectly still, waiting for their enemy to show its head. After the initial twenty minutes, Boiyd took his head away from the weapon to adjust for the current wind speed. Reese activated Boiyd's lane and watched for his reaction. One second after the target showed itself, Boiyd fired in reaction. The computer in front of Reese registered the target as a hit. When the simulated diagram of the registered impact displayed, it showed that Boiyd had fired center of the heart. Reese smiled with approval. Boiyd had made a last-second adjustment for distance since his scope was zeroed at four hundred meters. The target arrived at five hundred and fifty meters. Boiyd aimed slightly above the heart and nailed the kill zone.

After the hour was complete, only one person missed the kill zone. After the simulated display of the impact, Reese decided that no one could live through the shot for more than a minute. The round grazed the heart, which would have shredded the lining of the heart. Reese passed Wilson for this round.

The team gathered to the briefing area to reveal the scores for the simulated sniper training exercise. Most of the agents were speculating what their scores were. Since none of them had actual Special Forces or formal sniper training, they were not accustomed to this form of marksmanship. Reese walked out of the range shack with a small stack of papers showing each of the agent's results. The agents ceased to speculate when Reese stood to their front.

"Well, I am impressed with your marksmanship. For having strictly infantry training, I am very impressed. All of you reached enough points to proceed to the next phase. Only one of you was too close to easily decide. Here are your results if you care to see for yourself."

Reese passed around the result sheets to each person.

"This next phase is kinda fun, so I expect you to have a good time. Three targets will be moving from different directions. Each lane is programmed to cross at different points. At one point, all three targets will cross. You must hit only the blue targets. If the green target is hit, you will fail this phase. One of the blue targets must register as a kill. The second must register as a hit. It does not matter which registers hit or kill, but they must register each of them. Both can register as kills. Any questions? Oh, yes, the ranges will vary from one hundred meters to two hundred and fifty meters. Now, any questions?"

Boiyd had his hand up and lowered it when Reese answered his question.

"Okay, if you'll file to your previous lane, we'll begin."

The team returned to their previous firing lane and prepared for the next phase. Reese briefed the agents again on their instructions and rules of engagement. They had one hour to complete the mission with one round.

Trevor sat behind a desk with the validation kit to practice with. Michael was standing behind Trevor, guiding him through the verification process. Once Trevor successfully completes the process, he turned to ask Michael about the database they discussed earlier.

"Michael, I was thinking more about this genealogical database. Would it be possible to obtain the existing records kept by the Mormons? I heard that they had the most extensive genealogical database in existence. If we obtained a copy of those records and established a base for upload, we could have the updates arrive incrementally to give us a better basis of judgment. Sorry, how is your head right now?"

Michael laughed.

"I'm fine. I have some coffee in my system; I should make it through this. Let's try and map this out."

"Okay, what I recommend, and I have to admit I had the headache from hell thinking about this, we sit down and write a SOP regarding this that we will follow for all time. If there are any changes in the future, we must notify the past before the changes take place. The equipment as well as the software must remain the same or at least compatible with the systems in the past. This may pose as a problem, but we have to maintain consistency for this to work. Here is what I have so far."

Trevor pulled out a sheet of paper and drew a straight line across the sheet, marking the far left of the line "present" and placing incremented marks along the line to designate ten-year spaces. On each mark he wrote the designated year space, ten to fifty years from the present mark.

"All right, if this line is the present, and these are ten-year marks from the present, we plan to have the database complete ten years from now and send it to us exactly ten years back. Now each month we receive an update from ten years from now. The headache came from maintaining this forever. If ten years from now receives the update from twenty years from now, then twenty receives from thirty years, and so on. On our first update, we should receive at least fifty years of records. So if we were to arrange for a designated database to be installed tomorrow, we could have the update in the afternoon. Theoretically, we should have the ability to foresee the descendants' consequences far down the line tomorrow evening. I think we should do this.

If you want, I'll write up a proposition SOP right now before I leave for the simulation brief."

Michael finally understood what Trevor was thinking. They could have a database capable of receiving the backgrounds of all persons on today's genealogical records. All descendants would be accounted for as well as their accomplishments. All of this could be implemented tomorrow if a firm plan was made now. With a wry smile, Michael agreed to it and prepared to request funds and computer systems from the NSC.

"Trevor, you are a genius! Go ahead and make the plan now. You can always go to the simulation later and still be on time. I think you have been the first to realize the potential of owning time. I just thought of something that should make the budget committee smile. Whatever costs this system will take can be divided up over time. From now to a hundred years from now we could have the database set up to send equipment as well as updates sent to tomorrow. We could have a hundred years of advancement in computer systems in our office tomorrow simply by requesting and planning it today! Trevor, please get started and we'll see what happens. Whatever you do, make sure it is official. It must be policy for this to work; fortunately, I am the policy maker right now. Go ahead and write it up while I run this by Richard to get his opinion."

Trevor turned to the computer console to begin the orders to be followed to the minute. Computer shipments would be sent from thirty years from now to tomorrow's time. Database research would be sent along with the computer to be compiled by CIA or whatever intelligence agency they have thirty years from now.

The words seem to fly from his mind and place themselves on paper as Trevor writes all thoughts and ideas for future operations and delivery dates. Anyone in the agency thirty years from now would understand the consequences for not complying. The entire database would vanish if they fail to make the appropriate shipment. This was an exciting and historical moment for all of the national security agencies. The ability to have equipment and intelligence for the next fifty years was an idea never conceived outside of novels and movies.

After three hours of constant writing, Trevor finished the rough draft of the SOP. He had kept the orders simple and specific only in regards to basic and essential rules. Certain rules must be followed, such as selection of agents. Because agents would have a poor family life, the chronological background check must ensure that his lack of family does not impair the original time line dramatically. Future recruits cannot be recruited if their enlistment into the agency eliminates a Nobel Prize recipient who may be one of his grandchildren, for example.

Michael returned after a long talk with Richard regarding the genealogical database. Both scientists are excited about the idea and can think of no negative consequences.

"How is it coming, Trev?"

This was the first time that Michael had addressed Trevor so casually.

"Not too bad. I have finished the rough draft. I feel it would be best to keep it short and to the point. I also included a prime directive for the agency. The prime directive is 'whatever plans are agreed to be completed must be completed to prevent paradox from half actions. Finish what is agreed to begin and begin only after thorough research of potential consequences.' What do you think?"

"I think it's perfect. I am pleased to find that you have a grasp on this. It took all of my scientists speculating to come up with the same agreement when we were trying to recover you. When do you plan on receiving the first shipment?"

Trevor pulled out a large permanent marker and began to neatly write out a schedule on the wall. This was a simple list of shipment requests as well as specifics regarding system criteria. Dating the shipping for April 25, 2039, to be sent to April 25, 2009, at 0600 hours. Next to the dates, Trevor wrote the detailed request, including the preferred size of shipment.

"Hopefully we don't move our headquarters anywhere without moving the requests along. As long as we have this and maintain the request, we should receive it tomorrow. With the preferred size request, we would be able to have the room to implement whatever equipment they ship. The beauty of this is that the people who would be sending the equipment might very well be the same people here today. They already know what was sent and know exactly what it is that needs to be shipped."

Michael frowned as he attempted to analyze possible complications. As there were no complications in his mind, he decided to try it. Trevor completed the initial plan to have the equipment received and began to view over the files required for briefing for the NSC.

Michael decided to place the live fire exercise on hold until they found out whether Trevor's plan would work. One of the bank robbers could very well have children who might be successful.

Michael pulled out a restricted handheld radio and called Reese.

"Training, this is Ops."

Reese responds with the sound of gunfire in the background.

"Training here."

"Hey, we're going to place the op for tomorrow on hold until we receive new equipment. Go ahead and finish the training for the team. We might be able to deploy them tomorrow as planned. Just inform them that the plan may change considerably."

"Copy that. Complete training and inform of possible change to plan."

"Good. Copy, out."

Michael was still getting used to the military way of talking on radios. He found it difficult to speak certain things in a specific way as opposed to the natural way of speaking. There were certain things that combat units never say on the radio. Of those things, the word "repeat" was never to be said. When someone said "repeat" over the radio, it was directing artillery or mortars, who might be on the same channel, to fire on the last given coordinates. By a single word many friendly lives could be lost. Michael, though, was adapting well to the militarization process.

Trevor downloaded the information into his implant as he prepared his equipment for deployment. As he loaded into the Tahoe, Michael looked at him with a wry smile and said, "You may find some things odd about the briefing. I will only tell you that this was an experiment. You will see me there, and some of the staff members may look at you like an alien. I'll explain the details of the experiment when you return. Just get there and be precise on when you page General Maxwell. They are expecting you at a very specific time. Don't be offended at their reactions to you. Just deliver your brief and say what you feel needs to be done. This is for training. Good luck."

With a slightly confused look from Trevor, Michael smiled and turned away as Trevor started the Tahoe and activated the dark energy loop. As a retractable rod extended from the roof of the vehicle, a metal loop about the size of a tire was extended above the Tahoe. When Trevor activated the positive polarity of the dark energy loop, a field formed around the Tahoe as a cloud formed in the underground garage of the compound. With static discharge exploding in a brilliant flash of light around the vehicle, Trevor was gone. Michael looked back and sighed in a solemn approval of his own work. As far as Michael was concerned, Trevor's deployment was history.

25 APRIL 2009
0500 HOURS

Michael was still awake from the day before. Excited and anxious, he walked back and forth within his room as if he were afraid of being caught at something. When the time was right, he put his shoes on and walked down the living quarter's hallway to Trevor's room. After an anxious and hesitant knock on the door from Michael, Trevor opened it immediately. It seemed that both men were up all night, waiting and thinking about the plan they had made the day prior and watching a miracle of science come to life. With only one hour remaining until the arrival of the equipment, the men seemed beside themselves with excitement.

Trevor invited Michael into the room as they discussed the final and less important issues for the delivery. Michael asked Trevor, "Do you think we should have everyone there when the shipment arrives?"

Trevor laughed under his breath and said, "What if it didn't work? We are involved in an agency where our theories and our successful projections provide the agents with the confidence in our decisions. I'm not sure if I want to screw that up for them right now. On the other hand, if this does work, it could raise their confidence in us more than ever. Hell, I don't know, you choose."

"Well, I see your point, but I'm feeling that they should be here if for no other reason than understanding how this works. One day, any one of them could be in your shoes, or even mine. I think they should all be equally aware of how to manipulate the time line safely."

Trevor nodded and stood to put a shirt on. As the men leave the room, they stop by all doors to get the agents out of bed. As they come into the kitchen, one by one, coffee was given all around to help wake their minds to be able to receive the theories that Trevor and Michael suffered over yesterday. After fifteen minutes, all of the agents were sitting around the table with coffee in hand, groggily sipping them awake. Trevor began to explain what was about to happen in about thirty minutes.

"Well, good morning. Glad to see how you all look before a shower. I need you all to try to relax and listen to what I'm going to tell you."

Boiyd looked up at Trevor and said, "Trev, if you want us to relax then let us get back to our fuckin' beds."

Trevor laughed, though he knew that Boiyd was serious.

"What I have to say involves the mission that was scheduled for today, and every mission we conduct from now on. Michael and I have developed a plan to have the 'history' of all of our targets as well as their future descendants. This will allow us the opportunity to know in advance what kind of effect our target's death would have. In about twenty-five more minutes we are expecting someone who will deliver us some computer equipment from thirty years in the future. This computer will be a massive database, where all known terrorists as well as criminals will be included. Once we receive the equipment and are trained by the delivery person, we will be able to search anyone, in theory, down to a hundred years or more from now. Everyone following me?"

Segal looked over to Baxley, back to Trevor, and asked, "How the hell does something thirty years from now have a hundred years of future research?"

The other team members looked back at Trevor as if they had the same question. Michael began to explain.

"What Trevor did yesterday was develop a plan and a procedure that makes it so all updates will be sent ten years back. Since this will be a constant protocol for the database, the people a hundred years from now, if the agency still exists, will send it back ten years to ninety years from now. Ninety to eighty, eighty to seventy, and so on. When the people from ten years from now receive the update, they will send it to us, and we will have the complete series. When our agency is old enough to be able to send it ten years back, we will do so as well. You see, ten years from now we will be the ones who would be updating us, say, next week. All we are doing is relaying information to ourselves, nothing more."

The team seemed to have assimilated this massive theory easily. Trevor assumed it was because they didn't have to develop it.

Baxley asked, "So we are supposed to expect someone from thirty years from now in twenty minutes? How did we get a message across to them? Did one of you go to them and ask for it or what?"

Trevor answered, "I simply wrote the request in a large permanent marker in the briefing room. If the request is transferred with the agency, if we ever move, than thirty years from now the agents should expect and know what to deliver. Guys, this is all an experiment, so it may not work, but if it does we wanted you to witness it so you can understand what it is we are trying to do."

The team slowly nodded their heads as if in unison as Trevor stood from the table to call Marla and Walt from upstairs to let them know of a possible visitor.

The team fixed up a quick breakfast to pass the time. As they ate their cold cereal and hot coffee, the phone that was looped to the couple upstairs rang. Michael stood and rushed to answer.

"This is Michael."

"Yes, sir, I believe that I have something for you. Would you like me to bring it to you or would you rather come and get it yourself?"

"Oh, Marla, I hardly expect you to carry all that stuff down here. Why don't I go up with a couple of men and get it off your hands. Thanks a lot, Marla."

"Well, sir, I think I can manage, but if you want to get it yourself that's okay. It's sitting on the counter in the kitchen when you are ready."

"Thanks, Marla, we'll be right up."

Michael hung up the phone as Trevor entered the room from taking a shower.

"Well, Trev, it's here."

Trevor stood frozen in anticipation. Such a massive database with all the trimmings had arrived without a check or any direct contact; all he did was write on a wall. Stumbling over himself, he rushed to get his shoes on as he waved for Baxley and Wilson to follow to help carry the things down.

As they reached the main floor of the compound, the four men move to the kitchen, where a small package sat on the counter. Trevor, suddenly disappointed, picked the package up and returned to the briefing room. As the men sat in the room, they looked around, confused as to how the plan failed.

Trevor said, "Maybe I should have gone in person thirty years from now to make the request. Shit, I was convinced this would work."

Michael picked at the wrapping around the small package in equal disappointment for not receiving the computer system that they had hoped for. As Michael continued to pick at the wrapping, he found a small revealed portion of something that caught his eye. In a sudden movement, he ripped the remaining paper and sat frozen in shock.

As he turned it over in his hand, he studied it carefully. The sleek black object had a screen three inches by five inches, with no buttons. A small hole was at the bottom of the screen with some kind of tiny transmitter at the tip of the device.

A sheet of paper was taped to the back of the device that read: Genealogical Search Engine Ver. 2.01.

Keywords: Start, search, down, up, select, display, help."

Trevor held up the device and spoke.

"Start."

The screen lit up and showed a small menu. Trevor shouted aloud, "Holy shit! Get the team in here! Call Richard and Reese, they have to see this!"

Baxley shot from the briefing room and sprinted into the kitchen to get the rest of the team. Boiyd ran to the phone and called Richard and Reese.

Trevor continued studying the object and called over for Michael to get him the list of names of the men in the bank robbery. While Michael retrieved the intelligence file for the bank robbery, Trevor decided to experiment.

"Search, Trevor Sands, 2009."

The search engine displayed a service photo of him, as well as listed his parents, his wife and his daughter. Trevor looked down the list and said "Display." Instantly, a holographic projection of the family tree displayed in front of him. As he looked down the tree he saw his daughter's future family as well as his own future children. Trevor knew that he would have two more children, both sons, and with the same wife. This also told him that he would be successful with the prevention mission regarding the alphabet virus.

Michael brought the list of names to Trevor and looked at the projection as well as Trevor's reaction. Michael watched a tear slip from Trevor's eye as he said, "Thank God she'll live."

Michael slowly slid the list in front of Trevor and stepped back from him. Trevor, finally realizing Michael's presence, took the file and turned to the list of names. The names shown for the four robbers were Michael Rodriguez, James Mathewson, Timothy Green and Jason Weisman.

Trevor began going down the list, searching for potential genealogical conflicts. As Trevor searched the database, there were ninety-five years of future files compiled by the FBI, CIA and NSA.

As Trevor searched the list, Rodriguez, Mathewson and Green come up with almost useless life records. Weisman had a grandson who would develop safe atomic batteries and eventually receive the Nobel Peace Prize for nuclear research. All of the speculation regarding future Nobel Prize recipients flashes Trevor with a bite of irony. The call was made that these men could not be killed or placed in prison. If Weisman was placed in prison his daughter would not be born, and Dr. Weisman would never be. The final decision was to cancel the mission and leave the men alone.

Trevor paced across the briefing room as Reese entered. Trevor filled Reese in on the plan that was made, as well as the new device they received. Trevor also informed Reese as to the decision regarding the banks robbers. Reese, in awe of the power of knowledge they possessed, stood by and watched as Trevor continued to teach himself the new device.

This new device was set to display a three-dimensional photograph of the potential target as well as a holographic projection of the lineage of the target, with hyperlinks to each of his or her descendants. Each descendant had a complete file of notable accomplishments as well as a photograph. The system also was complete with an action database, which would tell the operator what events have taken place on a daily basis. Trevor was now equipped with the ability to see what missions he had in front of him as well as the ability to find out what actions were taken to prove successful. With this tool, the agency would be more responsible and much more effective. Trevor and Michael kindly call the new device their “cheat sheet.”

26 APRIL 2009
1005 HOURS

Richard was unable to be contacted the day before to learn about the cheat sheet. Michael briefed him when he came in this morning. The team was assembled and brought into the briefing room, and the room was sealed. Trevor stood at the head of the table as he looked at his agents as well as Michael, Richard, Reese and Quincy. As he focused his attention to the thick memo in front of him titled "New Option Standard Operating Procedures," he began to brief the agency.

"Good morning. You are all here to be briefed on the new SOP that was written to guide us in everything we could think of dealing with the agency. This should cover everything from missions, prime directives, recruitment, as well as restrictions.

"According to what was written, we would become the new judge and jury for anyone labeled as targets assigned under our jurisdiction. Be advised that we have no authority over any matters not assigned to us. When an incident is assigned to our unit, we are in complete control until one of us, just one, openly disagrees with an action or plan decided by the SAIC or director. When that person filed a formal disapproval, the matter for decision will fall to the National Security Council for decision. The decision made by the counsel was irreversible.

What we have decided regarding the recruitment protocols was somewhat difficult. People who are destined on this time line to die, such as soldiers in combat, covert operatives and various agents from FBI or CIA, if any of them die from unnatural causes we could go back and fake their death. Since the original time line follows around their death, children and grandchildren will not be affected by their recruitment. Unfortunately for them, they must follow a set of rules that are a bit more strict than what we follow. Since we were not completely aware of what consequences our new agency might have on our families or future families, some of us may be forced to leave to prevent a problem with the time line. We will conduct research on each of you, as well as me, to ensure that our enlistment into the agency had not made a dramatic change.

The other aspect to recruitment was selecting qualified persons with a lack of descendants. Those who never married or ever got a woman pregnant, these are loose strings to the time line and fair game as far as recruiting. Psychological testing will be done to better depict how the potentials would handle the power, as well as the massive stress, that will be issued to the new agent.

Restrictions that are going to be in place, once Michael and the president sign off on this SOP, are going to be severe. When this SOP is signed we will not be able to do anything that would affect our own time line. If one of us was supposed to marry a woman named Marlene Mitchell, then we will track the woman down and act as matchmaker to ensure that you do meet and marry. If you have children, we will make sure you are home on leave when the child was supposed to have been conceived. For us to be in this agency, no changes can be made. Because we own the knowledge of every aspect of importance, we should be able to prevent this, but if any of you have unsanctioned sex with anyone not originally recorded on the time line, you will be discharged and the child will be destroyed. When I say no changes, team, I mean absolutely NO CHANGES."

The agents look around at each other, searching for reactions, as the depth of the possessed knowledge and responsibility hit their minds. Their freedom of choice would be gone for as long as they remained agents. In a sense, the agency was acting as a god controlling what the people felt was their fate. They knew that there is no choice, there is no fate. There is only the "way." For any of them to stray away from the so-called way would be to change the world. What if one of the bastard children were to get angry in high school and beat the future president of the United States to death? All because a child who was never supposed to exist got angry at a destined president. None of the good, as well as the bad, decisions made by the future president would ever come to pass. The team now felt enslaved on a mind-splitting road of things that were supposed to be and not the road of the way things could be.

Trevor continued with his brief while the entire team's attention was lost in deep thought.

"What Michael and I have agreed to is to allow each of you to opt in or out of this agency right now. Those of you who opt to stay in will receive a complete layout of your own life to help schedule to allow you to make certain events take place. Keep in mind that we are the only agents who will have this option. Those we recruit will have no family or ties. So I ask you to retire to your rooms and think this over for the next hour. If you have no doubt in your mind what your intentions are, you may meet with us in Michael's quarters. That's all. I hope you all agree to stay, but this is a commitment that I can't ask you to make. We'll speak again two hours from now."

The team members stayed in their seats, none of them felt as if they could even consider leaving their new family for any kind of odd rules. Baxley shook his head and asked Trevor, "How are we supposed to choose this? We need some kind of confirmation that leaving would be to support the family we were supposed to have. We need to know what kind of life we lived if we are to choose."

Trevor and Michael exchanged glances and began to pull up the files. Baxley would have two children and die at the young age of thirty eight. Boiyd remained a bachelor and would never have children. Segal gets shot in the lower abdomen and would not be able to conceive. She never marries. Trits marries but never had a child, and Wilson, for some reason, never even dates a woman.

Now that the team had their lives, literally, in their hands, they chose whether to stay or leave. What Trevor didn't tell them was that he already knew who the original agents are from the records. This choice needed to remain a matter of free will.

Baxley stood and looked to all of his friends. Shifting his hands in his pockets, he rocked from his heels to his toes.

"As much as we fuck with each other, I need you guys to know that I would die for all of you. A man who was never there for me raised me. I can't do that to any child of mine. I hope you understand."

Trevor looked back at Baxley and nodded in expectation and understanding. The room was silent with the realization that one of their own would be leaving, never to be seen again. Michael pulled Baxley into the next room to perform the ceremonial non-disclosure oath. Baxley packed his things and left the compound for good.

According to the records in Trevor's hand, Baxley was the only one who did not remain with the agency. With one of Trevor's veterans leaving to live his life, the team was left with a loss as bad as death for their comrade.

27 APRIL 2009
0500 HOURS

Breakfast was a sullen occasion as all team members begin to adapt to operations and life without Baxley with them. Of all times for the team to conspire and ask the question Trevor had urged them to put aside, Boiyd stood to ask it anyway.

"Trev, we need to know, and we need to know now, what change was made to us and who it involves. This is driving us up the fuckin' wall; we need to know now!"

Trevor looked at Boiyd square in the eye and shook his head.

"Guys, the change deals with a team member dying. Let me explain it so you can understand. If you had just met each other when we arrived here, would you feel as strong of a bond with each other as you do now? Would you trust each other? Some of you can probably handle this, but some of you may not. I need to know without a doubt that you will be able to perform as normal, even with the news. Since Baxley had made his decision, I think we need to get used to one change at a time. I will decide when you are ready. This kind of news could make you or break you as a team. Looking through my notes, I know that I do tell you guys by at least next month."

Boiyd stood from the table and slammed his fists into the wall. The sudden outrage shocked the team members as they focused their eyes on him. The entire agency felt betrayed by Baxley's decision, but Boiyd was the only one to make it so obviously personal. Trevor walked over to Boiyd and put his hand on his shoulder. Boiyd turned to acknowledge the gesture and then turned away to go into his room.

After a moment, Trevor walked back to his seat and began the brief for the day's events. Since the cancellation of the live fire, the NSC was preparing a new mission to help the team practice against live targets. This mission was a chance for the next ranking person to take charge, finalize the details and deliver the brief. Trevor was informed that he would have a deployment later in the day to help with his own training.

This next mission for the team would have Boiyd in command to plan and execute. Hopefully he would have worked out whatever it was he needed to by then.

Trevor finished his coffee and walked into the operations room to find Michael and learn more about the deployment scheduled for the day. As Trevor reached the conference room he walked over to the counter and found the device he called the cheat sheet. Trevor held it up and scrolled through the file on Trits. Trits' future wife was named Kelly Malloy. As Trevor searched for Kelly's lineage, he was right when he learns that Kelly was the grandniece to the late Sgt. Malloy, the man who would be senator. Looking at this, Trevor knows that Trits tried to find out more about the family of the comrade they had all forgotten. He was scheduled to meet her in the end of May.

Trevor scrolls through the people he had searched for yesterday and came across the bank robbers. As he thought more about the situation they had originally planned to prevent, he remembered the one man that he had not checked: the dead security guard. Theoretically, if there was a record of the man's future, then the New Option was supposed to intervene. If they were supposed to intervene they were to use non-lethal means and allow one of the men the chance to have a family.

Trevor searched for the security guard and found no family lines beyond what he had already. Trevor sighed and sat back. The burdens of the multi-faceted responsibilities were beginning to weigh on him. As he felt the headache of too much thought sneak up on him, he calmed his mind by thinking about the day that seemed so long ago. The day that he had received the page for activation, the final kiss he gave his wife, the tears falling from her eyes as she helped him pack. Trevor shook the painful images from his mind and ran out to find Michael.

Michael was upstairs speaking with Walt about preparations for the evening meal when Trevor interrupted suddenly.

"Michael, I know what we need to do!"

Michael stood and excused himself from Walt as he stepped toward Trevor.

"Do about what? The mission or something else?"

"Both. Give me twenty minutes and I'll brief the team. We will deploy tonight for the mission."

Michael grabbed Trevor by the arm, walked him into the kitchen, and spoke hoarsely and quietly.

"Just how the hell do you plan to have the team ready in one day? What the hell are you up to? Do you not understand what's at stake?"

Trevor exclaimed in outrage, "I know exactly what's at stake; I know that we can go back fifty years from now and save these people. I know that we can do so in a hundred years. What I know for sure is that I am being tortured knowing that my daughter might be at some hospital without a mother and father. I know that there is a way to have these men ready today. I know that if you would trust me for one fucking second you will see something you have never known. I know that in twenty minutes a final brief will be ready for our men with a plan of action. This is what I know. Will you let me try this? Worst-case scenario is that my plan fails and we are stuck where we are. Do me one favor and keep my men here until I return."

Michael nodded without understanding and watched Trevor leave for the garage. Richard walked into the cottage as Trevor slammed the door behind him.

Richard leaned over to Michael and asked, "Where is he going?"

Michael answered, finally understanding what Trevor was talking about.

"He's going into the future to get his team."

27 APRIL 2010
1632 HOURS

As the cloud dissipated from around the vehicle, Trevor looked around to find the land around the cottage exactly the way he had left it. As he pulled the vehicle up to the front door of the cottage, he stopped the vehicle and opened the door. The sweet smell of lilac trees flooded his senses as he walked to the front door. Trevor knocked on the door and waited for Marla or Walt to answer. After a short moment the door opened, with Marla smiling back at Trevor. Trevor was welcomed inside as he was led to the elevator.

After the short and seemingly motionless trip down, he opened the door to the conference room. There were almost no changes except for the desks, which had been upgraded from the uncomfortable college-style to a large circular conference table with nameplates assigning each seat. As he looked at the names, his original team was there along with names he did not know. Five additional agents had been added to the roster in just one year. As Trevor walked toward Michael's office, he found his own room. With the curiosity of walking in to find himself reading a book or watching a movie, he restrained his temptations and continued moving to Michael's office. Trevor knocked three times before Michael's voice announced for him to come in.

As Trevor walked in, Michael studied Trevor carefully as he sat at his desk. A cup of coffee was poured as if he had been expected. Trevor took the seat in front of Michael's desk and reached for the cup.

Michael looked down at Trevor and asked, "Was your trip okay? Nice and smooth, I hope."

Trevor, now realizing that Michael would know where he went when he arrived back to his time, answered, "The trip was fine. Short. I see you were expecting me."

Michael answered, "The team is ready for deployment; they will not need a ride. You will meet them and remind them of the mission, though they have the brief ready to go. I have a feeling I said this when you returned, but I'm going to say it anyway. The more and more you keep doing your own thing, the more I have to keep track of and plan. Your trip here made me mark a calendar a year in advance to ensure that your men were ready to go. I only wish you would understand that your men must be back here along their time line. You are actually stealing their time. If they are gone for eight hours, they must be brought back eight hours after they depart. It is the only way to prevent mishaps. You are stealing their time in the present. You must understand this; it will bite you in your ass one day, believe me!"

Trevor laughed under his breath and said, "I'm sure you're right. Where are they?"

"In their rooms; just leave your room alone. Take the original team and you should be fine; the other men came after the alphabet, so leave them alone. Here is a note for you to read once the entire team is briefed. I know that you will have no one to brief you, but this note should explain what your actions should be during the execution of the mission. Just read it after the team returns here."

After a short pause, Michael continued as he remembered something he should not have forgotten.

"Before you go, I need you to not search for Boiyd. He came down with the flu and we aren't sure if this strain was around for last year's vaccination. It's too bad you didn't deploy for a year and two weeks. I have this other letter here for Boiyd. This includes what his mission is and exactly what is involved. The time line as well as the overall ops order is in there, so he shouldn't have many questions that you can't answer."

Michael reached his hand out with a second letter. Trevor smiled and collected the letter as he walked out of the office with the letters in hand. As he stopped in front of the first door, he looked closely at the nameplate. Ssg. Wilson. Some things, it seemed, had changed.

After five minutes of collecting his team, they met in the kitchen. All of them were briefed that morning to expect the Trevor from the past and deploy to deliver a detailed brief of plan of action. The team felt a haze of discomfort, since they were instructed not to give details about the events taken place in the past year. Trevor never asked. Without any hint, the team stood and walked to their garage as Trevor headed toward the elevator.

The team loaded up in their own vehicle and began to deploy, Trevor walked back to his own and programmed it for 0630 hours on April 27, 2009. The whirring hum swirled from above the Tahoe and enveloped the vehicle in the familiar cloud. As the flashing of static discharge blinded Trevor, he felt the faint sense of a single complete spin as he watched the cloud disappear from the windows to show the same cottage he had left. Looking behind him, he found the team waiting in their vehicle. The team and Trevor walk into the cottage and work their way into the elevator for the briefing.

27 APRIL 2009
1744 HOURS

Michael had come through again by having his team surrounding the conference room table. The support and understanding wasn't there when Trevor had left for the future. The agents at the table stood as Trevor entered the room. Almost all of them were beside themselves when they saw who Trevor had brought with him.

Trevor began to explain what his intentions were.

"Sorry for doing this without any warning. To save any kind of confusion, I decided to call the team from the future the 'red team.' My team here in the present will be the 'blue team.' Each double will meet with their partner and discuss the exact details regarding the mission for the prevention of the alphabet virus. I must stress one aspect of discussions. Red team cannot talk about items relating to anything other than the Alphabet mission. Any kind of conversation about personal information will not be tolerated. Changes that will take place must not be discussed as well, unless it is essential to the mission. Boiyd, I'm sorry, but your double had the flu. I have your instructions and orders here for you. Okay, let's begin."

Each teammate met with their double and went off to separate corners of the conference room. The two Trits sat in the far corner and just laughed at the odd occasion that they were in. The Wilsons were solemn and reluctant to begin their briefing. The Segals covered the details immediately regarding their roles in the mission. Red team Segal began the brief by giving details of the mission's plan.

"Okay, 'Blue,' the main plan was to have one man onboard the plane when it was supposed to have detonated to disarm the bomb. So, when Boiyd disarms the bomb, you are in Omaha to fire at the plane with an aerial napalm rocket to ensure it burns in the air in case detonation takes place. Now, you want to place yourself on the rooftop of the Hilton hotel garage here in Omaha."

Red Segal pointed on a map that she had brought with her. She continued.

"Now, what you need to make sure of is that you have the wind speed and direction in mind when you fire the rocket. The wind, when I was waiting, was fifteen miles an hour from 172 degrees. Just aim so that the wind will spread the flame into the blast and you should be fine. These are detonated by remote trigger. So you fire the rocket with the trigger mechanism on the modified Stinger and then detonate with the secondary trigger device near the front strap. Trits will be positioned a mile or so away from you so that he can get a second burst in for good measure. Now, Wilson is going to begin the last resort protocol. He will be at Offutt Air Force Base. He will fire a SAM at the aircraft in case Boiyd fails. Once detonated, there should be enough thermite to send the aircraft to over a hundred times its original detonation temperature. Once he fires, you and Trits will fire at the falling debris to ensure that it stays at a burning temperature."

Blue Segal writes notes as Red spoke and addressed the map. She noted that the entire plan was dependant on Boiyd's success. The rest of the team was waiting for him to fail to ensure that alphabet died in mid-air before infection could take place. The only question running through Segal's mind as Red spoke was, 'Where the hell is Trevor?'

As Blue scribbled the notes down as fast as Red spoke, Segal looked up at her double during the brief and asked the question nagging her mind.

"Excuse me, where the hell is Trevor while Boiyd is on board and the three of us are down below waiting? What is he doing?"

Red looked at her double and looked away as if in attempt to avoid a poor complexion in the mirror. Finally, she turned back to her younger double and replied, "We aren't allowed to know about Trevor's job. You see, he kinda becomes *the* agent."

Segal looked at her elder self in confusion as the elder quickly reacts to cut off her question.

"You see, well, okay, you know how we have to follow a certain time line forever. If you go back for three days you have to come back three days to the second after you left in order to stay in your own time line. Well, Trevor doesn't. A few days before you deploy, he goes into lockdown. He isn't allowed to be seen by anyone except Michael. Some of us think that he will never grow old because he isn't in his own time line. Its all bullshit and speculation, but that's what's going around."

Blue Segal looked down at the floor and back up to Red.

"You mean to tell me that we are not allowed to see him again?"

Red answered quickly, "No. I mean while he is in lockdown he cannot be with those he's in charge of. He had a different mission that none of us knows about. I do know that he recruited people, but no one knows where they come from or why they were recruited. We only know what their jobs are."

Blue Segal looked over in the opposite corner of the conference room at Trevor and frowned in pity for him. Red Segal looked at her younger reflection and smiled as she reflected about the things that the younger twin would not learn for many more months.

27 APRIL 2009
2200 HOURS

Trevor watched from Walt and Marla's windows in the cottage as the team of his own future disappeared into the mist from their vehicle. Turning away only after the mist completely dissipated, Trevor walked back toward the elevator. As he closed the door to the closet, Walt stopped him with an odd assertiveness.

"Boy, I think you and I should have a chat. Get on out here so I can look at ya."

Trevor delivered a look mixed with animosity and confusion toward the elderly man and followed Walt to the den. Walt walked to the end of the den where a small liquor cabinet was. Turning toward Trevor as if to offer a drink, he began to pour as Trevor nodded. Walt walked back toward a large sectional couch and motions for Trevor to sit as well. Once seated, the two men looked at each other in awkward silence. As Trevor began to ask what the meeting was about, Walt started speaking.

"You know, I actually know exactly how you feel. You see, Marla isn't my first wife. I was married to a beautiful woman and had a daughter long before I met her. Well, they died from a sort of flu when I was about your age. The whole time they were sick I assumed it was something else. It turned out they died of something I brought back with me from Asia. Doctors made the same assumption as I did and didn't catch the disease in time for it to save them. Anyway, I was working as an agent at the time, and I wasn't home when they were hauled off to the hospital."

Trevor looked at Walt and frowned with sincere empathy that he knew was now mutual. There was so much about Walt and Marla that he didn't know. All he knew was that they were both agents and maintained their clearance after they retired. Because of that, they were perfect for this new job as the cottage's cover. Trevor took a slow sip from his drink and flinched at the surprisingly harsh sensation that followed down his throat. Looking back at Walt, he noticed that the old man was now holding back his tears.

"Sir?"

Walt looked at Trevor with a new youth that scared Trevor for a brief moment. The sudden glance from Walt revealed more than anyone would ever wish to share. Walt swallowed a deep sip of his scotch. Swirling the drink in his hand, he looked back at Trevor and continued his thoughts.

"You see, son, there is more to life than just life. You must understand one thing. There is just one thing in order to become the hero that these people make you out to be. What you need to understand is that you aren't shit. You aren't a hero, you aren't even a patriot. What you are is a father and a husband searching for his way to find his family again. If you happen to save a few people along the way, that's fine too."

Trevor noticed that he had been leaning toward Walt, fully attentive and zoned into the world of elderly experience. Walt leaned back as if Trevor were violating some kind of invisible bubble around him. Trevor countered and relaxed back into the corner of the couch. Walt took a deep breath and another sip of scotch as he prepared to continue his thoughts.

"I know you think that you have the whole world figured out right now. I know that you think you know exactly how things will play out. Let me just say that some things are out of your hands, and the tools that are in your hands, well, just remember that the toolmaker had a purpose as well."

Trevor sat back and listened as he thought of the tools that he had just received. Remember that the toolmaker had a purpose as well? Exactly how much did Walt know about the project? Has he ever been downstairs, or was he just referring to general rules of spies or whatever the hell he was involved in? Trevor mentally shrugged off the advice and was now just listening to be polite.

Walt sat forward and placed his hands on his knees after setting his cup down.

"Well, I just thought you would like to know that there is someone who understands what it is that you're going through. You better get off and get some sleep. I'm sorry to take so much of your time. If it's any consolation, you made an old man happy by being my company tonight."

Trevor smiled and gestured as if it were nothing, but that wasn't true. This talk had not been a sign of hope for Trevor's situation. Trevor stood and headed to the elevator as Walt stood to follow him. As Trevor shut the door to proceed downstairs, he waited for another abrupt stop in his short journey. No stop came, and the door opened to the brightly lit operations room.

It seemed that all of the agents weren't in their usual collective this night. Each of Trevor's team was strewn about the entire underground compound, collecting their own thoughts. Trevor stood in the middle of the large room and watched each soldier in turn.

Trits was standing at a dry erase board with a map and a straight edge, planning his line of attack from where the flight originated. Wilson was reading several technical manuals about the surface-to-air missiles that he would be responsible for firing, as well as studying the best place on the plane to fire at in order to have the maximum explosive effect. Trevor looked behind him to find Boiyd and Segal. They weren't in the ops room; maybe they were in the living quarters.

Trevor opened the door to the kitchen and dining area and found Boiyd sitting on the couch, watching a movie. Nothing productive about this except maybe clearing his mind. Trevor patted Boiyd on the shoulder and walked back to Segal's room. With a gentle knock on the door, Trevor waited for an answer. After he heard a few things clutter through the door, Segal cracked the door open and smiled at Trevor in an almost sympathetic way.

"Hey, Trev, what's on yer mind?"

Trevor risked being nosy and peered above her head into the room and then back down to her.

"Well, I was just checking on everyone. You doing okay? Anything ya need?"

Segal thought about what her older self had said. Why was it that such a good man and hardworking leader should fall into a pit of solitude? She turned her head back into her room and searched for anything incriminating. Turning back toward Trevor, she said, "You want to come in? I think there is something we should clear up."

Trevor looked at her inquisitively and walked into the room. As he entered, he took the chair seated at the desk and sat facing Segal. Segal avoided eye contact as she searched her bookshelf behind Trevor. She soon ran out of things to search, and after a long, uncomfortable silence, she looked deeply into Trevor's eyes and asked, "It's me, isn't it?"

Trevor was thrown off by the vague self-implication from Segal.

"What the hell are you talking about? You what?"

"I'm the one who was changed, wasn't I?"

"What gives you that idea?"

Segal looked down at her hand and rubbed the implant.

"Ever since this was put in me I felt like I don't know anyone anymore. Tell me what happened."

Trevor stood and walked to the edge of Segal's bed and took her hand.

"Okay, you can't tell anyone what I am about to tell you, deal?"

Segal nodded her head dramatically. Trevor began to explain the change that was made in 1969. Trevor went into every detail about the sergeant who would be senator, and the son who was on their team. Every aspect and time line was given to Segal as she held herself tight and cried for the life she had that was now lost forever.

Thoughts now rushed through her mind of the life she held in the Army that was held in support positions. She couldn't imagine herself not being infantry. The single thought of being pushed aside by some politician sickened her. In a brief moment she found herself sitting on the couch she had as a teenager as her parents were fighting in the kitchen. A news report interrupted her show as she leaned forward to turn up the volume. A rugged-looking reporter was showing clips of a Gurney being carried by Special Forces troops. Apparently, a female POW was rescued and brought to a waiting aircraft for evacuation heading to Germany. As she watched the report from Iraq, she couldn't help but feel an urge to get as far away from home as she could. How much further from home could she be than Iraq or Northern Africa? She finally knew what she wanted to be when she grew up: a soldier.

Looking up with teary eyes, she gripped Trevor's hand tight and thanked him for the truth. Trevor didn't know if what he did was right, but he did know that he needed to assure her of something more important than the truth.

"A.J., listen to me. In all of our minds and hearts you have been with us since the beginning. You have to know that after this mission I am going to tell the team the truth about the change that was made. They all need to know, but I promise you that it will not change how they see you or trust you. Your training and your dedication to the team have always been there, and that is something that they cannot question. You have nothing to be afraid of."

Segal looked up, smiled and showed a beauty that Trevor had never seen in the tough soldier he knew. Trevor leaned forward and kissed Segal gently on the forehead as he walked toward the door.

28 APRIL 2009
0800 HOURS

Trevor dreamed about the early days he shared with his wife long before they married, the phase in their relationship where all physical contact sent shocks through their bodies. Each stroke of a finger or brush of the cheek was an erotic sensation. The fascination of their bodies as they joined, as well as the unknowns of their own finality as a couple made each encounter memorable. As they grew older as a couple, each day began to blend into a form of routine that hazed the memory and clouded the early days of true love. Only occasionally would a moment arrive that would show each partner how truly special they were to each other.

The specific memory that rushed through Trevor's mind was of his first date with Jessica as a couple. Jessi drove Trevor to his barracks two hours before he had to be ready for the morning physical training. They were sitting silently in the car as they were both finding the nerve to kiss each other. Trevor found the nerve first and reached toward Jessi's head, pulling her toward him as he kissed her for the first time. Trevor shook in his bed as he felt the electric lust rush through his body as if for the first time. Trevor shook himself awake as he realized there was a knock on his door.

Standing from his bed and walking to the door, he muttered for the person on the other end to wait a moment. Trevor put a pair of jeans on and opened the door. Boiyd stood there, looking very impatient.

"What's up, man. Whatcha need?"

Boiyd pushed through the door and closed it behind him. Trevor moved out of the way to let the man in. Boiyd sat at Trevor's desk and pulled out an envelope that held the mission details.

"Do you know what I'm supposed to do?"

Trevor sat at the edge of his bed and nodded.

"Yeah, you are onboard the plane to disarm the bomb. Why? What's wrong?"

"I overheard Trits talking about when he fired his rocket. Why would he fire if I succeeded? That means that I die, doesn't it?"

"No, you may have heard it wrong. You also were given a parachute to use in case you couldn't disarm in time. You could have bailed and then the team fired."

Boiyd looked down and then around the room, finally focusing on Trevor.

"Then why did my other self not brief me? The letter came from Michael. If my other self had the flu he would at least be able to write down a written brief of what I need to do."

"I know what you're thinking. I was told while I was with Michael a year from now that you were sick. I didn't think to question it. I'm sure you are gonna be fine. For safe measure, we'll set the phase line back further so you can safely jump. Sound good to you?"

Boiyd looked at Trevor and smiled.

"That'll work. Thanks, man."

Trevor smiled and looked at his watch.

"Shit, we need to get the debriefing finished so we can plan this thing right. I'll meet you in the conference room. Would you get the rest of the team there so we can begin?"

"Yeah, I'll get right on it."

Trevor closed the door behind Boiyd and looked down at his palm as he rubbed his own implant. Since he had received it, the chip had been a new tool for frustration. Rubbing the chip as he would twirl his hair if he had any, Trevor looked around and found his own letter that he had neglected to read. With a slight apprehension about what the letter would contain, Trevor opened it and read Michael's words.

Trevor,

By your own SOP we have implemented something that you need to ensure changes nothing in the time line. By April 28, 2009, you need to lock down and follow these rules for the safety of your team as well as the safety of the missions ahead. Once you have read this letter you must deliver it straight to Michael of the time. Enclosed is a disk that will guide Michael as to how to reprogram your implant.

From now on you will not follow your own time line. You will be in lockdown from your time line until such point as you have a replacement. Until that time comes, here are your new objectives:

1. Recruit agents or potentials as opportunities arrive.

2. For the purposes of national security, you will follow separate missions paralleling the agency's objectives to ensure a specific outcome.

3. At no time during a mission will you be exposed to other team member, with the exception of Michael or the NSC during briefings. At no time will you discuss your personal mission with anyone other than Michael.

4. Off-duty time is your own to explore and learn more about the time line and its possible consequences. You will be able to travel forward or back within the limitations assigned. At no time will you travel beyond the agency's existence. Your forward limit was September 23, 2104, 2342 hours.

5. Romantic relations are permitted within the agency, on off-duty time in the event of family loss. Keep in mind that this will only be permitted during allowed times while in lockdown. The purpose of such was to ensure a balance to your psyche. This will not make sense yet. It will.

The disk enclosed has the appropriate modifications to the implant. Ensure that the verification kits are modified to match. After the completion of the alphabet mission, you will be notified of all information hidden from you. Your knowledge will exceed most people on the planet, and you must ensure that your knowledge does not spread. Levels of code will be implemented for information arriving from your future. Omega code was the new assignment for all New Option agents' accessibility. Beta will require the intelligence to remain between you, the NSC and Michael. The most restricted code will remain with you alone. Alpha code was passed back to ensure that no time line disruptions will occur during a mission your team will conduct. This will be your eyes only.

Trevor, I know you have more questions than I can answer at this point, but you must trust in the system that you and I have developed. Because you will not be in your own time line, you will not age. The radiation running through you will prevent this from happening as long as you are not on your assigned time line. For this reason, you will remain ageless and will not suffer the effects of old age. You are mortal and can die from gunshots as well as any other unnatural means. This was implemented to ensure consistency throughout the agency's life span. Trevor, you will understand more the moment alphabet is complete. Your time line will alter every week to be offset ten minutes from your own natural time line. Once you read this, ensure that you see Michael immediately. He must read this as well and destroy this once he is finished. If you have any questions, you may ask Michael after January 2, 2010. You are more than welcome to visit at any time (no pun intended).

Your friend,
Michael Heimer
Director NOA

Trevor folded the paper in half and placed it next to him on his bed as if it were a newfound disease. After several minutes of staring at the blank wall in front of him, Trevor stood and walked out of his room with the envelope in hand.

28 APRIL 2009
0947 HOURS

Trevor sat in the chair opposite Michael's desk as he waited for Michael to finish his own future work. Once Michael finished the letter, he looked up at Trevor in a very sympathetic way.

"Good God, Trev, I had no idea it would go this far."

Michael reached under his desk and pulled a bottle of cognac along with two glasses. As he poured the drinks and slid one to Trevor, Michael raised one and whispered something under his breath, perhaps a prayer, or an old man's toast against old age, Trevor didn't know. Michael leaned back in his chair and pulled the disk out from the envelope. Holding the disk up against the light, he placed it in his computer to look at the line of code that would be used for Trevor's implant clock setting.

"Well, isn't that something."

Trevor leaned around to see the code. Though it would make no sense to him, Trevor couldn't help but read each line in its entirety. Michael looked over to Trevor and explained.

"You see, the line of code is designed to fool anyone who knows to look that you follow a specific time. What they don't know is that you follow two specific times ten minutes apart from each other. One is more like a ghost or shadow of your actual time. You see, the encryption hides that from them and will only show that your time is correct. The encryption needs to match the kits so that once you are verified, the computer lies to the NSC, stating that there is no change."

Trevor leaned back to take in the techno babble flying in his mind.

"You mean to tell me that we are to reprogram the verification kits to lie to the NSC so that I can still command the staff members during a mission? Doesn't the staff have their own techs to search encryption? Wouldn't they find out sooner or later?"

Michael shifted his body before he explained.

"Well, remember that I created this code. There is nothing like it because I needed it to fit in multiple dimensions in its writing. You see, there is no one, except myself and Richard, that can make out the code. No one would ever know."

Trevor nodded and asked, "So when do you want me locked down?"

Michael was waiting for this and didn't know the answer himself. He did know it had to be that day, and for that he said, "Trev, I think that I should be the one, with Commander Reese's guidance, to implement the brief with the agents. I'm not sure if there is anything that you would do to change the mission. Any change in the slightest way could do some damage yet. I recommend that you take the back door to the garage and deploy ten minutes back. From there I want you to stay in your room until I come to you for more instructions. What do you think?"

Trevor shook his head and decided to go along with the plan, not to mention a little bit of his own ideas thrown into the mix.

"I think I should get started. Don't be surprised if I come back pissed off."

"I won't blame you in the least. Dial my pager if you need anything at all. I'll explain the best I can to the agents. I have a feeling that Segal had an idea, probably something her counterpart mentioned."

Trevor didn't mention what Segal now knew, but he stood from his chair and hung his head low like a beaten dog as he left the room for the garage. As Trevor entered the garage, he felt an urge to speak with Michael again. He felt no urge to speak to the Michael down the hall, but he did wish to speak to the Michael ahead of time.

Trevor extended the rod from the Tahoe and activated the dark energy loop at the tip. Watching the field surround him like a slow gel, he felt a solid jerk as saw a slight darkness in the distance of his windshield. Finally, he found himself in the garage as he had left it. Looking down at the computer in the console, he realized the date was identical to when he had left. Why didn't he deploy? Trevor could think of nothing, until it hit him. There was no room for him in the garage from the future. There must have been a vehicle in the bay. Trevor opened the door, pulled out in front of the garage and decided to try again. Trevor activated the loop one more time and felt a fluid motion as he found himself sitting in place one year ahead.

Retracting the rod, Trevor left the Tahoe behind as he walked to the front door of the cottage. This time Marla answered the door, with a remarkable beauty for someone her age. She held her hands out and took both of Trevor's hands to pull him gently inside. Marla smiled and expressed as pleasantly as she always did her appreciation for visits. Trevor greeted Marla and walked to the closet to head downstairs. For some reason the elevator didn't move. Trevor flipped the switch several times but nothing happened. Trevor was thinking this was his day for malfunctions. Looking around the closet, he saw a small cell phone set into the wall. Trevor turned it on and it automatically dialed a number. After two rings, Michael answered.

"Hello?"

Trevor replied.

"Hey, it's Trev. It looks like I'm stuck in the elevator. What's going on?"

"Nothing's wrong except that you are locked down right now. Wait a minute and I'll unlock the door. Wait upstairs for me to get to you."

Michael hung up the phone. Trevor pushed open the door and waited in the parlor for Michael to join him. Marla heard the footsteps and met Trevor with a tray of snacks from the kitchen.

"Is everything okay?"

Trevor looked up at her and smiled graciously at the food in front of him. Taking a saltine cracker and a slice of cheese, he fed the hunger that he had neglected since he woke up. After several moments the closet opened and Michael met with him in the parlor. Trevor stood to shake his hand. After the formalities, the two men sat. Michael smiled and looked down from his glasses at Trevor.

"I take it you need some help with something. What can I do for ya?"

Trevor put his cracker down and answered, "Well, I just read the letter that you sent, and I wanted to know if there is anything that I did to make this easier. I had something in mind, but I wanted to make sure that there were no consequences."

"Trevor, you of all people should know that every little thing that you do has consequences. What is it that you had in mind? I'll check to see if it will work."

"Well, I wanted to send a letter of instructions back to when the cottage was being developed to allow for a self-contained facility that I could be in while in lockdown."

Michael smiled and stood from his seat. Trevor followed his with his eyes as Michael stopped in front of the window.

"Is that what you're talking about?"

Trevor walked to the window and found a small shack sitting at the edge of the wood line across from the driveway. The shack could probably fit a lawnmower and maybe a workbench. This shack was definitely not large enough for a living area.

"What's underneath the shack?"

Michael smiled.

"Wait here and I'll get you the blueprints."

Trevor took a seat and waited for ten minutes or so until Michael came back with the rolled blueprints for the shack and the lower levels. Trevor inspected every inch of the blueprint and looked up at Michael.

"Is there a rule against me visiting myself? I assume I'm down there right now."

"Well, being that the Trevor that is down there now knows the rules better than you, I know that nothing will be at risk of disclosure prior to you needing to know. Just don't ask anything outside of professional guidance. There are some things about your personal life that are better left unknown. If you want, you can head down there now. I need to get back to the team downstairs. It was good seeing you. Feel free to visit anytime."

Michael walked into the elevator and left Trevor standing alone in the room. Trevor collected the blueprints and headed out the front door as he hollered his gratitude for the snacks. Stopping at the Tahoe to drop off the blueprints, he walked to the shack, stopping at the door, hesitant to meet himself. Finding the courage to open the door, he walked in and found the lever to lower himself to the lower level.

At the bottom there was a large paneled room with a big flat panel television. Sitting on a couch covered with various files was Trevor, sleeping soundly with the background of a show humming indistinctly. Trevor leaned over his double and placed his hand on the sleeping shoulder. In an instant the sleeping Trevor woke to find himself staring at himself.

"Wha—what the hell?"

Trevor rose from the couch and stood face to face with the past Trevor.

"Holy shit! Of all the ways to wake up, this is one of the most fucked up. When did you get here?"

"I got here about half an hour ago. Came to talk to Michael about building this place. Thought I'd see it for myself if I'm going to spend so much time here. Are there more levels?"

"Hell yeah, there are three more. C'mon, I'll show you around."

Trevor followed the future Trevor down to a stairwell and walked to the next sublevel. In a large open area was all the equipment Trevor could want in a gym. Exercise bikes, treadmill, stair climber, and free weights filled the room. On the back wall, facing all of the equipment, was another television. Down another flight of stairs was a large kitchen and bar with yet another television. A small jukebox was playing old rock music. There was a chute leading God only knows where coming from the kitchen.

"What is the chute for?"

"That thing is my saving grace. Marla cooks up some pretty good meals and sends them to me. I don't know why, but she takes damn good care of me while I'm down here."

Trevor stopped at the stairwell going to the last level and looked at his past counterpart.

"Down here are some things that you shouldn't know about, but this is where I keep some of my most personal things. This is also where I get my briefings. There is a D.E. generator down there that allows my counterparts from past or future to send me information. Once you get this place built, I recommend you test it out. Just plug in this time and I'll shoot one back to return. For anything in here to work, a key code has to be entered at the shack. If that isn't entered, then all messages go to my room at the cottage. Either way, I'll get the messages. Any questions so far?"

Trevor looked up and was going to ask what the D.E. stood for when he realized dark energy was the answer.

"I do have one question. When do I need to go in order to have this place built?"

"March, Friday the thirteenth. The crews show up at about 2000 hours, and I think Michael arrived at 2100 or so. The crews stayed onsite until the entire cottage was remodeled. You would be better off arriving at the gate. The garage wasn't built yet. If you show up at 1900 hours you should be here before anyone sees you arrive. I think that's what I did. Either way, it will be built when you return to your own time. Just make sure you send a message for everyone to remain away from the area in your time. It could show up on top of someone."

Trevor laughed at the idea, though it wasn't funny. The future Trevor conceded to sending the message himself and making sure the area was clear for the building to arrive. As Trevor took his final look around his new home, he felt more comfortable about the idea. Heading upstairs, Trevor turned to his counterpart and thanked him for the tour.

Trevor returned to the Tahoe and plotted his heading to the remodeling time for Friday the thirteenth of March 2009. Once the course was plotted, Trevor moved the vehicle to the front gate and activated the system. In seconds he was looking at what the cottage used to look like. From the looks of things, there wasn't much of a change. The only difference was probably the sublevels. Trevor wondered how they could have done the sublevels without damaging the house. All things considered, he realized he had better things to worry about. Now all he had to do was wait for two hours until Michael arrived to receive the blueprints of the new addition.

28 APRIL 2009
0937 HOURS

As ordered, Trevor arrived ten minutes behind his departure to offset his own time line. Since he was locked down, he waited ten more minutes to ensure that he wouldn't run into himself. Trevor pulled the Tahoe around the backside of the cottage until his counterpart left. After several moments, he watched as the field radiate throughout the area. This was his cue to meet Michael. Trevor pulled the vehicle back into the garage and walked into Michael's office. Michael opened the door to let him in and handed Trevor the same drink that Trevor had just left behind. For Michael it had only been minutes since he had last seen Trevor, but for Trevor it had been several hours. Trevor took the drink and finished it off. After a bitter face, Trevor looked to Michael.

"Did you get my message?"

Michael laughed loudly and replied, "Yeah I did. I wasn't worried about it, but I made sure the area is cleared. Mind if I take a look?"

"Not at all. I'm kind of interested to see the rest of it myself. I wasn't allowed to see the lowest level."

"Lowest level? This I have to see."

The two men walked out the back door and headed to the shed. As they reached the entrance, Trevor keyed in the pin number on a keypad, hiding behind one of the trim panels inside the doorway of the shed. Lights in the shed came on, and the lawnmower moved to the right automatically. In place of the lawnmower, a small two-man pad elevator remained. Trevor and Michael stood on the pad and found themselves sinking into the sublevels below. Once they reached the first sublevel, they stepped off the pad. After a moment, the pad returned to the surface as they heard a scrape of the lawnmower returning to its place.

Michael, his head cocked to the ceiling, muttered, "This is the coolest thing I have ever seen!"

Trevor couldn't help but laugh at the man who had created time travel could be so awed by such a thing. The two men walked around the first sublevel, admiring the flat panel television that would entertain Trevor for quite some time. Walking past the exercise area and down into the kitchen and bar floor, the two men laughed at the home cooking chute leading to Marla's kitchen. As they walked down to the lowest sublevel, there was a large desk and a good-sized sleeping area. In the far corner, as described by Trevor's counterpart, was the D.E. generator for sending and receiving messages and equipment. Trevor walked to the generator to find a box setting in place with a date one week from now.

"Am I supposed to open this now or wait till this date?"

Michael replied, "I think it came from that date. Isn't that the day after the mission?"

"Yeah, I think so. Why would— "

Trevor looked closer at the box. In large bold print on the top of the box it read: Classification Beta.

"Oh, shit! Michael, let's take this to the kitchen."

After the two men walk their way up a level to the kitchen, Trevor placed the box on the table. Pulling a pocketknife from his jeans, Trevor slices the box open. Inside was a thick manila folder filled with personnel files, along with several surveillance-quality DVDs.

"What's you poison, boss? DVDs or the files?"

"Well, let's see what's on disk first. It might explain what the files are for."

Trevor placed the first of seven disks into the DVD input for the television. After a moment of white noise and static image, a video feed from what had to have been an air traffic control center appears. The display shows a Boeing 767 aircraft cross the center view when it explodes. After the initial explosion, two more air bursts detonated in the falling debris. Once the debris hit the ground, the picture ended.

"The question is, was that by our doing or by our failure?"

Trevor answered, "Not sure. Let's watch the rest and see."

As Trevor places the next disc into the feed, this shows what happens moments prior to the explosion. It looked like a man jumped from the plane and waited several moments before deploying his parachute. Once the chute deployed, the aircraft exploded, followed by the two more airbursts. When the fireballs faded, the camera followed the man whose parachute was on fire down to the ground. There was no way that he could have survived. It was then that they realized that they were watching Boiyd die.

"Oh my god. He was killed by the air bursts of napalm!"

Michael sat back in his seat and contemplated what this could mean. Why would they send us this intelligence update and still arrive to brief us on the original plan? This makes no sense at all, he thought. Michael turned to Trevor.

"I need you to deploy and clarify the situation. The team from a year from now came here to brief us on the original plan that apparently failed. Why would they do so if they knew that it would fail? Why not send us a brief that would succeed?"

Trevor nodded his head in agreement when he added, "We are forgetting about the files in the box. Let's read through these and then figure out what the hell this means."

Trevor pulled out the large manila folder and opened it up to find several personnel jackets. Pulling out the first file, he read the name. Master Chief Petty Officer Menendez. Served twenty-three years in Navy. Started out on the underwater demolition team (UDT) in 1986. Pinned on SEAL in 1989. Served in Iraq, Afghanistan, Panama, Somalia and undetermined locations in North Africa.

As Trevor read through the five files in the folder, he passed them to Michael and realized that they were classified KIA in an explosion at Coronado Naval Station in San Diego, California. The explosion took place April 22, 2009. The same day as the aircraft explosion. Trevor passed the death classification document to Michael and asked, "You don't think that they were onboard the flight, do you?"

"Trev, I don't know what to think, but I do know that you need to go and figure this out as soon as possible. Take the Tahoe and solve this. In the meantime, I am going to request from NSC that a second delivery vehicle be allowed to be kept here, with as much as you have been using it, and since you have a second mission from the team, I think it would be in our best interests to have the dual capability. I'm sorry, Trev, I'm rambling. Go on and get out of here."

Trevor stood and headed to the lower level to get changed into combat gear. For all he knew, this could be the last time he would be here before his team's deployment.

As Trevor changed into his BDUs, he started thinking about the men in the files. Are these the new recruits? On the original time line, they were slotted to die. If that were the case, they would be the ideal candidates for recruitment. They have Special Forces training, all have combat experience, and all are trained in covert tactics.

Trevor checked his equipment and loaded his load-bearing vest (LBV) with six twenty-round magazines for his rifle as well as extra batteries for the optics and his uniform. Trevor grabbed his helmet on the way out the door and walked right into Michael. Michael stood as if he were a father watching his son put on the high school football uniform for the first time. Holding on to both of Trevor's shoulders, Michael wished the man luck as he pointed him to the door. As Trevor began his climb up the stairs to the elevator, Michael followed.

2 JULY 2015
0500 HOURS

Trevor arrived in the humid Virginia summer in front of the cottage gates. He realized that his mistakes in the past were asking his questions of the wrong people. He was approaching the future one year ahead, when they may not have known the changes necessary to make. This time he decided to deploy to a future further ahead than one year ahead of his time line. Now sitting six years in the future, he hoped that Michael, if still around, would be able to help guide him better.

Trevor drove through the front gate of the cottage and pulled up the long driveway. Trevor stepped out of the Tahoe and walked to the front door. Walt answered the door and shook his hand. Trevor moved to the elevator and flipped the switch to go to the lower level. As he arrived, he opened the door to find the agents in the middle of a brief.

Trevor looked at each person in the room and found more faces he had never known. Five faces that were resting their eyes on him belonged to the SEALs from the personnel jackets. Trevor delivered an uncomfortable smile to the gazing crowd and walked forward toward Michael.

Michael shook Trevor's hand and introduced him to the team. With the awkward introduction, it seemed as though none of them had seen him before. Only his own team looked at him with familiarity, but there were two of his own missing. Trevor followed Michael into his office and closed the door behind him.

"Where are Boiyd and Segal?"

Michael looked at him and frowned.

"Let me see your date."

Trevor held out his hand and activated the implant.

"Sit down, Trevor. Let me explain the things that you weren't supposed to know."

Trevor sat down and focused on Michael.

"You're life started at the moment you stepped back ten minutes. For you it only happened today, but what you don't know is what made this your climax for your new life. I need to know if you are ready to begin your life, good or bad, right now."

Trevor felt the chill of horror and excitement run down his spine. What did 'good or bad' mean? Either way, any form of opposition might cause a dramatic change in the time line. Responsibility was the only thing that he had to fall on. He must be responsible for his life and for the lives in the future that he would impact. Any change made could destroy all of it.

Trevor answered, "I know what my role could involve. I know that if I choose that path in my future I will destroy my future by saying no. I'm tired of being told how to live and how and what to do. I do have a feeling that this is what my life will consist of from now on, so my answer is yes, I am ready to begin, good or bad."

Michael looked down at a sheet of paper and read back everything that Trevor had said.

"Trev, you have to know that whatever you do will be what you did. Does that make any sense to you?"

Trevor shook his head.

"Okay, what we have learned from the time line is this. If you decide to make a plan to strike a single man a certain way and for some reason it fails, you will likely send a message back to yourself stating what you would do instead of the planned mission. So the counterpart behind you will look at the recommended changes to the plan and succeed because of what you suggested. Now, for anyone else on this planet, they would look back and see that they had succeeded because of the fact that they were told to change in the past. You and your team have the ability to watch the changes made. What your confusion is based on is the thought of multiple time lines.

What you have to understand is that there is only one. One time line that changes with the flow of past changes interfered by the future. You confuse yourself by what you can see; what you don't know is what everyone else sees. No matter what you do, you are destined to do by the natural complications of conundrums. If you told yourself to shoot the man instead of bomb the man, you would shoot the man in the past by your own advice. If your counterpart in the past decided to ignore your advice and bomb the man, you would bomb the man anyway. Either way, you are going to do what your future self has done. The difference is that you are watching yourself from a third-person view and are blinded from your destiny."

Trevor was looking around himself in partial confusion as well as a blind effort to be comedic about looking what went over his head.

"Micha—wha—what the fuck did you just say? I'm going to do what I'm going to do because I told myself to do it when my future se—what the fuck?"

Michael smiled and pulled out the infamous legal pad and sketched out two lines. On the first line he drew a straight line. On the second line he drew a straight line and let it fork at a certain point. On one of the forked lines he branched it out further to several degrees.

"All right, Trev, this straight line is the normal time line as designed; there are no forks and there are no bends. The other model is the normal time line since time travel was discovered. Where this point forks is where a change was made. Now, the difference between the two forked lines is perspective. The line that branches off and remains straight is the civilian's perspective. They see and know nothing of changes made. The other forked section continues to fork and branch by every alteration you make to the time line. Now, the civilian end of each continuing fork will mesh to a consistent time line for them. They have no idea anything was ever changed. You have the blessing and curse of knowing all tragedies and events that required alteration.

"Because of your ability to maintain your knowledge, you confuse yourself as a person in control. You must understand that you have no control. You have the luxury of thinking that it is free will governing your decisions; it is not. You are going to do exactly what the person before you has done. The only difference is that you do not have the knowledge of the future counterpart in that regard. Do you understand now? You have no control; you are only doing what was already done. You may think it is the first time, but it is only the first time for you. Your future counterpart has already done exactly what you will do on one fork of the time line or another. Now do you understand?"

Trevor finally understood what Michael was saying.

"Then I have no choice but to agree to play my role. What do I need to know?"

Michael put down the paper with Trevor's future counterpart's dissertation of dialogue. Each word on the page matched Trevor's own words. This was one more piece of evidence of what Michael had just told Trevor. Michael began to brief Trevor.

"What you need to know is complete with happy endings and tragic development. You must know that whatever I have to say is something you need to know. From this point on we won't hold your hand and give you the brief you were supposed to have. From now on you are slotted to know everything available. Now, for starters, we need to talk about your family."

Trevor leaned forward to catch every word from Michael.

"What about my family? I saw on record that they survived. I saw that on the handheld!"

"Trev, your wife and child were killed. They died from a disease that happened to be during the alphabet crisis; everyone thought they had what the rest of the people had. I'm sorry, but there was nothing that we could have done. We needed you to have your head in the game during the planning, so we planted a record of their survival in your handheld. These things needed to be done to prevent a mishap. I am so sorry, Trevor."

Trevor's eyes filled with hatred and remorse at the loss of his wife and daughter. Trevor knew deep down that he was told the things needed to get the job done. He hated Michael for that, and still pitied him for being in a position to do so. Trevor held his head in his hands and cried. After his initial grieving episode, he looked up and asked, "What else do I need to know?"

Michael admired his dedication, but he also understood that the "job" was all that Trevor had left.

"Your job involves recruitment now. You will have to go and interview new recruits after their deaths have been imposed and ensure that this is the kind of life they can live with. They must have this interview before seeing anything that could be a security issue. That includes the vehicles. They must be drugged during all transits until they willingly enlist. Here are the dates that you must go to for your first batch. You must save them and isolate them until they are interviewed. This will be done by you and you alone."

Trevor nodded, avoiding the thoughts of his wife and daughter.

"What else do I need to know?"

"Well, for starters, your mission is going to parallel your team's at all times. You will be responsible for the briefings as well as any other peripheral changes necessary that your team may not have clearance for. To start with, the new recruits that you will have to recover will die on 22 April 2009 by the same aircraft that delivered the alphabet weapon. Once your man disarms the bomb, he will witness a terrorist take over. The flight will be diverted to Coronado Naval Station to eliminate the same SEAL team that killed the terrorist faction in Syria.

The demolition of the SEAL team will take place four hours and five minutes after the initial detonation was scheduled. Remember to factor in time zone changes and you should make it in time to recover the men. You must also ensure that no one witnesses you take the five men out of the compound prior to the strike. I recommend that you evacuate the men only minutes prior to the strike."

Trevor took the list and simply walked to the door. Michael said nothing and let his man go. As Trevor opened the door, he found the leaning ear of Segal eavesdropping. Segal looked up at Trevor with tears running down her face. Trevor looked at her and hinted a smile of gratitude for the gesture. Even though Segal found out about Trevor's family six years ago when he returned from the alphabet mission, she still ached for his pain.

Trevor walked past Segal and headed out the way he entered. As he passed the agents, they all stood and bowed their head for their leader's loss. Trevor stopped and looked at one of the faces he had never known.

"You, who are you?"

"Christopher Allen, sir."

"Do you like it here with us?"

"Sir, I lost my own family and was left alone by something that could not be changed. These people are my family now. I like it just fine, sir"

Trevor looked around the room and found the faces of his own team looking back at him with the deepest empathy glazing their eyes that anyone could find.

"Allen, what were you being briefed on when I walked into the door?"

Allen looked back at one of his team members and answered, "Sir, we were being informed that you were expected to arrive and that you would find out for the first time about your family. We were told that you had not known until now when you arrived and spoke to Michael. We are all sorry for your loss, sir."

Trevor stared deeply into Allen's eyes and said, "Allen, I look forward to getting to know you."

Trevor looked at each new face and smiled deeply.

"I look forward to meeting all of you. If you need anything from me past, future or present, just say 'Mali sent me.' I will do anything for each of you, as you should do for each other. Allen, you're right, this is our family now."

Trevor, the proven leader, stepped into the elevator and left the cottage to find his new brothers in San Diego. The agents of his future watched as he left the room and nodded in complete approval for his role over them all.

18 APRIL 2009
1130 HOURS

Trevor's main irritation with the project and equipment was the fact that the vehicle arrived in the same location regardless of when he traveled. He can't simply program in the computer to have him go to San Diego in March of 2009. He had to get to the date with enough time to spare to fly there and find the closest safe house to find another vehicle.

Trevor arrived at the cottage on April 18, 2009, with enough time to get on a private jet headed to California. As he unpacked the Tahoe, he headed down to Michael's office to request the flight. With flight vouchers in hand for one of the CIA's jets, he took a civilian vehicle to the airport to link up with the pilot.

As Trevor loaded the small jet, he took out the only suitcase that he wanted as a carry-on. The pilot fired up the engines and began to taxi for take off. Trevor pulled out the suitcase and opened it. Inside was his weapon and sidearm. Along with the weapons were his files on the new recruits. All recruits were Navy SEALs currently in a two-week training session at Coronado Naval Station. The station was scheduled for destruction on 22 April 2009. These men would be killed and have no idea that their lives would be over until Trevor broke the news to them.

Trevor read all of their files and discovered that they had all served together for more than a year. The youngest, Allen, had been with the team for seven months. Trevor studied each man's face and name and began to write them down to ensure that he remembered. In order of rank, Lieutenant Junior Grade (LTJG) Josef Papillion, Ensign (Ens) Anders Ritchie, Master Chief Petty Officer (MCPO) Cliff Menendez, Chief Petty Officer (CPO) Samuel Mickey, and Petty Officer First Class (PO1) Christopher Allen. The faces began to burn into his mind as the pilot called over the intercom that they were about to cross over Omaha.

Trevor looked out the window to find the exact buildings that his team would be perched from to fire at an airplane approximately where he was at now. With a shiver of the events flying through his mind, Trevor felt the sudden sickening jolt in his stomach from knowing that no efforts would save his family. Trevor began to think about the lies that he had been fed to ensure that he took the path necessary. What if the entire plan was a lie to make him find another way? Trevor pulled out a pad of paper and began to plot out the order of events that he was aware of. After all, what he was going to do was what he was going to do, according to Michael. In Trevor's mind, no matter what he decided, he would do what the future records would show.

Trevor knew for a fact that the bomb would detonate above Omaha, Nebraska, at precisely 1130 on April 22. Trevor also knew that the SEALs were hit four hours and five minutes after. Trevor decided to introduce a new mission plan. A hard hit of the scientist responsible as well as the destruction of his office while the agent was inside should prevent anyone else who may be involved from carrying on with the strike, just in case.

Trevor nodded with solid confidence as he placed his notepad away. Checking the settings on his weapons once more, he placed the suitcase under his seat and went to sleep the rest of the trip.

Trevor's dreams shifted between jungle nightmares and domestic pleasantries. Trevor's mind finally settled on a compromise as he found himself staring into the green-lit landscape of Vietnam through his night vision. Looking around for anyone near him, he found a silhouette of a woman in the distance. Trevor walked forward to make out who the woman was. As he walked closer to the shapely figure, the woman slipped further away with every step he took. Trevor stopped and leaned to see if the lighting around the face of the woman would change. It was as if the face lived in darkness. He called out to her and watched as she turned to face him. Trevor took a step closer as the woman took one to match him. Now that they were getting closer with each step, he rushed his steps in impatience. The woman, still shrouded in darkness, held out a hand, and Trevor reached to hold it. Trevor now stood face to face with the woman to find that he still didn't know who she was. Trevor held the woman's hand and recognized the touch of the skin he held. With a deep sigh of relief, Trevor kissed the woman on the lips to find his lips pressed against the mouth of a half-decomposed skull.

Trevor opened his eyes in horror to find the pilot's hand on his shoulder.

"Sir, we have arrived in San Diego. Are you okay, sir? Can I get you something?"

Trevor looked around him to gather his bearings.

"No, I'm fine, thanks. Uh, are you going to wait here or were you scheduled for somewhere else?"

The pilot helped Trevor on his feet and answered, "Sir, I have to be in Seattle in six hours. I'm sorry, but I thought that you had means of transportation planned from L.A."

Trevor, now fully awake after his horrid nightmare, recalled that he was going to find the safe house in San Diego and drive the suburban back to L.A. for a contracted flight on the 22nd. Trevor reached for the case under his seat and stepped off the plane into the humid California heat. As he stepped foot on solid ground, a bagman placed his luggage in an awaiting Chevy Niagara provided by the agency.

Trevor instructed the driver to move straight to the safe house's address. With strict obedience, the driver pulled off the tarmac and headed out to the highway, heading north.

Trevor arrived at the safe house and unloaded his baggage. Trevor instructed the driver to leave as he took his bags to the door of the house. Trevor opened the door and walked into the spacious house furnished by the agency. Walking into one of the bedrooms, he placed his bags on the bed. For Trevor, this was the first time he had been in one of these houses; so far it looked like any other home.

On the walls throughout the house were pictures of a family. The same families in different settings fill the home. Trevor looked in all of the closets and could not find anything that would allow him down to the lower levels. Trevor could find nothing. Now walking through the living room, he passed the banister of the staircase going up. On the telephone table next to the base of the banister he found a picture different from the rest. Trevor looked closer to find a beach photo of his wife and daughter. Trevor remembered taking this picture on the beach in Oregon. Haystack Rock was resting in the background with the hazy Oregon mist adding mystery to the scene. Trevor picked the photo up to look closer when a red line spread along the glass pane, scanning his fingers. The first eight steps in the staircase lifted up to reveal a hidden stairwell going down.

Trevor walked down the stairs. With each step going down, a light turned on to lead the way. At the base of the stairs a large room lit up with several doors along the back wall. Trevor walked in the middle of the room, where a large table rested. Trevor looked around as he heard the staircase lower back into position. Along the back wall were eight doors. Trevor opened each door to find a small bed and table in each. Now standing at the table in the large room, Trevor noticed another two doors on opposite ends of the room. Trevor walked to the one on his right and opened it to find the lower level of the garage. Seated was a duplicate of the Tahoe. Nothing else surrounded the vehicle. Trevor walked out of the garage and went into the last remaining room. The door was locked and there was no place for a key. Next to the doorjamb was a slot about the size of a credit card.

Trevor pulled out his ID card with the smart chip on it. In a couple seconds he heard a loud click from the other side of the door. Trevor turned the handle and pushed the door open. Inside was a well-lit room filled with weapon racks. Every type of weapon he had ever used filled the racks. The weapons included the experimental weapons they were all issued. Trevor counted nine types of pistols, twelve types of rifles, four types of assault rifles and three types of shotguns. Below each rack was a large case. Trevor opened one case to find hand grenades and C-4 explosives. Looking through the rest of the cases, Trevor found more than enough ammo for each weapon, as well as any kind of explosive he could imagine having a use for.

Trevor smiled at the measures the agency went through to ensure his supply. As Trevor walked out of the room, he noticed a small lock box on the wall next to the door. Inside there were ten secured cell phones. Trevor laughed aloud and walked to the large briefing table again when he noticed a first-aid kit below it. Trevor opened the kit to find no Band-Aids or gauze pads but several syringes of yellow fluid. On each syringe was a label revealing that they were sedatives for transport. Trevor closed the box and carried it to the awaiting vehicle. Trevor pushed the garage door remote to find that the floor was rising to ground level. What was in the garage above him? Nothing? Trevor shrugged off the questions and pulled out of the garage to find an old woman next door waving in courtesy. Trevor waved back and started his journey to stake out the SEAL Command Center at Coronado.

22 APRIL 2009
1200 HOURS

Trevor sat in the Tahoe and waited for the right time to find the men. He decided to pull all five men out by posing as DIA. Looking in the console of the vehicle, he found the set of fake IDs that the agency provided. Trevor pulled out the ID that was for DIA. Now Trevor decided to pull the men out for a brief inside the center. Trevor pulled up to the gate and showed the guard the ID. The guard looked at Trevor and compared it to the ID. As the guard should have, he took the ID inside and compared it to a list. When the name checked out, he returned the ID and waved Trevor through.

Trevor now pulled next to the main center and clipped the ID to his shirt. Trevor walked into the building and spoke to the man at the desk.

"My name is Special Agent Sands; I'm here to meet with—"

Trevor pulled out the list of names and read out the names.

"These men need to be debriefed from their previous mission. Do you have a debriefing room that you can call these men to?"

The desk petty officer looked at Trevor and squinted his eyes.

"Sir, I'm going to have to ask you to wait here. I'll see if these men are in here. This should only take a moment. May I use your list, sir?"

Trevor handed the man his list and waited for him to return. After a long moment, the man came back with the list.

"Sir, they will be with you in a moment. If you will follow me, I'll show you to our secured room."

Trevor followed the man into a medium-sized room. There was a row of chairs facing a podium with barely enough room to walk between anything. One good sign was that there were no visible cameras anywhere, let alone a large mirror.

After about fifteen minutes, five men began to file into the room. Trevor looked at his watch; he now had thirty-five minutes before the strike. Trevor decided to have these men out in twenty-five.

Each man found their seat and faced Trevor, anticipating another boring brief about their actions. Understandably, each man wondered why debriefings didn't take place with all interested parties involved at once.

Trevor waited another minute or two before he began.

"Lieutenant Papillion, could you walk me through you mission in Syria?"

Trevor asked this since he had no idea exactly why the Syrian terrorists were about to strike them.

"Well, sir, we were ordered to find the head of a newly developed extremist group and shut them down before they had time to develop a faithful gathering of anti-Western terrorists. When we arrived at their training camp, we found only half of the assigned group on scene. We infiltrated the camp from four directions and attacked in a simultaneous hit. The mission was over as soon as it started. I attacked the upper floor of the compound through an access hatch from the room. As I came down, I hit the two men pacing the hallway. While I was doing this, Mickey and Allen hit the lower level, consisting of five men. Menendez came through Aljira's window and hit him.

With the leader down, we were instructed to bring back two men to the regional command center in our Sinai compound. Ensign Ritchie was on post as distant cover with his M-88 sniper rifle. We regrouped and met our extraction five minutes later. There was no counterattack and no other men on scene. It was quick and straightforward. I don't know what else you would want to know."

Trevor looked at the men and down at his watch. He noticed he had little time before he had to clear. Trevor bit his lip in anticipation and drew his attention to Papillion.

"I need you men to come with me for an hour or so to look through some photos. We received word that some of the remaining terrorists were plotting to strike at SEALs. If you would remain patient and follow me, you would be a great help."

Papillion looked at his men as they looked to him in confusion. With a half-sincere obedience, the men stood and followed Trevor out of the building and into the waiting Tahoe. Trevor looked at his watch again and realized there were five minutes remaining. Trevor quickly pulled out of the parking area and drove straight to the main gate.

Papillion looked oddly at Trevor, trying to read his actions and gauge what his hurry could be. As they left the command center, Trevor pulled into a lot overlooking Coronado and parked. Trevor turned to Papillion and said, "I need your men to watch and trust me. I do not work for the DIA. I work for a new agency developed to prevent specific threats to the stability of our way of life. I know this is vague, but you must understand one thing. In three minutes you would have been killed. This is all you need to know right now."

Josef Papillion looked at Trevor and reacted like a combat soldier.

"Sir, who the fuck do you think you are? Is this a kidnaping? What the fuck do you want with us? You had better fill me in now or you will find out what five unarmed SEALs can do to you."

Trevor remained silent and kept an eye on his watch. One minute and fifteen seconds remained. Trevor lowered the window and heard the oncoming jet approaching. Trevor looked back at the men and said, "Do you hear that? That jet was supposed to explode over Omaha. Right now it is controlled by seven Syrian terrorists who are retaliating against the SEALs. They are going to fly this plane directly into the compound below. They have forty-five seconds until impact. This is going to be painful and confusing, but I swear to you I will give you plenty of opportunity for vengeance."

Trevor stopped talking and waited while he watched the reactions of the men in the vehicle. Two men got out and waited as they watched the large jet fly above them. The jet soared quickly and very low as it lowered directly level to the command center they were just sitting in. In a horrifically slow approach, the jet slammed into the building, leaving a path of impact. The jet hit the building and punched through the opposite end, leaving a trail of fire, blood and concrete behind. The SEALs screamed for their friends that had been inside the building with them only minutes before.

Trevor activated the extension rod for the vehicle and set the time back twenty minutes. As the cloud formed around the large vehicle, Trevor heard the men scream in panic indiscernible through the static discharge of the vehicle. In a bright flash, the men looked to find that they haven't moved. Josef looked out to find the aftermath of the jet's impact. There was none. The compound stood solid, with no indication of attack.

"What the fuck! What is this?" Josef yelled.

Trevor replied past the equal expressions from the men in the back seat.

"Men, my agency is responsible for defense against all attacks that will leave our nation in complete devastation. You fight in small wars that most people will never hear about. I fight wars that include millions of people who die and no one will ever know it.

None of you signed out of the center, so the database will list you among the dead. You must understand that you are only alive now because I pulled you. I am here for one reason alone. We want to recruit you as agents. I am now going to take you to our safe house, where I will explain everything I can, but I must do one thing. None of you can know where I am going, so I must inject you all with a sedative."

"Uh, no. Fuck you!"

This was the colorful voice of Allen in the backseat.

"Gentlemen, you have two options. Join our agency and live a life anonymous from the population you protect, or remain listed as the dead, where you should be in fifteen minutes. If you choose to continue with the only lives that you can live, stick out your arm. If you choose to follow the time line you are supposed to be on, sit tight and I'll put you back where you belong."

The men sat in a state of shock from what they had seen and heard. They have just witnessed their lives blown into a dust of flames and concrete. Now they were watching it all over again as if someone had hit rewind on the VCR of their life.

One by one, men held out their arms. Trevor pulled out the first-aid kit and drew five doses. Once each man was asleep, Trevor redeployed the vehicle about a half an hour ahead to place these men on their time line. Trevor began his short journey to the safe house.

22 APRIL 2009
1700 HOURS

Trevor sat at the large table in the center of the main room at the safe house, waiting for the first sign of the men to wake up. As soon as Trevor began to lose patience, a loud knock came from one of the five occupied rooms.

Trevor opened the door and brought the first man to the table for the briefing. CPO. Mickey sat at the end of the table as Trevor began the history of the agency.

"Do you go by Mickey or Samuel?"

"Sam, sir."

"I see. Well, Sam, you are sitting in the basement of one of our safe houses. We have twelve around the country. The purpose for these houses is to provide agents with a cache of weapons, ammo and delivery vehicles. Another use is for recruitment. Let me begin with how this all started."

Sam sat back casually and smirked throughout Trevor's speech explaining the accidental deployment for his team. Trevor explained how Michael and Richard worked to bring them back from 1969, and how the National Security Counsel was changed by the creation of the agency. Trevor briefed Sam about the alphabet crisis as well as the current deployment that his team was bound to be on. Once Trevor finished, Sam stood and faced the back wall.

"Sam, do you understand what I've said to you?"

Sam looked back at Trevor with no real sign of emotion, only confusion.

"Sir, I know what you're saying. I'm with you. Besides, if I'm dead I might as well act as a guardian angel."

Trevor laughed and forced himself to agree with the man. The mentality was appropriate.

"Okay, Sam, I need you to go back to your shitty room until I brief the rest of your team. Before you go, is there anything I need to know about the rest of your men?"

Sam smiled and shook his head.

"Sir, what you see is what you get. Five SEALs with nothing left now but a job."

Trevor nodded with approval at the remark and escorted the man to his room.

After three hours of briefing, Trevor finished the last of them as they were finally allowed to be together as a group. Now all men were sitting at the table as Trevor finished his remarks.

"Just so you all know, you are all about to learn more about this country than you would ever think was available. Each of you has shown the greatest courage and restraint I have ever seen. I trust you will make the greatest agents this country has ever known. Right now we move to our headquarters, and you will be drugged for that move as well. Please remain patient; soon this will all be over, and trust is all you will have."

The men took the sudden lives that they were offered with awesome adaptability. Trevor felt as though these men were meant for this job.

The men loaded into the suburban and deployed them all for the 28th when they were all sedated. Once they had arrived at the proper time, Trevor drove the men to Los Angeles and boarded a small jet headed to Virginia.

The plane touched down at a private strip only fifteen miles away from the cottage. An awaiting van took the sedated men to the cottage. The men were unloaded from the van from the lower garage and brought to the confined conference room, where they would stay until the sedation wore off.

Richard, Michael and Trevor sat in the conference room, discussing what Trevor had briefed already. Trevor continued his discussion.

"So once they were all briefed individually, I brought them all in and spoke to the group. They are aware of the situation. Hell, I made them watch their own command center get destroyed. After the attack, I deployed prior to the attack to make them watch it again. They are aware of the capabilities, and most of them are excited about being a part of it. There is one person who showed no real excitement, and that was Chief Petty Officer Mickey. He showed interest but seemed unsurprised about the whole system; it was as if he were aware already. That concerns me. Do either of you know Mickey?"

Richard and Michael shook their head and lowered their head in thought. Michael began to list the relatives of each person on the team and cross-referenced each person using the handheld. He could find no connection between any agency member and Mickey. Richard looked up from his shoes and muttered, "Don't forget the psychic factor."

Michael looked startled from Richard's remark.

"There is no basis that any kind of psychic activity ever existed. I don't think we need to go down that road."

Richard smiled.

"Sir, with all due respect, if that 'road' you referred to is the road of science fiction, well, look around you. There have been several studies that show that psychic behavior may exist. We have discovered that time is a continuing and closed loop. By discovering this, we have been able to relax on the notion that whatever we are supposed to do will happen due to destiny, for lack of a better word. With your permission I would like to fight my issue."

Michael looked back at Trevor.

"Rich, I don't think we are having a fight over this issue. We are just speculating about why this man might know something he shouldn't."

"Yes, I understand, but we are in the business of using strange phenomenon to benefit all concerned. There are autistic children who can naturally read complex encryption keys but can't read English at a first grade level. For all we know there are people out there who can naturally read the complex code of the time line and not know what it is that they know."

Michael shrugged his shoulders in an effort to give Richard something in that matter. Trevor raised his eyebrows and looked the other way toward the sleeping men. As he focused his eyes on Mickey, Trevor noticed the man shift his position. Trevor walked to the man and gently shook him.

Mickey raised his head and looked as if he was caught watching something he shouldn't.

"Mickey, we need to talk. Will you come with me, please?"

"Yes, sir, call me Sam."

Trevor led the man out of the room and took him to Trevor's quarters. As the two men sat facing each other, Trevor shifted in his seat, uncomfortable about how to ask the questions. Finally, Trevor found the words beyond Richard's remarks.

"Sam, were you awake when we were talking about you in the conference room?"

"Yes, sir, I was."

"What do you think?"

Sam shifted his weight onto the opposite side and replied, "Sir, the reason I wasn't excited or surprised, or the reason I hinted of knowing already, is because I dream things. I dreamed of gross and fucked up things in the spectrum of combat. I see things happen that never happened. Things like children dying of a sickness that can't be cured. Millions reported dead on the news. But the day that was said on the news was the other day, and nothing happened."

Trevor looked at Sam in wonder.

"Why don't we start with what you dreamed about and what this had to do with our mission?"

"Sir, I don't think you would understand."

"Try me."

Sam looked Trevor in the eye and began to explain his disturbing dreams.

"Sir, I dreamed as if it were a movie. It scared the shit out of me when I woke, but I know what I saw was nothing I have ever seen anywhere.

"I dreamed of a man bent over a microscope and repeating a phrase as if he were haunted by it. He kept saying 'Alphabet game.' After I saw that, I saw a truck pick up a large box and take it to the airport. The driver had short blonde hair with a name tag. His name was Dave. On the flight, the captain said over the PA that they were passing Omaha and said something about their cruising altitude. From the ground, I saw the plane explode and a mist come from the wreckage. I saw a playground inhale the mist, and I saw them coughing.

"I was now watching a doctor in a private room explain to a patient that there was nothing he could do. He walked out of the room and passed the waiting room that was filling so badly that nobody else could find room to stand. I saw a man on the same plane in a navigator's uniform disarm a bomb, and then he called—you."

Trevor raised his eyebrows and sighed with the heavy proof of what he didn't believe.

"You know that the bomb didn't go off because we prevented it, right?"

"Yes, sir. I assumed."

"You just succeeded in giving me a headache. I think there is something I need to say to return the favor."

Sam sat back and waited.

"You see, my team deployed to stop the device, but I don't know how. You see, I deployed ahead of time to find out how I needed to retrieve you. I then deployed to get you. From here, I deploy back in time to brief my team on how I decided to handle the strike. From there they go and make the change. A few hours after that you will see me at your command center, and all of this will happen again. Does your head hurt yet?"

Sam belted out a loud laugh and replied, "Yes, sir, you just confused the shit out of me. So you mean to tell me that I am speaking to you now and I know everything, but you are going to return to where you need to go and—what?"

Trevor returned the laugh.

"You'll get the hang of it. Your men should be awake right now; I think that you need to join them in the conference room. You will receive a similar brief to what I gave you all in San Diego."

Trevor patted Sam on the back and walked him back to the enclosed conference room. Trevor was right; the men were awake and very curious as to where Sam was. Trevor opened the door and called for Michael and Richard.

Michael and Richard stood outside the conference room door and waited for Trevor's thoughts.

"Richard, I give you credit for an open mind. If I didn't know what I know, I would have thought the man was crazy. Michael, he saw everything before it happened. Do with that what you will, but he did give me some information that I can use to stop the attack. If you'll excuse me, I have some catching up to do. I have to brief the team and the NSC to kick the show off. Good luck, guys."

Richard smiled at Michael and gestured as if he were right again. Michael grunted words back to Richard on his way into the conference room. Richard laughed softly and followed his own leader.

29 APRIL 2009
0900 HOURS

Trevor rushed through the garage entrance to the lower level of the cottage. As Trevor entered the kitchen area, he pulled Wilson from the table and dragged him to a computer console.

"I need you to find out what the current address is for Benjamin Phelps and cross-reference that address for any shipping company that would pick up parcels at home. Try UPS, FedEx and other couriers. Once you have the list, cross-reference it with drivers named Dave who had short blonde hair. When you find him, get me immediately."

Wilson didn't ask any questions; he began his search through the federal databases and found five companies that would pickup shipments from Phelps' address. Wilson called each branch office and found one that had a driver named Dave who met the description. Wilson smiled and wrote down the branch office address as well as the address for Dr. Phelps. Wilson took the sheet and ran to find Trevor.

Trevor was sitting at one of the desks, reviewing what he knew of the events. Trevor knew what the strike was by disguising Boiyd as a navigator, and he disarmed the bomb. Boiyd also died while the plane was destroyed from the ground team. What Trevor didn't know was whether he should make a change or not. Trevor sat back as Wilson ran to him with the sheet of paper.

"Trev, I have it. This is where Phelps is at now, and this is where you can find the driver."

Wilson watched as Trevor smiled deeply. Trevor reached back while looking at the paper and patted Wilson on the gut.

"You did good."

Wilson smiled and walked back to the kitchen table to finish his coffee.

Trevor sat back and decided to make the change. Besides, you're gonna do what you're gonna do, he thought.

Trevor began to sketch out the known order of events. He plotted when the package should have been picked up, which was easy to do if he assumed Dave's route for the company. Trevor would know Phelps' face if he saw it; all he needed to do was plan an attack around it and secure the package before delivery. Trevor made his plan and decided to stick with it. Now all he had to do was brief his team.

It took all of twenty minutes to get every person involved in the same place for the briefing. The agents were sitting at the conference room table along with Michael and Richard. Commander Reese stood behind the table with Quincy Roberts, while all eyes focused on Trevor.

"Hey, guys, we need to talk about something that you aren't going to be aware of. Okay, I have been under lockdown, but that is so I can do what I need to do in regard to the mission. I have done so. I deployed six years ahead and found some news out that wasn't so pleasant. Just so the rumor mill is stopped—my wife—"

Trevor took a deep breath and managed to find the wind to finish.

"My wife and daughter were killed by something that cannot be changed. They got sick from something other than the alphabet, and died. The doctors assumed it was outbreak related, but it wasn't."

The men at the table lowered their heads in sorrow as Segal slipped a tear out of her tough and hardened eyes.

"Now that everyone knows, you can all stop thinking that I am rushing the mission for my family. I have found a simple and easy attack that will eliminate, or arrest, Dr. Phelps and retrieve the device for discrete and proper disposal. Before I begin I need to request something openly. I request that all agents undergo training in detective work. They are simple procedures in learning what to look for. When I tell you what the plan is, you will see that it is so simple that my daughter could have thought of it. The plan is this that Wilson, Boiyd and Segal will be the entry team. Trits and Reese will handle the HAZMAT. Reese, you are not an agent, but for some reason we have been training on the things not needed, such as aircraft takeover and sniper. You are trained in HAZMAT transportation, so you are going to tag along on this one. Any objections?"

Reese lowered his head and replied, "No, sir. No objections."

Trevor felt a shudder within him as he heard a commander, the equivalent of a lieutenant colonel, call him sir.

"Ease up with the *sir* stuff, Commander. Now, we have all been in this complex mindset since we were activated. None of you is at fault; I am for missing the obvious. You are all well trained for almost anything out there, but we need to be well trained for simple and stupid things as well. Lessons learned, that's all this is.

"Now, here is the plan. A man named Dave drives a shipping truck with Stream Courier; he will be sent to retrieve the package from Phelps' house. I will take the man's place and pick the package up. Once at the door I will signal for the entry team to enter, but only when I signal. I must ensure that his guard is down; I have no idea what kind of shit he has in his home. Now, once the man is down, I need Trits and Reese to gather the package and take it to the shipping van. From there you will take it to the CDC field lab, where they will dispose of the device. Now, here is what I know. Ben Phelps resides in White Bear Lake in Minnesota. That's a little bit northeast of St. Paul, where he works. The shipping company is located in Brooklyn Park, which is northwest of St. Paul. So, do you all see how simple the plan is?

"The only difficult thing left to do is decide whether Phelps lives or dies. So, Reese, if you would drill them on the tasks necessary, I will run through the final decision with Michael. Once we have our story straight, I'll brief the NSC prior to your deployment. Get it right this time, team. Regardless of our freedom with time, now is all we have. Get to it!"

The team cleared out of the conference room as Trevor and Michael stayed behind. Trevor paced the room, furious with his own loss of the obvious. How could he miss the simplicity of the mission? He was about to kill a couple hundred people on a passenger flight for no reason. He was about to put one of his men on a flight destined for his own death. All he had to do was track the package. Ben Phelps used his own name on the shipping; all they had to do was have FBI flag any shipment under his name or address and collect it while Trevor's team hit the doctor.

Michael sensed Trevor's frustration and said nothing. Michael had thought too complex on the matter and made the same mistakes Trevor did. Trevor finally stopped pacing and focused his attention on the next step.

"Okay, I have the handheld here with me. Let's find out what's in Ben's future, shall we?"

Michael nodded in agreement.

"Benjamin Phelps, born December 13, 1974. Current age is thirty-nine."

A single name appeared on the handheld as Trevor opened the file. The genealogical listing appeared as Trevor selected holographic display. Ben would have remarried a woman who would deliver two children. Both children are male and both die bachelors, neither had children, neither had any significant effect.

Trevor looked up at Michael and said, "That settles it. Ben will die."

Michael confirmed the search results as Trevor left the room to prepare his brief for deployment.

The current plan was for Trevor to leave the following day, as the team would deploy in one week. The team should arrive three hours after Trevor. Hopefully, Trevor would have finished briefing the NSC in time to walk out and begin the assault on the objective. Trevor wrote out the rough draft for his brief, also including the mission time line for his team. The time line would include when to deploy and what training objectives need to be completed prior to deployment, arrival times and assault times. Trevor includes a series of go codes that would instruct the assault team to move in and secure Phelps. The follow up HAZMAT team would receive verbal instructions on scene as to when to secure the package.

Once Trevor finished his instructions and his op order, he filed his final brief for the NSC into the newly developed archives. He then collected his gear and moved to his lockdown area.

Trevor dumped his gear next to the couch and walked down to the kitchen to find a cold beer. After a moment of thought, he decided he should probably run downstairs and see if any kind of delivery was sent to him.

Trevor reached the lower level at the base of the stairs and glanced in the back corner to find several dozen items sitting in the generator. He pulled them aside and began to open them up. The first and smallest item was wrapped in brown packing paper. Trevor opened it to find a handheld with a handwritten note taped to the top of it.

> Trevor,
>
> I am terribly sorry for the news you received about your family, but please know that at the time of their discovery we did not fully understand the consequences of your knowledge ahead of time. Please note that you will no longer be deceived on any aspect of future missions.

Enclosed is an updated handheld with the correct information about your personal genealogical records. Though you are entitled to review this, I suggest you search your own records after your current mission.

Thank you for your professionalism,
Michael Heimer
NOA Director
P.S. Keep an eye out for the steel coffee cup; it will save us a trip.

Trevor folded the note neatly and looked at the handheld in front of him. Should he open it or shouldn't he? What kind of surprises could possibly remain in his life? Trevor heeded Michael's advice and set it aside until his own mission was complete. Now all he had left was his first briefing in front of the NSC. None of them would remember that he had trained with them. None of them would recall ever seeing him. When Trevor had last seen them, they had discussed how it would be his pleasure to work with them again. No one thought that they wouldn't have a clue.

Trevor sighed with the thought of never truly understanding how the hell his new world worked. Shrugging off the conflicting thoughts, Trevor continued to open the shipments. The second package was a picture frame of Trevor and his family from Trevor's house. Trevor held the picture up in the light and studied the contours on his wife's face. With the buildup of grief that he had been holding in, Trevor finally let loose the horrible pain that had tugged at his soul since he was told of their true and timeless death. Trevor balled into the corner of his bed and held the picture frame tight as he cried like a child. His tears flowed through the hour and into the night. With bloodshot eyes looking at the intricate detail in the photo he had walked past every day in his home, Trevor finally placed the photo down when he heard steps coming to him.

"Trev? Trev, you down here? Holy shit, how far down does this place go?"

Trevor picked the picture back up and placed it next to his bed. Stretching his legs and standing for the first time in hours, Trevor met his guest at the stairwell.

"I'm down here! What do you need, Segal?"

A.J. Segal showed her face from above the stairwell and looked down with extremely concerned eyes.

“Trev, I just wanted to see how you’re doin’.”

“Segal, I don’t think this is completely appropriate. What would the rest of the team think if they knew you were here?”

“Honestly, I think they would hope for the best. Trev, you’re their leader. Not just in combat but in life. Our whole world is upside down right now. They want you to be happy.”

Trevor looked up at Segal and realized that he had just walked halfway up the stairs without noticing.

Segal continued, “I’m not saying that I expect anything. I’m just telling you what the team would think if they knew I was down here. You have to remember that you are the only one who took me in and trained me to who I am today. I think the way I do because of what you taught me. Now you are in pain, and I want to help you the way you helped me. I want you to kno—”

Segal stopped and looked deeply into Trevor’s eyes. Trevor held up a finger and walked back downstairs. Segal didn’t know what to think, but she waited patiently, not knowing whether he would come back or not. After a moment, Trevor came back with the handheld in front of him.

Trevor, like most men, missed the key signs that had been in front of him the entire time, the new regulations regarding his private encounters within the agency, and the tears in Segal’s eyes when he left Michael’s office six years in the future. Trevor should have seen it coming. All of the signs pointed to him and Segal becoming a couple.

Trevor held up the handheld for Segal to see and turned it on. Trevor looked to her and asked, “This is the new version that had no alterations made. The last one showed that the deployment would fix my home life. This one would show the truth. If you are going to say what I think you are going to say, I think we should look to see if this is the road we would take eventually. Regardless of what this says, you have to understand that however you feel, I am going to need a lot of time to adjust to my loss. Do you want to see what it says?”

Segal looked at Trevor with the deepest thanks that she was afraid to say. Trevor had known what she wanted to say but couldn’t. Trevor seemed to know everything in her eyes. He was the man in her life who had the answers and knew when to say that he didn’t. For her, he was the highest and her only standard.

With a smile, she slowly and sincerely nodded her head. Her gleaming eyes looked down to the handheld and watched as he pulled his name up.

Within seconds, their entire futures laid out in front of them. Trevor would marry Segal in August of 2011; they would have one child and retire under an alias.

Segal, the tough warrior trained by hardened soldiers, had cried more for Trevor than she had in her life. She lowered her head and hid her eyes with her fallen hair. Trevor raised her head by her chin, saw the glimmering, satisfied look in her eyes, and set her hair behind her ears. For Trevor, he still had his wife in his heart, and the thought of kissing the woman in front of him never crossed his mind. Segal was trying to keep her mind on her heart and ignore the signs of a passionate kiss.

Instead, she turned her head and whispered to Trevor, "Now that we know how our lives end, just know that whether I was supposed to be on your team or not, I knew that I loved you from the moment you saved my life. You pulled me away at the last second before a bullet hit where my head was. It wasn't the fact that you saved my life, it was that it woke me to knowing that you would *be* my life. You would always catch me if I started to fall, guide me when I was lost. Because of you, I don't have to compete with men for status. Because of you, I want to be the woman that you will need in your life.

"I am so sorry for your loss, and I would never even dream of seeing you in this kind of pain. Just know that I'll be your friend to talk to or to be with when you need. Let's forget about our future and concentrate on where we were before I came down. Now that I said that, are you hungry?"

Trevor laughed and nodded while looking down at the handheld, which weighed more than it ever did in the failing strength of his hand. Segal walked into the kitchen and threw together some spaghetti. Trevor opened a couple of beers and set one in front of her. The two didn't talk for quite a while until after their dinner. They simply ate and drank while thinking of the complexities of their lives as well as the mission.

30 APRIL 2009
0700 HOURS

The sun began to rise over the treetops surrounding the cottage. As the light began to spread over the lawn and fresh flowers planted by Marla, Trevor stepped out of the front door of his shack and walked over to the main cottage. Michael was sitting at the table with Walt and Marla, having morning coffee, when Trevor came in. Trevor smiled politely and shook Walt's hand as he was offered a cup of coffee. Trevor accepted and glanced at Michael to see him raising an eyebrow in a perceptive leer. Trevor shook his head and drank the coffee black.

After coffee, Trevor excused himself and asked Michael to follow him to the lower floor. Michael looked up at Trevor while moving down the elevator.

"So, Segal wasn't in her room last night. The guys are beginning to wonder."

Trevor should have seen this coming.

"She was with me last night. I was having a hard time, and she cooked up some dinner and fell asleep on the couch. What's the big deal?"

Michael shrugged.

"I just said she wasn't in her room, just thought that would interest you. That's all."

Trevor laughed as the elevator touched the lower level. The two men stepped out of the elevator and walked to the briefing room.

"Okay, I'll head out to the NSC and begin the briefing. I need the implant updated for all intel we have so far. I have prepared the presentation, so it should be ready to go for loading. We need Reese to be implanted, if he chooses. If for some reason he gets separated from the team, we need to have accessibility to him. Worst-case scenario, he gets separated and comes here; we still wouldn't know for sure what time line he follows, so we need to maintain his time. He should be able to take care of himself, but I need accountability."

Michael nodded. "Done. What else do you need?"

"Here is the order of events for the mission. I need them to check in using specific codes. I will carry a handheld that a driver would have. The codes will be courier specific but on an encrypted channel. Here is the list of code as well as the times. I require them to be on standby for the objective when I receive word of the delivery. I'll take care of the rest. There is one last thing, but I need specific permission from NSC for the act. The bio-agent was created inside of the man's lab, which should be destroyed as well."

"No, I agree, the lab should be destroyed, but it was a government contract that Phelps was working on. I think they should have the say as to the destruction."

"I understand, but the contract was for a weapon that can be designed for specific people, not millions of people with a certain blood type. This weapon had to have been way out of the scope of its contracted objective."

"Ask NSC and make sure you give them the numbers of fatalities as well as the amount of the agent released. I'm sure they would like to know that all of the devastation came from one gallon's worth of material."

Trevor looked back at Michael in shock.

"The results came back?"

"Two million and seven hundred thousand dead from one gallon."

"Fuckin' lunatic! What the hell could he have been thinking?"

"I can guarantee that he will never expect agents at his door before he makes it happen; I know that for a fact!"

Trevor laughed; they all forgot sometimes how in the dark the world was on what was or was not possible. Trevor opened a small hatch located in the wall next to the projection screen and pulled out a mounted laptop. Trevor loaded the files on the laptop and fixed his hand into a glove equipped with an infrared upload device used for loading data into the implants. Once the time line and the mission brief were loaded, Trevor closed the hatch and walked back to Michael.

"By the way, the five SEALs that I extracted keep them in isolation until the completion of the mission. I'll take care of them when I get back, but I'll be sure to return before they know I'm gone. If they need anything, do me a favor and try to accommodate them. Make sure they know that they are welcome to all resources that aren't mission critical. They are soldiers, not prisoners; I can only imagine what's going through their mind. Anyway, can you think of anything else?"

Michael smiled and shook his head.

"I think you got it under control. Just relax; remember, in the briefing you are the only one who has done this before, so be patient if they seem slow to procedure. Just help them out along the way."

"Yes, sir. I'll be back soon."

Trevor smiled and stepped out of the conference room to the Tahoe. As he loaded in, he checked his combat gear as well as his notes. Trevor hit the garage door button and waited for his vehicle to rise to the ground floor. As Trevor pulled out, he saw a large covered vehicle resting to the left of the garage outside. It seemed that Michael got the second delivery vehicle after all. That was one less thing for Trevor to worry about.

Trevor drove out to the main gate and activated the dark energy loop to send him to April 18, 2009, at noon. When he arrived, he'd make the drive out to the Pentagon and make the call for access through security. Trevor prayed that Michael received the updated procedures for the new protocols so he could brief the NSC on how to deal with Trevor.

With the cloud forming around his vehicle, Trevor couldn't help but feel this to be routine. The vehicle hazed into the time ordered, and he was alone on the property. Trevor drove through the gates and began his journey to the Pentagon.

18 APRIL 2009
1532 HOURS

Sitting at the main gate to the Pentagon, security was sketchy considering what the visitor was wearing. Trevor was dressed in complete urban combat gear, with his weapon back slung. Trevor pulled out his cell phone and looked up the number for General Maxwell, chairman of the National Security Counsel. Once the pin number and code were entered for the assigned pager, Trevor waited without approaching the guard. He simply hollered to the guard that he was waiting for his escort. This didn't phase the guard one bit; Trevor still ended up with his face to the ground and his weapon pulled away. Within a few minutes, the expected Jeep pulled up to the gate, and the orders were given to the guard to return Trevor's weapon and let him through.

Trevor pulled into the assigned slot for the Special Agent in Charge for the NOA. Now walking with two lieutenant generals past all security, Trevor was no longer impressed by his power. One of the generals unlocked the elevator, and the three men step inside to go to the NSC command center. As they approached the sublevel, Trevor took a deep breath in anticipation. As the door opened, the men walked out of the elevator and went directly to their seats. Trevor stood at his place at the table and looked directly at General Maxell. Only three members of the NSC were at their places.

"Sir, has the NSC been notified?"

General Maxwell nodded.

"Yes, they should be here within about twenty minutes. The secretary of state will not attend, but someone will take his place. Is there something I can get for you? Coffee?"

"Yes, sir. Coffee, black, would be nice."

The chairman glanced back at his aide as the colonel walked to the coffee stand for Trevor's order. After a moment the aide returned with a Department of Defense mug filled with the stiff fluid. Trevor thanked the man and began to think about how he never imagined himself being served by a colonel before. Trevor was a squad leader for the infantry not even a year before. The highest-ranking person he had ever spoken with was a lieutenant colonel, and his battalion treated that man like a king. The changes in the past year had been dramatic, since Trevor would shortly be in command of the United States as soon as he was verified. Trevor's hand shook with unease, and he sat the mug down to prevent any kind of spill in the spotless room.

General Maxwell noticed Trevor's unease and looked back to him sympathetically.

"You should be aware, Agent Sands, that we are all aware of your actions in the past year, and we are fully confident in your abilities. You should be proud. I can tell you that you made the Army proud. Go ahead and relax; there is nothing that you can say that will screw up our opinion of you. I do need to ask you one thing—where did you deploy from?"

Trevor smiled and felt his body relax with the reassurance from the general.

"Sir, I deployed from the 30th of this month. Not too far ahead, I'm afraid."

General Maxwell nodded and leaned to his side as his aide whispered in his ear. The General whispered something back and stood. Trevor stood as the elevator door opened, revealing a group of sharply dressed men.

General Maxwell tightened up and announced, "Gentleman, the president of the United States!"

Trevor looked behind him to find the president watching him carefully. The crowd from the elevator included several high-ranking military, as well as sharply dressed civilians. Trevor recognized all of the men as they took their place at the table. The president walked briskly to Trevor and introduced himself, as if he had to.

"Agent Sands, I'm Dan Baker. I am so pleased to meet you in person. I wish I could say that I looked forward to this briefing, but I do look forward to your performance. I hear you have a hell of a brain in that head of yours. Shall we begin?"

Trevor remained standing as the president took the secretary of state's seat. One of the aides rushed quickly to remove the nameplate assigned to Honorable Durst. The aide returned with the plate for the president. As Trevor stood, he watched as all eyes were on him.

"Mr. President, gentlemen, I thank you for rushing here so quickly. Before we begin, I am hoping that a package arrived for this purpose. Is it here, General?"

General Maxwell nodded and leaned over to the side of his chair, pulling the heavy briefcase to the table. An aide brought the case to Trevor.

"Thank you, sir. Let me explain one thing before I am verified. There must be an imminent threat in case verification fails. General, have your security officer standby with a sidearm."

The officer chambered a round and walked quickly to Trevor's side.

"Now, during the verification process, the weapon must be pointed at my head in case of failure. I hope that this is the briefcase that has been configured."

The men at the table laughed uneasily at the morbid thought of the potential hazard. Trevor opened the case and slid in his ID card. Now entering the pin number, the artificial voice from the speaker instructed Trevor to the next step for the retinal scan. Trevor obeyed the voice and continued through the process of implant scanning. After the process was complete, the voice announced Trevor's identity and displayed the first screen of the presentation. Trevor sighed in relief.

The large clock on the back wall began to count down to zero hour. The remaining time showed 91:23:57 and counted down. Trevor had a little less than four days to resolve the problem at hand. Trevor watched everyone's reaction and began his brief.

"Gentlemen of the counsel. I hereby assume command of the presidency, Congress, as well as all internal agencies until zero hour in accordance to the National Security Act for Inevitable Catastrophic Event. To place your minds at ease, I am here for guidance and support. No choice made in the room will become policy or an act without prior time line data to reinforce the decision.

To begin my brief, in a little less than four days, this man—"

A picture of Ben Phelps was displayed on the screen.

"Dr. Benjamin Phelps, will have caused the deaths of almost three million people in the United States alone. The government, through the Department of Defense, contracted Dr. Phelps to develop a personalized biological weapon. It turned out that he had a personal vendetta against a certain blood type. He developed the alphabet virus, as he called it, to kill all people with AB negative blood type. His delivery means was a soda machine loaded onto a passenger plane headed to Arizona from Minnesota. The plane exploded from high explosives triggered by an altimeter with a binary timer above Omaha, Nebraska. The agent then spread all over the U.S. and continued to spread across the world. The body count I delivered to you was for the U.S. only."

The men at the table stared at the bloodied faces of the victims and shook their heads slowly. The president kept quiet and watched the horror on the view screen. Trevor continued his brief.

"After careful evaluation from my agency, an alternate time line attempted to eliminate the threat from the flight. The plan succeeded, but along with the bomb, several terrorists were on board killing a hundred and eighteen people at Coronado Naval Station. Our research shows that a dramatic disruption will occur if that is prevented. In other words, even more catastrophe will take place if that attack is prevented. By my notes issued from six years from now, when the terrorists failed in the aerial attack of Coronado, a larger and more populous area was attacked, more than tripling the body count. From the Coronado attack, all COMSEC and sensitive material that survived was accounted for. This attack must take place. The devastation from the virus cannot be allowed to take place. We have a plan of action that will recover the bomb from the doctor's home and allow us an opportunity to eliminate him. The only question remaining is, does the government wish the elimination of remaining biological agents within Mr. Phelps lab."

The men watched as the video feed filled their mind with horror. The men continued to watch in disbelief and awe as the remains of Coronado displayed on screen. The president looked to the Secretary of Defense and asked, "Just exactly what was he contracted to develop?"

Honorable Dean lowered his head and answered, "Mr. President, MedCorp was contracted to develop a case-specific weapon that could be designed to kill a single person from an aerial spray. It was never suppose to be a massive strike weapon. That was by his own making through our funds."

President Baker nodded and looked back at Trevor.

"Well, sir, you can go ahead and hit the rest of the bio-weapon, wherever it is. We don't need something like that around."

Trevor had to glance twice when the president called him sir.

"I'll take care of it then, Mr. President. Gentlemen, here is how we plan to strike Dr. Phelps. My team will be here in about twelve hours. From there we will place one man undercover with the Stream Courier Company in Brooklyn Park, Minnesota. Our man currently resides in White Bear Lake, just northeast of St. Paul. We know what man will be sent to receive the package, and we know our man's address. All we have to do is take the deliveryman's place and head right to Phelps' front door. From there the package will be recovered and taken to the CDC field office for destruction. Once the package is recovered, our team will strike Phelps and his office. I still need to finish the final plan for the strike against his lab. Until then, the plan is simple and should be efficient. Gentleman, what are your thoughts?"

Each member of the NSC looked around at each other, waiting for someone to speak. The first of them to say anything was the FBI director.

"Agent Sands, I am Director Allen. I think that the plan seems a little too easy. It seems that it can't be this simple. What other plans did you go through before arriving at this one?"

Trevor nodded.

"Yes, sir, it is easy. You have to keep in mind the basic elements necessary. Recovery of the weapon, covert or feinted elimination of Phelps, and elimination of possible assistance to Phelps. For all we know there may be others around who are in allegiance with Phelps. Once we take him down there may be someone else to make the strike happen. Therefore, we eliminate the weapon, the man and the possibility of another strike by eliminating the remaining agent in the lab. It is simple, but this plan counters these variables. We planned an aircraft recovery with bomb disposal, and we planned a strike from below using napalm to burn the agent in the air. These were effective in eliminating the agent but not in ensuring that the flight continued as planned with no knowledge of hazard. The simple plan was the last thing we were expecting. We thought so hard about the situation that we missed the obvious. Mr. Allen, sometimes the best answer is the simple one."

The men muttered to themselves as Trevor closed his folder and looked back.

"We have less than four days to make this happen. My team will be here in twelve hours to begin orientation. Director Allen, I request your assistance in retrieving false press involvement as well as tactical uniforms for my men. We would appreciate this man be labeled with some other kind of offense. It is important that we give the press something; the neighbors are likely to see everything. This is where I need your help, gentlemen. What other offenses would involve a package the size of a soda machine?"

The men thought for a moment when General Rebo, the Air Force chief of staff spoke.

"We could always say that he had a shipment of classified computer parts in the crate about to be shipped to high-paying rebels in Nigeria. Accuse him of espionage and leave it at that. When he was being arrested, he resisted and left us no choice but to put him down. What do you think?"

General Maxwell was the first to reply.

"I think that we have to go further than computer parts. I think we could use his job against him. Say he was sending terrorists the means to create their own biological weapons by sending a shipment of lab equipment along with instructions to create something."

Trevor smiled.

"I like that. Director Allen, if you could manage to leak this to the press the moment you are paged, it would help prevent conspiracies. If there is nothing further, I should prepare for my team's arrival."

The men begun to get up from their seats when the president spoke.

"Agent Sands, if it isn't too much trouble, could you allow us the privilege of meeting your team? We have followed all of your progress since your deployment to Vietnam, and we would appreciate an introduction. Besides, any one of them could be in your shoes in the future; it would be a good idea that they are aware of what you do, don't you think?"

Trevor wasn't sure if he was being asked or told. In all effect, he had supreme power over the president, but only until zero hour. Allowing his men to be briefed here shouldn't hurt anything.

"Mr. President, I apologize for not knowing already, but what military experience do you have?"

The president smiled and replied.

"I used to be Sergeant Major Baker with the 101st. I retired with twenty-five years in and somehow managed to get into politics by not keeping my mouth shut. I know what you were thinking. If you think now would be a bad time for your team to divert, don't worry about it. I don't want to put this mission at jeopardy for any reason."

Trevor smiled and reached into his pack for the messenger. Trevor wrote down on a piece of paper a message for his team to meet him at the Pentagon and closed the lid. Trevor scanned his implant and pressed the three side buttons. In seconds, the box vanished in a cloud of static. The men in the room were thrown back from the table in surprise.

"Oh, shit…I apologize, gentlemen. You have to keep in mind that I have been with you all before and showed you this device. I forgot this whole thing is new to you. The men should page one of you shortly."

The men raised their eyebrows as General Maxwell received his page. With a smooth motion, he waved a three-star general out the door.

After about ten minutes of waiting, the elevator opened to reveal six soldiers in complete combat gear. All of the agents looked around the spacious room and back to the large table in the center of the room. Trevor stood, waving his team to his side.

"Gentlemen, this is my team. Staff Sergeants Boiyd and Baxley, Sergeants Trits and Segal. This here is Corporal Wilson. Commander Reese, our training officer, will attend with us on this mission due to his experience in high-yield HAZMAT. They have served with me in Vietnam and proved themselves in every way. Team, this is the members of the National Security Counsel. Sitting in the secretary of defense's position today is President Baker."

The president stood and shook each agent in turn. He then walked slowly back to General Maxwell and whispered something in his ear. The general, in turn, called over his aide. The aide then walked over to one of the intelligence NCOs and took something from him. After a moment, the president returned to the team with something in his hand.

"Agent Sands, if you would." The president motioned.

Trevor walked over next to the president, a little confused. The president then looked to the team.

"Corporal Wilson, report."

Wilson walked from his team over to where the president was standing.

"Corporal Wilson, through exceptional performance and extreme attention to detail, I promote your from corporal to sergeant. As *former* commander in chief, I'm sure my replacement will not mind if I do so."

Trevor smiled and nodded back to the president. President Baker and Trevor pulled the corporal rank off Wilson's collar and placed the sergeant rank in place. After a moment, the president shook Wilson's hand and said, "Through what you have done and are about to do for your country, you should never be anything less than a sergeant. When you and your team are completed with your mission, come see me at the White House. Page me anytime and I will take care of one last detail."

Wilson smiled and raised a salute to the president. The president returned the salute and turned from Wilson. Trevor followed the president and shook Wilson's hand as well. The team stood there, not sure whether to applaud or wait. They did know that rank meant nothing within their team, but it meant more now for Wilson.

The president stood, being the politician he was, and said, "Agents, you have made us all proud, and we welcome any incident and any strike. Because of you there is nothing that can pose a threat. Agent Sands, lead them well and find that man. We have complete faith in your abilities as a soldier, a patriot and as a man. Godspeed."

The men around the table stood and clapped their hands toward the agents at the foot of the large table. Trevor smiled and waved his men to the elevator and followed behind them. As the doors of the elevator closed, the team looked to each other, forgetting the three-star general beside them. Trevor patted Wilson on the back.

"Trev, just what in the hell was that?"

Trevor laughed and shook his head.

"I don't know, but don't let it get to your head. None of that will mean shit if we fail. Keep your mind in the game. After we finish we'll give the president his photo op. We have better shit to do than play poster child. Remember your roles and you will live. Forget your job and you will get us all killed."

The lieutenant general smiled deeply in approval and escorted the young team out of the Pentagon.

21 APRIL 2009
0500 HOURS

Trevor placed his men at a local hotel, where not many people would ask questions. Now sitting in one room, the team suited up in the FBI tactical gear courtesy of Director Allen. Trevor was getting dressed in a jumpsuit issued by Stream Couriers and would head off to replace Dave in about an hour. Director Allen arranged for the company to know that Trevor would be undercover using their equipment; in return, he managed to give them five years of tax exemption for the company. The owner had no problem meeting Trevor now.

With the team suited up and ready to go, they went over the final plan. Now implementing the lab where the remainder of the bio-agent was resting, Trevor confirmed the plan with Reese.

"High explosives and thermite should destroy and kill anything in that room smaller than an ant, right?"

Reese nodded while taping his cuffs to his leg.

"Yes, sir, the agent will die in extreme heat. The only reason it survived in the fire from the aircraft was because it was laced with asbestos and frozen. Even after the blast I am sure that the majority of the virus was killed. You want to use three high-explosive grenades from a distance and simultaneously sending thermite charges. It could work better if the charges are already in the room when the HE went off. We have to ensure that the building is clear; what did you decide for me to do with that?"

Trevor loaded his sidearm, a 10mm automatic, and replied.

"I think you should have a second man gain access to the building and place the charge on the thirty-second floor where the lab is, and then start a small fire in the basement. This will set off detectors, and when smoke is visible the skeptics in the building will clear. I need one of you on an opposing rooftop to scan the area with your thermal scope and ensure that at least two floors above and below you are clear of innocents. Once cleared, fire the HE and clear out. I still feel we should send thermite with the HE in case the satchels in the lab fail to detonate. Is there a safe way to kill the virus in the lab in person?"

Reese considered and replied, "Sir, I can't be certain that I would know the alphabet virus when I see it. They all look the same in little petri dishes. I seriously doubt he labeled it, 'Weapon to Kill Millions.'"

Trevor nodded.

"Okay, bomb and burn. I just need the burn to happen before dust begins to settle from the bomb. If I had the nerve, I would simply napalm—wait! White phosphorous is just as effective and not as persistent. Okay, now all we need is WP grenades. We'll make a loop for them around the lab and set them to go by timer. Reese, what do you think?"

"Sir, Willie Pete should do it. It produces a shitload of heat and doesn't last long. A short burst of high heat will still set fire to the floor, but the fire department should be able to take care of it as long as they know it's WP that started it."

Trevor nodded and began to write down a request to send. Trevor places the request in the messenger and deployed it to their own time line. Not even ten seconds later, a knock came from the front door. Trevor opened the door to find Richard standing with a large box at his feet.

"Trev, I don't know what you need this for, but it's very heavy. Just don't ask me to carry it inside the room."

Trevor laughed and had Trits bring the box to the kitchenette. Reese looked at the box and then at his watch and laughed. After his moment of disbelief he began unloading the grenades and separating the fuses from them. With the amount of blasting caps and good old-fashioned time delay fuses, he would be able to make his bomb. Reese tied in about twenty minutes of fuse to equal lengths of detonation cord and connected the det-cord to the blasting caps. After only an hour of work, the bomb was complete with a twenty-minute timer.

Wilson helped Reese pack the bomb into a large duffel bag and set it in the bathtub. The team checked their gear as Richard moved frantically out of the way. Trevor placed his sidearm in the fanny pack given to the drivers for the company. Trevor looked out of the window and watched as the sun bled its way across the parking lot of the hotel. With all of the thoughts rushing past his mind in the past few days, he forgot how beautiful each sunrise could be.

Trevor thought of the mountains in Utah, where his wife and daughter joined him for vacation. The sun rose just as determined and gently over the mountain when he felt the surge of romance come over him. Trevor would lean over and kiss his wife the precise moment he felt the sun hit his cheek. These moments were over for him now. All he had left was the repetition of moments that he would never live down.

Trevor was still angry at the agency for hiding his family's death. The apologetic note, which he kept with him, wasn't enough, but it did help explain why they lied to him. Trevor grew more and more agitated as he thought about the efforts made to make him feel better about his family's death. As Trevor thought, he remembered something. Trevor read the note again and moved his eyes down to the P.S. note.

"Keep an eye out for the steel coffee cup; it will save us a trip."

What the hell does that mean? Why stress over a coffee cup? Where is the cup, in the home or in the lab? Trevor shook his head and decided to get the ball rolling.

"Okay, this is it. I am going to link up with the owner of Stream Couriers and take the truck a few blocks away from the objective. Reese and Wilson, I want you to take care of the office. I don't care what you have to do, but I want that office in flames the moment we put Phelps down. Before I go, I am going to give Director Allen a call to have him clear the building for whatever purpose. We'll use the same excuse we decided to give the press. We'll have him shut it down for an investigation. When the building is clear, plant the device and get the show on the road. Is there a way you can hook the TD fuse to a pager so you can remotely detonate?"

Reese nodded and said, "Sir, SEALs are issued pagers for that reason. Mine had a port for det-cord or TD fuse. I'll take care of it. Just call me when you need it pulled."

Trevor smiled. He had thought that the agency had cool toys. It seems that they still lack some equipment to make this smooth.

Trevor looked at each teammate in turn and gave them a confidant stare. Trevor walked out of the hotel and into the rental car. He would now drive to Brooklyn Park and meet the owner of the courier company.

The drive was relaxing and relatively sullen. He had time to reflect about who the man was that would create such a weapon. Was he the nutcase that he had been made to be from his file? Or was he simply a man who had a theory and nothing more? It would seem that a man who dealt with blood and its properties daily would have some kind of reasoning for why he did such a thing. Did he honestly believe that a certain blood type was responsible for the corruption and evil of the world? Are people with opposing blood types the cause of all the good?

Trevor almost felt sorry for the man, but he focused on the mission at hand, to kill Ben Phelps. Trevor pulled in to the large parking area for the truck company and walked into the building. As he passed the front desk, he saw a balding man with great concern on his face. Trevor approached him.

"Are you Mr. Freeman?"

The man walked to Trevor.

"Yes, I am, you Trevor?"

"Yes, sir, I am. Can I speak to you in your office, sir?"

"Absolutely. Donna, hold my calls, please."

The large man led Trevor into a spacious office and sat him down.

"Can I get you anything?"

"No, thank you, I'm fine. Sir, all I need from you is an empty truck and notification when this specific address is called for a pickup."

Trevor handed the man a sheet of paper with Phelps' address written on it.

"No problem. I thought this would be painful. When someone offers a tax-free company for five years I expect to have to turn over my entire resources."

The man looked at the paper and compared it to a wide spreadsheet printout on his desk.

"Sir, I already had a call requesting pickup for this address. It is assigned to my driver, Dave. This is the one you want, right?"

Trevor smiled at how predictable this was getting.

"Yes, sir, that's the one."

The large man opened his desk drawer and pulled out a set of keys.

"It's parked out back. It's unloaded now, so you should be ready to go. I won't mind if you bring it back on an empty tank."

The large man laughed as if it were comedy club material.

Trevor thanked the man and walked out the door to get the truck. Looking at his watch, the time was now something he owns. Nothing would happen if the package was not picked up. Phelps would simply wait until Trevor met him at the door.

21 APRIL 2009
1000 HOURS

Trevor was waiting three blocks away from Phelps' home as he finalized his plans with the two other units. The entry team, Trits, Boiyd and Segal, were on standby. Baxley, Reese and Wilson were at the front door of the MedCorp tower with FBI agents. Trevor was just waiting for word to come back that the tower was in control. Trevor looked down at the clipboard in his lap with the go codes.

"57 needs a dolly" would be the code for the entry team to assault. "57 will return to base for assistance" means for all team members to stand down. "57 picking up package" means that Trevor would take care of the man himself in case of imminent threat to his team.

Trevor repeated each phrase several times to ensure he remembered the wording. The vibration of his cell phone shook Trevor upright.

"This is Sands."

"Yes, sir, MedCorp secured. Moving to 32 will inform you when complete."

"Copy."

"Reese, out."

Trevor felt a skip in his heart, as he was about to cross the final stretch of a long nightmare. Trevor checked his sidearm and placed it in the pack for quick accessibility. With a deep breath, he waited for the next call from Reese.

It took nearly an hour before he got the call. Again, Trevor was shocked by vibration.

"Sands."

"Sir, all are in place. You should see this room. He is one sick bastard; we have exact plans in his private lab. It turned out he is the kind of guy to label what he made. Most of what we have is inside of the coolant locker for the agent. Any further orders?"

Trevor thought for a moment before he gave in on a warning he received.

"Reese, look around for a steel coffee mug. Do you see one around?"

"Hold on."

After a moment, Reese came back on.

"Yes, sir, have one here. Why do you ask?"

"Are you in full protective gear?"

"Yes, sir, Level A."

"Good. I want you to try and take the mug apart over the floor. Tell me if you find anything."

"Copy."

Trevor waited as he heard faint grunting on the other end.

"Holy shit, sir. A stream of compressed gas came out of the outer shell of the mug. We have more hidden inside of it, sir. The gas looked like a coolant. What do you want me to do?"

Trevor finally understood what the warning in the letter meant. When the bomb goes off, the agent would have survived and spread itself into the air, fulfilling its rampage for Phelps. All of their efforts could have been for nothing.

Trevor gave his orders.

"Leave the open container in the coolant locker and make sure no other mugs are in the room or the outer labs. Stay on the line until you have the pager in place. Give me the number. I'll handle the detonation."

Trevor got on his radio and called out.

"Entry team, this is 57."

"57, go ahead."

"Entry team, monitor this net for time synch. Set watch for twenty-minute timer."

"Copy. 2-0 mikes."

"Good, copy. 57 out."

Trevor listened for Reese when he heard a loud static blast from the other end. After a minute or so Trevor overheard a loud zip.

"Sands, this is Reese. Sorry about the noise, we're decontaminating. All items in place, pager set. Prepare to copy number. Secured area code 77453-424-7762. Key in 2666 to have it page in through the detonation port. How copy, over?"

"Good, copy. Well done. Out."

Trevor dialed the numbers on the phone and got on the radio.

"All stations this net, this is 57. Prepare to time."

"Copy, 57."

"Copy, 57."

Trevor pressed the send button and heard the loud tones repeating and accelerating.

"All units. Time now. 2-0 mikes until assault. Team one, get to my location and standby for backup."

The two units reported that they understood, and Trevor started the engine to the large truck and watched the timer count down on his watch. Trevor sat back and waited as patiently as he could. The nerves throughout his body caused him to shake as each second passed.

Twenty minutes was long enough for men to invent a new tool, long enough for a poem to be written, and long enough for two people to fall in love. Twenty minutes in the hands of the gifted was nothing. Twenty minutes in the hands of the impatient was an eternity.

As the final seconds continued to count down, Trevor got on his radio once again and gave his final orders.

"Entry team, proceed to phase line Harmony. Team two, what's your location?"

"57, this is team two. We are still fifteen minutes out."

"Entry team copies. Moving to phase line Harmony."

Phase line Harmony was referencing Harmony Street one block away from Phelps' house. With Reese's team still fifteen minutes away, they were going to be useless in the assault.

Trevor waited for the entry team to arrive at their next phase line before he began.

"57, this is entry. In position at Harmony."

"Copy, entry. 57 moving to objective."

Trevor pulled out from the side of the road three blocks away from Phelps' house and headed to his home. In a short moment, Trevor was parked in front of the house. So this is the house of a mass murderer, Trevor thought to himself. As Trevor looked around the house, he saw a man watching him through a crack in the blinds.

"Entry, this is 57."

"Go ahead."

"Entry, we have a single-level home with front door facing the street. Subject is watching the street through the window right now. I am moving forward to make contact. Out."

Trevor took the clipboard and walked over to the front door. Before he had a chance to knock, the door opened. Ben Phelps smiled at Trevor and looked back at his packed weapon.

"I thought you guys were never going to come. I put the order in yesterday afternoon."

"Sorry about that, sir. We are a little backed up. Do you mind if I take a look at the shipment?"

It made Trevor sick having to play nice guy to the man he had to kill. Ben opened the door completely and invited Trevor in.

"It was hard as hell getting it in here. I hope you have a way to get it to the truck. As a kid I always wanted my own soda machine, but it's just too damn heavy and takes too much room."

Trevor shuddered when he heard the man speak to him cheerfully.

"No problem, sir. Let me call in for a dolly. I was told it was a small package. I'll be right back."

"Sure. Do what you need to do. You need a phone? You can use mine if you want."

Trevor shook his head and walked to the door, where he could get better reception. As Trevor pulled out his radio, he heard something tumble from the kitchen. A shrill sound emanated throughout the home. Trevor walked back into the living room and looked at the floor of the kitchen to find a screaming little girl.

Trevor felt his own heart shrink with the thought of men coming in and murdering her father in front of her. How the hell am I going to get the girl out of the home? Trevor thought. Good at thinking under pressure, he acted.

"Oh, did you hit your head?"

The little girl cried in her father's arms and nodded.

"What's your name, honey?" Trevor asked.

The girl stammered her own name past her sobs. "Chelsea."

"Oh, Chelsea, how old are you?"

"Five."

Trevor had no problem with the girl. She seemed to act as his own did.

"Wow. Five is a big girl! Chelsea, do you want to ask your dad if you can see a big truck?"

Chelsea smiled and looked at her dad. Ben smiled back, picked her up to her feet, and told her to go.

"This way, Chelsea. Did you know that your daddy was five once, too?"

"He was?"

"Uh huh. Guess what?"

"What?"

"I was too."

The little girl laughed, and Trevor held her hand out to the front door. As he was about to pass through, Ben held tight to the door and looked at Trevor.

"You know, you're pretty good with kids. Thanks."

"Oh, it's nothing. All kids like trucks. I know mine does."

Ben smiled and opened the door for Trevor and his daughter.

Trevor lifted the little girl into the back of the large delivery truck and stayed on the ground, watching her. Trevor looked at Phelps and picked up his radio.

"Base, this is 57."

"57, go ahead."

"Roger. 57 needs a dolly."

"Copy. We have one in your area. I'll send him your way."

"Thanks, base. Could you put a rush on that I'm getting a little behind here."

"Copy. He's right down the road from you."

"Roger. 57 clear."

Trevor waved to Ben and announced, "The dolly is on its way any second now. I need you to check the parcel and make sure the address is legible."

Phelps looked coldly back at Trevor. Ben walked into the house and came back out shortly after.

"Could you give me a hand? The label is on the other side."

Trevor hesitated and asked the little girl if she was okay. She was running back and forth in the shiny steel cargo area. She cheerfully said she was having fun.

Trevor unzipped his pack and reached past his pistol for a pen. Taking the pen out in front of Ben, he began to write a receiving receipt for him. Trevor left the pouch unzipped.

"You just need to flip it over, right, sir?"

"That should do it. You look like you're in shape. Think you can manage?"

Trevor hesitated and began to place the pen back into the pouch. Trevor looked down briefly at the large crate and looked up to find Ben with a gun in Trevor's face.

"What do you think I am? I'm not stupid!"

Trevor froze in place with his hand still in his pack. Trevor said the first thing that came to mind.

"Sir, I don't carry cash on me!"

This infuriated Ben beyond his control. The doctor slammed the barrel across Trevor's face, knocking him to the floor. Trevor's pistol slid out of the pack and tumbled to the ground.

"Oh! I was right! Get up slow!"

Trevor placed his hand on the ground to push himself up. Easing his body upright, Trevor felt the throbbing pain from his temple.

"Dr. Phelps, your lab is destroyed and you are five seconds away from being killed. You have one chance to make your little girl think of you as a victim and not a monster. Put your gun down and lay face down!"

Ben laughed coldly at Trevor.

"I see, you want me to save your life before I die. Who are you with? How could you have possibly known what I was going to do? I know I'm a little paranoid; that's the only reason you are in this mess. What kind of deliveryman doesn't carry a dolly?"

Trevor felt the pain of stupidity strike him harder than being pistol-whipped. Trevor lowered his head in defeat. Ben placed the muzzle against the top of Trevor's head and pushed his head down.

As Trevor closed his eyes, he could only think of those he would see again. He pictured his child playing with his dog, his wife pressing her cheek against his, the warm flash of sunlight beating against his face as he kissed her in front of the mountain scene. Trevor loosened his body as his last thought passed through his mind. His last thought was over a simple beer and a plate of spaghetti made by Segal's hand. Trevor forgot all about his fate in this world and realized he was about to die.

Ben looked up from Trevor to find an odd shine coming from the window. He smiled widely, looked quickly down to Trevor, and pushed even harder against his head. With a thundering whirl of explosions and blood, Trevor laid still.

The back door crashed in with three agents swarming the room. The lead agent hollered, "Clear!"

Segal rushed to Trevor and threw Ben's body off of him.

"Trev! Trevor!"

There was no answer from Trevor. With the amount of blood covering the floor and the two bodies, Segal couldn't be sure. She lifted his head and held it tight in her arms. Trevor laid still as Reese rushed through the front door.

"Oh, Jesus, no."

Segal allowed tears to fill in her eyes as she lowered her head to kiss Trevor. Segal held him tightly when she felt something hard press against her forearm. She reached under Trevor's shirt and pulled out his dog tags. Segal read them to herself.

Sands, Trevor A.
AB
LDS

Segal pulled one tag away from the chain and slid it in her front breast pocket. It took no time at all for the men to fill the room and hover over his body.

As they carried Trevor away from Phelps, Baxley stepped on what was under Trevor's head. Picking it up, Baxley studied it closely. It was a steel coffee cup dented with a bloody imprint.

Baxley rushed over to Trevor and placed his hand on his chest. After his own shaking ceased, he felt it. Trevor was breathing. Baxley stopped the team and let Trevor down gently. The team looked down at Trevor, still in Segal's arms, and waited.

After five long minutes, Trevor opened his eyes to see Segal ecstatically crying, now out of joy. Segal leaned forward and kissed Trevor again. Trevor, still in a state of shock, returned the kiss.

Reaching in his pouch, Trevor pulled out a cell phone and dialed the number for Director Allen.

"Allen."

"Sir, this is Agent Sands. I need you to leak to the press right about now."

"Sure thing. It's over then?"

"Yes, sir."

Trevor looked up at Segal and smiled.

"The change had been made."

11 AUGUST 2010
1732 HOURS

The cottage seemed more like a home now than it ever did. In the bustling main level of the cottage, the team and their adopted parents were sitting down for dinner. With laughter and snide remarks, the team was finally joined by new experiences. It had been almost a year and a half since the alphabet attack. The men had been deployed twice more since then.

Trevor sat back quietly while Segal held his arm. Trevor had listened for many days and had heard no reference to Vietnam but through the past missions that they have embarked on. Trevor looked down at his arm and smiled, recollecting the tears in her eyes over countless occasions. In every occasion she had cried only for him.

Trevor squeezed the hands holding his arm and stood to face his team. As he stood, all eyes focused on him, as they always had. In brief moments the ten agents watched and listened obediently. In their experience with Trevor, nothing good comes after a good meal.

Trevor looked at each agent and at Walt and Marla.

“If I could have a moment. For the SEALs who weren’t with us in the beginning, this may bore you, but it should be interesting enough to listen to. We listened to Michael tell us about changes that were made to us in ’69. You wanted to know what they were. I’m going to tell you.

“A politician and Vietnam veteran named Senator Malloy fought a battle to keep women out of the combat arms positions. His son was Pfc. Malloy. He was one of us and we never knew it. Pfc. Malloy went with us to Vietnam and got sent back with us to 1969. Malloy was Baxley's assistant gunner. In the cleanup of the last battle, Malloy ran into Sergeant Malloy, his father. Apparently, Sergeant Malloy was reassigned to assist with our Green Beret friends over there. He was killed, and Pfc. Malloy was replaced in front of us…with Segal."

Trevor held her hand tight as he let his words sink in.

"You see, when Senator Malloy wasn't around after 1969 to fight against women in combat arms, Segal was able to become infantry. She joined the army and was assigned to our squad. She then came with us to Vietnam. So, you see, that was the change that took place that we didn't know about. That was why I didn't want you guys to know. There is one other thing."

The team looked shocked that there could be more. Segal looked at Trevor in wonder when her eyes went wide.

Trevor bent on one knee, held Segal's hand, and placed the dark ruby ring he held on her finger. The team watched reverently.

"A.J. Segal, you have always been a part of us, regardless of what changes were made. I ask you now if you will share your life with me. Amberly Jenna, will you be my wife?"

The room was silent as everyone hung on Segal's answer. With tears flowing from her eyes, she answered, "Oh God, yes! Hell yes!"

Trevor held his future wife as the men in the room cheered with excitement. The couple held each other tightly with closed eyes, except for one brief moment.

Trevor glimpsed at Walt and Marla, who were watching each other instead. Trevor smiled when he looked down at the hand Walt was holding to find a dark ruby ring.

Printed in the United States
57959LVS00004B/86

9 781413 770025